AT THE
BREAKFAST
TABLE

Also by Defne Suman

The Silence of Scheherazade

AT THE BREAKFAST TABLE

DEFNE SUMAN

Translated by Betsy Göksel

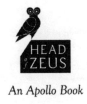

An Apollo Book

Originally published in 2018 as *Kahvaltı Sofrası*
by Doğan Kitap, Istanbul, Turkey.

First published in the UK in 2022 by Head of Zeus Ltd,
part of Bloomsbury Publishing Plc

9 7 5 3 1 2 4 6 8

A catalogue record for this book is available from the British Library.

ISBN (HB): 9781800247000
ISBN (XTPB): 9781800247017
ISBN (E): 9781800247031

Typeset by Divaddict Publishing Solutions Ltd

Printed and bound in Great Britain by
CPI Group (UK) Ltd, Croydon CR0 4YY

Head of Zeus Ltd
5–8 Hardwick Street
London EC1R 4RG
WWW.HEADOFZEUS.COM

For my mother

The writing of this novel was inspired by Ayfer Tunc's short story 'Burden'.

The truth is like a shutter made of iron and if you get caught underneath it you will be crushed. That's the most tragic aspect of historiography; in attempting to open the shutter, there are those who are crushed beneath its weight – and no one writes their story down.

Ayfer Tunc (transl. by Caroline Stockford), 'Burden'

Where my mama left me, hold me tight,
Where I've given up on love, set me right.

Metin Altiok (transl. by Betsy Göksel), 'Saril Bana'

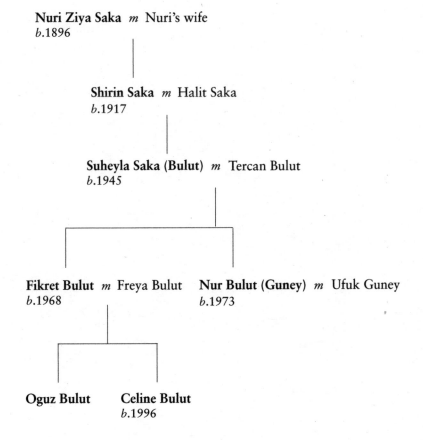

Nuri Ziya Saka *m* Nuri's wife
*b.*1896

Shirin Saka *m* Halit Saka
*b.*1917

Suheyla Saka (Bulut) *m* Tercan Bulut
*b.*1945

Fikret Bulut *m* Freya Bulut
*b.*1968

Nur Bulut (Guney) *m* Ufuk Guney
*b.*1973

Oguz Bulut

Celine Bulut
*b.*1996

1

Burak

Buyukada, an island off Istanbul
Summer 2017

The door opened a crack.

'Burak?'

I grunted.

'Psst, Burak! Are you asleep?'

The wood floor creaked and Celine slipped in.

I'm not asleep any more, Celine. Thanks to you.

I forced my eyes open. My head was thumping. Long, tanned legs entered my field of vision; hair brushed my face and tickled my neck. Celine plopped down beside me on the bed and grinned, realizing I was awake. I closed my eyes. High ceilings, white paint, a headache.

'I guess you're hungover, mister. You've got squinty eyes.'

'Mmm...'

'Burak, wake up. I want to tell you something.'

Just go away, Celine. I'm asleep. Find a man your own age to go to bed with. You might be young and beautiful, you might have hair the colour of straw and legs as shapely as columns, but it's your aunt I'm interested in, not you. And where is she? Asleep, of course.

The thought of Nur took me back to last night. We'd sat out on the wooden jetty below the house, Nur, Celine and I: aunt, niece and family friend, Burak. Nur's friend Burak. Drunk. Celine and I had polished off two bottles of red wine. Nur was drinking cognac, even though it was a hot summer's night, and smoking hand-rolled cigarettes. When she stubbed them out on the rotten jetty, instead of chucking the filters into the sea, she lined up the butts carefully, side by side on the boards. And then? And then you, Celine, went into the house and came back with a fresh bottle of wine in your hand. Because you were weaving all over the place, couldn't walk in a straight line, the bottle fell into the water. I retrieved it, and you and Nur clapped. 'Our hero, Burak!' So what? I saved a bottle of wine that had fallen into knee-deep water. We drank the wine, then Nur produced some weed and we rolled a joint. Then I was kissing one of you. Probably Nur. Or was it both of you? No, I didn't kiss anyone. That was a dream.

'Psst, Burak. Wake up, okay! I'm serious. My father's not here.'

'Uh-huh.'

'I'm telling you, he's not here. He's gone!'

'He'll be back soon, Celine. He'll have gone for a walk.'

Yes, it was a dream; a beautiful dream. I was kissing Nur. We were alone on the jetty – not the one in front of Shirin Saka's house but on the beach in the remote valley where Nur and I first met. Nur's naked body shone silver as the moonlight filtered through the clouds. There was something important I needed to tell her, but I stopped myself because I didn't want to come out of my dream.

Then Celine poked me and I had to open my eyes. Dream over. Forced landing into the present. When the wheels hit the ground, my headache returned. I ran through a mental checklist: me, Burak Gokce, forty-four years old, male, currently staying at Shirin Saka's house on the island of Buyukada. What day was it? Sunday. The second day of the holiday celebrating the end of Ramadan. Tomorrow was Shirin Saka's hundredth birthday and I was there both as a family friend and as a journalist.

Reaching for my glasses on the bedside table, I came face to face with Celine. The world was foggy, but Celine was so close, I couldn't fail to see how her big blue eyes widened as we talked. Her childishness, the way she aped the intonation of the girls in the local TV soap, irritated me.

'No, no... He's gone. His bed hasn't been slept in – it's exactly as it was when Sadik Usta made it yesterday morning. He took the backpack he always takes on his trips, and his laptop isn't there either, or his charger. My father's disappeared, Burak.'

I took a deep breath. The light sliding into the room through the open window had already faded from pink to yellow. Summer mornings are so unforgiving, so impatient, with the sun in a rush to rise in the sky, as if it weren't going to be up there for eighteen hours. I thought about Fikret, Celine's father. It was he who'd invited me to the family celebration for his grandmother's hundredth birthday. I'd be the only journalist, he'd said when he called me, his voice serious, as it always was. I smiled wryly to myself – as if the media cared about Shirin Saka. True, she'd been quite a well-known artist in her day, but who even remembered her name now? I didn't say anything, though. She was his grandmother, after all.

3

I was a bit upset that it wasn't Nur but her brother who'd invited me, but, still, I wasn't going to say no. I'd be staying in Shirin Saka's house on Buyukada for the entire holiday. I'd speak with Shirin Hanim, spend some time in the library where she'd created her masterpieces, look over old photographs and read through old letters, postcards and even diaries, if there were any. Most importantly, the whole time I was there, I'd be under the same roof as Nur, and what was more, for some family reason which didn't concern me, Nur's husband Ufuk would not be around. I did not turn down Fikret's invitation.

There was a time I'd have been on fire at the prospect of doing an interview with Shirin Saka. I'd asked Nur countless times to set one up for me, but she was always very protective, as if her grandmother were some kind of rare Indian fabric. Eventually I gave up. Now the opportunity was being handed to me on a plate, even if Fikret had warned me that his grandmother's mind tended to flit from here to there. That didn't faze me; I'd been conducting interviews with elderly people for years and was well used to piecing together their stories, like so many reflections in a shattered mirror. Making sense of the comings and goings of Shirin Hanim's mind would be a simple enough puzzle.

Celine was still there, right under my nose, waiting for an answer. I breathed in the sweet cinnamon smell of her. My mouth was like mud; I could barely move my dry lips.

'Maybe he's doing yoga. He told me he never starts his day without yoga.'

'Oh, come off it, Burak! Do you need a laptop to do yoga? And anyway, he always does yoga in his room before dawn – it's not as good once the sun's risen, apparently. Come on, get up. Let's look for my dad. Let's go down to the pier. I'm really worried – maybe he left on one of the ferries.'

I straightened the sheet wrapped around my legs and propped myself up on my elbows.

Celine laughed when she saw my T-shirt. 'Look at that – Metallica!'

Last night, in the dark, when I'd come in drunk, I'd felt around in the wardrobe for something to put on and found that T-shirt. My own shirt had got wet when I'd jumped in the water to rescue the wine, so I'd taken it off and hung it up somewhere on the jetty. This one presumably belonged to Celine's brother, Oguz.

'Where's Nur? Is she awake? Maybe she knows where your dad went.'

'Oh, yeah… If we waited for her! My aunt never wakes up before noon. She was probably writing all night. She's started on a new novel, a historical novel, commissioned by a rich businessman – didn't you know? While we sleep, she writes. A literal ghostwriter!'

Celine laughed at her own joke. I didn't say anything. It hurt me to think of Nur being a ghostwriter. Everything about Nur hurt me.

'Okay, I'll get up. Give me a few minutes to get myself together and wash my face. Wait for me outside.'

Grumbling, Celine stood up and walked to the door. How come she was being so familiar with me? Burak, my boy, this is what happens when you drink wine together in the darkness of the night. Most probably in my drunkenness I'd revealed things about myself, things that had made her think she was getting close to me.

I wrapped the sheet around me and sat on the edge of the bed. My head was still pounding. I filled a glass of water from the carafe on the bedside table, drank some and held the glass against my temple. The coolness felt good. I wasn't ready to get up quite yet. My gaze passed to the painting above the bedside table. It was one of Shirin Saka's. A ship was moving between shadows of light and dark blue, its outsized funnels billowing smoke that partly obscured the crowd of slender black silhouettes on the deck; faceless figures with handkerchiefs in their hands. In the background were green mountains out of which stone buildings had been hewn, or maybe they were tombs. Fog was rolling down from the peaks, into the foothills, smothering the prow of the ship. For some reason the painting made me think of Suheyla, Nur's mother, who'd died much too young. Shirin Saka's only child.

I never met Suheyla Bulut. She died on the day Nur and I came back from our holiday, the holiday where we met. We'd travelled back to Istanbul from Fethiye on the overnight bus. It's ridiculous, but for years I secretly held the poor woman responsible for destroying our love. As if Nur and I would have had a smooth relationship if her mother's heart hadn't stopped that day. Now, as I looked at Shirin Saka's painting, at the misty, elongated, tenderly rendered silhouettes, I realized that I had carried this angry resentment inside me for years. If her mother had lived, Nur would have fallen in love with me. I'd believed that in all sincerity. How absurd!

Another glass of water. My throat was like a desert, incapable of absorbing moisture. The water slid straight down into my stomach without touching my parched throat. Carafe in hand, I stood up, walked over to the window, pulled the curtain aside and stared out at the garden. The gardener, an extinguished cigarette stuck between his lips, was watering the desiccated earth with a hose. All the trees and flowers and pot plants had dried up. Shirin and Sadik must have got too old to look after the garden. It had once been lovely, full of roses of every hue, honeysuckle climbing the walls, bewitching expanses of purple and red bougainvillea.

I had a powerful urge to go and wake up Nur and reminisce with her about that morning we returned to Istanbul and went together to her university campus. I'd go through the bathroom separating our two rooms, tap on her door and lie down beside her. We'd replay the memories of our youth, as if we were watching an old film. But there was no way I could do that, not with Celine keeping guard at my door. And Nur would be furious at my interrupting her precious sleep. In any case, why would she want to remember the day she found out her mother had died?

I'd have to reminisce by myself.

I reminisced.

Nur, a prepaid phonecard clamped between her teeth, was waving at me, laughing, about to call her mother. We were on the Bosphorus University campus, with its beautiful red-roofed buildings and green surroundings, and I was sitting on the steps, watching students returning to their halls of residence, suitcases in hand. Pretty, suntanned girls were lounging like cats on the grass in the spring sunshine. It was as if the campus was a theatre set and my life was the most wonderful play being acted out within it. Nur's dress was lifting in the breeze and the boys were turning to look at her shapely brown legs. Her dress was too short for May and its bright colours – orange, red, yellow – too summery. I hadn't registered that it was so short until we got to the city, but now I felt uncomfortable. We'd made straight for campus as soon as we got off the overnight bus because Nur had a seminar that morning. Epistemology. I held my palms to my nose and inhaled the scent of her hair: honeysuckle, salt, sand.

'Don't go to the seminar,' I'd said on the bus back to Istanbul. 'You can get the notes off someone else later.'

The bus attendant was handing round cups of Nescafé. Sunday night was turning into Monday morning and real life loomed as our holiday receded. I held onto Nur so as not to break the connection between the idyll of the last week and reality ahead. I ran my fingers through her hedgehog hair. The bus was racing towards the city at full speed along the newly opened TEM highway and Nur was gazing out the window with sleepy eyes. To our right, the surface of the bay was like oil, totally smooth, purple, pink, lavender. This was not the crystal-clear turquoise sea that we'd been diving into with happy shrieks for the past week. It made me sad. I wanted to go back.

'I have to go. It's one of my options for my philosophy degree and I don't know anyone else in the seminar group. I wouldn't copy somebody else's notes anyway. I need to go.'

We went, but Nur didn't make it to the seminar.

The road up to the South Campus was extraordinarily beautiful, lined with pine trees and green bushes as it followed the elegant twists and turns of the Bosphorus; the Judas trees were in bloom, the hillsides were purple, and the sea was blue. Several couples passed us, walking arm in arm or holding hands, but I wasn't able to reach for Nur's hand. She was walking absent-mindedly beside me, lugging a backpack bigger than she was, to which were tied a sleeping bag, a tent and various metal camping utensils. There were streaks of white salt in her short hair from our final swim the evening before, and her tanned face looked gaunt. The overnight bus must have worn her out, I thought. Our canyon, our remote beach accessible only by boat, our nights of drinking wine beside the fire, roasting sausages, counting stars and then making love in our tiny tent seemed so distant now.

When we got to the green playing field, Nur turned to me. Her voice was soft, her face sweet like a child's. 'I can't miss this seminar, Burak, but after it I have a three-hour gap. I was going to go home and dump my backpack, but forget about that. Let's just sit on the grass. We can buy potato pies and tea from the canteen – I've even missed their horrible tea. What do you think? Or we could head down to Hisar if you like, buy some sausages from the kiosk and go to the Ali Baba Café.'

She gripped my hand, tightly, and my fears evaporated. I felt like laughing. If it hadn't been for her enormous backpack, I'd have pulled her to me, but as it was, I just nodded like an idiot. She put her pack down, unzipped the front compartment and took out a phonecard.

'I'll run and call my mum, tell her we're back so she won't worry. Stay here on the steps with our bags. It won't take two minutes.'

Let's pause it right there, Nur. Let's yell, 'Cut!' and make the film stop at that frame. You get to the phone booth, turn and wave. Let there be a girlish smile on your face. Let your short, thin, multicoloured summer skirt dance in the breeze. Let the boys passing to the right and left of you stare at your legs. Turn and look at me with the phonecard clamped between your teeth; smile, wave.

Let the hands of time not touch the happiest moment of my life.

It wasn't Nur's mother but her brother Fikret who answered the phone.

Suheyla Bulut had had a heart attack that morning. Nur didn't wait for her brother to finish talking; she dropped the receiver and came out of the booth, leaving the phone swinging on its cord. A boy handed her the phonecard she'd left in there. She raised her head and stared at me sitting on the steps. The girlish smile had gone. In its place was a look of utter desolation. I was stunned. Mine was the shock of a spectator who'd come to watch the most wonderful play of his life. Much later I realized that it wasn't time that had destroyed the happiest moment of my life but that look of utter desolation.

Nur never smiled in that beautiful way again. Not at me, not at anyone.

'Burak, what are you doing? Aren't you coming? Have you gone back to asleep?'

Celine opened the door and stuck her head in. Seeing me standing at the window in my underwear and T-shirt, she quickly backed out again. I walked over and put the carafe down on the bedside table. A lump had settled in my heart. Pulling on some trousers under my black Metallica T-shirt, I went into the bathroom between my room and Nur's.

2

Celine

I lied to Burak.

It wasn't this morning when I realized my dad had left. He came to my room last night and said goodbye. Actually, I'm not sure whether it was last night or this morning because I was asleep. I mean, I wasn't really asleep, but I pretended I was.

Dad had an old-fashioned laptop bag on his back. I saw it when I peeked. He leant down in the dark and kissed my cheek. Panic! I smelt of wine, tobacco and weed. That was kind of the reason I didn't open my eyes. I wished I'd only drunk cognac and smoked a little joint like Aunt Nur. Cognac smells classy and kills other smells. Why didn't I think of that?

A dim light was seeping through the curtains. Had the moon come out? I'm sure there wasn't a moon when we were on the jetty at midnight. Aunt Nur had been telling us about phosphorescence, how it makes the sea glow on moonless nights. When Burak jumped into the water to rescue our wine – Burak, my hero! – stars cascaded from his fingertips as he drew his hand out of the water. I'd never seen that before; it was magical. I wanted to get into the water too, but I was worried they'd think I was being childish. Then Aunt Nur rolled a joint and passed it to me. 'Don't you dare tell your father, he'd kill me for sure,' she said, laughing. I would never tell him.

My Aunt Nur has a beautiful laugh. It's like cognac: rough and warm. I took a puff of the joint and passed it to Burak. Our eyes met for a second and my heart literally jumped into my mouth. Such a great feeling – as magical as the phosphorescence.

My dad's moustache is as rough and warm as my aunt's laughter. When he kissed me, it tickled, and I really wanted to giggle like I used to when I was little, but I shut my lips tight, so he wouldn't smell my breath, and lay there like I was asleep. If he smelt the joint, he'd get mad at Aunt Nur. Actually, though, how would my dad know what weed smelt like? Anyway, I couldn't risk it. I didn't want to mess up my relationship with my aunt. She calls me on my mobile sometimes and we meet up. She takes me to places I'd never go on my own. We often eat a special pilaf dish with beans at the Suleymaniye Mosque, then we walk through Zeyrek and Fatih to Beyazit, the second-hand book bazaar in the old part of the Grand Bazaar. Before getting on the tram at Eminonu we always buy olives and cheese from the Spice Bazaar. Once she took me into a two-storey building with a big courtyard where there was a pile of second-hand leather jackets and stuff. She found a very stylish black leather trench coat in among the dusty jackets that smelt of sheep and bought it. She got it cleaned, and when she wore it she looked like an actress in one of those old films. My mother doesn't know about places like that; all she knows is Blue Mosque and St Sophia, and maybe the Grand Bazaar. My dad knows those neighbourhoods, but he wouldn't want me wandering round them; he finds them spooky.

Was Dad coming to my room in the middle of the night a dream? A tall, thin man bending down and tickling my cheek with his moustache in the weird blue pre-dawn light was just the sort of thing that happened in dreams, but this was real. I knew that. Although I was actually still very sleepy, my curiosity got the better of me, so I got up. With my eyes half closed, I put on the clothes I'd worn yesterday – denim shorts and a white vest top; I'd put on a bra later. I went into the bathroom that separated my room from Dad's and looked at myself in the mirror while I was brushing my teeth. Dad's door was half open. It squeaked when I pushed it. There isn't a door or hardwood floor in this house that doesn't squeak or creak; in the summer the house stretches, in winter it shrinks. It's like my great-granny's joints – crack, creak.

I went into Dad's room with my toothbrush in my mouth and, as expected, he wasn't there. His bed hadn't been touched. The tasselled bedspread was still tucked in tight. That's how Sadik Usta always makes the beds, like in a hotel. I have to kick the whole night to loosen the corners of the sheets and covers. Dad had left, no question.

Suddenly the detective in me woke up. I stopped brushing my teeth. Burak came into my head. Burak the journalist, the investigative journalist, famous for his interviews. He'd done an interview with old Sadik Usta a few years ago and it was published in the paper. When I was little and alone in the house with nothing to do, I used to go into Sadik Usta's room and look at the clipping of that interview. He'd cut it out and taped it to the red-tiled wall of his room. I used to take down the clipping really carefully, read it and study the faded, blurry photograph. That's where I saw Burak's face for the first time, in the photo. He and Sadik Usta were sitting side by side on the sofa, with one of Great-Granny's oil paintings on the wall behind them. The painting was of a giant man being tied up with rope by tiny little men. Behind them was a stone bridge, some huge candles, and a group of women standing in a pool of light. As always in Great-Granny's paintings, none of the figures had faces, not even the giant man. In the photo, Sadik Usta was wearing his usual expression, staring into the camera with anxious, owl-like eyes. Burak looked younger than he does now. His hair was still curly but blacker, his glasses were different and he was smiling bashfully. He's more handsome now.

I opened Dad's wardrobe and the smell of dust, soap and hot wood filled my nostrils – the smell of my childhood, the smell of every old wardrobe on the island. Someone should write a blog post about that smell. It's so unique; anyone who's familiar with it would recognize it straight away. Just as I thought, Dad's old backpack was gone, but his shirts and trousers were there; all he'd taken were his deck shoes, the ones I'd never liked. He'd put them on and walked out. I went back to the bathroom and rinsed my mouth. His pine-scented shaving lotion, his toothbrush, his razor? All there. What if I'd got it wrong and he hadn't gone anywhere? Okay, what about his old laptop, as heavy as a dead donkey? I looked around. It wasn't in its usual place. Good. He'd also taken the charger with the hefty cables. The laptop was so old, its battery didn't work any more.

The first clues were falling into place.

Fikret Bulut had left his house under the cover of darkness, taking with him nothing but his laptop, a laptop as old as the ark.

14

This would make the perfect opening of a detective novel. Great!

Curiosity swelled inside me, like a bubble of happiness. In my role as detective, I would enlist the help of Burak the investigative journalist. We'd go over yesterday's events together. When had I last seen my dad? He didn't come down to dinner, but Dad never eats in the evening. Where was he while we were drinking on the jetty? It was all very mysterious. Maybe he'd left a letter, like in the films. I scanned the desk in the corner of his room. An inkstand, a tiny notebook with a cracked leather cover, an old-fashioned phone directory. Nope. No letter, no note, no Dad. Nothing but the tickle of his moustache on my cheek.

Oh, how exciting! I'd have to wake up Burak – right away!

3

Sadik

Mr Burak and Miss Celine came out into the garden just as I was returning from the market. I was carrying my bicycle basket of bread and groceries into the pantry through the side door so I do not think they saw me. As she opened the garden gate, Miss Celine held the bell still to stop it from sounding. I hung that bell there myself, so that we might monitor arrivals and departures, for the island is not what it was and these days the ferries bring in an endless supply of hoodlums. Miss Celine's behaviour struck me as odd; she was acting like a thief in her own home, but it was none of my business, so I turned away.

Madam Shirin likes the boule loaves from Niko's Bakery. They must be purchased hot from the oven, before they get wrapped in plastic and go hard. Madam Shirin never says anything, but she always holds my gaze as she takes her first bite and I immediately know if she is dissatisfied. Here on the island, shopping is easy. I ride my bicycle down to the shops and while I wait for the bread, Niko's children serve me tea. Rest in peace, Niko; it's been several years now. All my friends from the market have departed. I am the last one left. The children say, 'You're as sharp as a knife, Mr Sadik,' and ask me how old I am. I don't even know myself. Some of them are surprised that I still ride a bicycle. I don't tell them that my knees ache, but even if I did, they wouldn't hear me. The complaints of the elderly are like dust in the ears of the young. 'He's like a horse, praise the Lord,' they say, putting me out of their minds.

Unknowingly, they are not wrong about that. Just like the wretched horses that pull our island carriages, I am as weak as anything, totally depleted, with no strength left in me. Only yesterday Madam Nur told me about a horse over at Viranbag, which, hot, exhausted and unable to bear the weight of his carriage any longer, lay down and died as blood streamed out of his mouth. What sinful cruelty! Madam Nur was almost in tears as she told me about it. Ever since childhood, she's been sensitive about animals. Should I distract her with some magic tricks? I wondered. When she was young, I used to make shadow figures on the wall for her with my hand and arm; the way the evening light hit the kitchen wall was perfect for that. I would press my fingers together and waggle my arm like a duck. Miss Nur, in tears over a lost kitten, a lame dog or an injured bird that had fallen into the fountain, would laugh at my shadow play and forget her sadnesses. The situation is quite different now, of course.

I drank my tea with Niko's children and we wished each other a happy holiday, smiled and bowed our heads. I didn't read the newspaper; I've not done that for years. When Niko was alive, we'd listen to the news on the radio. After he passed away, his children removed the radio. There's music in the shop now; Greek music, played softly. When Niko's daughter-in-law joins in the folksongs from behind the counter, it tears at my heart. I hear my dear mama's voice. I see a wild sea and a ship upon it. My lady and my humble self are on board the ship. As I stare down from the deck, waves burst through the fog, hitting the pier and sending out a spray of white foam. Our mothers stand on the pier waving us goodbye as the sea swells blackly. Clouds have descended on the mountains behind us and a light fog touches the green hills like a bridal veil then passes on. My heart tightens. My dear mama's voice comes and goes like the wind. A hand rests within my hand; it is soft and I feel comforted.

I always drink down my tea hastily and get up swiftly in order to dispel those disturbing scenes in my head. They wrap my bread in paper, never in plastic. I won't even pour cologne from a plastic bottle onto Madam Shirin's palms. Then follows, every morning, an argument over money for the tea.

'You are our uncle, we will not take it.'

'You must take it.'

'Definitely not.'

And so on and so forth. A bag of words. But this morning there were more purchases to make and the subject of the tea money did not come up. I bought Miss Celine's favourite doughnuts. With Mr Burak as our guest, I needed to buy things to please him. It was a holiday, after all.

In addition, tomorrow was Madam Shirin's birthday and the grandchildren wanted to have a tea party for her. In my opinion an afternoon tea was not appropriate for such an important celebration. In the past, my lady would often invite guests to our island home and many birthdays were marked with waltzes under chandeliers whose light shimmered like falling rain. The dining room would be filled to the rafters with the aristocracy of the island. Refined, elegant ladies would sit under the arbour in the garden or wander along the terraces that extend down to the private beach, arm in arm with well-dressed men. I, your humble servant, would walk among the guests throughout the evening, bearing trays of salami and platters of olive pastries, and serving champagne in long-stemmed glasses. Madam Shirin would be wearing a diaphanous dress and was always the most charming and gracious hostess. Confident in the knowledge that the party was functioning like clockwork, she would smile or sometimes wink at me over the tray of sparkling champagne. For me, those smiles, those winks, were an expression of gratitude greater than mere thanks. Despite my weary body and aching legs, I would fall asleep with a peaceful heart on the nights of my lady's birthday celebrations.

This year, however, Mr Fikret and Madam Nur were in charge and had insisted on afternoon tea. It is true that the era of birthday dances has passed, but I still hold that a gathering rather more elegant than afternoon tea is merited. They requested that I make no further arrangements, but it was a holiday and it would be inappropriate to present a pauper's table in Madam Shirin's home.

On holidays in the past, a crowd of neighbourhood children would congregate at our gate. I would open it and they would roam around the garden – children from government lodgings, gardeners' sons with shaved heads, children from neighbouring villas, little girls with white ribbons in their hair, polite young boys. They were always all so neat and tidy, dressed alike from head to toe, the wealthy families having passed the clothes their children had outgrown along to those of their servants. Madam Shirin would sit in the jasmine arbour and I would serve her tea from the porcelain tea service. You could tell from the children's faces how excited they were to be setting foot in our garden, the one day of the year they were allowed to do this. I would organize them into a line, and as they waited their turn to show their respects by kissing Madam Shirin's hand, they would gaze at the garden, committing to memory the different trees and flowers, and the house rising like a castle in the middle of it all. These days, children have telephones with which they take photographs of moments they wish to remember. I wonder if they ever go back and look at those photographs.

Madam Shirin keeps her photographs in old velvet-covered chocolate boxes. From time to time she takes a box from the shelf, opens it and goes through it. Sometimes she asks me to look through the boxes with her. In winter, when it's just the two of us in the house, we close up the other rooms and keep only the library open, where I light the fire. Madam Shirin has many photographs. I am always surprised when I see myself in one of them, in the background somewhere, caught in a doorway, like a ghost. Then I am minded to stop Madam Shirin and have her return the photograph to the box, though of course I would never do such a thing. At any rate, she never holds a photograph in her hand for long. They quickly fall from her fingers, back into the box or sometimes into her lap. She forgets what she was looking at.

Many years have passed since the neighbourhood children last rang the bell in order to kiss my lady's hand. It seems they are afraid. If they do not fear two old people in a huge mansion, who would they fear?

With these thoughts occupying my mind, I entered the delicatessen on the corner. They had spread sawdust on the floor and the boy was sweeping it. We greeted each other. Their goods are rather expensive, but they are courteous people. I bought salami, sausage, ham, and some of that Swiss cheese the name of which at my advanced age I cannot pronounce. Madam Nur likes to have the foreign chocolate that's only found in this shop with her evening cognac. That too I set down beside the cash register.

In the past, Madam Shirin used to give out chocolates to the children who came to kiss her hand. On the day before the holiday I would buy them by the kilo from the Haci Baba shop, little hemispheres of Mabel chocolate wrapped in shiny red, blue or green foil. Madam Shirin would place five pieces in each little palm held out in front of her. She would give Miss Nur and Master Fikret squeaky clean banknotes that she withdrew from her bank just before the holiday.

Nowadays the children of the neighbourhood rush headlong into the sea at the very mention of the word 'holiday'. Madam Shirin's family are loyal; they always come to the island on holidays. But this year Oguz was not with us. He had not returned from America. Apparently his friend, that foreign girl, doesn't want to come to Istanbul any more because she's frightened. The first year she visited with Oguz, she brought with her an American flag. Imagine my surprise when I went to tidy up the guest room and saw that she had hung the flag along the length of the wall. Seeing this, I myself was frightened, though I cannot recall why. I do not trust a person who travels with a flag in her luggage. Nor do I care for flags being hung out of windows and doors at every opportunity. Why so, you ask? I do not know the answer to that.

'Greetings, Uncle Sadik, what's up? Looks like your head's in the clouds, Uncle, but it's a holiday, you should chill out!'

The greengrocer Hasan was hosing down his racks of fruit and vegetables, which spread across half the street. I actually quite like this young man, though I do not make it obvious.

'Give me two kilos of tomatoes – no, that's not enough,

give me three. Not the bruised ones. Step aside. Cucumbers, but not these. Cengelkoy cucumbers. How much are the cherries? Where do your peaches come from? I can see that they were picked before they were ripe. Don't give me those. I don't want those. That's enough, that will be all.'

'No problem, Uncle Sadik. We'll get all that for you. These bags are heavy – you must have a full house for the holiday. You carry on with your shopping and I'll get the boy to deliver these to the house.'

I looked him in the eye. How could he think that would be acceptable? He would empty out the tomatoes I'd selected one by one and replace them with damaged ones. Miss Celine bought strawberries from there once, and instead of bringing them home herself, she had them delivered by the grocer's boy. The boy couldn't even manage to transport a kilo of strawberries in his bicycle basket. By the time they reached the house, they were squashed. Of necessity, we made jam.

'I shall wait. Weigh them now, in front of me, don't be going into the back.'

I loaded the bags and packages into my bicycle basket myself, one at a time. Greengrocer Hasan took up his hose once again.

'This morning when I was going to the mosque for holiday prayers, I saw Fikret Abi at the pier. Is all well? Heading to Istanbul on a holiday morning? Everybody else is coming to the island, but Fikret Abi goes in the opposite direction. Ha, ha. Was there an emergency or something? Since he left before sunrise—'

Saying nothing, I set off, pushing my bicycle. One does not ride one's bicycle within the market. Daytrippers don't know this, but it is the custom of the island. Hasan was still muttering something as I left. When you're old, you can get away with not seeing or hearing certain things. Greengrocer Hasan was clearly getting old. He should see a doctor, get his eyes tested, mistaking some gentleman he saw at dawn for Mr Fikret.

4

Nur

They left the house one after the other. First Fikret. Carrying his backpack, he walked to the gate. I was awake and sitting at my desk in front of the window, pen in hand, empty pages before me. As soon as I saw Fikret in the garden I turned off my table lamp and watched him from behind the curtains. It wasn't yet light, so the world was still veiled beneath a gauze of deep purple. Where could my weird brother be going? Had his interest in yoga and meditation given him a new enthusiasm for going to the mosque; was he intending to go to holiday prayers? The call to prayer hadn't even sounded yet. Where was he going at such an hour?

When he closed the heavy iron gate, the bell that Sadik had hung there echoed along the street and around our garden, but nobody took any notice. The gardener Huseyin's dog barked a couple of times down in the annex, but that was all. Fikret hurried up the hill, checking his watch, then turned towards the pier and disappeared from view. I stayed at the window for a while, wondering if he would return. Dawn broke and the call to prayer sounded. It was the end of a long night. Fikret did not reappear.

Once it was light, the stooped form of Sadik Usta emerged. He took his bicycle from its place beside the woodshed, rode off to the market, came back and unloaded his basket. Poor man, despite his extreme old age, he still considers it his duty to go down to the market at daybreak. We've suggested so many times that we should employ someone to help him, someone who would live in and see to all the chores, but neither he nor my grandmother will hear of it. Fikret hired a couple of people anyway, but those two stubborn oldies got rid of them. They do at least have the gardener Huseyin and his wife Sehnaz living in the lower annex and doing the heavy work and the bulk of the cleaning. Sehnaz does most of the cooking. Sadik Usta buys the breakfast food from the market every morning, prepares the breakfast table and clears it. The two of them eat like birds anyway. Let him go down to the market in the mornings. We can't ask the poor man to change the way he's been doing things his whole life.

While Sadik Usta was carrying his purchases round to the pantry door at the side of the house, Burak and Celine appeared in the garden. Celine got her retro 'made in China' Schwinn cruiser bicycle from the shed and, thinking no one had spotted them, they snuck away. If they'd looked up, they'd have seen me sitting on the windowsill of the top-floor bedroom. Celine muffled the bell on the gate so it wouldn't wake me. How about that! It turned out my niece was a wolf in sheep's clothing. Last night, when we were all drinking together on the jetty, she was practically throwing herself into Burak's lap. She laughed at everything he said. Was I jealous? No. Burak paid her no attention. He kept trying to catch my eye. I knew what he was thinking. Another fling. You cheated on your husband once; you can do it again. But that's not how it is, Burak. We made a mistake and then I felt guilty. Still do. Though you have no idea about that, of course.

With those thoughts in my head, and trying really hard to avoid Burak's gaze, which was becoming more intense with each mouthful of wine he downed, it didn't even occur to me to be jealous of Celine. But now, seeing them skulk out of the house like two thieves, like it or not, I started to wonder. What if, to spite me, Burak had slipped into Celine's room after we went back to our rooms drunk. No, Burak was honourable, a gentleman. He wouldn't jump into bed with a twenty-one-year-old chick to get revenge on me. Especially not when that twenty-one-year-old was Celine. I was accusing my old friend unfairly.

To tell the truth, I was too exhausted to feel jealous or anything else. I just wanted to sleep, to stretch out on the brass bedstead where my mother had once lain sick, the bedsprings squeaking as she tossed and turned, and sleep, sleep and forget. But I couldn't sleep, hadn't been able to close my eyes for so many nights. Not since Ufuk went. Since the evening he left the note on my writing desk – 'The clinic phoned. What you have done is unforgiveable, Nur' – and walked out of the house, the knot in my heart had not let me sleep.

Through the dusty curtains I watched them walk up the hill. Celine hadn't got on her bike, she was pushing it, leaning in towards Burak.

I wondered if Burak did sleep with girls Celine's age.

The question Burak asked me last night, half drunk, half sad, when Celine went to get more wine, came into my mind.

'Do you remember the night Celine was born?'

He was lying on the boards of the old jetty, his arms pillowing his head as he looked up at the stars, which seemed especially bright as they shone down on our private beach.

I was dangling my feet in the water. As my feet moved, they glowed with the phosphorescence. It was lovely. The night Celine was born was also lovely. I was with Burak at Fikret's house. We slept on the bed Celine was conceived in; slept, woke up, made love, slept again. Freya had gone to Norway for the birth and Fikret and Oguz went with her. I was staying in their beautiful villa in Levent, already one of Istanbul's most desirable districts, and looking after their dog.

'Was it New Year's Eve?'

Of course it was. I knew that perfectly well, but I didn't want Burak to think I placed too much importance on him or our past. I was suffering from a broken heart that New Year's Eve and didn't feel like going out. My lover had recently gone back to his fiancée and I was afraid that if I went out with friends to Taksim or Beyoglu I would bump into the two of them. If I were to see them at a bar, having a beer together, holding hands and sitting knee to knee as if I'd never come between them, happily celebrating the New Year, it would have been as if I didn't even exist, as if my ex was telling me to erase all memories of our time together, and that would have been devastating. It was better to stay in. Fikret's beautiful two-storey villa, complete with garden and widescreen TV, was warm and cosy. I invited Burak over. I'd split up with him a couple of years earlier, telling him it would be better if we just stayed friends. So now, as friends, we could cook, drink wine and watch a New Year's Eve film, which would be much better than traipsing around Taksim in a short, tight skirt, dragging my fragile heart from bar to bar, trying to have fun. It would be cheaper too.

'Yep. New Year's Eve 1995. At Freya and Fikret's place.'

Burak is the opposite of me. The more he remembers about

the past, the more empowered he feels. I didn't answer. He continued. 'It suddenly started snowing, do you remember?'

Of course I remembered. While Burak was kissing me and I was lying naked on the salmon-pink carpet, I was watching snowflakes falling from the white sky onto the garden.

'You'd gone out to bring the dog into the house, even though Freya had repeatedly told you to leave him in his kennel.'

I lifted my head and looked at the tops of the pine trees leaning into the darkness of the water. Burak clearly had no intention of shutting up. He was determined that we should reminisce together. He got up from where he was lying and came to sit beside me. As he dangled his feet in the water, the phosphorescence danced. I couldn't take my eyes off the light pouring from our feet. He leant against me and our bare arms touched. 'You were afraid he would freeze,' he said, in a whisper for some reason, 'but he was a Siberian Samoyed, he wouldn't have frozen.'

He laughed. His gaze was roving over my cheeks, my ears, my neck. If I'd turned my head, we'd have been eyeball to eyeball. I swished my feet around in the water. We fell silent and into our silence slid the memory of us making love on a salmon-pink carpet.

Right at the start of that evening, before we'd even finished the food we were going to eat as friends, we'd leapt into each other's arms, leaving the pilaf and chicken steaming on our plates. We'd both been looking forward to the dinner we'd cooked together in Freya's tiny, brightly lit kitchen, bumping into each other as we prepared the roast chicken, the pilaf with currants, the potato salad on the side, and the pumpkin dessert sprinkled with walnuts. We'd giggled when we stuck an apple into the chicken's bottom and we'd giggled again when tears started flowing down Burak's cheeks as he cut up the onion for the potato salad. We put the red wine Burak had brought on the table. Not exactly the right wine for chicken, but so what. We were going to watch TV after dinner, sitting there in our woolly socks, well away from the New Year crowds. Just friends.

We'd been 'just friends' for a long time. I'd left him because of my mother; because, even after seven months, I still hadn't come to terms with her death. I just couldn't accept that it had happened. I'd say, 'My mother's gone', or, 'After my mother went', because I couldn't put 'death' and 'my mother' in the same sentence. I'd seen the paperwork, though, which Fikret had organized, and in order to forget the 'Death Certificate' heading at the top, I distracted myself by sleeping around. Burak's love for me was intense, the last thing I wanted. So instead I flitted from one lover to the next, moving on whenever they got sick of my volatile behaviour. My mood swings had infuriated my last lover, the one who went back to his fiancée – I was well aware of that. If I'd make just a little bit of effort, he'd have stayed with me.

Burak and I had managed to remain friends in spite of his intense feelings for me. But as we raised our wine glasses to toast the New Year, the look he gave me was so passionate, so full of desire, that the memory of our breathless lovemaking on the beach when we first met shot through me like electricity. Within seconds, I found myself lying prone on Fikret's salmon-pink wall-to-wall carpet, stark naked and with Burak on top of me.

Then it started to snow.

'Here I am. It took me, like, five hundred hours to decide which wine to bring out. Sadik Usta's pantry is like an off-licence. Far too much—'

Celine didn't finish her sentence. When she saw us sitting side by side at the end of the jetty she stopped talking. Our shared history was hanging over us like a cloud and, who knows, maybe her antenna was sensitive enough to perceive the cloud and realize she wasn't included. She took a couple of steps towards us and stumbled, almost falling flat on her face. She let out a muffled scream and Burak jumped up and grabbed her. The bottle flew out of her hand and into the sea and we all started laughing. Burak rolled up his trousers and waded into the water as Celine and I cheered him on. Our reminiscing was forgotten. I rolled a joint and passed it round. The evening continued.

Yet again, I hadn't been able to sleep last night. I picked up my phone from the bedside table and dialled Ufuk's number. I stopped texting him a long time ago because I knew he wasn't reading them. Maybe it really was over. He once told me that there definitely was such a thing as, 'too late, Nur'. We were discussing having a baby. Ufuk wanted a little copy of himself that he could hold by the hand and stand with on the pier, pointing out the boats as they sailed by. His soul would be immortalized in a younger body. I wanted immortality too, but not embodied in flesh and blood. No, I preferred to follow the Platonic ideal, to have my legacy be the words I would write, my poetry, short stories and novels, and for these to be implanted in the minds of future generations and reproduced down the ages. But I was struggling with that. I doubted I would ever succeed in Plato's terms, and in my marriage I had assuredly failed. Was a marriage that was not committed to the furthering of the human race really a marriage? Anthropologically speaking, it was not. Anthropologically speaking, Ufuk and I had swapped roles: though I should have been the one wanting to reproduce, it was actually Ufuk who had the deep need to become a parent. If we had stuck to the traditional roles, Ufuk wouldn't have upped and left. Was that true? Even though I'd been fobbing him off for years and had repeatedly postponed the baby project with one excuse or other? And now? There was no part of what I'd done that could be forgiven. I knew that.

Feeling utterly hopeless, I gave up on the phone and put on my bikini. I draped the kimono that was hanging on the back of the door over my shoulders, left my room and went downstairs. The big hall, off which all the ground-floor rooms open, was empty and silent. Light streamed through the stained-glass fanlight above the front door and fell in a colourful mosaic on the floor, which felt cool beneath my bare feet. Grandmother was in the bathroom, which she called 'the powder room'. From behind the frosted glass I could just make out the motion of her tiny head with its wisps of hair. Sadik Usta was in the kitchen and I slipped out without him seeing me. The stones in the garden hurt my feet. The wine bottles were still on the jetty where we'd left them and the filters from my roll-ups were now scattered all over. I took off my kimono and dived off the end of the jetty as if it were an Olympic swimming pool. Fragments of last night's phosphorescence danced joyfully where the sun's rays hit them and tiny little lights sprayed out with each stroke of my arms. I swam through the cool, bright blue water until the Horoz Reis Tea Garden came into view and my grandmother's stone villa with its parched beachfront lawn and silent, grumpy facade receded, just another house in the Maden neighbourhood. I lay on my back and spread my arms and legs wide, all alone in the vast expanse of blue. This was freedom.

My mother was a great swimmer. It was she who taught

31

me, but she would never go out very far, always had to be able to touch the bottom with her feet. She'd sit in the sandy shallows on the beach, wearing a straw hat and big dark sunglasses, as the waves came in and out, splashing her bare legs and then withdrawing. When I came out of the water with purple lips, she'd wrap me in a big turquoise towel, hug me in her freckled arms and place a cream cracker on my salty tongue. Oh, Mum, for all those years you sat there so cautiously on the shore, and then you left in a great rush, diving deeper and deeper, drowning yourself in the bottom of a bottle, not caring that you might never resurface.

Dammit!

Tears pricked my eyes. Again. It was Fikret's fault; he'd set off that whole damn train of thought. My mother died of a heart attack, that was all there was to it. What was the point in digging up the past? The knot in my heart got bigger and it was then that I understood. That knot didn't settle there the day Ufuk left home; it had been there for years.

I started to cry, quietly, to myself, drawing the sobs inside me, one by one. The sea held me in its huge hand and softly rocked me as my tears mingled with the salt water.

5

Burak

'Shall we get some tea and cheese toast at one of the tea gardens by the pier? I'm hungry, and a hungry bear doesn't dance.'

It was obvious even before we got to the top of the hill that Celine's enthusiasm for tracking down her father was waning. I didn't slam the door in her face.

'Okay, but won't Sadik Usta and Shirin Hanim be expecting us for breakfast? I don't want to offend them.'

'Well, to start with, Great-Granny still needs to wake up and get dressed, and then my aunt has to get up, and Sadik Usta will need to make the tea and set the table. We'll easily make it to the pier and back by then. Anyway, we don't all have breakfast together in our house; it depends when we wake up.'

Celine was sitting tall on her bicycle saddle, pedalling right alongside the pavement, tempering her speed to my walking pace.

'But yesterday morning we all sat down to breakfast. It was an impressive spread.'

'That was different. Yesterday's breakfast was in your

honour. Today Dad's not here and my aunt will be hungover. You'll see. When we get back home, everybody will just be waking up.'

'Okay, okay. You've convinced me. I'm hungry too, actually. Why don't you pedal on ahead and I'll meet you at the pier.'

'No, I like it like this. Cycling is much more fun than walking – I get to sit down and move at the same time. We'll get you a bike from the rental shop, that'll speed things up.'

We were going to rent me a bike at the pier, then go and check out the places Fikret might be. My gaze kept resting on Celine's tanned, muscular legs as they moved in and out of view. She had beautiful legs, thanks to her mother's Scandinavian genes. Fikret's wife is from Norway. They met years ago in Bodrum, where their brief summer romance suddenly became a great deal more serious when Freya found she was pregnant. They got married, Oguz arrived, and then three years later, Celine was born.

Keeping her eyes on the road, Celine said earnestly, 'I have an idea – about Dad, I mean. A theory. Maybe... No, I'll tell you when we're sitting down. It's too hard to explain now.'

I smiled. Her youth amused me. There was something about her freckly little nose and big blue eyes that reminded me of a cartoon character.

She must have realized that I wasn't taking her seriously because she quickly added, 'And we'll ask at the coffee shops if anyone's seen him. If he got on the first ferry or motorboat, he'd have passed them.'

I nodded. Sure. Of course.

A refreshing salty breeze smelling of seaweed drifted up from the shore. It was still early and not yet crazy hot. The gardens we passed were silent. In some, automatic sprinkler systems were already in operation; in others, gardeners with hoses were watering the well-tended grass and many-coloured roses. Every so often, a horse-drawn carriage passed us.

'They're going to the pier to pick up the day-trippers,' Celine muttered. 'You should see the crowds. We'll be lucky if the island doesn't sink today.'

The street we were on was so peaceful, with its handsome wooden mansions that had been lived in by the same island families for four generations, that had I not witnessed the crowds for myself when I arrived yesterday, I'd have assumed she was exaggerating. The buzz from the marketplace grew louder as we approached and Celine got off her bike and began pushing it. As we walked through the market, shopkeepers to the left and right of us called out their greetings and Celine wished them a happy holiday in return. She wasn't bothered by the stares from the Arab tourists and the grocers' boys. She chatted a bit with the lady who was serving tea and pastries at the tables in front of the little bakery and greeted the greengrocer and the kind-looking man behind the till by name. Everyone wished each other a happy holiday.

'You've become a real islander, Celine. Everybody knows your name.'

'It's Great-Granny they know, not me. Her fame encompasses all of us: Shirin Saka and family. It's like the title of a book, isn't it?'

I didn't ask how it was that the shopkeepers on the island knew that Shirin Saka had been famous long ago when even the art crowd in Istanbul barely remembered her. Shirin Saka lived on the island year-round now and presumably there was plenty of scope for gossip and tall stories, especially during the quiet winter months, about an elderly woman who was once a celebrated painter in Paris and was now holed up in Maden, living alone in her mansion together with her servant.

We had arrived at the square with the clocktower. The crowds and the heat hit me at the same time: motorboats, ferries, bicycle bells, and a mass of loudly shouting people on the move. A ferry was approaching the pier, full of passengers ready to burst through its gates. They were shoving and pushing to be the first on land, like a wave that had been prevented from breaking on the shore. Celine cut through the crowds with her bike and made straight for one of the seafront tea gardens.

I followed. We sat at a table at the back, in the shade. The ferry passengers attacked the front tables, the square and the ice cream shop across the street like angry bulls. Unfazed, Celine leant across the table towards me. I looked away so as to avoid staring at her breasts, which were clearly visible down the front of her top. She immediately straightened up. She didn't want to arouse me; she wanted me to like her on her own terms. Being young is hard work!

'You know, I was really afraid you wouldn't recognize me when you got off the motorboat yesterday.' She gestured at the quay with her head.

'How come? Why wouldn't I recognize you?'

'Don't know.' She shrugged.

She must have figured out that I had no idea who the girl yelling, 'Burak! Burak Gokce!' at the top of her voice from somewhere within the crowd at the motorboat landing was. I was expecting Nur. Not expecting, of course – hoping. My eyes were scanning the crowd for her. It didn't occur to me that I'd be met by a Scandinavian beauty with hair the colour of wheat and eyes as blue as the ocean. I must have been staring at her quite stupidly, at which point she was forced to introduce herself. 'I'm Celine,' she said. And then, as if that might not be enough, 'Celine Suheyla.'

Our tea came, sage tea for Celine, regular tea for me. We ordered cheese toasts. I cleared my throat.

'The truth is, I didn't recognize you straight away. But as soon as you said your name, I knew who you were. The last time I saw you...'

I stopped to think for a second. I'd seen Celine as a child, and again during her teens. I must have. I searched my memory. At a coffee shop on a winter's afternoon. Where was that? The Ali Baba Café in Rumelihisar. A woodstove was alight in the middle of the room and the place was thick with cigarette smoke, but Fikret couldn't have cared less. He'd spread out his newspaper on the table and was absorbed in it. He was waiting for Freya to finish the lesson she was giving at Bosphorus University. Celine must have been around four or five years old. She was sitting like a doll in the middle of all that smoke, a piece of cheese toast with the crust bitten off in her hand. She was wearing a white beret and her cheeks and lips were pink with cold. When she saw Nur, she clapped her hands with excitement. But Nur didn't even notice her little niece. She was annoyed at having unexpectedly bumped into her brother, and then her eyes settled on his newspaper and in that moment her life changed. She immediately raced out of the café. Celine was astonished. Her eyes welled up and she was on the brink of tears.

'What happened? You seem lost in thought there, Burak.'

Celine was smirking. With a single sweep of her hand she gathered up her hair, exposing her long, tanned neck and delicate collarbones. When she saw my admiring glance, she got flustered and almost spilt her glass of sage tea. Once she's grown out of her youthful bashfulness, I thought, she'll be quite ravishing.

'I was trying to remember the last time I saw you.'

'If you have to think that hard, we've got a problem. C'mon, I'll give you a clue.'

How obsessed with clues and detective games this girl was! I nearly made a cutting reply, but something stopped me.

Her blue eyes were shining like the sea in front of us. 'Hisar.'

'What? The castle?' Rumelihisar. But how could she remember that?

'At a concert – at the Open Air Theatre. Does that ring any bells?' She flashed me a teasing smile, half-empty tea glass in hand.

I tried to remember, but my mind was preoccupied with memories of that other day, in the café, much further back. Nur and I were very young. We'd taken on a huge task and it was too much for us. We were miserable. After Nur fled the café, I tried to console her on the icy shores of the Bosphorus, but, by the end of the day, she'd given up journalism forever. When she saw that page of the newspaper, spread out in front of Fikret like a bedsheet, she realized something that I have only just recently understood. Journalism was not about revealing the truth, or calling people out or encouraging the powerful to admit to their failings. It was about fabricating a truth that didn't exist and then watching how that truth became the accepted version of reality. It was not at all the career I'd dreamt of when I was at high school. Years ago, at the Ali Baba Café, Nur had understood this, but even now, some fifteen years on, I was still trying not to accept this was the case. Was that stubbornness, apathy or simply optimism?

Our cheese toasts came: double cheese for me, and with sausage for Celine. Hers was well grilled. She'd admonished the waiter at length: it needed to be crisp and come with plenty of butter. She was still waiting for me to reply. I quickly made up something so as not to disappoint her. If we'd met relatively recently at the Open Air Theatre, it would have to have been for the Istanbul Jazz Festival.

'It was the Jazz Festival, I guess.'

In her excitement, Celine bit off a piece of burning hot toast. Steam poured out of her mouth and she fanned it with her hand, as if that would do any good. 'Exactly! A Joan Baez concert. You remember, right? My hair was shorter then and I was wearing glasses. We didn't talk to each other anyway.'

The toast got stuck in her throat and she thumped herself on the collarbones – knock, knock. For a moment I was confused. I lost all sense of time. This had been happening to me quite a lot recently. The past would come to my mind as if it were yesterday, yet I couldn't for the life of me recall where I went two days ago and nor did I remember faces or even names. What was Celine talking about? When Joan Baez performed at the Open Air Theatre, I was younger than she is now; I was in high school and I hadn't yet gone to that remote beach with Onur to have a manly adventure, hadn't yet met Nur and her Bosphorus University friends who happened to be going to the same beach on the same day, hadn't yet fallen in love.

Celine saw that I was confused, and elaborated. 'My aunt was just about to introduce us when you ran down the steps and disappeared off to the front row because you had a VIP ticket. I was so jealous.'

Suddenly it came to me. Celine was talking about the Joan Baez concert two years ago. She took another bite of her toast and carried on talking, with her mouth full, which made it harder to understand what she was saying.

'Aunt Nur had got us good tickets and in the end I went right to the front anyway. I bumped into some people I'd met at the Gezi protest and we danced together. Wasn't it a great concert! I'd never heard her before. I mean, I thought it was old people's music. Don't take it personally – you're not old. Then, you know, she started singing, and it took my breath away. It was magic. Sort of like Gezi, with people of all ages singing together like children. I know some people are angry at her for cancelling her concert last summer, but I don't care. I hope she'll come back.'

Now I remembered rushing away from them. I'd been trying to see if Ufuk was there. I thought he might have settled the women in their seats and then gone off to get food and drink. I'd never felt comfortable around Nur's husband, maybe because I wasn't sure how much he knew about us. I suspected his whole compassionate, intellectual, beardy, pipe-smoker thing might be a facade, but actually I know him to be a good and honest man. Being so on edge, I must have forgotten Nur's promise to introduce me to Celine.

'Sure, I remember. Nur is a huge Joan Baez fan, never misses a concert.'

'Yeah! She knew all the songs by heart, every line, from start to finish! She taught me "Donna, Donna" and "We Shall Overcome" when we were walking home. I looked them up on YouTube and the chords are simple, easy to play. Incredibly beautiful songs. It was a really great night.'

I recognized that happiness. When I went to my first Joan Baez concert, it was a beautiful night, the stars seemed so close, as if they might fall onto the stage, and the smell of meatballs being grilled outside the theatre was making my mouth water. The plastic cushions were uncomfortably hard. 'I'm now sending my voice to those of you outside the walls,' Joan Baez said, 'as well as to those of you squashed inside these walls.' And then she began to sing, unaccompanied, without even a guitar or a piano. Seven thousand people in the Open Air Theatre held their breath, and afterwards there was an avalanche of applause. Right then, surrounded by thousands of people all clapping together, I felt so full of hope. This is it, I told myself. I am not alone. This crowd is my country; I know where I belong. It was that night, there and then, that I decided to become a journalist.

'You know, Celine, we queued outside the Concert Centre all night to get those tickets for the Joan Baez concert.'

'Why was that?'

How could you explain to a generation that has everything at their fingertips that you used to have to fill in the Istanbul Festival forms with a pen and hand them over in person? It sounded absurdly simple now, having everyone register with pen and paper, like a child's game. I suddenly felt old, and like all elderly people, I wanted to share my memories out loud so that I could relive them. But I didn't, because I knew it would bore Celine.

My glance fell upon four elderly women who were playing cards at a table so far back from the waterfront, they didn't even have a sea view. The metal ashtray was filled with lipstick-stained cigarette butts. Over the years, as I've collected more and more stories from aged interviewees, I've become adept at guessing people's ages from a variety of clues – the wrinkles on their necks, the light in their eyes, the sparseness of their hair, the creak of their joints, the hoarseness of their voices, the smell of their skin. For example, the one sitting nearest to Celine, a little woman with a long chin, would be at least eighty-five years old. The one sitting across from her, who couldn't distinguish between the clubs and the spades in her hand, was even older, maybe ninety. Out of habit, I instinctively dropped my head and tried to catch what they were saying. What language were they speaking? I strained to hear, but I couldn't make it out. Greek? Portuguese? Armenian? No, none of those. I began composing an article about them in my head. It's always the same – I'll be halfway through one project when another one pops up and beckons to me. The title of this article would be 'Card-Playing Ladies'. It was a shame it wasn't bezique, then they'd have had the scorepad open in front of them.

Nur teases me about my 'fin-de-siècle' journalism, but she likes my stories. She says there's nobody better at finding interesting people and that I'm good at bringing out the humanity in their stories. It's the 'fin-de-siècle' comment that irks me, as if I'm out of date and only into old-fashioned things. Which is true, of course. What fascinates me is how people used to interact before the internet, smartphones and social media; if I don't document their stories, who will? Our generation is lucky, we've got a foot in both camps, a ringside seat at the transformation of society from the roots up; we're old enough to have known how people used to live but young enough to fraternise with the millennials, to act as interpreters between the two generations, in a way. Yes, a 'fin-de-siècle' journalist.

Suddenly I started paying attention again. Maybe my ear caught a few words I recognized, or maybe I put two and two together and got four. The ladies were speaking Ladino, the old Spanish dialect used by the Jews who fled from Spain to the Ottoman Empire centuries ago. I was excited. I'd thought there weren't any Ladino speakers left in Turkey, but here they were, right in front of me. The card-playing ladies. Who knew what tales they were harbouring. I'd been dealt an excellent hand! Proof, my darling Nur, that there are always stories there for the taking, if only you know where to look.

Even as you continued sleeping, up there in your ivory tower, and ghostwriting your novels.

I'd tried several times to talk to Nur about how she was wasting her talents, but the subject just made her angry. Her eyes would glitter with tears of rage. When her first and only novel, *The Stationery Shop*, failed to elicit the critical approval it deserved, she got mad at the literary world. Her publisher had set up several interviews and TV appearances to promote the book, but she wouldn't do any of them. She insisted that a good book had no need of publicity, that good literature would always find readers. Her arrogance was the death of her.

She was convinced she'd be singled out by the critics she respected, the heavyweights who wrote long, incomprehensible articles in the literary journals, and so, at the beginning of every month, she would race over to Pandora Bookshop and buy up all the new editions. Her patient publisher put up with her caprices, because he'd fallen in love with her. The publisher was Ufuk. In the end, even the bookshops wouldn't stock *The Stationery Shop*. Out of anger and stubbornness, Nur switched to ghostwriting other people's stories. So now she was writing cheap novels dreamt up by the shallow imaginations of high-society women who couldn't even string a sentence together. Ufuk published them. It was a family business.

Celine put the phone she'd been playing with down on the table, tilted her head and gestured for me to be quiet. I hadn't been talking – I'd long since forgotten about her. We listened to the gruff, garbled announcement coming through the loudspeakers.

'The boat now approaching the pier will depart immediately for Heybeliada and Bostanci.'

43

Abruptly, she jumped up, causing the tea glasses on the table to wobble. I grabbed mine to stop it from falling.

'I think I know where Dad went, Burak!'

'Where?'

'I can't tell you now. Quick, let's rent you a bike. We've lots of work to do.'

I had no choice but to stand up. Hoping that I would find the card-playing ladies at the same place tomorrow, I caught up with Celine.

6

Celine

I didn't really have a brilliant new plan, but I could tell that Burak was bored with me and his attention was wandering, so I had to invent something. It's a trusted technique of mine. At school, whenever a teacher asked why I hadn't done my homework, I used to say that I couldn't tell them right then but that I'd explain in detail later. Ninety-nine per cent of the teachers would never follow up. Did they forget, were they too embarrassed to ask or did they just not care? I don't think anybody bothers much about anybody else for very long. Which is both funny and sad, since I spend a lot of energy wondering what other people think of me.

As we made our way to Mesut's bike rental place, I glanced sideways at Burak, who was hurrying along beside me with his hands in his pockets. Could he be considered handsome? I wondered. Was he old? Since he was Aunt Nur's friend, he had to be at least as old as her, so, fortyish.

Wow, if Ayse heard about this, she'd say, 'Great, an older man, so he'll be good in bed.' She's got sex on the brain. Having sex with Burak would for sure be different to having sex with Emre. No question. Emre and I are the same age and neither of us had ever been with anyone else. Maybe he had now, since we split up, but I've only ever slept with Emre. That's why I was curious. I was dying of curiosity actually. What would it be like with another man? A few times I'd thought about bringing it up with Aunt Nur, but I was always too shy.

Burak didn't seem old at all. Right then, in Oguz's black Metallica T-shirt and with his hands in his pockets and a spring in his step, he was straight-up good-looking. With his glasses and all, he looked a bit like one of the scholarship nerds at school. Maybe he was one, back in the day. Ha, ha! I'd have to ask him. His curly black hair reminded me of lettuce; it was all tousled, had that 'just got out of bed' vibe, but it wasn't contrived, he really hadn't combed it that morning. It takes Oguz hours to get that look. He locks himself away in the bathroom and uses up all the gel; it drives me crazy.

It was chaos on the pier now and almost impossible to push the bike through the crowds. Every last day-tripper was making a beeline for the horse-drawn carriages the moment they got off the ferry, as if the carriages were lifeboats and their survival depended on securing one. The queue stretched right across the clocktower square, all the way to the door of the Princess Hotel. Assholes! Could they not even walk a few steps for fear of falling over and dying? 'Look, baby,' the mothers were saying to their kids as they pointed, 'it's a horse. We're going to get on one now and go jingle-jangle around the island.' You'd think they were about to cross the Amazon on an elephant. How ridiculous. They should make it so you had to get a visa to come to the island – but then Burak wouldn't have been able to come. Okay, then they should make it like the US visa so that you could only come to Buyukada if you had a relative or friend who lived there. Oguz gets really mad when I talk like that, says I'm a white Turk, an elitist, a fascist. What would Burak think if he heard me?

Mesut Abi was in front of his bike shop. He had a map of Buyukada in his hand and was pointing out the famous 'Grand Tour' route around the island to two French tourists who had somehow managed to make it there despite the holiday hordes. I had a quick look at the bikes that were left. He'd put the beat-up ones outside at the front. He's a shark, of course.

'Good morning, Mesut. Happy holidays!'

He wiped the sweat off his forehead with the back of his hand and nodded. The queues of noisy people waiting for the carriages were already driving him crazy. I left my Schwinn Cruiser in front of the spice shop on the other side of the road so that the idiots wouldn't think it was for rent, took Burak's arm and pulled him into the bike shop. In the back, leaning against the wall, was a white Trek.

'Let's get that for you.'

Burak looked at it and nodded. It was obvious he knew nothing about bikes.

I went over and picked up the Trek with one hand. 'See how light it is? A light bike is essential on this island. And it has gears. It's a hybrid: half racing bike, half mountain bike.'

I was about to flaunt a bit more of my knowledge when a huge row kicked off outside. There was yelling and shouting coming from the carriage queue. Leaving Burak at the shop, I went over to see. Two big fat men at the front of the queue were demanding that they be allowed to have five people in their carriage. The driver was refusing. Having more than four people in a carriage was against regulations, as decreed by the mayor's office.

The women who were with them were taking selfies with a selfie-stick, messing about with their puffed-up hair and giggling. 'Look, sweetie,' one of them said to the driver, 'the three of us only take up the space of two people anyway. The men can sit side by side, and we'll squeeze up a tiny bit. God, why are you making such a fuss – let's just get in and go. Can your horses not pull us or what? Ha, ha, ha!'

The driver was a tough nut. He stood his ground even as one of the fat men grabbed him and tried to pull him off to one side. I knew that driver. When he doesn't have customers, he sits over by the club and makes lewd suggestions to passing girls. He's grey-haired, old enough to be a grandfather, and he's always propositioning Aunt Nur, but she doesn't get mad. One time, we were buying rosehip ice cream and she stopped and said, 'One of these days, I'll go with you up to the pine forest, I swear, and you can show me all your tricks.' He doesn't make lewd comments to me any more, but whenever he sees us eating ice creams, he give us a leer. Old lech.

Anyway, my job was to protect his horses, not him. I jumped in among them like an Amazon warrior and with two jabs of my elbow I got rid of the women and bounded into the ring. The fat men were truly gross – their necks were as thick as temple columns and the backs of their polo shirts were sopping wet with sweat. Did they really need to stuff themselves that much? I barged past them, shouldered them aside and stood in front of them.

'Mister, did you not hear what the driver said?' I huffed breathlessly. 'The carriage is for four people. The two of you are the weight of four people anyway, and you want to squeeze in five of you? What gives you the right to torture these horses in this heat?'

'Are you nuts, girl? Get out of the way. You want us to fight you as well?'

I opened my arms wide. No passing, mister. The randy old driver was standing there like a bastard, not knowing whether he should laugh or join me. Yeah, he hadn't expected such attitude from the cute little ice-cream-eating girl.

I put my hands on my hips and shouted. It was fun.

'Do you know how many horses die on this island every day, from carrying arrogant people like you up to the top of the island? Their hearts stop and they collapse and die right there on the spot, poor animals. There are dead horses all along the Grand Tour road.'

'Listen, you little brat, you keep out of this and stop spoiling our day. We'll have as many people as we like in this carriage – five people; six. We're not taking orders from you! Get out of the way or face the consequences.'

I raised my voice. 'And what will you do if I don't?'

The jerk took a step towards me. I didn't move. His freshly shaved fat pink face was up close now and the smell of his vile aftershave mixed with the stink of his sweat turned my stomach. Where was Burak?

'Do you know who I am? If I want to, I'll rent every one of these carriages and drive them round and round the island until every last horse dies. Understand?'

A crowd of nosy onlookers had gathered around us.

One of the selfie women spoke up. 'That's enough, Osman. Our fun's been ruined now.'

I was just thinking how great it would be if I could grab the selfie-stick off her and break it over her head when Burak appeared at my side. He took my arm and pulled me away from the crowd.

'Come on, Celine, let's get the hell out of here.'

'Just wait a second, Burak.'

He yanked my arm again, quickly and powerfully, and spoke into my ear in a low voice. His breath was hot.

'Listen to me, Celine. There's no point in trying to take on that rich bastard. He can make your life hell, and if the police get involved, we're in real trouble. We live in difficult times as it is, we don't need more adventure.'

I shot one last hopeless glance in the direction of the carriages. The rubberneckers had already dispersed, but the driver was still resisting. Good. Stand firm, old lech. When Burak put his arm around my shoulders to lead me away, I felt like the heroine at the climax of a disaster movie. As the scene fades, we see a man and a woman in silhouette, their backs towards us. All around them is a burnt-out wasteland. As the mist descends, they link arms and walk away, towards the distant horizon.

In the commotion, my bike had fallen over. As I picked it up, I came eye to eye with the fat jerk. I smirked and muttered, 'You might lose a bit of that beer belly if they hitched you up to that carriage instead of the horses!'

I said it quietly, but the fatso still heard me. Hands on his hips, he lunged towards us.

'Jump on behind me, Celine – quick!'

Burak had got on my bike! My bike! Like a proper fighter. Burak, my hero! I sat on the metal rack at the back and put my arms around his waist and off he pedalled, away from the marketplace, slaloming through the crowd, avoiding the dawdlers and the befuddled. It was just like a Bond movie. Oh my God!

'Ring the bell! Ring the bell, Burak! Get out of the way, people!'

We were out of the market and on a dirt road. Burak was a

much better rider than I'd imagined. Bringing my face closer to his back, I yelled, 'Dad sent me to a karate class when I was in high school. If you'd let me, I could have tried a couple of numbers on him. I'd have folded that fat jerk in two, wouldn't I?'

The nape of Burak's neck was red, its blue vein was swollen, and sweat was trickling down his temples. Without taking his eyes off the road, he laughed.

'You would have! You have talent.'

As we started down the hill, Burak released the brakes. We were heading straight for the sea. My heart was in my throat and I loved it! I lifted my legs. 'Yippee!' I shouted. 'Faster! Here comes Celine Suheyla! Here come Celine and Burak, saviours of Buyukada's horses!'

We were both laughing as we neared the house. Gathering my courage, I wrapped my arms around his waist. Did he lean back more heavily on purpose, so that his back would press against my breasts, or was it just that we'd slowed down in front of the gate?

Either way, we got off.

7

Sadik

If I had not seen that the door to Mr Fikret's room was ajar, I would never have gone in there. I usually have no cause to be on the top floor at that time of the morning, but while I was carrying the parcels from the market into the kitchen, a cat had slipped inside, a playful grey kitten, so I gave chase and followed it upstairs. It began meowing outside Madam Nur's door. Madam Nur is particularly fond of cats, and with her being so sensitive to animals, the cats always know when she's on the island. For most of the year, they don't dare even come near the house, for fear of Gardener Huseyin's dog, but when Madam Nur is in residence they become daring, even to the point of going upstairs, where the bedrooms are.

It was Madam Shirin herself who found that dog's mother on the street, a tiny little thing. Back then, Madam Shirin was still strong and would go for a walk every morning. Her bedroom had not yet been moved downstairs; it was still upstairs, at the back, overlooking the sea. Nowadays we use that room for guests like Mr Burak. She used to walk all the way to the Lunapark Square junction, which is in the middle of the island, a significant distance, and involves going up- and downhill, not at all like simply going to the pier or the marketplace. One day she hired a horse-drawn carriage from Lunapark Square and continued on to Viranbag Tavern, on the Grand Tour route. I was not informed of this. My describing it as a tavern should not be taken literally; it used to be a tavern but now serves only coffee and tea. That day she returned home with a puppy in her arms, which she'd got from the grumpy old owner of the tavern.

It was only then that I became aware that my lady had gone all the way to Viranbag; she let slip this information in passing. I was extremely upset. 'But, Madam Shirin,' I said, 'I beg you not to go to such an isolated area unaccompanied.'

'When I have the strength, Sadik, I walk to Viranbag. If my energy is lacking, I take a carriage. There is no reason for you to be concerned.'

Madam Shirin has always been courageous and determined. When we were younger, and even before that, when we were children, she would race off along paths that only the goats would use, up to the tops of the mountains, into secret caves and down to underground cisterns. I was smaller than her but I always tagged along. As soon as I saw her crossing the stone bridge, I would run down from our hut and grab hold of her skirt. My lady would not say a word as we walked on together side by side. But where were we walking to and what were we looking for? What did we find out there – remote cells used by the monks from the old monasteries? I don't remember. The past has receded into the mountain mist. It is even hard to believe that those children were my lady and me.

The night after Madam Shirin returned from her morning walk with the black dog, there was a huge earthquake. I recall it vividly. How this house shook and shivered! Upon hearing the glasses rattling in the dining-room sideboard, I immediately dashed to the top floor. It was pitch dark up there. The electricity was off and the earth was rumbling ominously beneath us. 'The earth and the sea will devour us,' I muttered quietly to myself. 'Dear Lord protect us.'

I found Madam Shirin at the top of the stairs. She was gripping the bannister and shaking like a leaf. The candle in her hand was also trembling. Her hair shone gold in the candlelight and her eyes were as large and round as the grapes on the vine in our garden. Then something very strange happened. Even today, the memory of it gives me goosebumps and I can hardly speak of it. Madam Shirin, without relinquishing the candle, reached out and took my hand. I was already old, back then. My palms were calloused and my skin was rough, and when she reached for my hand, I was mortified, because hers was so cool and soft and moist.

For how long did the earth continue to quiver? Newspapers later wrote that the quake lasted forty-five seconds. I do not believe that. In the library downstairs, books tumbled off the shelves. I heard them thudding to the ground.

I took the candle from Madam Shirin's other hand and we descended the stairs. The puppy was whining somewhere in the dark. I managed to find it and bent down and tucked it under my arm. Was the puppy trembling or was it that the earth was still shaking? Madam Shirin's jaw was chattering and her hand remained in mine. I too was trembling, but not from fear. My mouth was dry.

As we entered the arbour closest to the garden gate, I took stock. Should the house collapse, that corner of the garden would be safe. It had a set of heavy wrought-iron chairs beneath it, and a matching table, but no cushions. I had removed those earlier, to prevent them from getting mildewed or spattered with droppings overnight. 'With your permission,' I said, 'I will fetch the cushions. The iron is too cold and uncomfortable to sit on.'

As Madam Shirin did not release my hand, I was obliged to sit down beside her, with the black puppy on my lap. Even when the candle guttered, scorching my fingers, I did not put it down; eventually it burnt itself out, or perhaps a breeze snuffed it out. The earth shook, then stopped, then shook again. The dog whimpered for a long while before finally it slept. Madam Shirin's hand continued to rest inside mine until the sky lightened.

Oh, this old head of mine! What was the story I was trying to relate? Where has my mind wandered to?

I was talking about the grey kitten and how I followed it to the top floor, even though I never go up there before breakfast service, especially when the grandchildren are visiting. I am always extremely careful. Madam Nur can never get to sleep before morning. I hear her footsteps on the hardwood floor: she opens the window, then closes it again, and in bed she tosses and turns, making the old bedstead creak. Finally, at the morning call to prayer, she dozes off, and it is always noon before she wakes. Mr Fikret rises early and does his morning exercises in his room. Miss Celine also sleeps in, though not for as long as Madam Nur. Since yesterday, though, there had been a change in her. She'd been going out before breakfast, and this morning she'd taken Mr Burak with her. I hoped that all was well. That darling girl greatly resembles our dear departed Madam Suheyla. It is my opinion that Mr Fikret made a mistake in giving his mother's name to his daughter, as her second name, though of course it is not my place to comment on such matters. May the good Lord ensure she does not share Madam Suheyla's fate.

When I went into Mr Fikret's room it was clear that

Greengrocer Hasan had spoken the truth. Mr Fikret had indeed gone somewhere. The bed was still exactly as I had made it yesterday morning. Only the bedcover was slightly wrinkled. I straightened it with my hand and opened the shutters that the room might get some air. The smell of old furniture pervades the rooms. I noticed that the wardrobe door was open. It is certainly not my custom to poke about among Mr Fikret's personal items, but Greengrocer Hasan had piqued my curiosity. His clothes were all there. Most probably he had found a quiet spot somewhere and would return for breakfast. Or perhaps he had gone to the city to fetch his wife. In recent years, Madam Freya has not spent the holidays with us, preferring to engage in one of her outdoor pursuits in the mountains or the countryside. Madam Shirin has never said anything about this – her grandson's wife is a foreigner, after all – and as Mr Fikret himself never complains about her absence either, it is not for me to pass judgement. However, this was not just a routine holiday and perhaps Madam Freya wanted to be present at the hundredth birthday of the eldest member of the family.

Mr Fikret's desk was neat and tidy. The inkstand, ledgers, old catalogues and grocery lists had all belonged to Madam Shirin's late husband, Halit Bey. Many years ago, this was his room. Time is so strange and the past feels so close, as if I could reach out my hand and step into it. Mr Halit would be right there, dipping his pen into his inkwell and writing his letters. The past is within touching distance, just the other side of a thin wall, but we seem to have forgotten how to access it. If I could remember, I would return to those days.

Fikret never knew his grandfather. None of them did. The gentleman died far too young and dear little Miss Suheyla was left fatherless. She went into a decline after that. She and her father were very close; every year, when the plum trees blossomed, Madam Shirin and I would come to the island to open up the house, but Miss Suheyla and her father would stay on together in the city, in the apartment in Moda, until the beginning of summer. After he passed away, Miss Suheyla would come into his room and stroke his possessions longingly, one by one – his inkstand; the scratched leather covers of each of his ledgers. I can still picture her as if it were yesterday. For that reason I don't have the heart to throw any of them away.

I closed the door tightly behind me. Madam Nur would know where her brother had gone. At an appropriate time during breakfast, I would inquire of her.

I found the grey kitten on the windowsill of the room in which Mr Burak was staying. It must have escaped there while I was opening Mr Fikret's shutters. I chased it downstairs and went into the kitchen. I had already put the coffee on. Although I do not care for the taste of coffee, I do enjoy the smell of it as it brews in the corner of the kitchen. Madam Nur becomes grouchy if her coffee is not ready when she wakes. I peeled the tomatoes, for Madam Nur will not eat them with their skins on. The gardener's wife made jam from the plums in our garden for Miss Celine and from the corner of my eye I glanced at the pantry and saw that it was there on the shelf. I sliced the doughnut in half and arranged it on a platter.

On the night of the earthquake Madam Shirin and I sat in the arbour until dawn. Her hand remained in mine as we drifted off into our own separate worlds; perhaps we fell asleep from tiredness, I don't remember. When I opened my eyes, Miss Nur and Mr Burak were standing in front of us. They were young then, practically still children, and as the dawn light streamed through the leaves of the acacia tree and lit up Miss Nur's hair, which was dyed a fiery red and cut short like a hedgehog's, I thought I was dreaming.

I immediately withdrew my hand, and my dear lady shook herself awake. My first concern was whether Miss Nur and Mr Burak had seen us holding hands. Had they or had they not? Do not assume, however, that I have been preoccupied with this question ever since. It merely came into my mind because Mr Burak was once again here in our Buyukada home. That is all.

8

Nur

I saw my mother in my dream. She wasn't dead after all. She'd been hiding, all these years – from me, from Fikret, from my father, but most of all from her own mother. She'd got tired of struggling in vain for Shirin Saka's love and attention and had decided to go into hiding until her mother died. 'Will you come back after that, Mummy?' I say. I am both upset and elated. I am a child again, and my mother and I are in the sea. She takes me in her arms and I curl my arms and legs around her. I become lighter, weightless. I am lying in warm water in her womb. I feel safe again.

When I woke up, the sun was already high in the sky, its rays lighting up my bed, dancing off the brass bedhead and legs. I hid my face in the pillow. My mother was dead, had died years ago, but I still couldn't accept that, so I let myself be seduced by my dream. I tried to convince myself that she hadn't really died. After all, I never saw her body. Fikret saw to everything – the funeral, the imam, the red tape, the grave. It was my spring break and I was on holiday, which was a more valid excuse than my father's at least. His plane from Bangkok was delayed and he almost didn't make it to his wife's funeral. 'My father's on a business trip.' Ha, ha. Even at that age, I knew his so-called business trips to Thailand were bullshit. The only thing he was working hard at over there was his midlife crisis, his solution to which was to party with young Thai girls.

He must have come back with all manner of venereal diseases; how could he not? But when I'd shared my concerns with my mother, she'd shrugged them off. 'My dear Nur, do you really think your father is still interested in me in that way?'

I was too embarrassed to ask her my other questions. Are you still attracted to him, Mum? If my father doesn't make love to you, then who caresses your beautiful peach-coloured skin, your long, silky hair? As if she'd heard me anyway, she wafted away the smoke from her cigarette with a dismissive wave of her slender fingers.

I couldn't decide whether the dark shadows around her eyes were from sadness or weariness. In the past she'd have had been stroking the rounded bowl of a wine glass, but she'd stopped drinking and we all now acted as if those days had never existed, as if she'd never touched a drop, wouldn't start on the red wine at noon and continue knocking it back late into the night, emptying every bottle she could get her hands on. Because we never talked about those days, it was easy to wipe from our memories a past we had vowed never to speak of. We erased it. We said nothing about the chain-smoking.

When I was leaving the house to go on my spring-break holiday, I didn't hug her goodbye properly. I had a huge rucksack on my back and I didn't want to take it off again. My tent was tied underneath, with my sleeping mat to one side of it and my metal camping utensils on the other. It was so heavy, I'd had to sit down on the living-room sofa while my mother pushed my arms through the shoulder straps. I staggered when I stood up and Mum laughed at the state of me. She felt sorry for me.

'Let's call Sukru,' she said. 'He can take you to the bus station.'

'I'll hail a cab on the street, Mum. Don't worry.'

I was in a hurry to get going. Freedom was always outside the house, in the shape of hotel rooms, hostel dorms, cheap guesthouses, tents. I barely had the patience to wait for the old-fashioned steel-caged lift in our building. My mother was at the door – in her dressing gown. Mum, it's evening already, why aren't you dressed? Well, okay, I can see there's not much point when my father's in Thailand. What would she do when I was gone? Fikret would stop by with baby Oguz. She'd see friends, play poker with them, and they'd make iced tea with lemon; no gin and tonics around my mother.

'Call me when you get there.'

The lift door was heavy and I barely fitted in with my house-sized backpack.

'I'll call you from Oludeniz, the town on the coast where we get off the bus. But after that I might not be able to phone you again. There aren't any facilities in the place we're going to, no one lives there, it's very remote.' There was a foolish pride in my voice, but my mother wasn't interested.

'Then call from Oludeniz.'

'Okay, we'll see. Kisses!'

But I didn't kiss her. I was already in the cage lift. Tired, beautiful, sad Suheyla was leaning against the door. First her face disappeared, then her body; the last I saw of her were her feet, then the lift was at the next floor down. My mother disappeared. Forever.

In my dream my mother was young, very young, Celine's

age or less. She was laughing, whereas when I was a child she was always tired and depressed and wearing a dressing gown in yellow, pink or green, depending on the season. She was always miserable when she was making our breakfast. I'd be spreading Nutella on a thick slice of bread and she'd be holding her head in her hands, counting the minutes until our father's driver, Sukru Abi, came to take us to school. We'd be in our kitchen in our apartment in Macka, which was spacious and airy, with big windows that opened onto the back courtyard. I loved that neighbourhood. Macka was in the middle of Istanbul, urban and yet quiet and orderly like a European city. Our courtyard was extraordinarily beautiful, even lovelier, I thought, than the view of the Bosphorus from the living-room windows that always left visitors in awe. It had a pool with a statue, palm trees, and little paths of white gravel like almond sweets winding through the greenery. My mother saw none of that – because she had a headache, was hungover. When I was a child, my mother drank. She could not tolerate Fikret and me squabbling at the kitchen table. She would button the collar of my school uniform the wrong way and go back to bed. Sukru Abi would take us to school.

Ah, Fikret, why did you have to open your mouth so wide? The memories won't stop raining down now.

I wonder if Fikret was trying to give our mother another chance at life when he gave his daughter her name. Actually, when Celine was born Fikret hadn't yet become interested in spiritual matters, didn't yet believe in reincarnation, past-life regression, inter-generational curses and so on, but maybe his intuition was stronger than I thought; maybe Mum spoke to him in a dream too.

Burak was with me when I got the news of my mother's

death. We met on holiday. Actually we met on the bus, but he chooses not to remember it that way. In his version, we met around the campfire under the stars on the remote beach where we'd pitched our tents.

Burak is an incurable romantic. I've told him countless times that we met at an awful transport stop for overnight buses – they weren't called 'rest facilities' back then and you didn't have turnstiles to get into the bathrooms. We were just four girls on our spring break, sipping bowls of lentil soup under the fluorescent lights at midnight and looking far from our best, our eyes drooping with tiredness, hair flat against our heads, sweatpants sagging. That didn't stop all the men in the place staring at us and laughing lewdly though: the bus driver and his assistant, who were drinking black tea and chain-smoking at the table opposite us; the kitchen boy wiping the tables; and all the other male passengers at the transport stop.

When Burak came over to our table with a metal tray piled high with food and asked if he might sit with us, we were relieved. We didn't let on, of course, just pointed to the empty chair and muttered okay, but we were glad. This skinny boy might not be our front man, but after he sat down, the driver and his assistant found something to talk about and the kitchen boy was sent to wipe the tables somewhere else. Burak's friend Onur wasn't so pleased. He didn't like us and he didn't like Burak's Superman rescue act. It was obvious when he shook hands with us. And when he heard we were all going to the same remote beach, he got really upset.

In the morning, when we got off the bus and onto the boat, Burak sat with us girls in the prow while Onur stayed at the back. The two of them were supposed to be on a manly adventure, fully equipped with knives, fishing gear, binoculars and the rest, and with nothing to eat save one bag of noodles, three cans of beans and a few packets of instant soup.

'What will you eat for a whole week? Will you go hunting after you've used up your cans?'

From behind his glasses, Burak smiled bashfully. The prow of the boat was parallel to the green shore, ploughing through the waves as it advanced. We girls had rolled up our sweatpants to our knees and were dangling our winter-white legs in the water, screeching. It was only April and the water was really cold.

'Well, bring us the meat from your hunt and we'll cook you spaghetti bolognaise.'

We all laughed. Burak was shy. Back then, he couldn't hold my gaze for long – unlike now; he's a master of that these days. With his curly black hair, square glasses and puny body he really did look like Clark Kent. I drew my legs up to my stomach and turned my face to the wind. The smell of the Mediterranean was making me dizzy.

Then suddenly the prow of the boat swung to the east and we saw the canyon, squeezed between two steep hills and in its shadow a long stretch of deserted beach. A sharp wind smelling of thyme blasted our faces. The only sound was the put-put of the boat's engine as we all fell silent at the sight of such wild, fierce beauty. Despite our hi-tech tents and other camping paraphernalia we would be entirely at nature's mercy once the boat dropped us off and left. All ties with civilization would be severed. There was a village at the top of the hill, but the only way to reach it was via the trail the goats used, and in some places that required hauling yourself up by rope. We were suddenly very happy to have bumped into Burak and Onur.

As the boat approached the shore, the sun rose behind the

village and settled on the highest point of the stony hill. The sea turned turquoise, the grass got greener and at the entrance to the gully poppies began turning their faces towards the sun. We gazed in awe at the extraordinary sight before us.

I have always found the sea more seductive than any man. No amount of lovemaking can match the feeling of wholeness that infuses my soul when I dive into the water. I adore the way my body gradually adjusts to the sea's hardness, its coolness. Even as a child, a most wonderful sensation would spread through me – a sensation that today I know as sexual pleasure – whenever I leapt off our wooden jetty into the sea. The sea was so vast and I was so tiny, so incomplete. Real life, a faraway port, would begin when I grew up. Until I reached that port, I would just be play-acting. This is meant to be my house. Here is the living room, the kitchen. I am meant to be the lady of the house and you, my dollies, are meant to be my children, but you aren't really. This isn't actually my house, it's a corner of my grandmother's garden, and I am not yet a beautiful, grown-up lady, I'm just practising right now.

When I was a child, I thought this game would come to an end when I grew up, that real life would begin as soon as I reached adulthood. Then I would feel complete, whole. But adulthood has proved to be no different; life still has an air of unreality to it, of play-acting, of waiting for things to start. We go about our days believing that reality will kick in sometime soon. It's only when I'm swimming, embraced by the turquoise sea, that I feel properly alive and fully in the moment; it was like that when I was a child and it is like that still.

Maybe that was why, as I sat side by side with Burak at the front of the boat on that cool April morning, I decided to test this boy who had come into my life. I wanted to see if he would commit himself and dance to my tune. And so, out of the blue, I yelled, 'Come on, Burak, let's jump in! Ready?'

Under Burak's surprised gaze, I shrugged off my jumper and sweatpants and went to the back of the boat. The girls cheered and Onur sulked. Turning to face Burak in my bikini, I watched as he shyly took off his T-shirt. With his narrow chest and long, pale legs, he looked like a feeble adolescent. I would never, ever sleep with this boy! I tumbled into the water from the back of the boat. Whee! It was really cold. My brain froze. Screaming, I began to swim. The boat was speeding away, leaving foam in its wake.

The girls were shouting, 'Jump, Burak! Jump! It's cold, but you'll get used to it once you're in.' Poor, shivering Burak duly jumped in, just to impress me. The girls cheered. 'Bravo, Burak!'

He was a better swimmer than I'd expected. He approached me with strong, steady strokes of his thin white arms and we swam together in parallel. The sea, contained within the steep cliffs of the canyon like a turquoise pool, was so clear that you could see the pebbles on the seabed. Schools of little blue-grey fish darted here and there, nipping between our white legs as we powered through the water. I looked at Burak. He'd obviously spent his childhood in the sea; it was his home too. As the blue of the sea was reflected in his eyes, they shone like plump, oily black olives. Without his glasses, he could even be considered handsome. Give him a tan and muscles and maybe I could sleep with this boy.

Together, we swam to the shore.

9

Burak

When the telephone rang with the news of Celine Suheyla's birth, Nur and I were asleep in Fikret and Freya's bed. Nur reached for the phone without opening her eyes, but I immediately propped myself up amid the mound of sheets, blankets and quilts. She could hardly hold the phone, she was so sleepy, and it almost fell onto the pillow. I strained to hear what was being said. Phone calls in the middle of the night make me extremely nervous. I had been asleep when the call came through telling us that my father had died.

It was the year the bulldozer uprooted our trees, the year I finished primary school. The ringing of the phone woke me up. Mum was not in bed beside me and an ominous purple glow was seeping around the edge of the curtain. My father wasn't there either. He'd stayed over in Erdek, as he sometimes did when he and his work friends met up at my uncle's place. 'I missed the last minibus, Nebahat,' he'd said, 'so I'll stay with my brother tonight.'

I'd been having frequent nightmares recently, especially on the nights my father stayed in Erdek. I'd wake up in tears and beg my mother to stay with me until I fell back to sleep, but that always took so long, because I was so scared from the nightmare, that in order to get some sleep herself, my poor mum would let me sleep in their bed when my father wasn't home.

That night I dreamt the orchard was still ours and hadn't been taken away from us. This made me so happy. But then the atmosphere changed and the bulldozer came rumbling and grumbling into our yard, as if it were alive. Straightaway it set about tearing out our cherry trees with its gigantic claws, and spitting them into the dirt. The churned-up earth was littered with severed branches and stained crimson from the fallen cherries. Mum was standing at our front door, repeatedly twisting a strawberry-patterned tea towel in her hands.

My father wasn't there in my dream, and nor had he been there in real life on the day the bulldozer came. It was his fault that they'd ripped out our orchard, but I didn't know exactly why. Was it a signature that was missing, had a document been mislaid, or had the land not been ours to start with? My father had neglected to finalize something during the inheritance process and we lost the court case. The government won the right to build a road directly in front of our house, a road that would enable trucks to carry coal to the new government lodgings nearby. I was angry with my father. It was his fault.

The bulldozer didn't just demolish the cherry trees, it attacked the laurels and then the plum trees too. Those trees were tall and they fell heavily, as if in shock. For so many years they'd lived in each other's shadows, and now their branches, their trunks, lay side by side on the earth. The bulldozer wasn't strong enough to uproot the mulberry tree. It would have to be cut down, its branches hacked off with saws and axes. For days my father didn't say a word. That mulberry tree had been in our yard since my grandfather's time, or even before. The land belonged to that tree more than it belonged to us. Its roots passed under our house and into the neighbour's yard. The government workers tied ropes around it and even as they struggled to chop it down, they were rubbing their hands in anticipation, as if the tree was now theirs. What did that mean? How could a tree belong to someone once its roots had been torn out, its spoilt fruit scattered across the earth? 'They'll burn it,' my mother said. 'Use it as winter wood for the stove.' Her voice was low, so that my father wouldn't hear.

The tank-like tracks of the bulldozer had flattened my mother's lavender, her rosemary; now it turned towards me. Its scoop was raised high, as high as it could go, ready to plunge down at full power and grab me!

'Dad!'

The scream I had not been able to utter was echoing in my brain when I woke up, slick with sweat. The loud ring of the telephone tore through the gloom. Throwing off the thin yellow sheet, I raced barefoot out of the room. Mum would be angry that I hadn't put my slippers on; she'd fuss and tell me I'd get a stomach ache. But no! Mum was standing in the living room in her short-sleeved cotton nightdress, holding the red telephone receiver in her hand like a candle in the pale blue dawn light. Her feet were bare too. Her brown hair was loose around her shoulders, her eyes were wide and her face was pinched. I'd never seen her like this. She looked like one of the village girls, not like my mother. For some reason I was most frightened by the fact that she was barefoot. I ran and hugged her legs.

My uncle's voice was coming through the receiver. 'Nebahat, are you there? Can you hear me? Don't go anywhere. I'm coming over right now. You understand? I'm setting off right now. Don't think of coming here.'

He stopped talking and the dial tone sounded. I could hear its long A note – 'diiit' – from where I stood, clasping my mother's legs. Though she was holding the phone to her ear, she didn't hear it. I stood on tiptoe, took the phone from her hand and placed it back on its hook. It made a small ping, and that brought my mother back, as if she were coming out of a trance. Taking me by the hand, she sat me down on the sofa facing our wrecked garden. The sky was getting lighter, the stars dimmer, and inside me something was fading. My mother didn't need to say anything. A horrible thing had happened. The most horrible thing.

'Freya's had a daughter,' Nur mumbled, putting the phone back on the bedside table. New phones didn't make a ping when you replaced them, and you didn't dial numbers any more either; you tapped them. Technology has made us so impatient, presenting us with a never-ending supply of faster, slicker devices.

I let out the breath I'd been holding as I sat there, naked, in the bed.

Nur drew her knees up to her stomach and mumbled sleepily, 'They're calling her Celine. Celine Suheyla, in memory of my mother.' She buried her little head in the biggest, softest pillow I'd ever seen, and almost disappeared. As we'd made love, she'd sweated, leaving a stain on the pillowcase from the bright red punk hair dye she'd bought the previous summer in Canada, when she followed a lover there. I stroked her neck. She inhaled and drifted back to sleep. I wondered if she'd even remember the news about her baby niece when she woke up later. Though she finds it impossible to fall asleep before daybreak, once dawn's broken, she sleeps so deeply, not even a bomb exploding would rouse her. I'm the opposite; if I wake up anytime after dawn, I can never get back to sleep. And so, wrapping the quilt around my bare shoulders, I got up.

Since we'd made love all through the night, in every room of the house, it was hard to find my clothes. The house was ice cold and my teeth were chattering as I walked from room to room. We'd turned off the heating before we went to sleep. Freya had repeatedly warned Nur that gas was extremely expensive and that she should turn off the radiators and keep the doors closed in the rooms she wasn't using. I finally found my underwear in Fikret's son Oguz's room, among the Lego, and my trousers on the carpeted stairs. My shirt and sweater were downstairs in the living room. Somehow one of my socks had made it all the way to the kitchen. The other one was stuck in my trouser leg.

When the dog saw me coming down the stairs, he got up, stretched, and wagged his tail. I stroked his soft head and scratched his neck. He was pure white, with black lines around his eyes. After Nur had brought him into the warm house from his kennel, he had happily curled up on a corner of the rug and gone to sleep.

'You watched our lovemaking out of one eye while you were lying there like a bagel in the corner, didn't you, you rascal?'

As if he understood what I was talking about, the dog turned and looked at Nur's leather jacket with the fur-collar, which was lying on the floor. She'd slipped it on over her naked body when she'd run out into the snowy garden to bring him in. When she came back, her stomach was like ice. I became aroused just thinking about it, recalling how I hadn't even given her the chance to take it off before I was on top of her. My penis stiffened, as if it hadn't been filled and emptied countless times through the night. Nur's warm, strong, naked body was under the quilt right now.

The dog stretched some more, then stood up and walked around in a circle, making half-whining, half-barking noises. He definitely needed to pee. I went over to the window. It had stopped snowing. The squatter neighbourhood that had colonized the hill across from Fikret's house looked very ugly under the dull white sky. The ramshackle homes, knocked up overnight by villagers who continued to stream into the city in search of a living, were flimsy and filthy. I picked up Nur's jacket and hung it on the hook beside the door. The dog's leash was there too. He'd taken his place beside the door and was gazing at me with his black eyes. I put on my boots, put the leash around the dog's neck and we went out.

As soon as I'd pulled shut the front door, I realized I didn't have a key. Damn it. What an idiot! I'd planned to walk the dog and then come back and get under the covers with Nur. Why had I gone out? I had to stop myself from punching the glass door in frustration. By now the dog was pulling me and I had no choice but to follow him.

The big freeze had thawed and last night's snow had turned to muddy slush. It's always like that. Just when we're all rejoicing that the ugly bits of Istanbul have been buried beneath the snow, the city turns into one big squelchy mudbath. The dog dragged me out of the garden and down towards the muddy ditch that formed a natural boundary between Fikret's villa and the squatter neighbourhood on the opposite hill. Nur's Fiat Uno was parked in front of the house on the sloping dirt road. As soon as it got warmer, we'd need to park it on the level. If it iced over again, she'd never get out.

I glanced up at the bedroom window on the second floor. Nur was in there asleep. Nur... She was mine again. Not 'again', really; for the first time. When we were together two years back, we were so young, so raw and inexperienced, and she was so childish. We hadn't managed to continue our summer romance in the city and after a few months she dropped me. We'd gone to the house of one of her film friends in Cihangir to celebrate New Year's Eve and she left that party on the arm of another man. As she and I stood shivering together on her friend's freezing cold balcony with its magnificent view of the Bosphorus, she announced that from now on she wanted us to be just friends, nothing more. And so, as soon as Nur left the party, I headed off with a dark, skinny girl I'd found in the kitchen. We went to her basement apartment in Firuzaga and spent the night having passionless sex in the semi-nude, beneath a fluorescent strip-light.

But now Nur and I were embarking on a real relationship, as adults. In the new year, great things would happen. Fikret now had a daughter and Nur had become an aunt for the second time. Aunt Nur. The next generation was coming through. I tried to laugh, but the heaviness that had settled in my heart earlier wouldn't go away. All because of that phone call. But why? The call had been a joyous one, sharing news of a birth, not a death.

Having peed against a car tyre, the dog was now dragging me further afield. For a medium-sized dog he was really strong. Were these the dogs that pulled sleds in Siberia? I had to wonder what Freya had been thinking, to bring a Russian sled dog to Istanbul, to be tied up in a garden in Levent. I let him off his leash so he could do his business in comfort. He found a tree on the slope just above the ditch, circled it a few times, laid his ears back and took up position.

I looked across at the squatters' houses. Could they have spied on us last night as Nur and I, both stark naked, had raced breathlessly from kitchen to living room to the stairs, then back to the kitchen and living room? Our lights had been off, but the television was on. Its blue light could have given them quite some New Year's show. Did poor people have binoculars, actually? Anyway, New Year's Eve was only celebrated on our side of the ditch; on the other side it would have been just another night.

Perhaps because my focus had shifted to the squatters, the dog suddenly ran off down the hill. I couldn't shout for him because I didn't know his name. Nur had always just called him 'the dog' or 'Freya's dog'. If I were to lose Freya's rare, snow-white Russian Samoyed, there'd be a high price to pay. I chased down the hill after him, grabbing at clumps of weeds to keep from falling as my boots repeatedly got stuck in the thick, icy mud. The dog reached the ditch, wagged his tail joyfully, then took off for the opposite hill and waited for me partway up, gazing at me with his coal-black eyes, his black lips seemingly almost grinning. I caught up with him and clipped on the leash. He didn't object but immediately pulled me on up the hill with all his strength.

I was now in the squatter neighbourhood. Houses lined both sides of the hill's muddy dirt roads, each one a different colour – blue, yellow, pink and so forth. Most of them had gardens, but unlike in Fikret's neighbourhood, these gardens had no clear boundaries, so the arbours under which people sat on summer days, the vegetable gardens planted with cabbages, and the fields where little boys with shaved heads and plastic shoes played football threaded the land together. Neither the children nor the women carrying buckets of charcoal to their homes paid me any attention. I looked like them, I thought. I too am a village boy. I was born in my father's village on the shores of the Sea of Marmara. My mother being from a family of civil servants in Edirne and my having studied at Istanbul High School for Boys did not change this fundamental fact. A village was a village, whether it was in the mountains, which was where these squatters had come from, or whether it was a fishing village, as ours was.

Because of my roots, I could only get into the Taksim bars that Nur and her Bosphorus University friends frequented when Nur was with me. If I was on my own, the bouncers wouldn't let me in. 'You look too revolutionary, that's why,' Nur joked. 'What do you expect, with your parka, your combat boots, your long curly hair and your dirty beard.' But there were plenty of men who looked like me inside those bars. The rock musicians that Nur and her friends whistled at and cheered so crazily looked just like me, hair and all. For sure they bought their boots from the same place I did, that dusty military-surplus shop in Kadikoy that Nur adores. And yet they got red-carpet treatment, while I was sent packing.

I was upset now. I was tired and cold from being dragged behind the dog anyway. If Nur was still asleep, I'd ring the bell and wake her up, I thought, as I stopped at a bakery for bread. But when I got back to Fikret's I didn't need to ring the bell. Nur was up and dressed. When she saw me from the kitchen window, she opened the door. The dog raced into the living room, wagging his tail joyously. Nur looked at the bread in my hand. It was hot and fresh, still steaming when I broke the end off. Her face was cloudy.

'I need to go. I have an essay to write by tomorrow, so I'm going to the library.'

I understood right away. Nur had no intention of having breakfast with me, of beginning our relationship over again.

Our lovemaking the previous night didn't change our status as 'just friends'. She took the bread and placed it on the counter. Then she turned and looked at me with a wry smile that really irritated me. She was waiting for me to verbally acknowledge that this was fine – silent acquiescence would not be sufficient. She needed me to tell her, with sincerity, that I wasn't upset about it. Nur doesn't like to break hearts, cannot step away until she has effected a repair; she needed the decision to be mutual.

I recalled the New Year's party two years back, this time with anger. She had expected the exact same response from me then. I was supposed to pretend I hadn't seen the horse-faced idiot waiting on the other side of the balcony door, hiding in the curtains with a nasty, impatient look on his face. Not only was I supposed to forgive Nur and let her go, I was supposed to want to do it. I was supposed to be excited at the prospect of making mechanical love with that dark, skinny and very drunk girl and to be wholehearted in my enthusiasm for Nur's proposal that we just be friends. Only then would her conscience be clear. I said nothing then and I said nothing this time. If I say nothing, she suffers. Let her suffer.

After a moment of silence, I handed Nur the dog's leash and left the house. She muttered something, but I didn't look back. She hadn't changed at all; I'd been deluding myself. Slipping and sliding in the snow, I walked to the market in Levent and got a bus back to Kurtulus, where my mother was waiting for me. I'd been a brute to leave her by herself on New Year's Eve.

10

Celine

I left Burak at the kitchen door and went up to my room.
After the excitement of the fight over the carriages and the
warm closeness with Burak on the bike, my heart was beating
like crazy. I wished I'd leant my cheek against his sweaty back,
or, I don't know, the back of his head. I paced up and down
between the window and the bed, saw my sweater and T-shirt
that Sadik Usta had folded neatly and put on the couch –
stupid, childish clothes – and my guitar, leaning against the
wall behind the door. Yeah... carry your enormous acoustic
guitar on the ferry, then don't even take it out of its case. I felt
depressed. I'd been meaning to write some songs. I downed
a glass of water in one, got up, looked out the window. A
couple were walking innocently down the hill towards the
sea, arm in arm, presumably expecting to find a beach at the
end of the road. But all they'd find when they got there would
be an old boathouse, a place where all sorts of shady goings-
on were said to happen. I'd never once seen a boat tied up
there.

I needed to make a plan. I'd cast my hook and caught Burak
by telling him I had an idea, even though I didn't. I needed to

come up with something, but my mind had gone blank. My body, on the other hand, was on fire. Everything was racing madly – heart, pulse, breathing. I was panting as if I'd been running, but I hadn't been running, I'd been on a bike, on a bike but not pedalling, because Burak was pedalling and I was sitting behind him. He'd leant backwards, into me, into my breasts! When me and my school friends used to go to amusement parks, we'd go on those big circular rides where people sit behind each other and it spins you round and round really fast. I'd refuse to sit in the front because then they'd put their arms around you, to protect you, and say, 'Oh, sorry, was I holding you a bit too high up? Let's get on again and we'll swap places and I can lean back against you.' Idiots. Burak wasn't like that. But what was he like? I didn't know. He was grown up, for one thing, had had his fill of breasts. If he wanted to touch me, he wouldn't be underhand about it. Which was why he did what he did. Or didn't do. Whatever.

I took off my shoes and sat cross-legged on the bed. Sadik Usta had tucked in the corners of the bedspread really tightly. I needed to focus on the problem in hand – Dad. Where could he have been going, skulking off in the dark with his old laptop bag? No, really, where? I felt a twinge of worry in my heart. Lately, what with his yoga practice and his sessions with the therapist, he'd not been himself. Should I call Mum? But then I wouldn't be able to play detective with Burak. And Mum was on the top of some mountain somewhere, at the final retreat of her training course to be a yoga teacher, or something like that.

Dad acted weird at breakfast yesterday. If I didn't know better, I'd say he was stoned. He was stuck on one subject, totally obsessed. He took zero notice of me, or my aunt, and he never takes any notice of Sadik Usta anyway. Great-Granny wasn't there, though she might have come in later, after I left. They'd all pissed me off. Dad was entirely focused on Burak, as if there was no else in the room, only Burak Gokce. And by the time Aunt Nur, Burak and I were drinking on the jetty last night, he'd already retired to his room.

Okay, so what happened at breakfast? I got angry because they were all ignoring me. What else? Well, Sadik Usta had prepared the most magnificent breakfast table, an amazing spread, as if not four but fourteen people would be sitting at the table all day, right through until the evening. It was that kind of feast, because it was both a holiday and a birthday, and, of course, because of Burak.

Tea was brewing in the kitchen and the thermos was full of filter coffee. Slices of white bread and the boule bread that Great-Granny likes were stacked like a tower in a basket. Sadik Usta had found the wholewheat sourdough that Aunt Nur loves and toasted it just a little, the way she likes it. It had been put next to Aunt Nur's place, of course. Logistics are important at a breakfast table, otherwise passing stuff round becomes a problem. In the middle of the table, on one of the thick wooden boards, were all kinds of cheeses – full-fat feta, Roquefort, goat's cheese. On the other board were spicy salamis, smoked salmon, turkey ham, sausages from Budapest...

When I'd settled myself in my place beside my aunt, I noticed that the plum jam and hazelnut-chocolate spread had been put on my side of the table. What a sweetheart Sadik Usta is! How does he know what each of our favourites are? Between Aunt Nur and me were cherry tomatoes festooned with sprigs of basil. Beside Dad's place were olive-wood bowls filled with fat black olives and green olives sprinkled with paprika and olive oil, and there were also little glass dishes of tahini, molasses and organic butter. The empty chair next to Burak was for Great-Granny when she came down. In front of each of us was our egg. Mine was hard-boiled, my aunt's was soft. Dad doesn't eat eggs any more.

Dad was sitting at the head of the table. Did I notice anything different about him? Not at first. He was wearing his sky-blue linen shirt and he'd tied a beige cotton napkin around his neck so he wouldn't stain his special holiday outfit. Out of stubbornness, Aunt Nur had come down to breakfast in her kimono, the one Uncle Ufuk had brought back for her from Japan, a gift from the hotel he'd stayed at. Actually he brought two back and my aunt gave one of them to me. It's navy blue silk with red cherries and white dots, but I've never worn it; it's still in its packet. My aunt's looks really good on her. With her slanted, sleepy eyes, pale face and skinny arms, she has a sort of Japanese look about her. If I put mine on, I'd look like a sumo wrestler.

I glanced over at Burak. He was sitting across from Aunt Nur, on Dad's right, on the side of the table that faces the window. The guest always gets the best view. He was tearing his bread with his stubby fingers and nodding at something Dad was saying. When he lifted his head to take some salami from the board in the centre of the table, our eyes met and he gave a small smile, so small that only I could understand it. My insides were churning, and heat rose from my cheeks to my temples. There'd been a special bond between us ever since I'd gone to meet him at the motorboat landing a little earlier. I took a sip of coffee. Delicious.

Neither Dad nor my aunt had said good morning to me. Don't worry about it, I told myself, they're busy talking among themselves, adults discussing serious subjects, and at this table you will always be a child. If marriage kills love, the family dinner table infantilizes the adults around it. I took my phone out of my back pocket and hid it under the rim of my plate so that Dad wouldn't see it. I'd uploaded a selfie of Aunt Nur and me on Instagram, with Great-Granny's roses in the background. I'm never going to take a selfie with my aunt again. She's tiny, like a miniature, and my face always looks huge next to hers. Anyway, no one had liked it. And it came out too dark, you couldn't see the roses or the garden. It was just a boring photo of Celine and one of her relatives. I'd delete it. I surreptitiously refreshed my Insta feed; it was full of holiday wishes and prayers, blah, blah, blah. Boring!

Dad had turned to Burak with his most professorial expression on his face.

'I've read your articles, Burak. You are doing a fine thing, documenting forgotten histories, preserving stories that our nation would prefer to erase entirely from our collective memory. If it wasn't for your interviews, the histories of our minority peoples would remain untold and unacknowledged – their way of life, the things that happened, the very fact of their existence would be lost forever. It's hard to be a journalist these days, but you've stuck to the path you believe in and I admire you for that.'

I don't think Burak had expected such praise. He blushed and cleared his throat. So cute. I smiled into my plate.

'I do what I can. You see—'

'Don't belittle what you do. It's so important – essential, in fact. If only everyone used their pen the way you do, to illuminate the hidden corners of history. In order to understand the present, we need to know what we've forgotten, isn't that right, Nur?'

My aunt's mouth was full. She just nodded. Dad was right: Burak is a really great writer. The sweet old people he interviews talk to him about their lives back in the day, about a time when there was just the one TV channel, and sometimes about life before even that, like when you had to go through the operator if you wanted to phone someone in Ankara. Compared to life nowadays, when everything's available in an instant, at the tap of a finger, it's like they're talking about another planet. I adore Burak's interviews, and not just because they're his. I really love them.

'The interview you're going to do with my grandmother is particularly important to me.'

'Fikret, my dear brother, don't start all that again, please!'

My aunt's voice was shrill. I looked up at the two of them in surprise. What the hell was going on?

Dad continued regardless. 'This is how I see it, Burak. Shirin Saka is an important artist, a Turkish painter who made a name for herself in Paris, and maybe that hasn't been emphasized enough. In her time – in her youth, I mean—'

My aunt interrupted him again. 'Her star waned when she got married, that's why. How could the ravishing beauty that was our grandmother, the artist who was the talk of Paris, possibly continue to live and work as she once had, after she moved here, to a big house on Buyukada? Was she to present herself as the exotic creature that everyone in Paris was in love with or as the wife of the maths professor Halit Saka? It was only after her husband died that she was able to return to her art. At least he died young, God rest his soul.'

'Nur!'

A black cloud had descended on our grand holiday breakfast table and it was up to me, the naive little family clown, to despatch that cloud back to where it had come from. That was my most important role, as the little girl of the family.

'Oh! Great-Granny had lovers in Paris?'

Aunt Nur gave a theatrical wave of her hand. 'You cannot imagine, Celine, darling! During the Second World War every last writer, painter and sculptor in Paris was in love with your Great-Granny. And in Istanbul—'

'Nur!'

'What? Is it not the truth, Fikret? Did Grandmother not sleep with Sartre?'

'What?'

As I laughed, crumbs of bread flew out of my mouth and onto Burak's plate. He was laughing too. It was wonderful that both of us were laughing together; it sounded like we were making love. My stomach was in turmoil again.

'Excuse me, Burak,' I mumbled as I put my hand to my mouth. 'Aunt, what are you saying – that Great-Granny slept with Sartre? The Sartre we know, you mean?'

It would have been good if I'd remembered Sartre's full name. Burak would have been impressed. Without making it obvious, I googled him from under my plate. 'Jean-Paul.' I knew that.

Aunt Nur ignored Dad and turned to me. Her eyes were a bit puffy, and there were slight shadows underneath them, but she was still pretty.

'There was a rumour, Celine, darling. Sartre was taken prisoner during the war, then he was hospitalized, and eventually he started giving lessons at a university in Paris. At that time young Shirin was a scholarship student at the Fine Arts Academy. Your father will get cross with me again, but we know she was the lover of a professor at the university.'

Aunt Nur paused and took a sip of tea, for maximum dramatic effect. She was enjoying making Dad angry.

'Wow, I can't believe it! Jean-Paul Sartre and Shirin Saka!

Burak, you will get Great-Granny to tell you all about that, won't you?'

'I could do. If the subject comes up, I'll ask.'

Diplomat Burak. Switzerland Burak. Not taking sides. Cool-headed Burak. I wondered if he'd noticed my 'Jean-Paul' detail.

Dad cleared his throat, and, literally turning his back on the women at the table, once again addressed Burak. 'My grandmother's artistic legacy is important, of course, but so much has been written about that already, has it not? I think it would be interesting to explore her, um… not what we've just been talking about, but… her roots.'

'When you say "roots", you mean…?'

'Her family. Her mother, and particularly her father.'

'Fikret! Leave it, for God's sake!

'Why, Nur? Why does this subject make you so uncomfortable? Does it trigger some anxiety in you?'

Aunt Nur set down her tea glass with a bang. 'Burak, pass the bread, please – that white bread. I need to eat in order to suppress my "anxiety". And please don't use that New Age jargon with me, Fikret – "trigger", "anxiety"! It sounds ridiculous coming from a man pushing fifty.'

Dad ignored her, just lowered his voice and carried on. 'What are you so angry about, Nur? Don't you think, Burak, that there's an unhappiness in Nur that's she's never been able to understand, never been able to address? You've been friends for years, you must know that better than I do.'

Dad didn't use to talk so softly and patiently; it's only since he took up yoga that he's become like that. I can't get used to it; it seems fake. I preferred it when he was his old, stroppy self. If Aunt Nur had talked to him like that in the past, he'd have dropped his head and glared at his newspaper or something. He'd have been angry. Does he not get angry any more?

Aunt Nur shrugged. Then she tapped the top of her egg with her teaspoon and began very carefully to peel off its shell. My aunt's hands are really beautiful. Exceptionally beautiful. Nothing like mine. Her fingers are slim, and she's got big nails, which is why she doesn't grow them long. She'd painted them a deep burgundy. Burak was watching her peel her egg, just like I was. What had Dad meant when he said they'd been friends for years? What kind of relationship did they have – in the past, I mean. Were they lovers? No, they've always been like siblings, otherwise I'd have known. And if there'd ever been something between them, Uncle Ufuk would have objected to Burak staying here this holiday – wouldn't he? Why wasn't Uncle Ufuk here with us, anyway? They must have told me and I'd forgotten. Or maybe they hadn't told me. Should I ask now? I wondered. No, I couldn't. I wasn't sure why, but I knew I couldn't.

I refreshed my Insta feed. One person had liked my selfie with Aunt Nur – 'Demirrrr_Sevvda', a boy I've never met. He's harmless; he likes everything I post anyhow.

'It is my belief that there's a curse affecting this family,' Dad continued quietly. 'A dark energy, the shadow of something unresolved that makes every one of us feel somehow incomplete.'

Burak stared at my father, his slice of bread spread with Roquefort and smoked salmon paused in mid air. Aunt Nur nudged my arm with her elbow. She was laughing softly.

'What kind of dark energy, Dad?' I asked. 'Like somebody put a spell on us?'

He took a black olive from the dish in front of him and chewed it for a long, long time, as if he was solving a maths problem. The Adam's apple in his skinny neck bobbed up and down. I felt like laughing. I wondered if he'd noticed that Sadik Usta had grated lemon zest onto his olives, but I doubted it. We were like a Renaissance painting – me looking at Dad, Dad looking at Burak, Burak looking at Aunt Nur, Aunt Nur looking at the half slice of buttered white bread on her plate. Nobody was looking at me. It was as if I wasn't there.

'I'll give you a brief explanation, if I may, Burak. Freya and I have recently attended a series of what I'll call psychotherapy seminars in which we learnt that the traumas suffered by senior generations of a family can have an effect on their children, grandchildren and even great-grandchildren. By traumas, I mean losses, so that could be the children of a man who lost his land, or the grandchildren of a woman who lost her child. Even the grandchildren's children can carry that loss in their souls. They don't know why, but they feel incomplete, as if there's something missing. What I'm talking about is abstract, a curse that has endured and continues to be passed down because a family secret has remained untold.'

Aunt Nur took her packet of tobacco from the pocket of her kimono and began to roll a cigarette. With the filter gripped between her teeth, she muttered, 'Is there such a thing as "a concrete curse", brother? As opposed to an abstract one?'

Dad drank drown his tea, held the empty glass up to the light and examined the swirl of leaves at the bottom for a while, as if he might find the answer there. Then he abruptly raised his head and looked towards the door.

'Where could Sadik Usta have got to?'

We all glanced over at the door. Aunt Nur licked her

cigarette paper, rolled it tight, and inhaled as she gathered up the tobacco that had stuck to her fingers. I felt like smoking too. She'd have rolled me one if I'd asked, but Dad would have been very upset.

'For the love of God, Fikret, do your ears hear what your mouth is saying? Is there a grandfather in this country who hasn't been dragged from his land? Or a grandmother who hasn't lost a child? Are you forgetting that you live in a country that has been nourished by the blood of its children? Not a day passes that we don't wake up to the news of some massacre. If you want to trace every individual's psychological problems back to some event in their ancestral history, you've got your work cut out. Just look at the state of our generation, let alone that of our grandparents.'

Dad just shook his head pensively.

Ding! A message popped up on my screen – 'From Demirrrr_Sevvda' – but I didn't want anyone to notice my phone, so I didn't open it.

'The barbarity and inhumanity we read about in the newspapers every day, Nur, could well be the consequences of unresolved historical trauma. If people like you, me and Burak don't make an effort to heal our psyches, if we don't acknowledge the weight of our losses, the suffering in this country will never end. When you decided to stop being a journalist because you couldn't bear to witness any more injustice—'

Click! My aunt took out her Zippo and lit her cigarette, drowning out Dad's words. There was a smell of gas. She waved the smoke away, dismissing Dad's comments at the same time, but he wasn't interested in her opinion, he just wanted to impress Burak. Maybe we all just wanted to impress Burak, the famous journalist, author of the *Saturday Extra*'s popular 'Portraits' page, guest of honour at our breakfast table. VIP Burak Gokce. Burak, my hero!

'The fact is, Burak,' my dad continued, 'that for some time now I've been preoccupied with the truth about my grandmother's childhood. You'll be familiar with the interviews Shirin Saka has given over the years. When she was rediscovered in the 1980s, many prestigious magazines and fine art journals published articles about her. I was a child then, but I remember the house being full of literary and artistic figures who treated my grandmother with respect and awe. Recently, I've been going back through those interviews and I've discovered that not one of them goes into details about her childhood. Whenever she's asked about her mother and father, she sidesteps the question. She talks about her high-school years after she came to Istanbul, but she never says who she came to Istanbul with. We assume she came with her family, but she never mentions her mother or her father and nor does she ever talk about where they came from. It never occurred to me to wonder about that either, so I didn't even think to ask her about it back then, and now when I try to talk to her about it, she says she doesn't remember. In my opinion she remembers perfectly well but chooses to gloss over it. So my request to you—'

Ding! Ding! Messages began popping up on my phone one after the other. Ding!

'Girl, how many times do I have to tell you not to bring that phone to the table!'

Dad calling me 'girl' really upset me, and in front of Burak too. I pushed my phone back under my plate and hurriedly wracked my brain for a retort. But just then Sadik Usta appeared at the door and Dad redirected his grumpiness at him.

'For God's sake, Sadik Usta, where have you been? We've finished our tea, my throat's parched.'

'I do beg your pardon, Mr Fikret. I was taking your grandmother to the bathroom. She's rather tired this morning.'

Sadik Usta's wrinkled hands were trembling slightly as he quickly gathered up the empty tea glasses and took them to the kitchen. I put my phone on silent.

Aunt Nur glared angrily at my dad. 'You're the limit, Fikret! You scold a ninety-year-old man? Couldn't you have got your own tea? What a fine effect all those therapists and mentors are having on you. Your heart has really opened up – not even the hills and mountains can contain it now.' Cigarette in hand, she stood up and went to the kitchen.

Dad lowered his gaze and retreated inside himself, like he always used to. He was ashamed. I felt sorry for him, and my anger at him having called me 'girl' passed. This thing about Great-Granny was really getting to him and he just wanted to explain it to Burak.

I should have gone and helped my aunt and Sadik Usta refill the tea glasses, but I was caught in the crossfire, glued to my seat across from Burak, so I said, 'Dad, if you give me the name of Great-Granny's father's, I can look him up on Google. We could learn some things, couldn't we, Burak? Research it together.'

Dad took two slices of turkey ham from the board in the middle of the table and stuffed them in his mouth, entirely unaware of what he was eating. He'd given up meat! Silence hung like smoke over the table. I was bothered not about my dad but about Burak not having answered me. So that they wouldn't realize I was on the verge of tears, I began very carefully spreading plum jam on a piece of bread. Aunt Nur came in with the tea tray. My throat was dry and I sipped mine right away. Shit, it was hot! It scalded my mouth and burnt my tongue and tears rushed into my eyes, but nobody so much as looked at me. I stood up from the table in a fury and ran out.

Sadik Usta and I bumped into each other right outside the dining room. Or rather, I ran into him. He was just standing there, like a statue, behind the door. Standing there and – I'm embarrassed to say this – his head was bent and he was listening to what was being said inside. When he saw me, his face went white – even his blue eyes went pale – and his hands shook even more than usual. He murmured something. 'Miss Celine, Ciss Meline...'

I was more embarrassed than he was. I felt like I'd seen a very shameful act that I shouldn't have seen. I threw myself outside. Through the window overlooking the garden I could still hear Dad's voice. It was loud with excitement.

'Yes, that's the way to go, Burak. Let's explore that avenue and see what we come up with.'

'I'll do all I can, Fikret.'

Switzerland Burak!

I sat down on the side of the old fountain, turned on the tap and splashed my hands and neck with icy well water. It was a terribly hot day. The crickets had gone crazy. I kept thinking about Sadik Usta, not about his listening at the door but about the expression on his face. He'd looked frightened, very frightened, as if he'd seen a ghost.

11

Sadik

I was most certainly not eavesdropping on the conversation in the dining room. I was standing by the door so that I could be of service as soon as I was needed. That was all. Why, you ask? Shortly beforehand, because I'd been looking after Madam Shirin, I'd been tardy with the tea. That was why.

My lady had woke up late and had been unable to get to the bathroom in time. This was my fault. I should have woken her earlier. A similar accident happened last month, at which time my lady warned me, 'Sadik, you mustn't let me sleep in like that again. My bladder doesn't have the patience.' Even so, I decided not to interrupt Madam Shirin's rest this time, because I knew she hadn't slept well. I'd heard her wooden floor creaking as she paced up and down it in her slippers, right up until midnight. Even though my room is the other side of the kitchen and the pantry from hers, my ears are on constant alert for my lady's movements.

As soon as I had taken the bread and groceries to the kitchen and put the coffee on, I went to Madam Shirin's room. Even though she hadn't said a word about Mr Burak's visit,

I knew she was looking forward to it. When Madam Nur telephoned the previous week with the news that he would be coming to stay, she asked Madam Shirin if she would grant him an interview. My lady was in the library and when I passed her the cordless telephone, she was sitting on the sofa across from the fireplace, staring at flames that were not there. She was most happy to hear her granddaughter's voice. At first she pretended to be reluctant to do the interview, but in the end she agreed. She's had so many requests, after all, from newspapers and journalists and even from people from the television.

'Let him come, your journalist friend,' she said to Madam Nur. 'Let him ask his questions and if I find the answer inside myself, I will give it.' Those were her exact words. She has a special love for Madam Nur. It is my opinion that she sees a tiny reflection of herself in that child. 'That girl takes after me, Sadik,' she used to say.

Miss Nur was a most rebellious child. When she was no more than thumb-sized, she would run off by herself to the pine forest, and once she even managed to stuff the gardener's daughter into a large suitcase, wheel it all the way to the Seferoglu Club and go into the club. When she reached the swimming pool, she opened the case like a magician and released the gardener's daughter. The clerk on duty immediately telephoned Madam Shirin, and I, your humble servant, was despatched to the club forthwith. I found Miss Nur and the gardener's daughter sitting in a smoke-filled office marked 'Director'. The gardener's daughter was a stunted little thing, dark and with legs like matchsticks. Miss Nur's old skirts and T-shirts were always too large for her, which was why she fitted into the suitcase. She was terribly embarrassed about it all and as soon as she saw me she darted behind the smoke-stained curtain that was rippling in front of the window.

My lady and I had been coming to Buyukada for very many years, but I had never set foot in the Seferoglu Club, so as I approached the entrance on Cankaya Street I was a little anxious. However, when I saw how dilapidated the wooden buildings were, it would be untrue to say I was not disappointed. The red carpets were in tatters from the humidity and the sea air and the interior smelt of mould. How could this be? The members of that club were from Buyukada's most elite and respected families. Madam Shirin had explained to me the difference between the Anadolu Club and the Seferoglu Club. Those who owned things that money could not buy were members of the Seferoglu Club. In which case, those carpets surely had to be replaced.

'Come out from there,' I said to the gardener's daughter, who was sobbing behind the curtain. 'You'll get covered in dust.'

At that time the gardener's children were frightened of me, but Miss Nur, that thumb-sized girl, was not. She took the hand of the gardener's daughter, extricated her from the curtain and then stood confidently in front of me, her eyes daring me to reprimand her. There was not the slightest trace of shame in her face. I understood then why Madam Shirin had said the child resembled her. The child's mother, little Suheyla, had had hair like honey and eyes like grapes when she was a girl. She knew nothing of trickery or lies. If you ask me, she was sacrificed. But this little girl, dear me, this child surpassed even Madam Shirin in her courageousness. Recognizing no obstacle, she would take aim and shoot.

'Come along now, we're leaving. Madam Shirin will speak to you both when we get home.'

I was trying to frighten Miss Nur, but as soon as those words had left my mouth, I heard Madam Shirin's laughter ringing in my ears. She had contained her amusement when the man from the club called to complain, but once he had hung up she could hold it in no longer. At that time there was only one telephone in the house. It was green, supplied by the postal company to its subscribers. We had had it installed on the marble-topped console table with the mirror above it, in the hall, just outside the dining-room door. Beside the table we placed a comfortable armchair, upholstered in the same shade of green. It had small wheels. Of an evening, Madam Shirin would sit on this green armchair and call her many friends, with whom she loved to have long chats. She was sitting in that green armchair with the telephone in her lap when she told me about the incident at the club. Tears of laugher rolled down her cheeks as she kept repeating to herself, 'Child... oh, what a child! What will we do with you, child? Sadik, come and listen to this latest naughtiness of Nur's!'

My lady has a beautiful laugh. Her eyes narrow into slits when she laughs and when she stops to catch her breath, they open wide and change from blue to green. They shine like beautiful Riesling grapes. Her laughter resembles the tinkling of little bells arounds the necks of kid goats gambolling on a mountainside. When she laughs like that, I recall the days when we ourselves would race along goat trails. Time stands still and as if in a dream, the foaming waters beneath the stone bridges appear in my mind, my lady picks me up in her arms, my heart swells, and a warm feeling envelops me.

In short, once I'd removed Miss Nur and the gardener's daughter from the smoke-stained curtains and tatty red carpets of the director's office, I could not stay angry with them for long, even if I'd wanted to. Miss Nur understood this very well. As she dragged the empty suitcase back home with us, she had a smile on her face. She knew she could charm her grandmother into forgiving her. I am sure she was wearing the same expression when she telephoned Madam Shirin about Mr Burak's visit. It's not that Madam Nur is arrogant but that she knows she is loved. That's all. Though her grandmother might have pretended to be reluctant about the interview at first, Madam Nur would have known that she'd very soon be looking forward to it with eagerness.

And that's what happened. Over the following week my lady made various preparations for Mr Burak's visit, some obvious, some subtle. This morning's accident was the last thing she'd have wanted. Unsurprisingly, she was very upset. Although it was definitely my fault, she did not throw that in my face. Only after I had cleaned her up, laid out fresh undergarments and sat her on the pouffe in front of her three-way mirror, did she say to me in a low voice, 'You better go and see to the dining room, Sadik, in case they need anything.'

As Mr Burak was our guest, Madam Shirin required me to be extra attentive at breakfast. The unfortunate accident had prevented her from joining the others at the table on time, and it would only make things worse if I were to be tardy with my duties as well. I immediately left the room, passed through the hall, and waited outside the door. It was at that moment that Miss Celine burst out in her fury.

Madam Shirin is well aware that my hearing has been poor for some time. Madam Nur raises her voice when she calls me. Mr Fikret does not have much to do with me, but he did once have both my own and Madam Shirin's ears examined by a young doctor friend of his. He most definitely knows I am hard of hearing. Madam Shirin keeps a bell to hand that she rings when necessary. But Miss Celine? If Miss Celine got the wrong impression, that was partly my own fault, for it was silly of me to rush away. I was frightened, and if I happened to have muttered a few words, it was for that reason.

However, I cannot lie. I'd heard two or three words as I collected the tea glasses that had made me anxious. Those words had caused tension at the breakfast table. When the family gathers on a holiday morning, the atmosphere should be joyous; disagreements should be forgotten and those who have become estranged should make peace. But Madam Nur and Mr Fikret were bickering just as they used to as children. Of course, I did not linger there long enough to ascertain why. I gathered up the empty tea glasses, then approached the table again to clear the silver eggcups. They were deeply involved in their discussion and both of them looked angry, wearing expressions that had changed little since they were children. I think Madam Nur was angry with her brother for things he'd said about the family. I did not hear that, so this is purely conjecture.

There was also this, however: as I was passing through the hall, I thought I heard Mr Fikret mention a curse. My ears were not to be trusted, of course, and he was surely talking about this in relation to a different subject, but were my ears playing tricks on me again when I heard Madam Shirin's dear father mentioned? Was it possible that Mr Fikret, Madam Nur, Miss Celine or Mr Burak might have information concerning Mr Nuri? It could not be. Years had passed since that matter. Our Miss Suheyla herself knew nothing of her grandfather, so how could the next generation, or the one after that, know anything of this?

Yes, I was the plaything of my ears. I had not thought about Mr Nuri for years, but now that he had come back into my head, my mind froze temporarily, was transported somewhere. I was among high mountains in a fierce wind. I saw people scrambling up goat trails, old women being rolled down cliffsides, old men's feet covered in blood, babies submerged in water to silence them. I asked, 'Mama, is this a fairy tale?' and my mama replied, 'Yes, a tale, my son. Sleep.' I was hidden in the crypt of a church. They took away my mama, my papa. Could a person remember something that never happened?

I was so deeply immersed in this strange vision that for quite some time after Miss Celine pushed open the door in anger and came out, I remained stationary, as if I had lost consciousness. She ran off and I stayed standing there for a moment, under the influence of that faraway memory. Then Mr Fikret asked something of Mr Burak. I listened, in case I might be of assistance. As I served the tea, it stayed with me. In my opinion it was not right to tire Madam Shirin by bringing up the past. Broaching unsettling subjects is not proper, especially not on a holiday. Naturally, however, it was not my place to do anything about that.

12

Nur

The dining room smelt of coffee and toasted bread. There were two places set at the table, mine and Fikret's. Fikret obviously still hadn't come back from wherever he'd gone so early in the morning. Sadik Usta must have cleared away the other places and then disappeared. The chairs had been pushed back under the table. There wasn't a sound in the house – even the seagulls were quiet – and the squeak of the floorboards under my bare feet was getting on my nerves. It was hard to believe that yesterday morning Fikret, Burak, Celine and I, and eventually Grandmother, had sat around this table until noon, enjoying an elaborate breakfast and drinking coffee, then tea, then double espressos, then dark Turkish coffee, and then, finally, frothy iced frappes with Bailey's added. With Fikret now gone, that togetherness had been fractured. I was to eat alone, it seemed. Had Burak and Celine come back? It was past noon by now.

I walked over to the music system on Grandmother's walnut dresser with the mirror above it and pressed 'play'. Albinoni's Adagio in G minor filled the room. That was more like it! The dining room felt incomplete without Albinoni – an

Adagio, an Allegro, a concerto for strings in G minor or F major. I strode round the room in time to the music, stamping my bare heels down heavily for the double bass and coming to a stop at the head of the table. The sorrowful violins grew louder and the violas that followed kept time with the sorrow. A thin, dull ache, the ache left by my mother's passing, spread through my heart. I pulled out a chair and sat in Fikret's place from yesterday.

Since when did Fikret get to sit at the head of the table? When we were children, we used to sit side by side, facing the window, and the head of the table remained empty. It had once been the place of the grandfather we never knew (not the great-grandfather that Fikret was obsessed with but my mother's father, the maths professor, Shirin Saka's husband) and Mum wanted my father, who rarely came to the island, to sit there, but my grandmother wouldn't allow it. She made no secret of the fact that she disliked her son-in-law. Maybe that was why my father came to the island house so rarely. He wouldn't have appreciated the Albinoni anyway. When he and my mother were alone together, he'd make fun of my grandmother's eccentric ways and the two of them would laugh about her, about the silver rings that held the linen napkins, the Thonet chairs with wicker seats from Vienna, the library filled to the brim with books signed by their authors. Mum never once defended her own mother against her husband.

We used to stay here in the summer, my mum, Fikret and I. Dad would have work in Istanbul that seemingly went on and on, and when he was finally done with it, he'd take us to Cesme in our two-door, navy blue BMW. As we drove along the dusty village roads, children would run behind us shouting 'Beee-Emmm-Veee!' It was from those flocks of little boys with shaved heads, seen through the back window, that I learnt that our car was one of a kind, something special, though that didn't mean anything to me, nor to my mother, who'd be sitting in the front seat peeling an apple with her knife. But Mum did relish the luxuries my father provided her with and she adored him for that. This was her way of rebelling against Shirin Saka, who could not abide such materialistic things as fancy cars, new technology, holiday villages, American TV series and video cassettes.

The Adagio had ended and the Allegro movement of the next track had begun. Boom, boom – with joy! The light filtering through the acacia leaves onto the wooden floor changed colour. Music echoed the vibrations of the heart in a way that no other art form could. The violins were conveying joy with their short notes as they approached the Adagio movement. Life is joyful, life is full of sorrow, they were saying. Grief is always with us, and happiness too; there is sadness and there is passion; rhythm and melody; double bass and violin. Music is never silent. The universe vibrates, and so does the heart. If the tune played by the violins wasn't encapsulating time itself, then what was it doing?

For me, my childhood was not about going to Cesme in a BMW and sitting in the back seat next to Fikret listening to that year's Eurovision songs on a Walkman with two earphone jacks. I got car sick on long trips and my father was so afraid I'd vomit on the BMW's grey velvet seats that every few minutes he'd pull over into the emergency lane and open the door. When we were at the holiday village, my mum and dad used to go to the bar in the evenings, once Fikret and I had gone to sleep. The bar was only a few steps away, so close that Mum would have seen me if I'd stepped out onto the balcony of our room, but I never even left the bed in which

Fikret and I lay side by side, let alone the room. I hated that our parents ran off like that; it made me tremble with fear and rage at what I saw as a betrayal. Fikret was the boy, but it was me who was jealous of my father being with my mother.

My childhood was not about riding in the back seat of a BMW. It was about this house, on this island; it was about Albinoni, Bach and Vivaldi; about this dining room and the smell of toasted bread. I twirled around in the circle of light coming through the window, reprising my girlhood ballet moves, doing a rond de jambe, forwards, back, forwards. My childhood was Shirin Saka sitting at this breakfast table across from the ghost of her husband, always stylish, always upright, spreading butter and olive paste onto her bread with her long, slender fingers. After breakfast, Grandmother would retire to the arbour and talk to the cats as she drank her coffee. The cats would curl around her legs and she'd talk to them in a sweet, childish tone of voice that she never used with us. Childhood was being jealous of a tabby cat; it was buying rosehip ice cream from a blue cart and selecting my own piece of corn on the cob from a chrome cauldron as shiny as a mirror. When we'd finished our breakfast, mother and daughter, we'd run away from the house, away from Grandmother, Fikret, Albinoni, modern art. We'd cycle along the Grand Tour road and get our arms and hands all scratched from picking the fruit off the strawberry tree.

I filled my coffee cup from the thermos. Sadik Usta had left sliced tomatoes, olives and goat's cheese for me and he'd covered my bread with a napkin to keep it warm. He'd put olives in front of Fikret's place. That was my brother's breakfast – three olives. Fikret the ascetic. Yogi Fikret. No, this had nothing to do with yoga; Fikret had never had a big appetite. Who knew what he was on to now. How obsessed he'd been at breakfast yesterday, repeatedly bringing the subject back to Grandmother's father, to roots, curses, trauma, warnings and all the rest of it. But it was too late for all of that. We'd lost our mother years ago and still hadn't come to terms with it, so how could we grieve for anything else?

Tears flooded my eyes. Again. It had been happening a lot lately. My mother came into my head and then my eyes welled up and ghosts from the past began to crowd their way in. Here they were now, in that room, gathered around Sadik Usta's carefully prepared breakfast table. As Albinoni plays in the background, there's a glass of dark, sugary tea in front of me and I am pleading with my mum: 'Let's go to the beach, Mummy. Please, Mummy! We can build sandcastles, dig holes, make canals and hold hands underwater.'

From her place at the end of the table nearest the door, my grandmother, the artist Shirin Saka, sixty years old and once again in the ascendant, admonishes me. 'Child, we have sea right in front of our house, open sea. Why would you want to go to the public beach?' Her hair is pulled into an updo and secured with combs and I can smell her talcum powder. I know she wants me to stay there, with her, but she doesn't say that because that's not her style, or she doesn't dare.

Whenever the south wind blew, it would dump seaweed, beer bottles, jellyfish, plastic bags and watermelon rind on our beach. The seaweed-encrusted steps of our jetty would be coated in filthy foam and the boathouse would stink of sewage. My mother would forbid us from going swimming when that happened. By contrast, Yoruk Ali Beach, which I called 'Sandy Beach', was not affected by the direction of the wind. It was surrounded by pine forest and looked out at the green hills of Heybeliada, the next island, across the endless blue.

Also, to get to that beach we would take a horse-drawn carriage. My mother and I would sit side by side on the blue leather seat, being rocked to and fro as if we were in a cradle as we contoured the hills and curves of the island. I adored carriage rides, loved everything about them – the shiny wheel rims, the tasselled curtains, the buttons on the upholstery, the ringing of the horn. Fikret would sit up front. 'Young man,' the driver would say, 'you come and sit with me.' Then he'd call 'Giddy-up!' to his horses, and Fikret would solemnly echo him with his own 'Giddy-up!' and Mum and I would laugh. Men were funny. Mum smelt of peach blossom.

My tears seeped through my fingers and dropped into my cold coffee. Crying was normal, to be expected, according to the internet. It was the hormones. Not that the snake-eyed doctor had told me anything; all she did was make a telephone call, disclaiming all legal responsibility.

My crying intensified. It was good that Sadik Usta wasn't around, otherwise he'd be very upset. What would I say to him? Sadik Usta, my hormones are all messed up, because I... because a very bad thing happened to me. Yes, if Sadik Usta were to come in right then, I would act like one of those naive young girls in the old Yesilcam movies and tell him that it wasn't my fault. Maybe the curse that Fikret was talking about was to blame, maybe it forced me onto this bad path. Great. I'd just say it was the curse and get out of it like that. I'd blame a previous generation – my grandmother's father, whom we never knew. We were accursed and suffered as a result of his sins. Hopefully, Fikret had gone to consult his curse-breaking yoga instructor and our family would be brought out of the darkness and into the light.

What was the difference between blaming my hormones and blaming Fikret's curse? If our brains are controlled by our hormones, there's no such thing as free will. But we all know that there is such a thing. Of course there is. One makes a choice to go down a certain route. To go to a clinic, for example; the clinic where the snake-eyed doctor worked. To hand over documents with a signature that was forged in a nearby fast-food restaurant. Oh, you need my husband's written permission? Here you are, signed and delivered. Were hormones responsible for that? The story also has a beginning, before the hormones kicked in. Where a choice was made to go to Kurtulus rather than to return home.

I pulled out my phone and called Ufuk, again, while my eyes were still wet. He's used to my crying; I'm the tearful type. The only time my eyes stayed dry was at my mother's funeral, when not a single tear ran down my cheeks, even though the emptiness she left behind should have been filled by a lake of tears.

The emptiness my mother left behind... The real emptiness was in the living room in Macka, in that vast room, big enough to ride a horse through. This was not a metaphorical emptiness but a material one. Just as, at the scene of a crime, investigators sketch an outline of the victim in chalk, so on the floor of our family living room lay a white, long-haired sheepskin rug encircled by empty bottles of alcohol. Fikret found our mother lying unconscious in the middle of them. He scooped her up and took her to hospital. My mother, who had vowed 'never again' and had not touched a drop for seven years, was lying on the white sheepskin surrounded by bottles. There's where she put her head, between the whisky and the vodka. Her hair was a mess, all tangled up with the bottles. At her fingertips were the expensive wines, and between her legs were the champagne bottles. Mum wouldn't touch raki or beer and I didn't think she liked gin either, but there, to the left of her neck, was an empty gin bottle, along with bottles of whisky, vodka and cognac. After seven years of abstinence, in her excitement at rediscovering them, she'd guzzled them all.

When I returned from my spring break, I stood in the living room with that huge rucksack on my back, gazing at the emptiness left by my unconscious mother, at the bottles with their tops off, at the sheepskin matted with spilt cognac and the sticky patches of whisky on the parquet floor. Their smells mingled together. She had died much earlier and was now waiting at the morgue in a closed coffin.

She took her last breath at 5.28 a.m. The only person with her at the hospital was Fikret. He'd woken up at midnight to the crying of Oguz, who was just a few months old at the time. 'You go, please,' Freya murmured. 'I just fed him.' Fikret picked up Oguz, shushed him and took him downstairs. From the window of their uncurtained living room, he looked across at the squatters' neighbourhood. A few of the houses had a single lightbulb burning, in other windows the blue light from a TV was reflected. Then 'Tik!', the electricity went off and the hill went dark. For a brief while, Leica, Freya's Russian Samoyed, barked intermittently, and then a deep silence settled over everywhere. Baby Oguz's eyes were open, but he wasn't crying; it was as if he too were watching the darkness, listening to the silence.

Fikret is quite vague about what happened next. He handed Oguz over to Freya, left the house, got in his green Fiat Tempra, which was parked at the foot of the hill, and drove through the dark, empty streets. The electricity was out in all of Levent, on Nispetiye Street, in Zincirlikuyu, and all the way to Gayrettepe. His mind was absolutely clear, but it was as if some higher power was guiding him. In Macka the streetlights were on. They were on in the living room of our fourth-floor apartment too, illuminating the large, ugly but comfortable black leather sofas and chairs, and Dad's hi-tech music system. Beneath the hissing halogen lamps in each of the four corners, the mirrors and cut-crystal decanters and matching glasses sparkled in all seven colours of the spectrum. The only things not sparkling were my mother's half-open eyes.

The weight of that backpack must have been too much for me, or maybe it was the story Fikret had related on the phone in a voice devoid of personality or feeling, a 'this is a recording' kind of voice. As the story went round and round in my head, my knees gave way and I fell to the floor, slowly and heavily, like a building being demolished. I put my head down in the emptiness left by my mother and inhaled the sweet smell of expensive alcohol. The rucksack slid off my back, sending my sandy tent, ripped sandals and pots and pans flying.

I lay there among the bottles, whisky and vodka within licking distance. Was it worth it, Mummy? I was on my way home, would have been there soon, and you wouldn't have been on your own any more. Liar! I'd met a boy on holiday, Mummy, and most probably I'd have forgotten you while I was hanging out with him, knowing full well that the most painful thing for you was being forgotten. I'd have been going out with Burak, leaving you dozing at the kitchen table with a long-ashed cigarette in your hand, and coming home at dawn. Or maybe not coming home at all.

I remembered that I hadn't hugged her when I left for my holiday. From the door of the cage lift as it descended, I had watched as first her face, then her body, then the skirt of her yellow dressing gown, and then her feet vanished. I began to cry. I cried and cried until the emptiness left by my mother was filled with tears.

Albinoni had gone quiet. The coffee had gone cold. I sat there frozen, with my phone in my lap. Ufuk hasn't answered my calls for days. Not since I'd forged his signature at the fast-food place. He'd left before I got home that evening. It had been a week now. I cried.

If he did pick up, I'd tell him the truth. The truth might make him angry, but eventually he would calm down and come back to me. I'd hurt Ufuk very much. If he'd only answer his phone, I could explain everything.

13

Burak

The islanders sitting at the plastic tables in the Horoz Reis Tea Garden were indifferent to the holiday crowd arriving at the pier, who may as well have been from another planet. Most of them were over eighty. They sat there contentedly, chatting quietly to each other, surrounded by open newspapers, tea glasses, cheese toasts, dice and playing cards, as if this were just another summer's afternoon. As I settled at my table under the awning, several of them turned around, to size me up. I greeted them with a nod and signalled to the waiter to bring me some tea. He rose languidly to his feet.

The sea around the pier was a dark blue. Every so often, the wind ruffled its surface, then it smoothed over again. Everything sparkled in the afternoon light. Boats of all sizes – little sailing dinghies; fishing boats moored along the shore – shone yellow, white, green and red in the sun, their colours harmonizing with the deep blue of the water. I got my phone out and, like a teenager, took some photos.

My tea came and I ordered a cheese toast as well. I placed my dictaphone on the table, together with my earphones, notebook and pen. I wanted to listen to the recording of the hour-long interview I'd done with Shirin Hanim at breakfast yesterday.

Shirin Saka came into the dining room just after Celine jumped up and raced out to the garden. Nur, Fikret and I had finished stuffing ourselves and were talking lazily about this and that. I'd given up hope of seeing Shirin Hanim that morning and was counting on perhaps finding her in the library before lunch. When Sadik Usta shepherded her in, I sprang to my feet and pulled out her chair, and Nur and Fikret both quickly sat up very straight.

As she settled into her place, Shirin Hanim greeted me with a slight inclination of her head. Sadik tied a linen napkin around her neck. She was wearing a navy blue silk blouse and thin, comfortable trousers. It came to me that I hadn't seen her in almost twenty years. Had she changed? Naturally. She'd shrunk, for one thing. Her eyesight was poor and she was prone to lapses in concentration. But she was still alert and talkative. She laughed, drank coffee, buttered her own bread. As soon as she saw me take out the dictaphone and place it between us, she began to talk. She had no need of input from me and simply chattered on about whatever came into her head. This suited me perfectly and meant Fikret's questions probably wouldn't even get an airing.

My toast came. I put in my earphones and pressed 'play'. Shirin Hanim's shrill voice rang out against the clink of spoons in tea glasses.

'I was well developed for my age and when I grew tall my mother sent me to stay with my uncle. He was the manager of a factory. He wasn't my real uncle, just some distant relative of my mother's. He spoke Arabic, Persian and Greek. Sadik, do you remember? Where's Sadik gone? We were just children, no bigger than your thumb, when they put us on that ship.

The captain was supposedly an acquaintance of my father's, but we never once saw his face. Was I frightened? Of course not! We got seasick when the ship rolled, that was all. Sadik ran up on deck and vomited over the side, but because I ate nothing but dry biscuits, I was fine.'

Elderly people do have moments like that. A floodgate opens and memories spill out into the present. Shirin Saka's memories streamed out like a fast-flowing river. The challenge comes in keeping that gate open. I know from experience that you mustn't interrupt the speaker and that you should refrain from pointing out any inconsistencies or contradictions. Suggesting that the past might not be quite as they remember it can cause the barriers to come crashing down again, and then confusion sets in, the memories dry up and the connection is lost. I was afraid that Fikret would interrupt Shirin Hanim in his eagerness to discover the truth about his great-grandfather.

For the time being, however, Shirin Hanim, was still talking away.

'I never saw my mother again. Supposedly I was sent to Uskudar to study, but that was a lie. After my dear father... my mother had many suitors. She was a young, beautiful widow. Hold on, Sadik, don't take my tea away! I'm still drinking it, can't you see? Leave it, for God's sake! Just add a spoonful of sugar. That's enough!

'My mother didn't want me in her new husband's house. I was a young woman, after all – if you understand what I mean. What to do? The man we called uncle, that distant relative, had just recently had a baby and so he said, "Let her come and help her aunt." He had quite different intentions, however. He wanted me for himself. But my aunt, his wife, would never have allowed anything like that. Uncle Nevzat never got what he dreamt of, if you know what I mean. Where's Sadik gone? Anyway, while Sadik's mother, Meryem, who was our servant, was packing my trunk, she begged my mother to let Sadik come with me so that he could go to school in Istanbul too and later go on to help Uncle Nevzat in the shoe factory. "Otherwise the boy will just rot here," she said to my mother. "Please do this good deed, my lady. Sadik will keep watch over Shirin and he will study and become a man." Meryem did everything she could to try and persuade my mother. Sadik! Where the hell have you gone? Nur, hand me the bell. Right. Ring it like this and Sadik should come to the table.'

I stopped the recording to make some notes. Uncle Nevzat was an interesting character. His name had come up before, years ago, when I did an interview with Sadik. Sadik had talked about him with respect, but Shirin Hanim painted a quite different picture, of a debauched old man who wanted her for his harem. Interesting. While she was talking yesterday, Shirin Hanim had repeatedly wanted Sadik to join in the conversation, but he always managed to not be around. The two of them grew up together and lived through an entire century side by side. I would have loved to have heard the pair of them reminiscing and discussing their different recollections of the experiences they shared – what a fascinating conversation that would have been. But during our interview yesterday, Sadik rebuffed all Shirin Hanim's attempts to get him to remember their past. It evidently made him nervous and unhappy. In various indirect ways he repeatedly suggested we cut short the interview, using Shirin Hanim's weariness as a pretext. It was absolutely clear that he was afraid of what she might say. But why?

I made a note of that question. It wasn't relevant to my

article but it might illuminate Fikret's issue. As I ate my cheese toast, I thought about the opening line of my article. The first sentence of an article is important; it sets the tone. What tone should I take? Since I was close to the family, I should write with warmth and familiarity. Readers always like it when my 'Portraits' pieces are personal, when there's as much about me in the article as about my interviewee. I put my earphones in again and looked through my notes. The room I was staying in at the house had once been Shirin Hanim's. When it became difficult for her to use the stairs, she moved downstairs, to the living room across from the dining room, and her old room became a Shirin Saka museum. Yesterday afternoon I'd looked through her old sketches and browsed the piles of gallery guides and magazines that featured her work, as well as the postcards and ornamental dolls that she and Halit Saka had brought back from various European cities. But none of it spoke to me. The room was sterile, had been arranged to create a certain image of Shirin Saka. What I was interested in was her day-to-day life, her lived experience.

I suddenly remembered the first time I met Shirin Saka. It was there, on Buyukada, in the garden of Shirin Hanim's house. She was asleep in a chair under the jasmine arbour and Sadik was beside her. Their heads had dropped onto their chests and Sadik's bald patch, which he'd tried to cover up with a couple of strands of hair, was shining in the sun. It was the morning after the great Istanbul earthquake of 1999.

Nur has a crazy kind of courage. She often attempts the impossible. That night of the earthquake, she'd set out to rescue her grandmother and Sadik. Those two oldies were stuck on Buyukada without electricity and with no telephone, radio or television. Nobody had any idea what sort of damage had been wreaked on Buyukada or any of the other Princes'

Islands, so Nur decided to go and check on them. She dragged me along with her.

I picked up my pen. I could begin my article with that scene.

Less than an hour after the earthquake, Nur's car drew up in front of my building, its ancient brakes making a 'zink' sound. I had my camera bag slung over my shoulder, but I had no idea what the best thing to do was. Should I go into the newspaper office or should I stay with my mother? Should I run up and get my mother's gold, the title deeds of our apartment, my chequebook and the money we'd hidden, or should we stay away for fear of aftershocks?

By the time Mother and I ran bewildered downstairs the first shocks had subsided. Like everybody else we took shelter in the garden of the church behind our street. The whole neighbourhood had gathered there. Crazy Cavidan Hanim, who used to throw plastic bottles full of her own urine from her window into the church garden every Sunday; the middle-aged widow who sat on her back balcony and spied on my mother and Nur on summer evenings; the arty young couple who yelled at each other in broad daylight – every single person who lived on our street had fled to the backyard of the old Greek Orthodox church. Lives that had previously only been glimpsed through the windows that overlooked the courtyard of our building were now brushing up against each other. Though nobody knew anybody's name, the faces were familiar. As the earth shook beneath our feet, we huddled together in terror beneath the hundred-year-old pine trees.

Leaving my mother with our neighbour Efterpi Hanim and her daughter and son-in-law, who'd just come from Athens to Istanbul for the baptism of their baby, I went back out onto the street. I didn't feel good about that, but I was a reporter

113

and on a night like that I needed to do my job. When I saw Nur's maroon Fiat Uno pulling up in front of our apartment building, I was impressed. What a woman, I thought! When an earthquake strikes, she gets in her car and comes to get me. Completely fearless. She loves me, this woman – in her own way, but she does love me. She loves me like a hero. At that time I had a girlfriend, Cigdem. She was studying law at Istanbul University, and she was sweet and pretty and smart. Nur and I were both working at the newspaper. Nur was an intern and I was a reporter and we'd be sent out on stories together. We made a good team. I was convinced that I'd got over her, that I'd put my obsession with her behind us, and I genuinely thought that we really were 'just friends'. Nur was right. We shouldn't put our friendship at risk by trying to be lovers as well as friends; it was too precious for that.

When I jumped into Nur's car, I assumed we were going to the newspaper. I was so preoccupied with observing and taking notes on the desperate people who were filling the streets, squares and parks that it wasn't until the last moment that I realized Nur had turned onto the highway that would take us onto the bridge and across to the Asian side of Istanbul. We weren't going to the newspaper, we were going to the marina at Pendik.

The earthquake had caught Nur home alone. She woke up when a heavy glass vase fell on her foot. She was very frightened. Her father was away on yet another business trip, her mother had died long ago and Fikret was living in his villa in Levent. The living-room walls were echoing to the rattle of the glasses in the sideboard. Scared out of her mind, Nur grabbed the car keys and ran outside in her underwear. Luckily, she had a spare set of clothes in the boot of her car. Nur had lots of lovers during those years. Most evenings, she'd get dressed up in some stylish outfit, go to the Taksim bars with her Bosphorus University friends, and then spend the night with one of her lovers. In the morning, when she left the lover's house, there'd be jeans, a T-shirt and tennis shoes ready for her in her car. Which was why she'd been able to get dressed in the car on the night of the earthquake.

It was only after we'd crossed to the Asian side that Nur told me that we weren't going to the newspaper but to the island, to Buyukada. I was angry. She'd deceived me. Again. I should have been at work, but instead, there I was, with Nur. I stared out of the window as we speeded along. The city was in total darkness and the sky was full of stars, just like it had been in that faraway valley where I'd met Nur. I began musing to Nur about the stars, about how every star evolves, twinkles and then collapses, about how we humans should not forget that we resided on a small, insignificant lump of rock that didn't even produce its own light or heat. In the grand scheme of things, we were dispensable, I told her. We could easily have died in that brief period of less than a minute during which our insignificant lump of rock had got the shakes. Maybe people had died, I said. At that point we didn't know that the earthquake had claimed thousands of lives already.

Nur wasn't listening to me. In the pitch black, she was driving at 140 kilometres an hour in the fast lane of the empty dual-carriageway. The little Fiat was clanging and rattling, but it kept going. Nur had heard that the epicentre of the earthquake was Buyukada. Or maybe she just made it up, or was hallucinating. Her grandmother didn't have a mobile and no one was answering the house phone. Nur had me calling it over and over, but to no avail. Phone lines all over the country were down.

As we drove, she was cursing the parking attendant, Niyazi, who'd parked her car for her on Kucuk Parmak Kapi Street the previous week. Niyazi had stolen her radio, or had had it stolen, or had closed his eyes to it being stolen. Whatever. Because of that damn bastard, that son-of-a-bitch, that faggot Niyazi, Nur couldn't tune into a radio station and therefore couldn't get any reliable news. She was sure that the earthquake had hit the islands and that her grandmother had been buried under a heap of fallen debris. If we were lucky, we'd be able to save her. There was still time. Her grandmother's bedroom was on the second floor; maybe only the roof had caved in; maybe she was still alive.

Nur was not in her right mind. And nor was I, clearly, given that not only did I jump into the car with her but I then went to the marina at Pendik and helped her take her father's speedboat out. When I boarded that boat, I knew that Cigdem would never forgive me. She would leave me for having gone with Nur to Buyukada instead of stopping by her digs in Cemberlitas to check that she was okay. And she did break up with me. I would also be in big trouble with the newspaper. Nobody would notice that the young intern Nur wasn't there – no, they'd notice, but they wouldn't pay much attention – but my not being there on such an important night, as a promising young reporter for the Istanbul News Service, would certainly draw the attention of my boss, Omer. Yes, Nur's craziness that night would get me in big trouble in more ways than one. But when we got to Buyukada, just as the sun was rising, and found Shirin Hanim sitting, asleep, at the wrought-iron table under the jasmine arbour, hand in hand with Sadik, and when Nur hugged her grandmother's knees and began to sob her heart out, I knew that witnessing that scene was worth all the trouble that would ensue.

Because those of us who live on this insignificant lump of rock are united by such strong bonds that even if every one of the millions of evolving, twinkling, collapsing stars in the sky were to come together, they wouldn't tremble like the love in the heart of this person who had been so distraught at the possibility that her grandmother might have been lost.

While Nur was weeping into the blanket on Shirin Hanim's lap, she was also shedding the tears that she'd been holding in since her mother's death. Seeing this, I understood why ascetics and dervishes who pledge themselves to God are called 'lovers'. Love is vast and all-encompassing. In the physical world there is no equivalent to the love that lives in the heart. Love is God's blessing. It is hidden in a person's heart so as to guide them to the truth, for there truly is such a thing as the heart's eye. I realized that I had not got over my love for Nur. Not at all. Nur had come into my life so as to awaken the love in my heart. As long as she was near me, I would be able to distinguish a lie from the truth.

While these thoughts were passing through my mind, I caught Sadik's eye. He knew exactly what I was thinking. He knew because he too had found the person who had awakened the love in his heart. And he had never left her. He hastily got to his feet and set down the puppy that had been curled up on his lap, a cute little grey-eyed, black-haired thing.

When the puppy's wet nose nuzzled Nur's ankles, Nur lifted her head. Shirin Hanim took her granddaughter's face between her purple-veined hands. Her blue-green eyes glistened as she gazed at Nur and a line of tears trickled down her wrinkled white cheeks. Shirin Saka was crying. The irascible artist, whose notoriously short temper intimidated not only her family but also Istanbul's entire art world, was crying, gasping for breath, as she looked at Nur, as if the love in her heart were too great for her to bear. Side by side for I don't know how long Sadik and I stood and silently watched the crying grandmother and her granddaughter, the women we loved.

My dictaphone suddenly came to life and Fikret's voice brought me back to the interview.

'So, Grandmother, where did you see the priest?'

The recording hissed. I repositioned my earphones.

The swirling of the teaspoon in the glass, the fork hitting the plate, the click of Nur's Zippo lighter, Sadik mumbling, 'You are tired, Madam Shirin, why don't you continue in the afternoon? Mr Burak can also take a rest.'

Nur says something. She is scolding Fikret. 'You interrupted Grandmother's flow. She was doing so well. What do you want with the priest? The churches were full of priests. Back then, they weren't yet attacking the churches and forcibly circumcising the priests.'

A clattering sound. Sadik had dropped the wooden pepper grinder. And then, just then, right in the middle of an hour's recording, something was said, a detail that Sadik and Shirin Hanim argued about. My interest was piqued. The voices mingled together: Sadik and Shirin, Nur and Fikret:

'We came home that day, the day the priest found the icon… the next morning… we told the family about it at breakfast. Sadik, your ma was serving breakfast. She'd lit the samovar.'

'No, Madam Shirin. I beg your pardon, but—'

'Silence! Do you know better than me? You were just a kid then—'

'Grandmother, could you say that again? Which icon are you talking about? Whose icon was it?'

'God, Fikret, you do go on! Can't you hear? She's trying to

explain something else. Burak, it would be better if you spoke to Grandmother on your own.'

'Madam Nur is correct. Madam Shirin, allow me to take you to your room so that you may rest for a short while.'

Fikret, Nur, Nur and Fikret, Sadik, Shirin Hanim's broken sentences. 'Buried... Priest... We were drinking tea... The stove was alight...'

'When we told them about the priest, my beloved father buried his head in his hands... Then? Then, what happened? What was I saying, Sadik? Where is Sadik?'

A bell sounded. It got louder and louder. It began disturbing the people around me in the tea garden, disrupting the tranquil torpor of the afternoon, confusing them. Had I turned on the speaker on my dictaphone? No. My earphones were still in. But where was that piercing sound coming from? Everyone was now looking in the same direction. What were they looking at?

'Burak! Burak! Buraaak!'

Celine was careering through the Horoz Reis Tea Garden on her bike, approaching the seafront tables at speed. She braked in a cloud of white dust. I was embarrassed. Trying to appear calm, I took out my earphones and raised my eyebrows. What was up? That noise had been Celine ringing her bell like crazy. Throwing her bicycle on the ground between two tables, she came over. Her cheeks were red and her navy blue eyes were lit as if with electricity.

'Burak!' she yelled breathlessly. 'You won't believe what I've just found out! Get your stuff together. You've got to come back and talk to Great-Granny before she loses her thread. Come on! Let's go!'

14

Celine

The door squeaked as I went into the library.

Great-Granny was sitting on the sofa across from the fireplace. She was so tiny, if I'd hugged her, she'd have slid through my fingers like soap. One touch and she might turn to dust. She was wearing her silver hair up, secured with ivory combs, and was dressed in a multicoloured silk nightdress, and knee-high stockings (despite the heat) for her varicose veins. With her translucent skin and straight back, she looked like a doll sitting there. Baby Shirin. Sartre came into my mind. Could she really have slept with Sartre? Had this little old lady, lost in her own thoughts in front of an empty fireplace, once moaned with pleasure in Sartre's arms? What if I were to sit down next to her and say, 'Shirin, dear, tell me, what was it like, sleeping with Sartre? Did he give you an orgasm? Or did you fake it so as not to make him feel bad, pretend that thanks to his expert petting, you'd climaxed?'

The library was dim and stuffy. Sadik Usta had closed the thick red velvet curtains again. I walked over to the window with the sea view, drew them back and opened the window. Much better! A moist, salty breeze now mingled with the smell of dust and old furniture. The sea was flat calm. The next-door neighbours were getting ready for a barbeque. They'd arranged a line of tables in their garden, squeezed close so that they all faced the sea. White plastic tables, white plates, plastic chairs with wobbly legs... They were probably having guests over from Istanbul for the holiday. They were laughing as they brought out the meatballs, tomatoes and peppers ready for the shish kebabs. Their blonde son was swimming off the concrete jetty in front of the house, watched over by his Filipino nanny. The neighbours' garden could have been on a TV commercial, with its evenly mown emerald green grass and yellow roses, hydrangeas, and white and yellow daises swaying harmoniously in the breeze, like players in a symphony orchestra. In comparison, our garden looked like it was from a different climate zone, a botanical embarrassment, all dried up. The branches of our mulberry tree overhung their garden, staining their gravel paths with dropped fruit, but we wouldn't let them prune it. No wonder they didn't like us much.

Turning away from the glare, I stumbled across the living room as my eyes adjusted to the dimness, feeling my way round the hefty wooden table, the side tables and the shelves, until I stood in front of Great-Granny.

'Shall we look at some photos, Great-Granny?'

She didn't answer. When I was little, I used to spend hours on my knees in front of those shelves, looking at old photos. Great-Granny was sharp as a tack in those days. Not like now, when she sometimes stares vacantly into space. She used to tell me long stories about every photo, which is lucky, because now I can repeat those same stories back to her. I reached up and took a red velvet-covered chocolate box from the bookshelf next to the fireplace. The set of Oxford

World's Classics on the shelf were in tatters and covered with a thick layer of dust. Those two old crazies, Sadik and Great-Granny, won't let a cleaner in the house, even though my dad repeatedly insists that they should have one. They won't hire a caretaker either. They're like hermits, those two.

I sat down beside Great-Granny and put the box in my lap. She reached in with her crooked, bony fingers, took out a photograph and brought it close to her face. I leant over and looked too. It was a picture of Dad and Aunt Nur on swings. The swings were suspended from the iron poles that supported the grapevines. My aunt was really little, but she was dressed so stylishly, in a fancy navy blue and white dress and white socks with tiny pom-poms. There was a hand on her back to keep her from falling. Dad must have been seven or eight. His hair had been carefully combed, wetted and parted on the side. He was standing up on the swing, looking tall, thin and grouchy – just like now. Aunt Nur was cute. She was laughing, and in the light filtering through the vine leaves her eyes looked huge and green.

Great-Granny put the photo back in its box and took a deep breath. Did those children on the swing mean anything to her? I reached up and pulled down a different box, the one with the green velvet cover. Almost all the photos in that box were black and white, only a couple were in colour and they were Polaroids. Polaroids are cool now, among my friends. Let them come and learn who is a hipster and who isn't from Shirin Hanim.

'Let's look at these, Shirin. Let's see who's here.'

When it's just the two of us, I love calling Great-Granny by her name. She doesn't mind. Maybe she doesn't hear me. It's like we're friends. Shirin and Celine.

I picked up a photo at random. A black-and-white shot of

three girls sitting in the stone courtyard in front of this house, with blankets spread out under them. The oldest was a nice-looking blonde girl of fifteen or sixteen and she was doing some kind of sewing, with fabric in her hand. The youngest was a chubby-legged nine- or ten-year-old with short hair and an impish face. In the middle was my namesake, Suheyla, who even as a child could mesmerize strangers on the street with her radiant eyes. The grandmother I never knew. Because she died so young, it's impossible to imagine her as my grandmother; she's like a character in a novel, a name, the forever youthful Suheyla.

'Who are these two other girls, Shirin? Suheyla's friends? Look, Suheyla is the prettiest. Do you see?'

Great-Granny took the photo from me and put on the glasses that were hanging on a chain around her neck. She traced each of the girls' faces with her finger. I held my breath. Sometimes out of the blue she'll come out with such weird stories. Once she told me about how she had posed naked at the academy in Paris to earn money when she was a student. That was when we were looking at a photo of Suheyla, like now. What was the connection? I wondered. She told me she caught a cold, posing nude, and was sick in bed for days, without anyone around, and thought she would die. Those kinds of stories.

But this time she put the photo back in the box without saying anything and handed me another one. Suheyla again. Riding a horse on what looked like the Grand Tour road, with Heybeliada in the distance, the sea going on forever, and little puffy clouds in the sky. Somebody was holding the reins of the horse and Suheyla's long hair was blowing in the wind. She had an innocent smile on her face. There are tons of photos of Suheyla because her father, my great-grandfather, the maths professor, was very keen on photography. He tried to catch every moment of his daughter's life with the Kodak camera he brought from Germany.

And there was Suheyla eating ice cream, with a kiosk in the background, maybe a hotel. And there she was sunbathing on a chaise longue on our jetty, shading her eyes with her hand and laughing, with a big straw hat on her head. The boards of the jetty hadn't rotted or broken off yet. And there was Suheyla, tall and slim and small breasted, in the ballroom of the Splendid Palace Hotel, dancing with a tall, dark boy. That one was taken by the hotel photographer. Suheyla wasn't smiling in that shot; she was looking thoughtful, not sad, and still pretty, very pretty. She had a neck like a swan's, and slender arms. She was prettier than me, or Aunt Nur, or any of the women in our family. Maybe because she looked like she knew something we didn't. But what?

Great-Granny abruptly tossed away the next photo, aiming it at the empty fireplace as she muttered something angry and incomprehensible. It floated down onto the dark blue rug at our feet.

'Leave these! Bring the blue!'

I knelt down and examined the photo. It showed Suheyla as a child, with short hair and a fringe, sitting on her father's lap. She was wearing shorts with braces, a scout uniform, I think. She and her father were reading a book, one of the Oxford World's Classics from the bottom shelf of the bookcase. The maths professor was wearing round glasses. Suheyla's grasping fingers were long and thin, very clean and white. Why had Great-Granny jettisoned this photo so violently? Was she jealous of the father–daughter intimacy? I looked at the photo again. Father and daughter did look very close, like they clearly belonged together. I turned and gave Great-Granny's knees a reassuring pat, to show her I understood, but she recoiled. This was obviously one of those days when she didn't want to be touched. Understood!

She stamped her stockinged foot on the floor, like a child. 'Bring the blue!'

She was talking about the dark blue box, the one containing the oldest photos, the photos from Shirin Hanim's youth. They were small, with torn edges; some had been taken in studios and some were printed on postcard paper. In my childhood these were the photos I was least interested in, but that wasn't the case any more. Before I'd even sat back down on the sofa, Great-Granny had snatched the box from my hand. She rifled anxiously through the dusty sepia prints, searching for something. Then she found it. Holding the photo in her gnarled fingers, she nodded.

I stretched and looked at it over her shoulder, inhaling the scent of the powder she applies with Sadik's help every morning. It was a smell both familiar and from a dark, faraway time, like the inside of the drawer lined with flowery paper in the room my dad stays in. That room used to be my great-grandfather's, the great-grandfather in the photo Great-Granny tossed away. He died when Suheyla was fifteen. From bits and pieces that Sadik Usta has told me, I know that Suheyla became very depressed after that. As soon as she finished high school, she married a rich businessman, Tercan Bulut, my grandfather, Dad and Aunt Nur's father. Tercan Bulut is really rich now, but he pays no attention to us. After Suheyla died of a heart attack, he married a young woman he'd met in Thailand. She's younger than Dad, and Dad and Aunt Nur don't speak to him any more. So I don't know him at all; instead, I make do with tales about Dad and Aunt Nur's grandfather.

We were now looking at a photo of a young Shirin Saka in a café in Paris. She was sitting at a round table with a cup of coffee and a croissant on it. Her hair was short, with finger curls, her hat was on the table, and her lips were painted some dark colour. Her legs were crossed, and the straps of her pointy-toed shoes were tight around her slim ankles. All she needed was a cigarette in a long holder; that would have been cool, but as far as I knew, Great-Granny never smoked, despite leading such a bohemian life and being a nude life model at the academy. Maybe on the morning that photo was taken she'd come straight to the café from Sartre's bed.

'Wow, you're beautiful, Shirin! All the men must have been dying for you.' I laughed and nudged the saggy, wrinkled skin of her elbow with mine.

She remained serious-faced, found another photo and handed it to me. A little one. Dark, sepia-tinted and with torn edges, taken in a studio. It showed a group of children and in the middle was a woman. I studied their faces carefully, trying to work out which one was Great-Granny.

'Is that your mother?'

No answer.

'Are these your brothers and sisters, Shirin? Which one is you? What a lot of children! How many siblings did you have?'

She handed me another photo. Also with tattered edges. Also in dark sepia tones. Also taken in a studio. A man. Alone.

'Look carefully! Do you see it?'

I looked. So what? What was going on? Why was she so nervous? The man was resting his elbow on a tall table. His head was turned slightly sideways and he had a thin, pointy moustache and was wearing a stylish suit. He looked so much like Dad! The same tall, thin silhouette that looked like it might not be able to support his body. He looked as if the world owed him something. I had no idea what. Maybe Great-Granny knew. Exactly like Dad, I swear!

'Is this your husband, Shirin? Halit Bey, the maths professor? It is, isn't it, Shirin?'

Silence. I turned it over. Ottoman Turkish words written in Arabic script. I saw the year. 1927. So? Since Great-Granny was a hundred years old, born in 1917, this man couldn't be her husband. Was it her father? Could this be the grandfather my dad was so keen to find?

'Great-Granny, this is your father, right? I'm going to have to take this photo so I can show it to Dad, okay? I promise I'll put it back. See how much he looks like Dad – exactly the same! I can't believe it.'

Great-Granny didn't make a sound. Where just a minute earlier she'd been asking me to look, to look very carefully, now there was a deep and ominous silence between us. Was it the silence before a storm? I heard a sort of hum, like when your computer is working too hard and the hard drive is overheating and the system is about to shut down and lose everything you haven't saved. I felt nervous.

'Great-Granny, are you all right? Look at me.'

And then... Great-Granny's rattling breath and... Boom!

'My father shot himself.'

'What? What did you say? I don't understand.'

She put the dark blue box beside her on the sofa and turned to me. In the dim light her chin and her nose seemed longer and thinner. Emphasizing each word slowly, she repeated, loudly and clearly, 'My father shot himself. What's not to understand?'

I stood up. I needed to do something. Right away. With the old photo in my hand, I walked to the door. Then I changed my mind, came back, and passed it to Great-Granny. She took it but didn't look at it, just held it. Her eyes were fixed on the empty fireplace. She put on her glasses then spoke as if her mouth were full of pebbles.

'We had just finished breakfast. The stove was alight and Meryem was pouring tea from the samovar into our glasses. The windows were all steamed up. Father turned and took the Kirikkale shotgun off the wall. He put it in his mouth and pulled the trigger. His head fell onto the plate in front of him. The plate broke in half. Blood splattered all over the wall behind him. We scrubbed and scrubbed for days, but the stain would not come out.'

I ran out of the library, clattered down the hall, grabbed my bike from the garden and raced at top speed to the Horoz Reis Tea Garden. Burak had just posted a photo of the tea garden on Instagram. Stay there, Burak, I urged. Don't go anywhere. You've got to hear this story, before the gates to Great-Granny's brain clang shut. I'm coming! Wait there, Burak! Hold on!

15

Sadik

Madam Shirin did not eat a single mouthful of the breakfast I took to her room this morning. The joyful mood of yesterday morning, when she sat in the dining room with the grandchildren, had vanished. What a shame. If I were asked, I would say that the conversation at the breakfast table fatigued her. The grandchildren were not aware of this. They asked questions, they probed, they encouraged her to recall unnecessary details about the past. My lady's strength was exhausted. I took her to her room to rest. Thank goodness, the grandchildren and Mr Burak did not tax my lady again yesterday, but today she woke up with neither energy nor appetite. Even though I bought her favourite bread fresh from Niko's Bakery and prepared it the way she likes, dipped in egg, she didn't touch it. She merely drank her coffee, without milk. Her hands shake when she drinks that pitch-black coffee. Some evenings her soupspoon cannot find her mouth and droplets of soup spill onto the napkin I tie around her neck. Then she will raise her hands, hold them in front of her face and stare at them without saying a word. I know she is suffering inside. Her silence also causes something inside me to ache.

From those hands once flowed works of great creativity, works of art that unlocked something deep within my soul and spoke to a part of me that I did not know existed. Madam Shirin needed only to brush a single colour onto the canvas and I, your humble servant, could straightaway envisage what she was painting. She would know from my reaction, however subtle or unconscious, that I had understood. I might simply have held my breath or unknowingly cleared my throat, and she would say, 'Sadik, what do you see in this painting?' But I would remain quiet. How could I say anything? She would become angry then. 'Speak, man! What do you see?'

I couldn't say, 'I see the leaves of the acacia tree in front of the window beating against the glass during the June rains.' How would I say such a thing?

As I stood there in silence, my lady would lower her hands – hands daubed with orange, blue, crushed cherry – and say, 'True art should touch a person's soul, Sadik. If my work does not even come close to touching yours, then it is not art.'

These thoughts came to my mind as she handed me the tray with trembling hands, having not eaten the tiniest bit of her breakfast. In the evenings, when, exhausted, she would sit in front of the fireplace, I would remove the paint from her fingers with turpentine. Her skin would emerge from the blues and oranges like a white lily. I took the tray and as I went through the hall to the kitchen, I heard music coming from the dining room. Gently, I pushed open the door and looked in. Madam Nur was sitting all by herself at the head of the empty table, crying. She was holding the coffee cup in both hands as tears streamed down her cheeks. The dear girl used to cry like that when she was a child too. I withdrew. She hadn't seen me. Silently, I left Madam Shirin's tray in the kitchen and went to my room. I would tidy the house later, in the afternoon. For now, I would leave Madam Nur to weep as much as her heart desired.

It is not my custom to spend time in my room during the day, it is not appropriate, and so I was now at something of a loss as to what I should do there. My room, which Madam Shirin generously offered me many years ago, is relatively spacious and it warms the heart. Or it seems so to me, anyway, for it is the only room whose walls are lined with deep red tiles. I have often thought that this is the sole room in the house where I could sleep comfortably. Because Madam Shirin is a generous person, after Professor Halit passed away, she moved me here and allocated the annex beside the sea to the gardener and his family.

When Mr Halit first bought this house, I myself lived in that annex. I had no complaints, thanks be to God. Quite the opposite. I would wake up to the sight of the milky sea in front of my window and watch the fishermen casting their nets from their boats. It made me happy. But on winter nights, when the wind was wild and the waves beat against the wooden jetty, I would be reminded of our childhood, willingly or not. I do not think that Madam Shirin remembered those days, which was why she thought the annex suitable for me. In the old days, we lived on a remote mountain. Madam Shirin resided with her lady mother and her esteemed father, Mr Nuri, in a large stone house, and my beloved mama and I lived in a small dwelling connected to the big house by an underground passage. The passage was dark and damp. Candles burnt in niches carved into the mildew-encrusted walls and I would feel the gaze of the strange beings contained within them as I walked along it, which frightened me. In the night, if Mama was needed in the big house, the sound of a bell would echo through that passage and she would run to their aid, heedless of my tears. As I lay all alone in the bed that Mama and I shared, I would cry, afraid that the howling wind and raging storm on the other side of the wall would snatch up our little hut and rip it away from the large house, separating us forever.

By the time Professor Halit bought this house, that old mansion was gone. Madam Shirin had sold it and I presume the money was used to purchase this one. The life we'd lived there had long ago been consigned to history. In the years since, a great deal had happened. Madam Shirin studied art in Paris, returned, and married Professor Halit. When she said, 'The cabin by the sea shall be yours, Sadik,' it did not occur to her, of course, that she was repeating the arrangement of our childhood.

My room overlooks the backyard while Madam Shirin's has a view onto the front garden. In between us are the kitchen, the pantry and the bathroom, but in spite of the distance, I am on my feet at the first sound from my lady's room. Although I do not hear well, as I have said, where my lady is concerned I hear like a wolf in the night. I even hear the shuffle of her slippers as she walks from the bed to the window, stands there, and then turns and sits in front of the mirror. On some nights, when she does not get up from the mirror, I become concerned. Fearing that she might have dozed off and, God forbid, could even have hit her head on the edge of the dressing table, I go into her room. The scene I am met with is invariably even more alarming that that. My lady will be sitting in front of the mirror. In the darkness of night the mirror reflects nothing, but Madam Shirin, as if she sees what I do not, will be using her eyebrow pencil and drawing her own image on the surface of the mirror.

In the morning I always fetch a soapy cloth and wipe away the image, and as I wipe, I will be full of wonder at how uncannily the self-portrait resembles the original. Not one wrinkle or shadow will have been omitted. Sometimes Madam Shirin draws a trio of figures, one on each of the mirror's three panels. The three figures gaze at each other and as I erase one, the other two keep their eyes fixed on me. It makes me extremely uncomfortable, but I do not baulk. I make sure to take the same care in wiping clean each panel as I used to when wiping clean my lady's hands. From the glass that I have cleaned appear not lilies but my old and wrinkled face.

Oh, dear brain! A person should always keep themselves busy, otherwise the brain wanders and conjures illusions, memories. Unlike Madam Nur and Mr Fikret I am not used to spending time alone in my room. Even in winter, when it is just Madam Shirin and me left in this house, when my work in the kitchen or with housecleaning is finished, I sit in the library, in a corner behind my lady's armchair. I come to my room only at bedtime, to sleep.

When Professor Halit was alive, musical instruments were kept in this room. Our little miss, Suheyla, was a talented musician. She played the violin and the piano very well. Her father's double bass was huge and took up a quarter of the room; it stood in the corner, which I now keep empty. It was from the professor that I learnt the name of this instrument. Soon after we moved into this house, he leant over and whispered to me, as if imparting a secret, 'Sadik, do you know that the reason I bought this house was because they were selling the double bass along with it.'

He'd apparently had a long-held desire to learn the double bass. When the former owners, an Italian family, were taking

Professor Halit and Madam Shirin around the house, they mentioned that in addition to the furniture they would also be leaving behind the double bass and the piano in the music room. Professor Halit immediately shook hands on the deal. It is true that the money came from Madam Shirin, but perhaps Mr Halit contributed to the fund with his salary from the university. I do not concern myself in such matters.

To tell the truth, when Professor Halit first began to play the instrument I did not understand the music that came forth. I rarely entered this room, as a matter of fact. My workload was excessive. Miss Suheyla had just been born and life on the top floor was busy. We had settled the baby into the room on the street side, where Madam Nur now stays. Madam Shirin was ill, with no energy, and also a little bad-tempered because she was unable to come down to the library, which she used as a studio. She had no tolerance for the dum-dum-dum musical efforts of Professor Halit. When the double bass instruction began, the wooden floors would reverberate noisily, giving her a headache. She would shout from the child's room where she lay, and when her complaints went unheard, she would begin to cry. When she cried, Baby Suheyla would also cry. Professor Halit paid no attention. I would take the infant onto my lap and rock her to sleep.

Time passed and Miss Suheyla grew up. She began to play the violin. It was only then that I understood the sound produced by Professor Halit's instrument. In the same way that Madam Shirin could bring a painting to life with the addition of a single colour, so the deep, moaning echo of Professor Halit's double bass gained meaning when accompanied by Miss Suheyla's violin. With the bowing of a single note, the sound became music. From then on, I was addicted; music haunted my soul. Whenever I heard music starting up in this room, a complex, incomprehensibly strong feeling would overwhelm your humble servant, and, even as I told myself to stay away, I would find myself standing at the door.

From time to time Professor Halit's nieces would come to Buyukada from their home on neighbouring Heybeliada. They would arrive from their island on the daily ferry and bathe in the sea with Miss Suheyla. They were very sensible children. After afternoon tea, they would gather in this room. The eldest daughter – I have forgotten her name – was an excellent pianist. She would sit at the piano, and little Suheyla would take up her violin and incline her lovely neck. As soon as I heard Professor Halit playing the first note on his double bass, I would leave whatever I was doing in the kitchen and go into the pantry, which is adjacent to this room. Or I would dally a while in the hall, on the pretext of fetching a broom from the cupboard under the stairs. From where he stood behind the double bass, Professor Halit would crane his neck and say, 'Come in, Sadik,' and I would approach the door, embarrassed and a little nervous. I was anxious lest Madam Shirin get angry, for my lady desired that I be ready to assist her with anything she might need while she was painting in the library, but the music touched me so deeply that I was not able to drag myself away.

I later learnt that sound resonates differently in this room. I will never forget the day Professor Halit told me this. He was at the breakfast table, in the chair upon which Madam Nur was now sitting and crying. He was alone. Madam Shirin had shut herself up in the library, as she always did as soon as she woke up. The professor did not mind that. He was hungrily spooning up the egg that I had served him, and at the same time he was listening to Miss Suheyla, who was in the music room. He closed his eyes as he listened, and kept time by rapping his hand on the table. Miss Suheyla's singing instructor was teaching her an opera and as her voice filled the dining room, it sounded more lovely than the splashing of the most beautiful river and as full and strong as if she were using a microphone. I was overcome. I was young then and some daring must have come over me that I asked Professor Halit about the sound.

'It's because there are special acoustics in that room, Sadik. It was built especially for playing music in.'

He appeared to wish to speak further, but I had been tactless enough. I was silent. He again closed his eyes and gave himself to Miss Suheyla's voice.

Professor Halit left this life at a young age. God rest his soul. It was in the evening. The three of them, Madam Shirin, Miss Suheyla and Professor Halit, were in the dining room and I was serving the soup. It is still fresh in my memory. It was a rice and leek soup, cooked with carrots, potatoes, onion and abundant parsley and fresh mint. A light, summer soup. The school term had just finished and Miss Suheyla and Professor Halit had arrived that very day. Madam Shirin and I had been here for almost two months. That year, as usual, as soon as the plum trees blossomed, my lady had had me pack our trunks and suitcases and, leaving Professor Halit and Miss Suheyla to fend for themselves in Moda, the two of us had come to the island, opened up the house, aired it, and got it ready for summer.

Madam Shirin was a trifle upset that the flow of her inspiration would be interrupted by the arrival of her husband and daughter, but it was my opinion that the house becoming livelier would make her happy. The previous month there had been a coup d'état in the country. Madam Shirin had been pleased that the military forces had taken control. 'When provincial people try to govern the country with their narrow minds, this is what happens,' she'd said. Miss Suheyla related how she and her friends had gone to Taksim Square to give flowers to the soldiers who were taking over the government. It was obvious that Professor Halit had some concerns about the military regime, but he did not go into detail. Madam Shirin had just completed her last painting and was in high spirits. The Splendid Palace Hotel would soon be holding a gala at which her most recent works would be exhibited.

The curtains were open and so were all the windows. The mimosa leaves were rustling sweetly and the branches of the mulberry tree were bowed low with fruit. It was a bountiful year. A piano concerto was playing on the radio and Miss Suheyla was tapping her foot to it under the table. In honour of Mr Halit and Miss Suheyla, I, your humble servant, had prepared roast lamb sprinkled with rosemary from the garden. Having cleared away the soup bowls, I brought the lamb to the table on a tray.

Miss Suheyla and Professor Halit were discussing a book. This book had greatly affected dear Miss Suheyla. The professor was cutting the meat I had placed on his plate and laughing at the same time. 'Why did she have to write such a long book? We understood what she was trying to say after just two chapters.'

Miss Suheyla disagreed. She was of the opinion that the book would change the world. The author, although born in Russia, had written her book, as thick as a brick, in English. As she spoke, her eyes lit up, her cheeks reddened, and the tapping of her foot accelerated. It was the first time I had heard her speak about something with such passion. From my position beside the door, where I waited in case I might be of service, I caught Madam Shirin's eye. She was as astounded as I. Our dear Miss Suheyla had changed. My lady was also enjoying this. She raised her eyebrows at me and I smiled very subtly. So subtly that only Madam Shirin would notice.

Mr Halit laughed again. 'The story of the individual's struggle against the stifling power of the state is a tale that's been told many times, dear Suheyla, from Homer onwards. Your Russian lady should at least understand something of literat—'

Halfway through his sentence, the professor fell forwards in his chair and hit his mouth. One side of his mouth was still laughing, the other was scowling furiously. I ran to his side, but I was too late. He dropped to the floor with a tremendous crash. He had grabbed at the tablecloth as he fell, so his plate also tumbled to the floor. Pieces of lamb, mashed potato and salad were strewn everywhere. I was too upset to move. Miss Suheyla was trembling like a frightened bird in her chair. Madam Shirin threw down her napkin and knelt on the ground. Her hands, those gifted fingers that I had cleansed of paint before dinner, found Professor Halit's carotid artery.

'Sadik, go and find a carriage immediately and fetch Dr Kemal.'

Her voice was so calm, it brought me to my senses. I put on my shoes and rushed out onto the street.

I've often thought upon this since. Had Professor Halit not been on the island but at the apartment in Istanbul, might he have been saved? At that time there was no hospital on Buyukada, and crossing to Istanbul was nothing like as easy as it is today. You had to wait for the ferry, unless you could find a fishing boat to take you to the Numune Hospital in Haydarpasa.

As Dr Kemal knelt beside the professor in the dining room, one hand on the back of his head, the other on his pulse, he gave his diagnosis to Madam Shirin. Professor Halit had had a stroke and would not survive the swaying of a fishing vessel. The doctor advised that we should bid the professor adieu. I held little Suheyla's shoulders, but she broke away and shut herself in the music room. Dr Kemal carried Professor Halit into the living room across from the dining room and laid him on a sofa. He did not return to his home up in the hills but spent the remainder of the night in that room. Madam Shirin did not sleep either. She sat in the glittery armchair in front of the window. Miss Suheyla did not emerge from the music room until morning. The dear little one understood from the hurried footsteps on the stairs and in the corridor in the morning that Professor Halit's soul had passed over. From where she sat, Madam Shirin watched as Dr Kemal closed the professor's eyes. I brought down a white sheet from upstairs, covered his face, bound his jaw and laid a knife on his stomach. All colour had drained from my lady's face, her lips and even from her eyes. She was like a transparent white statue. It was as if she had died along with her husband.

Then, suddenly, we heard a violin. Miss Suheyla was playing a piece of music steeped in excruciating sorrow. It was a piece she had practised many times with her father. The magnificent acoustics of the music room carried the notes into every room of the house, whence they reverberated from the walls, the windowpanes, the wooden floors and the fireplaces. Nothing, however, could compensate for the lack of the double bass. The absence of that instrument, whose name at one time I didn't even know, carved a hole in my heart.

We remained motionless where we sat until the piece ended.

From that day on, Miss Suheyla never again took up her

violin. Madam Shirin donated the double bass to the Istanbul State Opera and Ballet. The piano was moved into the living room and no one has touched it since.

I myself settled into the now empty music room. At certain times, when I lie alone in my bed, the ghosts of Miss Suheyla and Professor Halit come to visit me.

The music that Madam Nur was playing over and over as she wept in the dining room now filled my ears. I became emotional. Though it was not my custom, two tears fell from my eyes.

16

Nur

I dried my tears when I heard Celine hurtling out into the garden. The whole house shook with the thump of her footsteps. I got up from the table and went over to the window. She was in a tearing hurry, hadn't even put on a bra. She thrust her bike out through the gate then jumped on and began pedalling furiously up the hill, not bothering to shut the gate or look behind her.

In the hall, I bumped into Sadik Usta. He too had been curious at Celine's leaving so noisily and was muttering something, deliberately not looking at my face. He knows me well and understood that I'd been crying. Sniffing, I followed him to the kitchen and jumped up onto the marble counter next to the sink, just as I used to when I was little. I swung my legs and the marble felt cool under the thin fabric of my kimono. Sadik Usta was clearing my grandmother's lunch tray. I turned to look at the garden through the window behind me. Everything was so dry. Then, just to make conversation, I said, 'Sadik Usta, where do you think Fikret went?'

He didn't look up. He was decanting leftover noodle soup into an old yogurt pot. He put the cheese back in the paper the shop had wrapped it in, then crumbled the uneaten bread, moistened it, and sprinkled it along the windowsill for the birds. Sadik Usta does not like waste. If it had been me, I wouldn't have saved Grandmother's leftover bits of chicken. They wouldn't get eaten anyway. But Sadik Usta tipped them into a glass pot and put them in the fridge together with the cheese.

I took some tobacco out of my kimono pocket, rolled myself a thin cigarette and held it between my fingers without lighting it.

'I saw him leaving really early – Fikret, I mean. It was still dark. For a moment I wondered if he might be going to the mosque. He's become so strange lately, so fixated on mystical stuff, that I wouldn't have been surprised if he'd gone for holiday prayers. Being religious is pretty much de rigueur in this country these days, if you want to get on, though that's not what Fikret's spirituality is about, it has to be said.'

I sniffed. Sadik Usta pulled a handkerchief out of his shirt pocket and handed it to me. He still wouldn't look at my face. I put my cigarette down and took the handkerchief. It was white, with thin blue stripes, sparkling clean and carefully ironed. All of a sudden, my eyes filled with tears once again. My heart cracked at the thought that this man, who had been with my family for almost a century, who had passed all of us handkerchiefs when we cried – me, Celine, my mum, Grandmother – this giant oak tree would die soon. He would leave a hole in our lives that could never be filled. The force that united us was Sadik as much as it was Grandmother. It might be Sadik more than Grandmother.

'When I was a little girl, I would dry my eyes with this handkerchief when I cried. Do you remember, Sadik Usta?'

I couldn't bring myself to blow my nose. The handkerchief

was so clean! The mascara I forgot to wipe off in my drunkenness last night would ruin it. Sadik Usta was arranging some things in the fridge. He nodded imperceptibly, then turned round, removed the gold filter from the coffee machine, tapped it against the side of the plastic bin – tuk, tuk – and dumped the grounds into the rubbish bag. I lit my cigarette. As I took the first puff, I examined the blue stripes of the handkerchief.

'Do you remember when I fell over and bashed my nose on one of the garden steps? It was bleeding like crazy, dripping all over the floor. I ran to your room and you didn't know what to do. Do you remember? My nose got all swollen later. I looked like an owl.'

'You were a rascal, Madam Nur,' Sadik said quietly as he tied up the top of the rubbish bag. 'Crowds of children used to follow you off the street and into our garden. If Madam Shirin hadn't had a special soft spot for you, that sort of behaviour would not have been tolerated.'

Finally he straightened up and looked me in the face. His small blue eyes had begun to lose their colour, like babies' eyes. They'd become a sort of milky blue, the colour changing in the light. I rolled a cigarette for him too.

'Shall we have coffee, Sadik Usta – you and me? Turkish coffee? Let's smoke a couple of cigarettes together.'

He looked away. I thought he was going to say something along the lines of, 'I have to prepare the dinner, Madam Nur,' but he surprised me.

'Of course, Madam Nur. You take it with a little sugar, am I correct? I will have it like that too. It will be easy.'

'Great!'

We stayed in the kitchen. After all, that was where Sadik Usta was most comfortable. And I was used to dangling my legs off the marble counter as we talked. Taking my coffee, I handed him a cigarette. Sadik Usta didn't smoke regularly, but I knew that in the mornings when he went to the market, he would sit at Niko's Bakery and roll a cigarette. I could see the yellow stain on his fingers and I'd also heard the boys at the bakery mentioning it.

He sat down across from me, at the kitchen table, took a drag of his cigarette and closed his eyes.

'Your mother was very upset when she saw your nose all bandaged up.'

'Yes, she went to Istanbul once in a blue moon, and I picked that day to fall and hurt myself.'

'Madam Nur, every day you hurt some bit of yourself, you just didn't notice. You would climb up onto the top of the garden gate and sit there as if you were riding a horse. The gardener's children would swing it backwards and forwards so that you could play the acrobat. My heart would be in my mouth.'

I smiled. It was true, I was very keen on acrobatics as a child, but I wasn't as wild as Sadik described. I was just curious.

'Sadik Usta, that day when my nose bled so much and I came to your room and cried because I was so frightened, after you'd cleaned my wound with hydrogen peroxide and iodine, you laid me down on your bed and sang me a lullaby, do you remember?'

'I do not remember, Madam Nur. Forgive me.'

'It was in a foreign language. You said you'd learnt it from your mama. Do you really not remember?'

'Unfortunately, Madam Nur, many years have passed since my childhood. I do not know any lullabies. You must have imagined it. You were very small at the time.'

He stared at his slippers in stubborn silence.

You are lying, Sadik Usta, I said to myself. You know it, and so do I. You speak that other language fluently. Remember that day that you and Mum went up to the Monastery of St George? It was midsummer, years and years ago, way before Fikret and me. A hot day. You would never normally have abandoned your housework or your Madam Shirin and gone to the other side of the island, but you couldn't disappoint your dearly beloved Suheyla, and she wanted to say a prayer for her father's soul and light a candle in the church.

Exactly forty days had passed since Professor Halit had crashed onto the dining-room table and never got up again. When Suheyla said, 'Let's go to the church together, Sadik Usta,' unshed tears quivered in her green eyes. It was only two days since you'd saved her from drowning.

Suheyla was a good swimmer, but that day she had gone out too far. She hadn't realized how strong the current was and it had carried her a long way. She was in the middle of the sea, all alone, and she panicked. The sea, which she had always known as a friend, that watery mass in whose embrace of greens and blues she was usually so comfortable, had become dark and hostile. Suheyla thought of her childhood. Life was fragile, pathetic, when confronted by death. Her ears heard nothing but the pounding waves; her breath was fast and ragged. The shore was just there, in front of her, with its stepped terraces and familiar trees and their beautiful house with the wooden shutters whose every brick she knew so well. But her strokes didn't bring her nearer to the house, they drew her further away.

She gave up swimming freestyle and switched to breaststroke. I mustn't struggle, she told herself. I must conserve my strength and stay calm. As if it were baiting her,

her panic intensified, submerging her calm, logical side beneath a flood of fear. She understood now how a person drowned. There came a point when death seemed the preferable option, the only option, when the terror became impossible to endure and surrender seemed sweeter. Let me drown, she decided. Let me die. And as soon as she thought that, she realized that this was what she really wanted. For a long, long time a part of her had longed for death. This had nothing to do with her father's recent passing, it preceded that; it was a seed that had taken root inside her long ago, to spite her mother. The only way to get the attention of the mother who used to leave her in a cradle and shut herself in her studio was to kill herself. That was the only way Suheyla would secure a place in Shirin Saka's heart. Finally. She would become an everlasting ache in her mother's heart, and that pain would creep into Shirin Saka's art; it would be there for eternity. Suheyla surrendered. She began to sink. But her lungs would not give up on her and with the first gulp of seawater, she started to struggle.

It must have been then that you saw her, Sadik. Perhaps you were looking at the sea as you shook the sheets out of the bedroom window. Maybe at first you thought it was a seagull, whereas in fact it was a white hand, sinking and resurfacing. Nobody knows how you managed to hurl yourself out the door, run to the jetty at the bottom of the garden, dive into the sea and swim so rapidly to where the waves had marooned Suheyla. Where had you learnt to swim so well?

You were weeping when you finally got Suheyla back to the jetty. My mother's beautiful head was tipped back. Her hair was plastered to her scalp like seaweed, her face and neck had turned blue, her skin was cold and wrinkly from the saltwater. Her pulse had almost disappeared and she wasn't breathing. You thought she was dead and you weren't far wrong. Her soul was hovering there, watching the drama being played out under the round midday sun. Letting go would be easy. If she went, she would leave a mark on her mother's life. If she stayed, she would remain unheard, unseen.

You had taken the seaweed-haired Suheyla onto your knees. Water was streaming from your shirt, your tie, your nose. You were sobbing. Suddenly, Suheyla gave a cough and woke up. As the two of you looked into each other's eyes, a pact was made. I will live, Sadik Usta, my mother told you with her eyes. Your crying is so heartfelt, so terrible, that, for your sake, I will endure this life.

The two of you never told anyone this story. It was only when, many years later, I asked Mum why she never swam very far out with me when we went to the beach together, that she shared it with me. That's how I came to be a partner in your secret.

You hovered over your little Suheyla more than ever after that, and when she asked you to accompany her to the church (Mum wasn't the sort to insist on things, as I do; she requested) you couldn't refuse. In any case, Madam Shirin was taking her afternoon nap and you assumed that you would simply light a candle and then come back. You didn't know that Suheyla was intending to walk all the way up St George's hill, like a pilgrim.

You went as far as the Lunapark Square junction in a horse-drawn carriage. There was hardly anyone around, just horses standing in the shade with their heads buried in their nosebags and their drivers asleep in the back seats of their carriages. From there, Suheyla wanted the two of you to go on foot up to the monastery, along the steep and dusty dirt road. You would have been young then, though, Sadik. How old, exactly? Nobody knows your age, but you probably weren't even forty then. Younger than I am now. Even as a child you had an old soul, I'm sure of that.

You and my mother made your way slowly up the long, steep hill. The sun shone in your faces as you walked. On both sides of the road the bushes were hung with offerings placed there by pilgrims, Muslims and Christians alike, who trod this route in the hope that their prayers would be answered: colourful ribbons, bells and little votive offerings or keyholders representing houses, babies, books, quite unlike the filthy paper napkins that get tied there today. But you didn't see those. Your capped head was bowed and you were gazing at Suheyla's feet, which were bare in her leather sandals and covered in dust and dirt. 'We could have hired a donkey, Miss Suheyla,' you said. 'I could have led it by its halter and pulled you to the top.'

'What a thing, Sadik Usta,' my mum replied dismissively, gesturing with her slender chin at the three tiny women, clad in black from head to toe, who were walking ahead of you without complaint. Her eyes looked greener than ever beneath the shadows cast by her long lashes. Suheyla was like your own child. You'd been with her since the day she was born and you were terrified that something might happen to her. Just the other day she had almost drowned. And Professor Halit was dead. What if some prowler were to jump out of the bushes and grab her? Her beauty made your heart tremble with fear, not pride.

When you reached the church, Suheyla lit a candle in the courtyard. She had covered her head with a blue silk scarf and her little white hands, which she had spread open in prayer, were shaking. You didn't know what to do with yourself during this strange ritual. With your cap in your hand and your head bent, you waited behind my mum. From below, near the holy spring, three black-cloaked priests appeared. They were speaking softly among themselves as they walked towards the church. When they saw Suheyla praying fervently with her eyes closed, they nodded to you and went inside.

At that very moment, the bell began to ring. The sun had lost some of its strength as it passed behind Heybeliada, and the encircling sea sparkled blue, turquoise and yellow beneath you. From the seminary on Heybeliada came a responding bell. The two monasteries, built on opposite hills on neighbouring islands, sang out to the skies, unaware that one day they would be silenced. First one rang out and then the other. It was as if that sacred hilltop, the highest on Buyukada, was beyond the reach of the evils of politics, a place to shed one's earthly identity and become a purely spiritual being.

For a while the church bells echoed among the blue-green hills. Your heart tightened. A memory from long ago, maybe not even your own, began to take shape in your consciousness. Suheyla raised her head, looked into your eyes and smiled. 'Let's go, Miss Suheyla,' you said. Anxiety was rising inside you like an unstoppable tide.

But Suheyla wouldn't listen. 'Evening prayers are beginning, Sadik Usta,' she said. 'Let's sit in the church for a while.'

With her blue scarf wrapped around her face, she was as beautiful as the Virgin Mary. For no reason, your mother came into your head. Not for no reason, of course. Your mother's name was Meryem; Mary. Suheyla's innocent beauty, the bells, the murmured prayers and the smell of incense would have certainly invoked the memory of your mother, Meryem.

Inside the church, as you sat side by side with Suheyla on a wooden pew at the back, you suddenly felt very faint. The priests under the dome were chanting the same prayer over and over: 'Kyrie eleison, Kyrie eleison, Kyrie eleison.' Just as Suheyla's beloved father had fallen off his chair forty days earlier, you now fell sideways onto Suheyla's shoulder. One of the young priests rushed over and laid you down on the cool stones of the church floor. 'It was because of the heat, the incense, the steep climb up the hill,' you said to Suheyla later. She did not reply.

It was then that Suheyla heard for the first time that other language coming out of your mouth. When the young priest turned to her and said something in a language she didn't understand, it was you, Sadik Usta, who answered him, as if you were speaking from deep within your subconscious. Your words mingled with the smell of the incense.

The two of you didn't talk about it on the way home; you didn't talk at all. By the time you got home, the sun had set, but it was still light outside. You went into the kitchen, Sadik, resumed your position in front of the stove and began preparing the evening meal. Suheyla went to her room. On her lips was a tiny smile. This was your second secret. Years later, Mum told me this secret when I asked her about the lullaby you'd sung for me on the day I fell and bloodied my nose.

We both know all this, Sadik Usta, I continued, carrying on my silent conversation with him as we sat there in the kitchen, but we don't talk about it; we choose to stay quiet, to forget. We push what we know into the darkest recesses of our consciousness. We know of no other way to live. That was why I was so angry with Fikret, because I was afraid he'd force us off that path. That was why we wanted him to come home right away. Let him sit at the head of the table and behave like he was supposed to. Let him not delve into the past.

Sadik Usta's cigarette had gone out and lay forgotten, half

smoked, in the ashtray. He'd finished his coffee long ago. Eyes still fixed on his slippers, he sat motionless. I jumped off the counter, went over to the table, reached out and touched the arm of his long-sleeved brown shirt, the one he never took off, even on summer days. He raised his eyes as if he were waking from a dream. Out of habit, he straightened up the salt and pepper and the bottle of olive oil on the table and cleared his throat. He was trying to remember what we'd been talking about before I mentioned the lullaby. I was sure his mind had travelled back to the same memory that mine had settled on, but now he caught hold of the present.

'Is there anything more to be done for the tea party tomorrow, Madam Nur? You were to order the cake and Mr Fikret was to see to the food, but—'

'Don't worry, Sadik Usta, we've ordered everything for tomorrow's celebration. It will all be delivered here in the morning, including the cake. You can relax.'

He inhaled, looked steadfastly ahead, and began to speak.

'Madam Nur, Greengrocer Hasan said he saw your brother at the pier this morning, before the ferry was due to leave. I thought he must have been mistaken, but now that you say Mr Fikret left the house very early, perhaps Greengrocer Hasan was right. I pray that your brother is not in any trouble.'

I smiled. 'Oh, don't worry, Sadik Usta. Fikret is having a midlife crisis and is forever distracting himself with some new enthusiasm or other. He's probably decided to make a family tree or something. He'll have got interested in something Grandmother said yesterday, when she was telling Burak about her childhood, and now he'll have gone back to his home in the city to look through photo albums or old newspaper cuttings. He'll be back with us this evening. He wouldn't miss tomorrow's celebration for anything.'

I rolled another cigarette, lit it and handed my Zippo to Sadik Usta so he could light the one lying in the ashtray. He didn't take it.

'To delve into the past does not bring peace to the present, Madam Nur.'

'Why not, Sadik Usta? Fikret believes that if the secrets of the past are brought to light, we will all feel better, more at peace.' I said this sarcastically, to hurt Sadik's feelings. Let the unknowns of the past be revealed, the shell broken. Let whatever was hiding there come out.

He turned his deep-set eyes on me and looked me full in the face. 'Is something troubling you, Madam Nur?'

When Sadik Usta asked me straight out like that, something moved inside me. It was as if inside my chest, in my belly, there was a locked safe, or a cave with its entrance blocked by a boulder, just waiting to be opened by Sadik Usta's question. I muttered something, stuttered, as if I had done a very bad and shameful thing. I, who all my life have been a vociferous supporter of women's rights. How could I think that what I did was shameful? Was it seeing myself through Sadik's eyes that made shame flush from my cheeks to my temples, setting my whole head on fire?

Sadik Usta was gazing at me with his cloudy, milk-blue eyes. 'Are you all right, Madam Nur? You are not sick, I pray?'

I put my arms on the table and buried my face in them. My voice was muffled.

'Sadik Usta, I had an abortion. I... For the first time in my life, I fell pregnant, at the age of forty-two. It was clearly a blessing from God, a miracle, but I went ahead and murdered that life, Sadik Usta. I did a terrible thing.'

He reached out and touched my head. He brought his chair closer to mine and stroked my hair with his calloused fingers, the skin as wrinkled as a turtle's. I began to cry, quietly, without sobbing. My warm tears flowed down my face and onto the sleeve of my kimono. Sadik Usta bent his head to my ear. I closed my eyes.

I don't know how long we stayed like that. I must have fallen asleep at the table where I'd lain my head. When I woke up, Sadik Usta was no longer beside me, but the old lullaby was still echoing in my head.

17

Burak

We practically ran back to the house from the Horoz Reis Tea Garden. Celine was bursting with excitement. Still, that didn't stop her from trying to get me to ride two-up on her bicycle again. We would get there faster that way, so she said. What a little Lolita! I pretended not to hear her. I wasn't sure I had the strength to pedal a Scandinavian-boned Celine today. She didn't insist but instead walked swiftly beside me, pushing her heavy, retro bike and talking nonstop.

It seemed that she and Shirin Hanim had been looking at old photos together in the library when her great-grandmother came out with something quite extraordinary. A family secret. I would love it for sure. It would change the whole direction of my article and when the paper came out on Saturday morning, it would sell out. She would post a link on social media so her friends could know what a weird family she's from. Shirin Hanim had laid a golden egg, but if Celine told me the secret herself, it would ruin the effect. I definitely had to hear it from Shirin Saka herself. So we needed to get to the house as fast as possible as this might be our last chance before her great-granny fell silent on the subject again.

I wasn't expecting this huge secret to be anything earth-shattering. It was no doubt some snippet of sensational gossip that I'd heard years ago, but so as not to rain on Celine's parade, I made an effort to seem interested, excited even. She was upset anyway because of the bike thing. In truth, I was mainly thinking about the last part of the recording I'd just listened to. I was eager to listen to it again more carefully.

The house smelt of coffee and I could hear classical music, a familiar piece. It was coming from the dining room. I glanced in quickly as we passed; the room was empty and the table had been cleared. Celine gestured for me to follow her down the hall. Out the back, beside the door into the garden, Sadik Usta was distributing bits of leftover food to three tabby cats who were winding around his feet. He didn't hear us. He was murmuring a song as he bent over. I would rather have chatted with him in the garden than gone to the library, not for the article but to have a one-to-one conversation. I was certain there were lots of things he could tell me, not about himself but about me, for I'd glimpsed an understanding in his eyes, though I hadn't been able to decipher it. But Celine was determined and wouldn't let me linger. She'd already opened the door and was waiting impatiently.

We went into the library, Shirin Hanim's studio, her refuge, her space. Or rather Celine went in. I stayed on the threshold.

I stood there aghast.

If any room in that house were to affect me, it would be that one, of course. It was a miracle that it hadn't hit me until then. Since the previous morning, I'd been wandering around the two floors of the house, protecting myself from the ghosts of those three days seventeen years ago. What with Fikret's disappearance, Celine's flirtatiousness, Nur's troubles, Ufuk's absence and Shirin Hanim's story, I'd convinced myself that those ghosts would not return. Almost.

But now there I was in the doorway of that room and I could not take a step further. The ghosts were there, waiting for me: on the sofa where Shirin Hanim sat stiff as a poker, at the window with its view of the sea, in the empty stone fireplace, in the drawers of the decoratively carved rococo desk with a broken leg.

I leant against the doorframe to keep myself from falling.

Celine walked round the sofa, knelt down on the rug and took the old lady's hands in hers.

'Great-Granny, Burak's here. Turn round and look. Over there, in the doorway. Burak, come on in. Why are you standing over there like that?'

Did the room still really smell like that? I read somewhere that the part of the brain that processes smells is right next to the part that processes memories. That's why smells bring back memories associated with them. But what about vice versa? Could the memories permeating that room create the illusion of a smell? Could a person look at an empty fireplace and smell burning wood? Could the curtains, the sofa covers, the rugs hold the sweet fragrance of cognac drunk so many years ago, of tea brewing on top of the stove?

'Great-Granny, tell us about it! Tell us about your father. You were just saying...'

Celine's excitement had made her insensitive, like anyone who's fixated on their own concerns. Shirin Hanim had become flustered at the sight of me. As for me, I was immobilized, trapped behind an invisible barrier fashioned from smells and memories. If I crossed it, they would turn to dust. My most precious memories, which had never been touched, would vanish into thin air and become nothing, overlaid with Celine's self-important dramas and Shirin Hanim's nonsensical stories. I'd spent the best three days of my life in that room. Seventeen years ago I'd lived a winter fairy tale in there. No, I couldn't allow a different set of memories to be imprinted over the top, couldn't allow the present to alter the past. I had to preserve that room in its former state in my memory.

Celine sat down on the sofa, one foot tucked under her, and turned to Shirin Hanim.

'I was sitting here with you just a few minutes ago. You remember, we were looking at photos. We looked at pictures of Suheyla, and then there was one of you at a café in Paris. You told me about modelling, how you caught a cold and were sick. Then we were talking about your childhood and you saw a photo... Wait a minute, let me find it for you.'

Shirin Hanim was not listening to Celine, who was sorting through the photos in the box on her lap. She was staring fixedly at the fireplace. Did she too see a fire burning there? At a different time, in a different dream, that same fireplace had been blazing. Nur lay on the sofa beneath a red and green plaid wool blanket. Her eyes were bloodshot. I had piled on the logs. 'What if the chimney smokes?' we asked each other. But Sadik Usta would never have closed up the house for winter and left for Istanbul without first sweeping the chimney. Nur didn't have the energy to even raise her arm. She'd caught a cold and was feverish. From where she lay, she was directing me in a weak voice.

'You're supposed to stack them like an Indian tepee. The middle should be empty. Then you feed the twigs into the space.'

'Twigs? There aren't any twigs.'

'Why aren't there? Aren't there any in that basket?'

'Nope.'

'Then let's gather some from the garden. Wait, I'm coming too. I'm getting up.'

'Are you nuts, Nur? The garden's covered with snow. Anyway, where do you think you're going? You're to stay lying down with that fever. You're burning up. Lie down. Like this. I'll find something to burn.'

'Sadik keeps old newspapers in the pantry. Look there.'

'I've found some. Kindling too.'

'Of course, Sadik Usta would have left the house provided.'

'I'll make some tea. And I'll make you some soup too. I found tomato paste and rice. There's dried spearmint too.'

'Bring it in here. Let's cook on top of the woodstove. The kitchen's too cold. Oh, you're frozen, Burak. Come and get under the blanket, quick. God, your hands are so cold! Don't touch me – especially not my stomach!'

'I'm not doing anything, just checking your temperature.'

'Liar!'

'You're burning up, Nur.'

'Wait. Don't, Burak! Your nose is like ice. Get it away from my neck. Just hold me. Hold me tighter.'

Do I really have the words to express how those three days we spent in front of that fireplace were the best three days of my life? At the same time, I can't forget what had brought us to the island in the first place, what we were fleeing from. Even if I wanted to, I couldn't forget; this country of mine will not let me. I can't erase my shame at having abandoned those people on the hill, even as Nur and I made love nonstop on that sofa, under the red wool blanket, almost fully clothed. I would like to remember only the intense pleasure that coursed through me every time I touched Nur's burning stomach with my hand; our kisses, which began as the snow fell gently outside;

158

the unhurried lovemaking that kept changing its character, becoming deeper and more fulfilling, not just a race for simple gratification. But in coming to the island we had left behind the hilltop squatters' settlement we had only recently come to know, a world of steep, muddy slopes, of children with wary eyes, of houses with iron rods sticking out of their flat roofs in hopeful anticipation of adding another floor, a world that made our hearts ache. We had run away from it and taken refuge in Shirin Hanim's place.

We needed to believe in a different world. And to make love. The plan was to arrive on the island on the Thursday evening and to take the first ferry back to the city the following morning, back to those muddy, dusty, pain-filled hills where we'd spent every day of the last two months researching stories for our newspaper. Then it snowed. The ferry service was cancelled and we couldn't get back. We called the newspaper. Or rather, I called. I thought Omer, my boss, would be disappointed, but he reacted as if that was what he expected of us. He didn't even listen when I told him we'd take the first ferry back or maybe hire a motorboat. He just cut me short and said, 'I'll see you at the office on Monday.' I didn't know then that Nur wouldn't ever be going back to the newspaper, but Omer must have sensed it.

On the Friday, instead of letting up, the snow got heavier. It became a blizzard. Everywhere was white – the sky, the ground, the sea, the opposite shore. We closed all the rooms in the house and shut ourselves up in the library to keep warm. Perhaps making love was our defence against the cruelty out there. We had listened to accounts of cruelty and oppression as we spent time on the hill, researching our articles for the paper, but listening wasn't enough. We had witnessed cruelty first hand, but nor was witnessing it sufficient. As long as we remained spectators, we were complicit in the cruelty.

The pain enflamed us. Losing myself in Nur's skin, in her depths, for hours at a time, I understood for the first time as an adult man what it meant to become one with a woman. Not with the haste of an adolescent boy but with the satisfaction of a complete human being. Did Nur feel the same? I don't know. She wanted me, that was for sure. It was she who pushed my hand down when I touched her stomach, down into the trousers she'd unbuttoned, guiding my fingers into her warm, oh so warm, hidden places. How many times did she wrap herself around my neck, pressing her body into mine ('Tighter! Hold me tighter!'), climaxing with only the rhythm of my fingers.

I wasn't all that young then. I had made love to Nur as well as to other women, but this was the first time I'd experienced a woman's sexual pleasure so intensely. Nur's body became my body. The ecstasy at my fingertips jolted through me as if I were being electrocuted. Maybe this was intimacy, experiencing another person's sensations as if they were yours. It was a secret, private thing, like reading someone's thoughts, and it excited me. I read somewhere that having a high fever arouses women. Maybe that's why, when she was lying there exhausted, her hands would suddenly creep under my sweater, my shirt, finding my skin. Or maybe she just wanted to forget. Nur is one of those women who make love to forget.

Those hills were a 'liberated ghetto', self-determining and therefore supposedly off-limits to the police. During her university years, Nur had driven past the fringes of those squatter neighbourhoods many times in her maroon Fiat Uno. While we were on the island making love in front of the fire, over there on those hills people younger than us were lying down ready to die for a cause. Teenage girls, young boys, mothers who'd lost sons, women who'd lost husbands, scores of people, hundreds of people. They would go into what were known as 'resistance houses' and, after a brief ceremony, would start the hunger strike and lie down to die.

In the autumn of the year 2000, there were hunger strikes in prisons throughout the country in protest at the transfer of political prisoners from dormitories to isolation cells in high-security 'F-type' prisons, which inmates considered inhumane and feared would result in increased abuse by jailers. Relatives and supporters of inmates took up their cause and joined the hunger strike, and the resistance movement spread to Istanbul's hillside squatter settlements. The hunger strike continued for two months. Our newspaper had decided to allocate a whole page every day to the hunger strike and it sent a team of reporters, which included Nur and me, to the hills every day, come rain or shine, to knock on doors. Nur would interview the young girls who'd recently entered a resistance house. They were dressed as brides, with red bands tied around their heads, and they were so young, they couldn't really say why they were sacrificing their bodies, their life's breath. Nur approached them with an open heart, keen to understand their point of view, even as they were fading away in front of her eyes. Sometimes doors would be closed in her face, but most of the women could sense Nur's good intentions and invited her in, offered her tea. Mothers who had lost their sons asked Nur to find them. Young women would say, 'Write the truth, Comrade Nur. Write about our resistance. Write about our cause.' They had a childish hope that the world would hear their voices through us. It was this hope that finally finished Nur.

At the end of every day, as we walked down from the hill, exhausted, or while we were stuck in traffic on our way back to the newspaper office, Nur would talk nonstop about what she'd heard that day. She'd go into every last detail, as if I hadn't also been there in the same neighbourhood, talking to the same people and hearing the same horrific stories. It was her first big assignment and she was excited. She was hooked.

We were working long shifts, getting back to the office in the evening and writing furiously into the night. Sitting side by side at our monitors, we'd bash away at our keyboards, fast and angry. We wrote about how, day by day, life was seeping out of those young bodies; we documented the dimming of the light in their eyes, the greying of their skin. They were pawns in an ugly game and so we kept writing in the hope that we might save a life, that we might catch the public's attention and help bring about an end to the intransigence on both sides. Those people's pulses were beating through our pens and if we stopped writing, their pulses would stop – that's what we thought. We ascribed great importance to our profession. But the negotiations between the big powers and the little lives continued, somehow never reaching a solution. Our hearts ached.

Then one day Nur stumbled. She choked up. She couldn't do it any more. The hand holding the pen shook.

It was the day after the military's so-called 'Return to Life' operation designed to put an end to the hunger strike resistance, the day we ran into Fikret at the Ali Baba Café in Rumelihisar. It was a sunny day, very cold but sunny, the kind of weather that presages snow. One or two people were sitting at the café's outdoor tables but most had gathered around the woodstove inside. Fikret was at a table beside the window. The windows had steamed up, and the smell of panini mingled with the smell of cigarettes. Celine was in the chair next to him. She was wearing a white beret and her cheeks were pink with cold; she had beautiful dark blue eyes. Celine. I'd known about her since the day she was born, and for a moment I was confused that she'd grown up so fast. Surely a child born just yesterday should stay a baby for a while, whereas this little girl was not just the unformed offspring of her parents, but a walking, talking little person with a will of her own, capable of making decisions. I quickly totted up the years. She had to be almost five years old.

Fikret was reading the paper. He was surprised to see us. I realized immediately that Nur was upset. She tensed. When Celine saw her aunt, she clapped her hands, jumped off her chair and ran over to us. Nur didn't even register little Celine with her blonde pigtails; she was looking at the 'Return to Life' article in the newspaper that was lying open on Fikret's table. She was searching the photo for faces she knew among the group of miserable, exhausted women being dragged out of the prison, crying as they held onto each other. In each face she saw the stories she'd heard with her own ears. Surrounding the emaciated women with withered skin and wounds under their fallen-out hair which they were trying to cover with bits of cloth were soldiers in gas masks and camouflage, carrying machine guns. As she stared at the photograph, Nur's face got paler and paler. I thought she was going to faint. I gripped her arm. It was rigid.

We knew a lot about the 'Return to Life' operation headlined in Fikret's newspaper. More than what was in the article. Much more. We'd seen and heard from its victims just a few hours ago, on those hillsides that were both a mere stone's throw from the Ali Baba Café and yet also a world away. By that point we already knew that our profession had the power to distort the truth and rewrite history. But what we read in that article in front of Fikret was so far from what we'd seen and heard ourselves. We were young and idealistic and it floored us. Nur couldn't take her eyes off the newspaper lying there beside Fikret's tea, his panini, Celine's Barbie doll. She could not fathom the chasm between the story she'd heard from Elif that morning and the article that purported to be news.

Elif was one of the women who'd opened her door to Nur. She'd been taken into custody during a raid and, two nights ago, during a military operation inside the prison, she'd been injured in her cell. Later, she was released and as she was walking back home, Nur happened to be passing and gave her a lift. Elif showed Nur the palms of her hands. 'They burnt us,' she said, crying as she talked, almost delirious with pain and grief. 'They scorched our skin.' She begged Nur to write about it. A hose had been lowered from the ceiling of the cell, with black smoke spewing from it. The women's skin had immediately started to burn. Elif told of screams, of people suffocating, of women who died at her feet, of being dragged out by her arms, of the hair, faces and bodies of her neighbours being scorched.

Nur dropped Elif at her home, parked her car in the empty lot across the street, and came to the coffee house where I was talking to the neighbourhood men about the military's operation in the prisons. It was what everyone was talking about. Everyone had a son, a grandson or a brother in one of the prisons. Some of them were members of the resistance, some weren't. They were all burnt at the same time. Were they alive? Would they live? The faces of men who didn't know how to grieve had hardened with the pain they kept inside. When Nur came in, all talk stopped and every head turned towards her. With her fur-collared leather jacket, short red hair, slender white neck that she never covered with a scarf no matter how cold the wind from the Bosphorus, and hazel eyes shining with tears, she looked like a frame of colour film that had been inserted by mistake into a black-and-white movie. I went over to her. She wasn't crying. She couldn't cry. She was trying to write something, but the hand holding the pen was shaking. I'd known her almost seven years and had never seen her like that.

I led her out of the coffee house of gloomy men. Without saying a word, we headed down to the Bosphorus. I drove. We would get some tea in the Ali Baba Café, which had been a favourite of ours during Nur's university days. We had no intention of giving up on our weeks of research and the thousands of words we'd written about Elif and those hill settlements, about the troubled men in the coffee house, about the young people lying down to die in the resistance houses.

Then Nur saw the newspaper on Fikret's table. She read that the violence Elif had experienced had been part of an operation named 'Return to Life'. She recalled how Elif had sobbed as she talked about what had happened and she immediately understood that the barbaric policy of poisoning individuals with nerve gas and burning them to death would be reframed in the collective memory as being a 'Return to Life'. Nur glanced at the headlines of the newspapers open on other tables. Each one talked of the kindness and compassion of the state… She read with disbelief that the protestors had set themselves on fire… that the illegal organization was responsible for the burns and that the soldiers had saved them… that it had been a fake hunger strike… that this was a bloody climax to the fasting… As Nur's eyes passed from one headline to the next, she realized that even if you were the world's boldest journalist, with all the power and means you needed to report the evidence of first-hand witnesses, the government would still produce new, false accounts, and your story would never be believed. As she glanced around the tables, she also understood that sovereign power did not rest only with the state, the party, the political establishment and the police, it derived from the fact that the masses believed whatever they read in the paper and then forgot about it. Sovereign power was Fikret and people like him. It was in the hands of those who would never be convinced of Elif's innocence.

Nur pushed aside Celine, who was trying to hug her legs, and ran between the tables to the door, almost knocking the teapot off the stove. Behind her, Fikret yelled, 'You shouldn't treat a little child that way, Nur!', but she didn't hear him. She'd already raced out of the courtyard and on across the busy street, not looking to left or right, oblivious to the drivers honking their horns and sticking their heads out of their windows and shouting at her. She turned towards the sea and hid her face in her wool-gloved hands.

Before racing after Nur, I apologized half-heartedly to Fikret and stroked Celine's long blonde plaits. Her eyes had filled with tears and she was biting her lower lip. When I made it across the street, I pulled Nur into my arms. She was trembling with cold and anger. The wind had strengthened. Taking off my beret, I put it on Nur's head. Her cheeks were bright red, and the hazel of her eyes had turned to green. I wanted to kiss her but didn't dare with Fikret looking on. At any rate, we weren't officially together at this point. After the Great Earthquake we'd been lovers again for a short while, then Nur had decided we should return to being 'just friends' once more. Even so, she didn't object to me holding her tightly. I told her that we would stand together against this inhumanity. We would write. There were good people with consciences in the country and in the world. Good would always conquer evil. We could change the world, the two of us, and even if we couldn't, we might at least save one person's life. We could convince Elif, for example, to not join the hunger strike. She would live. If Nur talked to Elif, she could persuade her not to go into the resistance house and sacrifice herself.

I said things like that. I didn't realize that Nur had already given up. She didn't answer. We walked to Bebek, and from there to Arnavutkoy, and from there to Besiktas. I kept my arm tight around Nur's shoulders. The wind was bitter and the Bosphorus had turned a melancholic light blue. The surface of the sea was like glass, as if it were holding its breath.

When we got to Besiktas, in an unusually sweet voice, Nur said, 'How about we go to the island, Burak? What do you say?'

I didn't ask what we would do with the car. Anyway, we'd be back soon. The car would be waiting for us in the back street where we'd parked. The stereo had already been stolen.

While we were on the ferry, the sky darkened and it began to snow. The sea exhaled and the surface became choppy. The ferry gave a long, hooting whistle and had difficulty reaching the pier. And then I spent the most beautiful three days of my life. Right there, in that house, in front of that fireplace, on that sofa, after we'd left the people whose stories we had promised to write, left Elif with her burnt palms on the hillside where people lay down to die.

Celine had already given up on me. She was pulling photos out of the velvet-covered box and stuffing them into Shirin

Hanim's hands, which were clasped tightly in her lap. Celine was also trying to turn back time. She was sure that if she could only bring her great-grandmother back to that point a half-hour ago, she'd be able to impress me with her incredible story, that huge secret. Whereas the truth is, that there's no turning back time. I'd tried so hard to do that. I realized then that for the past seventeen years I'd been living in hope of reprising those three days I'd spent in that library. Happiness was held captive there, a dazzling mixture of shame, pain, pleasure and love in a young man's heart. But the past can't be dragged into the present. There's no such thing as being 'in the moment', despite what Celine's generation says. The second you think of 'a moment', it has already become a frame in a film called 'The Past', a memory. Life is nothing but a series of memories, and memories are made up of losses.

'Celine...'

'One second, Burak. One second. Great-Granny, look at me. Are you listening? You'd just finished breakfast. Your servant was brewing tea. Then your father...'

I left the library without saying anything. Sadik Usta was no longer singing in the back garden. I couldn't see him anywhere. I stopped beside the stairs when I got to the hall. At first the light shining through the door blinded me, but then I saw her. She was leaning against the kitchen door, wearing a dark blue silk kimono patterned with bright red cherries. In her hand was a pouch of tobacco. She was looking at me with eyes swollen from crying, or from too much sleep, eyes that were cleansed, eyes that shone. I stopped and looked at her. I saw the years we had spent together in her face, in her gaze. The woman I loved. My closest friend. Sole witness of my youth.

We stood there across from each other for a while, she at

the kitchen door, me beside the stairs. When I heard Celine's footsteps, I carried on down the hall. Nur held out her hand and I took it. The skin of her palm was as soft as the earth after rain. Hand in hand we went into the dining room and shut the door behind us. The wooden floor was streaked with the lazy orange glow of afternoon light and the air was warm and sweet-smelling. Side by side we sat down at the table where we had breakfasted the day before. The delicate leaves of the mimosa in front of the window trembled in the faint breeze. Nur's hand was still in mine. I knew her well enough to tell from a single glance that, inside, her heart was breaking.

18

Celine

When Burak disappeared, I left Great-Granny's side and sank down into the armchair by the window. I was so angry, I could have died. My eyes were spitting flames. I wanted to pull the fancy gilded cushions off the sofa and pound the floor with them over and over. I wanted to beat them, kick them, thump them until their cotton stuffing flew into the air. Actually what I really wanted to do was shake Great-Granny, grab her by her skinny shoulders and shake, shake, shake. You made a fool of me, Shirin! Burak must have thought I'd tricked him into coming back.

I went out into the hall. Great-Granny was dozing on the sofa with her head tipped back, a lost cause. Something made me pause, but at first I didn't know what. The light coming through the stained-glass window above the front door was dancing on the floor. Then my brain made sense of what my eyes were seeing. Two shadows had flitted into the dining room, two people with their hands entwined. The door closed. I ran up to it, but just as I reached it, the key turned in the lock from the inside. What the...? Every room in the house has a great big, black, heavy iron key, like the ones in fairy tales, but I had never heard one being turned in the lock before. They were just decorative, as far as I was concerned. What was going on? I pressed my ear to the door. I could hear Aunt Nur's voice and then Burak's. Muffled murmuring. Footsteps on the wooden floor. The squeak of a chair. And then music. Albinoni.

The blood rushed to my head and I was just about to grab the doorknob and force them to open the door when something stopped me. What was I doing? Who cared what *I* was doing – what were *they* doing in there? Man, what an idiot I'd been! Why hadn't I seen it? Those two were in a relationship. They were having an affair! My aunt was cheating on Uncle Ufuk right in front of our noses. In front of my nose. Like an idiot, I'd been expecting something from Burak. I thought he would come to my room last night, whereas it was clear whose room he spent the night in. That was why Dad left. He didn't want to be party to this disgusting situation. And that was why Uncle Ufuk hadn't come to the island.

My Uncle Ufuk is the sweetest, coolest person in the world. He didn't deserve this. Shit! Fuck you! I hate you both! I leant down to try and peep through the keyhole, but I couldn't see anything because the key was in the way. Blocked at every turn. What were they doing? Why weren't they talking, or was it that I couldn't hear them because of the Albinoni? Were they making love? Why would they make love in the dining room when there were so many empty rooms upstairs? For kicks, of course. Aunt Nur would be lying on the table with the sash of her kimono undone, its skirt draped over the sides. Burak would be on top of her, kissing her long, white neck. For the first time in my life, I felt a stab of jealousy that actually hurt, like real physical pain. I tormented myself by imagining Aunt Nur's skilful hands caressing Burak in all the right places, pleasuring him, and them kissing each other breathlessly. But it wasn't just in my imagination, for sure. Why else would it be so silent in there?

'Miss Celine?'

Shit! Sadik had caught me! I turned slowly towards him but kept my eyes fixed on his brown leather slippers. Sadik Usta's bony, crooked big toe had made a mark on the front of his slipper. I had nothing to say to him. I was a shameful person. But wait... wait a second, I did have something to say. Wasn't it Sadik who only yesterday had his ear pinned to this same door while we were at breakfast?

I straightened up, and as we came eyeball to eyeball, Sadik Usta took two steps back. He must have realized what I was thinking. This would stay between the two of us; we were even now. No one else will ever know what went on behind this door, Sadik, I imagined myself saying in a deep voice, like a villain in an old Turkish movie. I could even laugh like a psycho. Sadik Usta looked weird. Was his hair messed up? But he doesn't really have any hair, just one long strand that he combs over to one side and a few grey bits around the ears. No, something else was messed up. His clothes? The look in his eye? God! Now was not the time to worry about that. I had more important things to worry about.

I grabbed my bike and went out onto the street, purposely slamming the garden gate. The bell made a lot of noise on our quiet, hot hill. I coasted down to Resat Nuri's house without touching my brakes. The wind ruffled my hair. I closed my eyes. I wanted to be rid of everybody, everything. About halfway down, I turned my handlebars to the right and began pedalling uphill. It was a really steep hill, which would be tough in the heat, but at least I'd avoid the crowds. Tourists never used the island's backstreets, not unless they were lost.

Sweat was dripping down my chest to my stomach and my lungs felt as if they were about to burst, but I still couldn't erase the mental image of Burak and Aunt Nur making love. The scene just kept on playing. Aunt Nur was having an orgasm on the dining-room table – it was disgusting.

I stopped at the Monastery of St Nicholas to get my breath back. I was panting hard. Steadying my feet on the ground, I rested my forehead on the handlebars. The monastery's white wooden building stretched silently into the forest. Its windows were closed, the curtains drawn. If there'd been a caretaker in evidence, I'd have asked for a glass of water. My tongue was stuck to the roof of my mouth.

Two assholes passed me. Sweat was rolling down their greasy hair onto their cheeks and down their red necks. 'Hello baby, need hand?' one of them said in pitiful English. Then they laughed like idiots, as if he'd said something hilarious.

I glared at them contemptuously. I wasn't afraid of them and their idiot, cracked voices. I had a bike at least. If they came anywhere near me, I'd take off. They couldn't catch me with their pathetic lungs, they'd die.

I pedalled off, not stopping till I got to the Lunapark Square junction. I had got my breath back and found my rhythm now. My head had cleared too and my fury had abated. Nur and Burak had to have finished making love by now. Maybe they felt guilty. They'd momentarily lost their heads. Maybe they hadn't made love. What difference would that make? They were doing something so secret they had to shut themselves up in the dining room and lock the door behind them. Did they make love or did they not? Let them not have made love, please. I felt awful imagining them moaning and writhing. Then don't think about it, Celine. But I couldn't stop thinking about it.

Lunapark Square was a madhouse. The miserable horses pausing there had their noses buried in feedbags. They'd only get to eat a couple of mouthfuls of hay before it would be giddy-up and time to hit the Grand Tour road again, time to please the crowds of unsophisticated tourists and fill the pockets of the carriage mafia. I stopped and dried the sweat off my face with my T-shirt. A group with selfie sticks attached to their phones were gathered round the donkeys waiting to ferry trippers up the hill, taking selfies like crazy. In the background a donkey's head with its beaded necklace and mascara-lined eyes, in the foreground a chorus of daisy-crowned idiots.

I locked my bike and started walking up St George's Hill. Taking my phone out of my back pocket, I put in my earphones and hit 'shuffle'. Tori Amos began with 'I'm Not in Love'. Perfect for the mood. I'd downloaded it off Uncle Ufuk. He has a great collection of albums on CD and vinyl as well as on his computer and thanks to him I discovered lots of songs for my band – enough to keep us going until we write some of our own. Uncle Ufuk knew right away what would work for me and my girlfriends, even before I did. He'd only heard Ayse on the piano and me on the guitar and immediately he put four records and two CDs in front of us. Hence Tori Amos. Oh, Uncle Ufuk, how could they do this to you! How will I be able to look you in the eye when I next come and stay at your house? You've ruined everything, Aunt!

I'd been walking so fast, I was nearly at the top of the hill already. I turned around to see the whole of Buyukada spread out at my feet and Hristos Hill right opposite me. Maybe I should have gone up Hristos Hill instead. All the tourists went up St George's Hill, but hardly anyone knew about Hristos Hill and the monastery up there. If Dad hadn't taken me there at the end of last summer, I wouldn't have known about it either. We'd been out walking and we'd gone to the Haunted House, then down Lovers' Road, through the pine forest, past the Greek orphanage, and finally on up to Hristos Hill. There was an old wooden building up there, an Orthodox Greek monastery with all its doors and windows shut up; it had a sullen air about it, looked as if it hadn't been used for a long time. The weeds were as high as the ground-floor windows, and plants were sprouting out of the green wooden shutters on the top floor. Even so, Dad rang the doorbell. I was surprised. I didn't think anyone would come, but then a boy of about my age opened the door, a quiet, calm, polite type, and we went in. There were candles burning – he must have raced around and lit them when he heard the doorbell – and Dad got very excited when he saw an icon of the twin healers, St Cosmas and St Damian, on the wall. Apparently you didn't see that icon in many places. It didn't make much of an impression on me, but I took a picture of Dad and the icon.

That's one of my favourite things about Istanbul. You think you know a place, but then a gate opens and you feel like you've stepped into a foreign country. Aunt Nur once took me to see some old churches in a district I can't remember the name of. I had no idea there were so many churches in Istanbul, I thought there were only the big ones on Istiklal Street in the city centre, but that neighbourhood was nothing like as cosmopolitan or sophisticated as Istiklal Street. It was a conservative Muslim area where women walked around in black burkas and little boys wore Islamic-style skullcaps, and yet there were Greek Orthodox churches on every corner. I would never have gone there by myself and definitely wouldn't have had the courage to open a door squished between two old apartment buildings so that I could see what was inside. But when the door opened, we found ourselves in a garden full of roses, mulberry trees and cats. It was incredible. Just like *Alice in Wonderland*. 'If you live in Istanbul,' Aunt Nur said, 'you don't need to go on any fancy trips, you just need to open your eyes and you'll soon find yourself in a different space, a different time.' Oh, Aunt Nur, what a minx you turned out to be.

When I got to the top of St George's Hill I didn't go into the church. A guard at the door was handing out beige blankets so that girls like me, who'd walked or cycled up the hill in shorts and T-shirts, could cover our exposed flesh, but I didn't want to wrap that filthy blanket around myself. I looked for a rock to sit on, so I could contemplate the view out over Heybeliada, but couples had grabbed all the vantage spots on the slope, so I practically had to walk halfway to Viranbag to find my own rock with a view. Eventually I found a place down by the Holy Spring. I was worn out, and because of that I'd sort of forgotten what it was that was burning me up. The sun had moved round to the Heybeliada side and the sea was sparkling silver in the bay below. I wished I'd brought my swimsuit, then I could have gone down there and had a swim.

Aunt Nur finds joy in small things. When we're out walking somewhere, she'll stop suddenly and her face will light up as she points out a magnolia tree squeezed between two walls or some pigeons taking a bath in a puddle. Of course Burak was in love with her. Everybody was in love with my aunt. Actually she's not that pretty. When my mother walks round Istanbul's swanky Macka district, people turn and stare. She's tall, blonde and tanned, and she's a stylish dresser. Aunt Nur's not like that. Her hair, eyes and skin are okay but not striking, and yet as soon as she walks in somewhere, the place falls silent. Why? Because people take her seriously; they respect her. It's as if she exudes gravitas. The revered Nur Bulut. If they knew she was cheating on her husband, would they change their opinion? If they saw her spreadeagled on the dining-room table, making love to Burak, would they continue to respect her? Would the waiters at the tea gardens, the hairdressers, the guys who work at the House Café still follow her around, saying, 'Welcome, Madam Nur. Come this way. What can I do for you?'

I got my phone out and stared blankly at the screen. I didn't feel like seeing all the pseudo holiday posts on social media, as if everybody's family was a Coca-Cola ad. If only we could see the bits between the ads. My dad, for example, left us on the first day of the holiday. If I put a post like that on Insta – in big print, with a purple background – what would people say? I'd share it on Facebook so that our oldies would see it too. Dad would see it. Where was he? I called his number. 'The person you are calling cannot be reached at the moment. Please try again later.' No, I wouldn't try again later.

The church bell began to ring. From somewhere below me, three priests appeared. The skirts of their long black robes streamed out behind them as they walked towards the church. One of them had a long white beard and a fat belly; the other two were fairly young. They walked right past without noticing me in my rocky hollow. What could it be like living there as a monk, I wondered, waking up to that wonderful view every morning as the church bells sounded, then going to pray before sunrise, having a meal of bread and holy water, then praying again. Maybe such a life would sort me out, purify me. They say that children fulfil the dreams their mothers and fathers leave half finished, a sort of 'hopes and aspirations' inheritance passed through the genes. Last summer, Dad shared a secret with me the day we climbed Hristos Hill. Actually, I don't know if it was a secret, but he said it should stay between us, so I guess it was.

'Between you and me, Celine, I'd like to join a monastery like this.'

It was getting towards evening when Dad said that, and the light was turning orange. Pine needles crunched beneath our feet and the pinecones were giving off a sweet, hot, woody smell.

Did Dad feel the same undefined incompleteness as me? He had the air of someone who was waiting for their life to begin, which was exactly how I felt. As if he was marking time until something happened, as if, up till now, he'd just been making do with a temporary, interim life, like a spare tyre. He was such a great big man, it was hard for me to see him as a person and not just Dad.

As I sat in that rocky hollow on St George's Hill, I suddenly had a terrible thought, a premonition of disaster. I leapt up. What if Dad had committed suicide, killed himself, like Great-Granny's father? What if the kiss he'd given me when he came into my room the previous night had been a farewell kiss? Oh, my God! Was that possible? Don't be stupid, Celine! Why would Dad commit suicide? What possible reason could he have? Who does have a reason? Did Shirin Saka's father have a reason?

He put it in his mouth and pulled the trigger. Blood splattered all over the wall behind him. We scrubbed and scrubbed for days, but the stain never came out.

Insanity, severe depression, a sudden breakdown. In a panic, I dialled Dad's number again. My fingers were shaking. 'The person you have called cannot be reached.' Shit! I opened Facebook and typed in Dad's name. He hadn't posted anything for a week. There was nothing on his wall except some post he'd signed at change.org and three crap photos taken at a symposium, without a filter, in awful lighting, unedited. He didn't have Instagram. What could I do?

My head was spinning. The cliff edge, the sea, zoomed in close, retreated. There was the hum of prayers from the church. The breeze was gathering force. I was at the highest point on the island and below me was a rocky cliff face. Don't look down! Look straight ahead, at the horizon. Take a deep breath. There was Dog Island, Heybeliada, Burgazada, and beyond them it was pure blue sea all the way to the horizon. What if Dad had thrown himself into the sea? Plenty of people did that. Aunt Nur had two friends who'd jumped off a bridge, and another friend of hers hanged himself in his backyard. I wasn't panicking for no reason. There was a suicide epidemic. Could you kill yourself by jumping off St George's Hill? No, Celine, you couldn't. By putting a gun to your head? Dad had taken just the one backpack with him, containing just a gun and nothing more. Why would a person who was going to kill himself need a shirt and a pair of trousers? That was why all his clothes were still in his wardrobe. Okay, but why did he take his computer? To record his last moments, of course. He doesn't have a smartphone, so he does all his digital work on his old-fashioned brick of a laptop. Fikret Bulut went down to Viranbag Bay with his laptop in his backpack in the early morning and... Boom! Oh my God.

What I did next was not very adult, I admit. But I wasn't acting out of spite – that didn't cross my mind. Not at all. I was only thinking of my dad. I panicked. With my phone in my hand, I was stuck on that rock like a stork. I was staring blankly at the screen and my fingers moved completely independently of me. I swear I didn't know what I was doing. It was only when I heard a man's voice saying, 'Hello? Celine? Are you there? Can you hear me?' that I realized I had called Uncle Ufuk.

19

Sadik

I fed the pieces of chicken Madam Shirin had left on her plate to the cats. The playful grey kitten didn't come. Had it slipped into the house again? Madam Nur was asleep with her head on the kitchen table, just like when she was a child. I heard Miss Celine and Mr Burak enter the library and hoped they would not tire Madam Shirin unnecessarily. However, it is Mr Burak's job to speak to important individuals; otherwise he would have nothing to write about. Many years ago he conducted an interview with me. I myself am not an important individual, of course, but at that time he had just begun to write his 'Portraits' column and it is my belief that when he spoke with your humble servant it was to practise. Now his column has grown and Mr Burak has been allotted a whole page.

When I first saw the interview Mr Burak conducted with me, I will be honest, I felt proud. I cut it out of the newspaper and I keep it in my drawer. A photograph of us was also printed in the newspaper. It is very fresh in my memory. We posed for it in the living room of the apartment in Moda. Madam Nur took the photograph and wanted us to sit on the sofa with the gilded upholstery and delicate legs, the one beside the wall. I refrain from touching Madam Shirin's furniture, especially in the living room, and never sit on her sofa or in her armchairs, but my lady considered the living room to be the proper place for that day's interview.

I had prepared the tea ready for the guests. I brought out the gold-rimmed cake plates and arranged on a platter the savoury pastries I'd bought at Baylan Pastry Shop that morning. I would remove the chocolate-covered cherry cake from the refrigerator later. Madam Shirin had chosen what we were to serve. I lit the samovar, brewed the tea and lined up the tea glasses and silver coasters on the sideboard.

When Madam Shirin came out to inspect the table, she said, 'Put out a plate for yourself too, Sadik. Today you are the guest of honour.'

Hearing this, I was greatly embarrassed. But as I am obliged to do as my lady wishes, I arranged another plate on the table. As it turned out, there was no reason to do so.

After Madam Nur had taken our picture, she invited Madam Shirin to go for a drive in her automobile. They would have their tea at the Divan Pastry Shop in Erenkoy. My lady could never resist an excursion. She immediately requested her handbag, hastily got ready, and left the house on Madam Nur's arm.

When Mr Burak and I were alone, he asked a number of questions, most of them concerning the past. To start with, the dictaphone that was recording our conversation, which he had placed upon the white tablecloth, made me uncomfortable. To my mind there was nothing about my past that merited being published in a newspaper. The individual who should have been interviewed was Madam Shirin. Mr Burak paid no heed to my objections. He was a young man at the time and his eyes were bright behind his glasses. As we drank our first glass of tea, I described my youthful years in Uskudar, which was, back then, a traditional Muslim neighbourhood on the Asian side of Istanbul. We lived in her Uncle Nevzat's mansion, on a hill that overlooked the Sea of Marmara and was not far from the shores of the Bosphorus. What a beautiful garden it had, containing every species of fruit tree – mulberry, apple, cherry, almond – and even two palm trees. There were rafts tied up on each side of the ornamental pool and goldfish swam among the waterlilies. There were roses of all colours and a magnolia tree whose flowers were so beautiful that passers-by would stop and ask whether they were real.

Mr Nevzat was a magnanimous man. It seems he was not in actuality Madam Shirin's uncle but a distant relative. At a later date, certain evil-minded people would claim that there was no family relationship between them at all and that his intentions were of a suspect nature. Not so. I know the truth. He hurt no one, offended no one. After all, it was Mr Nevzat who arranged for Madam Shirin to go to Paris, to the Fine Arts Academy for her diploma. It was said that Mr Nevzat's wife, our auntie, forced him into doing that. Mouths are not bags that we can draw them shut. Mr Nevzat enrolled me at a school in Uskudar, where I stayed until the end of middle school. Rumours also circulated that he engaged in black-marketeering during the war, and something called 'railway trade' was mentioned. These were unfounded and one should not believe such slander. I pointed this out to Mr Burak. It was important.

Mr Burak took many notes in the notebook he had opened beside his plate. I offered him the savoury pastries and he seemed to particularly like the ones with sesame seeds. While refreshing the tea, I brought in more from the kitchen and took the cake out of the refrigerator and set it in the middle of the table. Mr Burak drank his second tea slowly. He asked a question concerning what I did after middle school and included my answer word for word in the newspaper article. Occasionally I take it from my drawer and read it. This is what I said:

'Mr Nevzat's wife, Auntie Melahat, saw that I was interested in housework. During that period the head house servant was indisposed – he was later found to have consumption – so Auntie Melahat showed me his duties. Mr Nevzat was the manager of a shoe factory in Beykoz and he found a job for me there, turning by hand the big vats in which the leather was softened. I would return home for the midday meal with Mr Nevzat and in the afternoons I remained with Auntie Melahat. She was a very pleasant, knowledgeable lady who had come from the deserts of Syria. It was she who taught me proper table etiquette, how to cook, how to polish glass and clean upholstery, how to beat rugs, how to shine silver candlesticks.'

That was all I said. If I am not mistaken, I was overcome with a coughing fit just then. It was not my custom to speak for such a long time and these were anyway unimportant subjects and I was sure that Mr Burak would prefer to hear about things concerning Madam Shirin. When my coughing subsided, I mentioned that she had exhibited an aptitude for painting when she was just a young girl.

Mr Nevzat enrolled Madam Shirin in a girls' high school in Camlica. He used to drive her to school himself, in his private car, on his way to the factory. At noon he would collect her and bring her home. After I had completed middle school, we would go together in Mr Nevzat's car in the mornings. He taught me how and when to open the car doors and in what order everyone should board. The ladies were to get in first and always sat in the front. Then I would run round and open Mr Nevzat's door for him. After we had dropped Madam Shirin at school, he would give me driving lessons, in the hills of Camlica. He was a very kind and humble man. He did not like to discriminate against people on account of their class and he never got angry at my inexperience.

Soon, Auntie Melahat called me over and said, 'Sadik, my boy, from now on you will take Miss Shirin to school in the automobile. Then Mr Nevzat can leave for the factory a little later.'

Mr Burak raised his head from his notes at that point, but I was caught up in my journey into the past. In the mornings, when I used to drive Madam Shirin to her school, there would often be a thin layer of fog hanging over the Bosphorus and my lady would ask that I divert via the top of Camlica Hill, the highest point in all of Istanbul, so that she could enjoy the view. At that time a pine forest covered the hill, and as the wheels of the car crushed the cones beneath them, the cool, minty smell of pine would waft in through the windows. When we got to the top, my lady would request that I stop the car, even though that would make her late for her first class, because she wished to watch the fog shivering over the water as it lifted. I would park under a tree and wait for her. Madam Shirin would gaze intently as the fog thinned, gradually revealing the hills of the European shore, turning the sea blue where the sun touched it, and sending shadows flitting between the domes and minarets of the old city. I believe she was engraving the scene in her mind in order to paint it later.

I came to my senses when Mr Burak said, 'Why haven't

you poured yourself any tea, Sadik? Go and get a glass. Your plate's empty too. It's not right that one of us is eating while the other watches. Please, get yourself some tea.'

In one gulp he finished the last of the tea in his glass. I took it and filled both our glasses from the samovar. When I returned to the table and sat down, I noticed that the sky had darkened. We were in the last days of March and coming towards the end of a harsh winter. There had been snow on the ground for weeks and although that day was sunny, and warm, I was concerned that my lady might be getting cold outside. I hoped that with her youthful enthusiasm Madam Nur would not tire Madam Shirin needlessly.

I put half a sugar lump into my mouth and held it inside my cheek. Mr Burak looked at me and smiled. 'When I was a boy, the men in the coffee houses of my village used to drink their tea like that, with a lump of sugar in their mouth.'

Embarrassed, I shifted the sugar to the other cheek. I'd done that without realizing it. It would have been more proper to have stirred the sugar into my tea.

'Could we talk about your school a little, Sadik Usta? What did you say the name of the school was?'

I was quite upset when I couldn't remember the name of the school. It was a local school in the Uskudar district. On holidays, Mr Nevzat would take us all to the travelling funfair and we would ride on merry-go-rounds, throw hoops and win cigarettes, which we gave to Mr Nevzat in exchange for chewing gum. But I did not think Mr Burak would be interested in those kinds of activities, and why did he wish to know the name of my school? I again mentioned the pictures Madam Shirin had painted of the magnificent garden. Mr Burak had put his pen down and was listening to me with his arms folded. His plate was empty. I immediately cut a slice of cake for him. I took a slice onto my plate as well, so that he would not object.

Of course, I cannot speak with authority on the subject of art. However, I can say that even at such a young age, Madam Sirin had great talent – her painting of the magnolia tree, for example, was unequalled, as Mr Tugrakes Hakki immediately understood. Here was a story a young journalist with a powerful pen such as Mr Burak should definitely be told. While he was eating his cake, I tried to recall as much as I could regarding that important evening with Mr Tugrakes Hakki.

Mr Tugrakes Hakki was Mr Nevzat's neighbour and good friend. He was a calligrapher and I believe he had made a name for himself on both shores of Istanbul. He lived in a two-storey wooden house with bay windows, the ground floor of which was set up as a shop. He worked there alone. Every evening, he would close the shop and pay Mr Nevzat a visit. They would sit on the veranda facing the Bosphorus and watch the silent sun setting behind the hills on the opposite shore. I would serve them raki that had been cooled in the cellar, just as Mr Nevzat had taught me, accompanied by roasted hazelnuts and peanuts.

One evening there was an incident at the factory and Mr Nevzat sent a message to say that he would be late home. Mr Tugrakes Hakki, however, did not know this, and so he arrived, as was his custom, shortly before sunset. Auntie Melahat welcomed him out to the veranda and I prepared his raki as he liked it, but he did not want it. 'I will wander round the garden until Nevzat returns,' he said.

It is my opinion that our situation today is as it is because of what happened that day. If it hadn't been for the coincidental encounter that evening, what direction would

Madam Shirin's life have taken? Would she have gone to Paris? Would she have achieved the fame she enjoys today? In a person's lifetime many factors contribute to an event having happened at a particular moment. If just one of those details were altered, would the outcome have been different? There is no way in this world one can know the answer to such questions, but still we cannot stop ourselves from asking them. Naturally, I did not bore Mr Burak with such thoughts.

When my tongue loosened, I told him of Mr Tugrakes Hakki coming by chance upon Madam Shirin painting a picture of the magnolia tree while he was strolling in the garden. In describing that evening, details which I had long forgotten crowded into my mind. I had taken my place under the magnolia tree, waiting with palette, tubes of paint and brushes in hand. As Mr Tugrakes Hakki approached, I saw that he was looking at the flower appearing on my little miss's canvas. He gestured to me to keep silent. I nodded. Even as a young girl, when Madam Shirin was absorbed in her painting, she would forget the world around her. That evening she was painting hurriedly in order not to miss the reddening light. She had even forgotten me, standing right beside her with her palette in my hands, taking the place of a table. Naturally, she did not notice Mr Tugrakes Hakki watching her brushstrokes over her shoulder. After standing there for quite a long time, he departed just as he had arrived, with quiet footsteps.

Upon Mr Nevzat's arriving home, he and Mr Tugrakes Hakki sat on the veranda overlooking the ornamental pool as was their habit. I served the raki, adhering precisely to Mr Nevzat's instructions. As the raki in their glasses turned cloudy, I heard Mr Tugrakes Hakki say, 'Your niece has an amazing artistic talent. Let's send her to Paris, my friend. Perhaps she'll become another Mihri Musfik.'

I had truly learnt how to serve raki perfectly. There was no one superior to me in not spilling a single drop upon the cloth while filling the glasses. However, at that moment my hand suddenly shook. It was not the accustomed hour of their gathering, the weather was rather cool and dusk had fallen. I must have caught cold. Perhaps in the twilight, my eyes did not see so well. As I poured the raki into Mr Nevzat's glass, one drop fell onto his coat. I panicked. However, our gentleman being a very courteous person, said not a word. He continued to scratch his beard as if nothing had happened.

For reasons which I did not understand, Mr Burak was not very interested in this extremely important story. Of course, while relating it, I did not add the unnecessary detail of my having spilt the raki. The important point was that, due to that evening's coincidence, Madam Shirin's fortunes changed. What enlightened persons Mr Tugrakes Hakki and Mr Nevzat were that they did everything they could to further the education of Madam Shirin, one of this country's most important artists. However, rather than asking questions about that, Mr Burak returned to the subject of my schooling.

'Did you like school, Sadik Usta? Were you a good student?'

I couldn't tell Mr Burak that my liking or not liking school was something I never thought about. I studied hard in order that Mr Nevzat would not be in receipt of any bad reports. I was very grateful. I had known how to read and write before, but that school taught other lessons as well. My mathematics was good, and I developed an interest in reading books from the library. Compared to the naughty neighbourhood boys, I was well behaved. If this was what was meant by 'good student', I was good, but I was not inclined to say these things. It is not becoming to praise oneself. I tried to talk instead about what an extremely bright student Madam

Shirin was. Some of the female teachers at her high school were prominent intellectuals and had played a role in the founding of our country, which was surely of interest, and they could never stop praising the young Madam Shirin.

Mr Burak pushed his plate away and put his notebook on the table. 'Sadik Usta,' he said in a kind voice, 'a great many journalists have talked to Shirin Hanim and much has been written about her. Of course, your perspective is very valuable and if I get the chance to interview Shirin Hanim in the future, your stories about her youth will be of great use to me. But for now I am interested in you. Did you have friends at school? Did you play games with your friends? That kind of thing. Could we talk a little about that, and then we'll get to the years you worked at the factory, your youth.'

I had a lump in my throat. What could I say about the children at my school? Only bad things came to mind, including several very unpleasant instances that I thought I had erased from my ageing memory long ago. My classmates used to corner me in the yard and try to make me recite prayers that somehow they had perceived I did not know. One day, they jumped on me and said, 'Recite the Shahada,' but I had no idea what that meant. I'd been given no religious education, neither in Mr Nevzat's house nor before. I did not want to ask Auntie Melahat, for fear of revealing my ignorance, and although I did not think Mr Nevzat would be angry, I thought he might be sad at my being troubled. The next day at break-time the boys attacked me again. This time one of them shouted, 'Pull down his trousers. Let us see whether you are circumcised or not. If you are not, we'll circumcise you ourselves.' They all laughed meanly. A teacher came out and the boys scattered, but I was too frightened to tell him what had happened. I almost died of shame. After that, I went to school very reluctantly, and as soon as I finished middle school, I begged Mr Nevzat to take me on at the factory. He was disappointed and did not understand. 'You love studying, Sadik, and you could easily finish high school and get your diploma. Why don't you do that?' Even so, he accepted my decision. In any case, it was then that the head servant was diagnosed with consumption. Auntie Melahat wanted to train me to take his place and so my school life came to an end.

While these memories were passing through my mind, Mr Burak must have seen something in my face. He leant over and turned off the dictaphone beside his plate. 'Forget about school then,' he said. 'Tell me about your mother and father.'

I was bewildered. When Madam Nur had told us that Mr Burak wished to conduct an interview with me, Madam Shirin and I did some preparation. I was to relate to him how, thanks to the training I had received from Madam Shirin's family, I had become a butler the like of which could only be found in the finest aristocratic households of England. Today, you cannot find servants as loyal or as well versed in household etiquette in Istanbul nor anywhere else in the world. I was to speak of Auntie Melahat, who was the daughter of a famous noble Arab family, which detail I was to be sure to include, and had come to Istanbul upon her marriage to Uncle Nevzat. Had we lived in the days of the Ottoman Empire, I could even have attained a position in the palace.

I was to have spoken in that way. We had determined which subjects it was assuredly not necessary to mention. We were not to say a word concerning our dear departed Madam Suheyla. If by chance Mr Burak were to mention her, I was to change the subject. Madam Shirin and I had practised this. I could talk on the subject of Professor Halit's untimely death, but only if I were obliged to. My lady appeared to know that the musical evenings at the Buyukada house had had a great effect on me and if I so desired, I could speak about my interest in Western classical music and what I had learnt from Mr Halit.

However, neither I nor Madam Shirin had considered that Mr Burak might ask about my mother and father. We had not imagined that he would be interested in the distant past. This article would be published in a newspaper. For what reasons would a journalist ask prying questions concerning the father and mother of a child from a poor family like mine?

When I was finally able to speak, I said, 'Mr Burak, this Sadik sitting across from you is an old man who doesn't even know his own age. Forgive me, I beg you. The distant past is too much for my memory to hold on to.'

Mr Burak smiled. Outside the window, the sky had darkened considerably. I got up and turned on the light, which sparkled above the table. It was a waste, but if my lady should arrive and find Mr Burak in the dark, she might become angry.

'That's fine, Sadik Usta. You don't have to go into detail. Tell me your mother's name. Did she live in Uncle Nevzat's house with you? What work did your father do?'

'My father died when I was very small,' I murmured. 'I didn't know him at all.'

He asked me how he had died. I stammered. From within the fog inside my head, the stories my mother used to tell me during the night as we lay together in the bed took shape. My mama was by nature a silent woman. In the daytime, while serving the grand lady, Madam Shirin's mother, she rarely spoke. She did not like me getting under her feet and so I often went into the mountains and forests by myself. But once night had fallen and we were lying side by side in the small hut in the garden of the big house, she would whisper stories into my ear. There was a condition, however. I had to be asleep. If I were not asleep, she would not tell the stories. And so, while my mama was undoing her plaits before joining me under the quilt, I would close my eyes. Perhaps that is why I remember her stories as if they were dreams. Some of them are mixed up in my memory. For example, had I truly seen my papa or was it only my imagination? At my advanced age, there is no way of knowing.

My papa, like my mama, used to work at Mr Nuri's mansion. He looked after the horses. From what I heard, when Mr Nuri died, Papa left in shame, because Mr Nuri died falling off a horse that Papa had groomed. Mama never stopped waiting for his return. However, this may have happened only in my imagination. My past is a complex mix of dreams and memories. And there are some memories in my head that I recall even though I did not experience them.

Mr Burak was waiting for an answer to his question about my father. He got sick and died, I said. I felt sorry that I did not know more and was anxious lest he ask me what the sickness was. A strange silence grew between us.

Mr Burak took up his notebook and leafed through it. 'All right, what about your mother? She worked for Shirin Hanim's mother, is that correct?'

I nodded. Mr Burak continued looking through his notes. I got to my feet to refresh his tea and bring some more sesame crackers from the kitchen, but he held onto my arm.

'Please sit down, Sadik Usta,' he said in a firm voice. 'I will not have any more tea.'

Anxiously, I sat back down in my chair. As I said, the

living room in Moda is used only for important guests. That I should be sitting in an armchair like the host of the tea table I had set was unheard of. My stomach ached, as it sometimes does after drinking tea.

Mr Burak glanced up from his notes, took off his glasses, and looked into my eyes with a very sincere expression. His eyes were like olives marinating in oil, black and shiny. I did not know what I should do.

'Sadik Usta, your mother's name was Meryem, wasn't it? Meryem was a servant of Madam Shirin's parents and you were born in their house.'

I swallowed. Hearing my dear mama's name after all these years brought a lump to my throat. Much later I thought that I should ask Mr Burak how he learnt her name. He turned back to his notebooks and his brows furrowed.

'There's something I don't understand, Sadik Usta. You described Shirin Hanim's uncle's mansion in Uskudar very well. You have recalled many details, for example the fish in the pool, even the neighbour's shop. That's good. But I don't understand why Shirin Hanim was staying with her uncle. Did something happen to her parents?'

I lowered my voice. 'Mr Nuri died.'

'This Mr Nuri you say was Shirin Hanim's father?'

'Yes.'

Mr Burak wrote a few sentences in his notebook.

I felt the need to explain. 'He fell off a horse.'

Without raising his head, Mr Burak wrote that down. 'Her mother, Shirin Hanim's mother, where was she?'

I swallowed. The pain in my abdomen intensified. 'Madam Shirin's mother was a very beautiful lady. When she became a widow, a suitor appeared soon after.'

My voice came out very feeble, but Mr Burak still heard

me. I immediately went silent and lowered my head. I had said too much. That detail had been buried deep in my memory and I had not even known I knew it. But that the subject had reverted away from myself and back to Madam Shirin gave me some comfort.

Mr Burak cleared his throat, leant back in his chair and traced his fingers over his notebook.

'Okay, let's see now. Nuri Bey falls off his horse and dies. His wife is an attractive woman. Right away a suitor arrives. She remarries. Have I got that right so far?'

I nodded.

'How old was Shirin Hanim at that time?'

'She was a child. I do not quite remember, Mr Burak.' My voice was hoarse.

'Why didn't her mother take her daughter with her to the house she was entering as a new bride instead of sending her to a distant relative?'

I thought about his question. I tried to remember. It was as if my memory of that period was covered with a thick grey cloth.

'I do not know, Mr Burak.'

Every time I said I did not know something, I felt guilty – towards Mr Burak, Madam Nur, and my lady. I had heard evil rumours as to why Mr Nevzat had invited the young Madam Shirin to join his household and these were flying around in my mind. 'Mr Nevzat was wealthy,' I said quietly. 'He wanted his niece, Madam Shirin, to receive an education. That may have been the reason.'

Mr Burak scratched his chin. 'I see. Well, that makes sense. But what about you?'

'I, your humble servant, sir?'

'Yes, you. Why were you sent to Uncle Nevzat's house?'

What an absurd question!

'Why, to assist Madam Shirin, of course.'

He nodded. His pen was suspended over his open notebook, but he wasn't writing anything down, just muttering to himself, 'To assist Madam Shirin...'

I felt the need to elaborate. 'And so that she would not be alone on the journey.'

'What journey?'

It was my turn to be surprised. Was an intelligent journalist like Mr Burak having difficulty following my story?

'Our journey to Uskudar, Mr Burak. From Madam Shirin's mother's home to Uncle Nevzat's mansion.'

'Where was Shirin Hanim's mother's house?'

For a moment my head became foggy again. Although Mr Burak's question was very easy to answer, I continued to stammer. My anxiety increased. I made a great effort to remember the name of the place in which I was born. That I had forgotten the name was impossible. It was on the tip of my tongue. A name I had known forever, like my own name. I was on the verge of remembering when Mr Burak spoke, and the rope whose end I had caught flew away from me. He brought his head close to mine.

'Sadik Usta, I want to ask you something else. This will be the last question. I know I've tired you. Your mother, Servant Meryem, did she go with Shirin Hanim's mother to the new house?'

I nodded. My insides twisted. An image of my dear mama waving her handkerchief on the pier as we sailed away came into my head.

'I understand. They sent you to Uncle Nevzat so he could put you through school and employ you in his factory. You would also attend to Shirin Hanim. Your mother went with

Shirin Hanim's mother to her new husband's house. Where did you say that house was?'

I had not said anything. But all at once my mind's eye was filled with a vision of the mountains there, the great expanse of green, the wave after wave of peaks and ridges. It was such a powerful vision that I could feel the wind whipping my cheeks and smell the hazelnuts on the branches. And with that vision the name of our village slipped into my memory.

'Macka.'

'I beg your pardon?'

'Macka, Mr Burak. Madam Shirin's parents' house was in Macka. I myself lived there with my dear mama.'

I was relieved that at last I had been able to answer one of Mr Burak's questions. Pensively, he made a note.

'Macka, was it? They lived in Macka as far back as then, did they? Macka. Very interesting.'

I left that question unanswered.

20

Nur

One evening a while back I went to Burak's house. 'A while back' is just a figure of speech. It was almost two months ago. Burak knows me well and right away he understood that I wanted to talk to him about that night. But he didn't know what had happened before I went to see him, or what happened afterwards. We locked the dining-room door behind us.

I'd been in a good mood that day, two months back. Istanbul in spring always smells of hope to me, and as I was walking around Macka I got caught up among a group of high-school students. Then, by chance, I bumped into Fikret. It wasn't really by chance – he was on his way to my house. I got upset. If I hadn't got so upset, I wouldn't have gone to Burak's that evening. If I hadn't gone to Burak's, a whole lot of other stuff wouldn't have happened. Ufuk wouldn't have left me, and Burak and I wouldn't have now been sitting at the dining-room table like two young lovers who didn't know how to talk to each other.

I'd just received a commission for a new ghostwriting project. A rich, ostentatious, middle-aged businessman, a fat cat named Metin (no need to give his last name), had found me independently of the publishing house and emailed me direct. Ufuk didn't know about it. 'Nur Hanim,' he wrote, 'I have the outline of a novel in my head. Would you help me bring it to life?' His last name seemed familiar. Was he in engineering? Or communications? I couldn't remember, but he was the son of a family of prominent businesspeople. I could have googled him, but I wasn't that bothered. Sometimes not knowing anything about a famous person puts you in a stronger position when you meet them.

Of course, I should really have forwarded the email to Ufuk. After all, he owns the publishing house and it's his job to deal with the clients. He tells them what ghostwriting entails, talks to them about how much influence they, as the so-called author, will have over the story, informs them how long the process will take and sets the price according to the number of pages. I don't even see the client until the contract has been signed, and after that we always meet at the publishing house. We roll up our sleeves and set to work on creating a bestseller out of a mediocre plot, trite ideas and two-dimensional characters. I'm the writer, but Ufuk is the one who shapes it into a bestseller. If the client is sufficiently articulate, they can express their opinion on what we've come up with. Since the books I've ghostwritten have sold really well, Ufuk and I could be considered a good team.

Fat cat Metin had bypassed Ufuk and come straight to me. Short, plump and thick-necked, with grey eyes behind frameless glasses, he was an unattractive type. He'd got to the café before me and was sitting inside, at a table beside the window. Who sat indoors on such a beautiful spring day? I glanced around and was surprised to see that all the tables were full. Then I remembered how Burak preferred to sit inside even in beautiful weather because the outdoor tables were always smothered in smoke. Fat cat Metin was probably a non-smoker, so I wouldn't be able to light up.

When the fat cat client-to-be saw me, he got to his feet and, without buttoning his jacket, held out his hand. Though he was plump he didn't have a beer gut, which meant he watched his health. He knew what I looked like. Well, of course, who can remain incognito these days? As I shook his damp hand, I was already regretting having agreed to this. I would tell Ufuk everything that evening. He'd be angry that I'd made the appointment and met the customer without telling him. And because I couldn't see myself telling the fat cat to talk to my husband about the money, it would be up to me to do the negotiating. But the man had no intention of negotiating. The first thing he did after we sat down was to take a fat envelope stuffed with money out of the inside pocket of his expensive jacket and lay it in front of me. I was startled and wanted to put the envelope out of sight immediately. But Metin was relaxed. He was clearly used to laying fat envelopes on the table and anyway it was me and not him who was doing a deal behind my husband's back. He might even count out the money right there, repeatedly licking his fingers as he did so. Or, worse still, he might insist that I count it too.

We were in Tesvikiye, at the House Café, the one on the corner, beside the mosque. I had chosen it thinking that since it was open on all four sides, he wouldn't try to take advantage of me. We were sitting diagonally across from each other at a square table. If he pressed his knee against mine or anything like that, I decided, I'd throw his money in his face. Though how old did I think I still was anyway?

My client had no intention of being fresh with me. He got straight to the point and started telling me what kind of novel he wanted. It would be a work of historical fiction, set in Manisa during the Turkish War of Independence. I was aware, was I not, that when the Greek army withdrew from Manisa, they razed it? They filled the mosques with men and set them on fire. And the women... My God, we were in trouble, I thought to myself. If he had the time, he'd write it himself. He had lots of notes, he could send me the notes if I wished. I didn't wish. In his mind he envisioned scenes of extreme sex and violence. As he said this, his grey eyes stared into mine, a stare not of desire but of ownership. He saw me as a machine. No, not a machine, a device. I was a writing device. Fat cat Metin inspected his device carefully. He was trying to figure out whether this model could write scenes of extreme sex and violence. The Russian-American author Ayn Rand came to my mind. She had sat down at the table and said to herself, 'You are a writing machine from now on. Write!' Mum had filled the house with not only her novels but also her sayings and her diaries. I had read them as a child. Wasn't she the one who tied her hands to the typewriter – or was it to her chair? She wouldn't let herself get up until she had written a certain number of words. 'You are a writing machine now.'

Give the envelope back, Nur! Right now! Push the envelope politely under the man's cup of green tea and get up. A high quota of sex and violence could mean only one thing: rape. And the kind of rape scenes that filled the imaginations of men like him were those where the woman resisted at first, with a bagful of words like 'no,' 'don't', 'stop' and 'please', but later went on to writhe with pleasure and have multiple orgasms. Even if this fat cat covered the entire table with his thick envelopes, he would never get me to write scenes like that. No way.

'You write erotic scenes so well. I really like the way you

convey real passion without veering into melodrama. I won't
interfere with your style. We'll outline the plot together and
then I'll leave the rest to you.'

Wow! I hadn't been expecting that. It seemed that people
did know which books I'd ghostwritten. His grey eyes were
searching my face. I felt uncomfortable. High-school kids
were laughing as they passed the window. Carefree Friday.
Once upon a time I'd gone to high school near there, and
on Friday afternoons, unburdened by homework, I'd sashay
down that street. A boy I had a crush on lived down there,
on Husrev Gerede Street, and I used to stand on that very
corner and watch him loping down the hill, his schoolbag on
his back. The weekend lay ahead, a long slice of time full of
anticipation and excitement. Momentary thrills and pleasures
that would influence us for months as we relived them over
and over could be squeezed into a single Saturday. Monday
was the faraway future, not worth thinking about. I knew
exactly how those passing teenagers were feeling.

We shook hands and I put the envelope in my handbag.

I was going to write fat cat Metin's novel all by myself,
in peace, without seeking any advice or support from Ufuk.
Ufuk interfered in everything, from the number of pages in
each scene to the development of the characters. How many
times had we sat around the big rectangular table in the
meeting room at the publishing house, from where you could
just glimpse the sea, as he convinced us that the client's story
should be set there and not here, should take place during
that time and not this, should have yet another plot twist
added just at that point. If we – I – objected, he'd explain
that if we didn't make those changes, the book wouldn't sell,
which wouldn't please the client. He was always right, but it
still annoyed me.

Most of our clients were women in their late thirties who were fed up with corporate life but unable to find the courage to quit, and they were always prepared to accept whatever Ufuk recommended. They were determined to prove – to others, but primarily to themselves – that the business world had not sucked all their creativity out of them. By creativity they meant the wonderful ideas that dropped into their heads. Putting those ideas on paper was a mere detail, craftsmanship, which was why they came to us with their clichéd dreams and sterile visions, so that they could become part of the literary world. When they sat at the book-signing stands set up by our company, signing books for friends and rivals, they really believed the book was their own creation. The likes they received for the photos they went on to post on Instagram gave them genuine satisfaction. They didn't sleep with my husband, but he gave them very real pleasure. They had planned the story 'exactly' as Mr Ufuk had described; he had read their minds. Nur Hanim, would you rewrite that chapter precisely as we've just agreed?

But fat cat Metin and his historical novel set in Manisa were mine. The scenes with lots of sex and violence were mine. So was the money in the envelope. When I got home, I shut myself in the study and counted the money. Necla was cleaning the windows in the living room. I drew the curtains and counted again. The 200-lira bills were crisp. His accountant must have placed them in the envelop with care. Fat cat Metin had paid more than he needed to – an amount that could have covered the printing, distribution and publicity as well as my writing of the book. He didn't care. The only thing he wanted was a book. A book that I would write. That was all. Maybe he had his own publisher. Maybe he was just wanted it for his friends to read. Maybe there was a woman he had his eye on. Look, I wrote this, he would say to her. It was none of my business. We hadn't talked about where and by whom the book would be published. Another minus point, Nur. I should have asked, but I didn't. The man was probably going to take my text and offer it to a prestigious publishing house that published real books by real writers. Every minus point was making it harder to tell Ufuk the truth.

I put the money back in the envelope and searched the internet – should I buy euros or dollars? The Turkish lira was in such a pitiful state that the money in my envelope was losing value by the hour. I should have gone straight to the exchange bureau next to the House Café. I put the envelope back into my handbag. Just as I was leaving the study, the computer pinged. I turned and looked: an email from Metin. Not one to hang around, it seemed. 'Nur Hanim, the relevant documents are attached. Please let me know when you've completed the first part. Best wishes and good luck with the writing.'

That was all. As if I was his secretary. Well, I was, wasn't I? His writing machine. Without looking at the 'relevant documents', I grabbed my handbag and left the house. I had to exchange what was in the fat envelope into something else – euros, dollars, gold, whatever – before Ufuk came home. Hide the murder weapon, Nur. And hide yourself. The sky had clouded over and the Friday evening brightness was lost. Walking up from Macka, back to Tesvikiye, I suddenly felt exhausted. What a stupid situation! Why was I behaving like this, as if I'd slept with the man? I should tell Ufuk: it was like this and this and this. What was it to him, anyway? Was he my boss? Let him get angry. As long as I didn't neglect my other projects, what business was it of his? It made no sense to stress myself out by keeping it a secret, and if I delayed telling him, he might start wondering if there were other things I hadn't told him about.

I immediately got my phone out and called Ufuk. My heart was beating too fast. What was happening to me? What was triggering this guilty feeling? 'The person you have called is busy at the moment. Please hold the line.' I didn't hold the line. I would go and exchange the money first. Euros seemed sensible. Not that I understood the stock market, the arrows, the numbers on the panel, just that Europe was nearer. What would I do with dollars? Was I going to America? If I had a nervous breakdown, I'd go to a Greek island. Not that I'd ever done that before, but that wasn't important; there was a first time for everything. I'd go to that island where Leonard Cohen had a house and I'd stay there for a week, by myself. Of course! I had money. My own money. My own euros! I'd write the fat cat's book on that island. There'd be a taverna under the sycamore trees, and music, and in the evenings I'd drink a carafe of white wine and maybe even dance with various elderly, courteous, intellectual Greek men. When you went to a different country by yourself, you could be whoever you wanted to be.

As I came out of the exchange bureau hugging my handbag, I bumped straight into Fikret.

'What happened, sister? Did you win the lottery or something? You're smiling.'

Fikret! The enemy of happy moments, my brother. You had no right to smile, because the country was weeping tears of blood. Fikret's role, his goal in life, was to call people to seriousness. What did I care if the world was going to hell? If our country, not exactly the epitome of heaven on earth, was going belly up along with the rest of the world, would my sitting at home crying and complaining change anything? I was happy, okay? I had dreams, and euros in my handbag. I was happy at that moment.

'What are you doing here, brother?'

Since Fikret and I had grown up in an apartment just down the street, that could have been considered a stupid question, but Fikret rarely came to that part of the city, or at least not any more. Around the time I married Ufuk, they moved from their villa in Levent to Zekeriyakoy in the northern suburbs. He left Istanbul Technical University and started teaching at a private university a long way away. Now we only saw each other for holiday celebrations, at New Year, and for a meal in a fancy restaurant whenever Oguz over from America. We saw Freya even less. So my question wasn't so stupid. What was strange, however, was Fikret's answer.

'I was coming to see you.'

Wonders never ceased! My surprise was no doubt obvious from my expression. Fikret explained.

'The mother of a friend from university passed away and I came to the funeral. So I thought I'd come and see you while I was in the area. What's going on around here? There's construction work everywhere. There's barely room to walk in Macka any more.'

All my happiness evaporated. If Fikret was coming to see us, he'd definitely want to discuss selling the apartment. Which was why he'd randomly mentioned the construction work. Damn. The whole way home, I sulked. I unlocked the door. Necla had finished the cleaning and was melting butter into red lentil soup. Red pepper and dried spearmint were sizzling in a pan and the whole place smelt like a kebab restaurant. I opened the living-room windows. The noise of building work and the smell of spring wafted in.

'I'll tell Necla to make us both some filter coffee. Or would you prefer tea?'

Fikret was standing in the middle of our oversized living room, looking at the furniture of our childhood. When it had been just Dad and me living there, it had never occurred to us to change it. He was often away on trips and I just wasn't interested in things like updating the soft furnishings or stripping and staining the floor. I'm still not. By the time Dad relocated to Thailand and Ufuk moved in, our old Scandinavian-style furniture had become fashionable again. The workshops in Cukurcuma were selling similar things at outrageous prices, and I thought how good it was that I hadn't changed so much as the slipcover on an armchair. My laziness had served me well. The bookcase Dad had had made by a friend of his in Ankara before we were born was still full of Mum's books.

'I won't have anything, thanks, Nur. I've given up tea and coffee.'

'We have herbal tea – sage, chamomile, mint and all that. Necla, would you come here a minute?'

I collapsed onto the sofa in front of the window. Where was my tobacco? Fikret's looking around at the furniture, the books and the paintings on the wall was making me nervous.

'Do sit down, Fikret. Don't stand there like a stranger. This is your house too.'

I hadn't meant to insinuate anything, but a cloud passed across Fikret's face. We hadn't worked out the ownership business of the apartment. It belonged to both Fikret and me, but he wouldn't accept any rent from us. This upset Ufuk and no doubt Freya nagged Fikret about it too. Fikret wanted to sell it. He would take half the money and the problem would be sorted. I couldn't agree. Like all unresolved money issues within a family, this had divided us, and we'd never been very close anyway.

'This is the first time I've been here since that day.'

I was about to ask which day but decided not to when I saw that he was looking at the sheepskin rug on the floor with great sadness.

'That can't be true, Fikret. You must be mistaken,' I said and hurriedly tried to think. Had Fikret visited us since I'd married Ufuk? I couldn't remember. After Dad fell in love with a Thai woman and moved to Bangkok, I lived in the apartment by myself. Our new stepmother was just three years younger than Fikret and two years older than me. Before Dad gave up his share of his business and moved to a Bangkok skyscraper, he did the responsible thing and put the title deeds of the apartment jointly in my name and Fikret's. Fikret was furious with him, perhaps because he wasn't properly honouring our mother's memory or perhaps because of his new wife's age, I don't know. He was angry at me too because I had the huge apartment all to myself. Did he come and see us before Dad left? After Mum? He was busy with his children: Oguz was little and Celine had just been born. Did the children never come over to see their grandfather? I didn't remember. I was a novice reporter at the time. I'd wake up in some lover's bed, briefly stop by the apartment and then rush out again like the wind, chasing a news story. Compared with world affairs and people that needed saving, visits from my brother were of no consequence. Before that? Before that, Fikret had scooped Mum up from among the empty alcohol bottles and carried her to the hospital.

'Don't bother trying to work it out, Nur. I have consciously stayed away from this apartment. How many years has it been? Have you counted?'

Necla came in, bringing coffee. Fikret didn't want any. He also refused herbal tea. I took my coffee and sat down on the sofa. I wanted to curl up with my foot underneath me, but because my brother was sitting ramrod straight and acting so serious, I was too tense.

'Twenty-four, Nur. It's been exactly twenty-four years. Time enough for a whole generation to have grown up. Oguz is a man now, and as for Celine, she's dreaming of the day she can leave home.'

I got up and retrieved my handbag from where I'd left it under the mirror in the entrance hall. Necla was putting on her coat and tying her scarf. As I fumbled around in my bag for my tobacco, my fingers came across the fat cat's envelope, now full of euros and therefore no longer quite so fat. I felt really depressed. I still had to explain all that business to Ufuk. Necla closed the door behind her as quietly as a mouse and left. I wished Fikret would leave. I wanted to have a glass of cognac and get myself together.

Bag in hand, I went back into the living room and collapsed onto the sofa again. This time, while searching for my tobacco, my fingers found my mobile. Ufuk had called, but I hadn't heard the phone ring. Should we celebrate Fikret's coming over after so many years? I was thinking that maybe I should ask him to stay for dinner, when he said, 'Do you have access to old newspaper archives, Nur?'

'What? How old?'

'Really old. The beginning of the twentieth century.'

'Archives of newspapers that pre-date the Republic, you mean? Of course not. How could I access them? I don't even know which newspapers' archives are kept where. And even if we did find them, we wouldn't understand them because they'd all be in Ottoman Turkish. What are you looking for?'

'I'm looking for... Don't laugh, okay? There's something I can't stop thinking about, to do with our great-grandfather.'

'Which great-grandfather?'

I finally found my tobacco in the front pocket of my handbag and hurriedly rolled a cigarette. Yogi Fikret would definitely be annoyed by the smoke and would no doubt make a snide comment.

'Shirin Saka's father.'

'Nevzat? Or was that Grandmother's uncle? Who was the one with the mansion in Uskudar?'

I licked the cigarette paper, stuck it down, shook the tobacco strands off my fingers and lit up. Smoke hung there in the middle of the living room, between Fikret and me. I leant back to put the Zippo on the table. Fikret waved away the smoke but didn't grimace.

'No, not him. That's Uncle Nevzat. I don't think he even has anything to do with us. The one I'm talking about...'

He stood up again and walked to the window. He was like that when he was little too. I wouldn't get up from the table until I'd finished my homework, but Fikret couldn't focus on anything even for five minutes. He'd walk over to the window, the bookcase, go to the kitchen, open the fridge and stare blankly at the shelves, then sit down at his books. Five minutes later, he'd start the whole tour all over again. Nowadays they'd diagnose him as having ADHD and drown him in medicine. Even so, despite his poor concentration, he became an engineer, and, as if that wasn't enough, went on to become a professor. It was me that lacked focus now. The scatterbrained writer, the ghostwriter.

'... the one I'm talking about is Great-Grandfather Nuri.'

'Great-Grandfather Nuri? What was his last name – was it Nuri Ziya? Was he Shirin Saka's father? Wasn't he a member of the Committee of Union and Progress or something? His name sounds familiar.'

'No, he wasn't a Committee member. He was too young for that. If you count—'

I interrupted him. Something was making me uneasy. 'There were plenty of young idiots in the Committee. What did you say his name was – Nuri Ziya? Nuri?'

'Yes, so what?' He turned and looked curiously at my face.

I smiled. 'Maybe I was named after him.'

'What do you mean? What's the connection?'

'Nuri, Nur. Nur, Nuri. How much more of a connection could there be? And I wondered why the name sounded familiar. Ha, ha!'

Fikret had sat down across from me again and was pulling at this moustache. I took another drag of my cigarette, turned and blew the smoke out of the open window behind me.

'I doubt it. By the time you were born, who was left to remember Great-Grandfather Nuri's name?'

'Grandmother, of course. Couldn't Shirin Saka have given me her father's name?'

Fikret pursed his lips and I immediately felt bad. I was always Grandmother's favourite. She never paid much attention to Fikret. If it came out that she had chosen my name, my brother's childhood hurt would resurface.

'Forget about that, Fikret. Sorry, I interrupted you. What was it you wanted to learn about our great-grandfather Nuri from the newspaper archives?'

It was then that Fikret first mentioned the curse hanging over our family like a black cloud. According to him, the identity of this Great-Grandfather Nuri was shrouded in mystery. Why didn't Shirin Saka ever mention him, and why did she never say much about her mother either? We had been told only about the uncle in Uskudar, the rich uncle who sent her to Paris to the Fine Arts Academy, so our attention had been deflected from Shirin Saka's father. If this mystery continued to be kept secret from generation to generation, we would never be free of the curse.

To hide my amusement, I pretended to be wiping stray flecks of tobacco off my lips, but hearing words like 'dark energy', 'a curse', 'trauma passed from generation to generation' and 'genetic memory' coming out of my brother's mouth was so incongruous that I couldn't stop myself from giggling.

'I asked you not to laugh.'

'Okay, I'm really sorry. Okay, look, I'm not laughing. But you have to admit that—'

'Nur, about Mother's… I think Mother's alcoholism was connected to this curse.' He stared at the sheepskin rug again.

My uneasiness was rising from my stomach to my throat like a volcano about to erupt. Oh, God!

'Don't go there, Fikret!' This time I laughed right in his face. I knew where he was going with this. 'You think Mum became an alcoholic because of her grandfather? Let's think about that, shall we? Her famous mother hands her over to Sadik and returns to her art. Her father dies young. The rich husband she put all her hopes in never comes out of the Bangkok bars. Her son marries a tourist girl he got pregnant on holiday in Bodrum. Her daughter hangs out in Taksim bars till the early hours, then wakes up in God knows whose bed… It was none of that that turned Suheyla into an alcoholic, but rather Gentleman Nuri, our great-grandfather, identity unknown. Is that what you're saying?'

By the time I'd finished, I was almost shouting. Fikret was being ridiculous and I should have just laughed it off or joined in the game. We could have looked up this Nuri together on the internet. I could have used him as a character in fat cat Metin's historical novel. Why did I have to go and raise the tension between us?

My brother wasn't bothered by my shrillness. He'd leant forward and was staring at the square coffee table between us. His elbows were on his knees, his fingers folded under his chin. He looked like a Christian confessing his sins to a priest.

'I'm sick of feeling guilty all the time, Nur. Do you understand?'

I got up. My foot had gone to sleep from where I'd been sitting on it. Half-limping, I went over to the sideboard, picked up the cognac bottle and poured myself two fingers. Out of sight of Fikret, I swigged it down, then refilled my glass. Leaning against the sideboard, I took a deep breath. What was going on? Why were my nerves so on edge? Of course I understood. I knew exactly what Fikret meant. Guilt clawed at me all the time too, had done for as long as I could remember. Whenever I tried to follow a dream, assert myself, do something I wanted to do, I was wracked with guilt. And shame. But this wasn't something we could escape by solving the mystery of a great-grandfather. This was the pressure felt by every autonomous individual who cared about what society thought and said about them. The antidote was courage, and I didn't have that courage. I acted like I did, but I didn't. I thought of *The Stationery Shop*, my first and only novel. Its shelf life was about as long as a butterfly's. My stomach cramped. I drank my second glass of cognac in front of the sideboard and, taking my third, returned to my place on the sofa, across from Fikret.

He lifted his head and looked me straight in the eye. 'Nur, you know that Mum committed suicide.'

The round cognac glass quivered with the trembling of my

hand. 'Are you okay, Fikret? You know better than anyone that Mum died of a heart attack.'

I combed my hair back off my face with the fingers of my free hand and looked up at the ceiling cornices. Wonderful carton-pierre plasterwork. Once upon a time, the city had been home to master craftsmen adept at producing such delicate work.

'Do you not remember, Nur, what Dr Kemal said to Mum when she got sick?'

'Got sick when?'

'Come on, Nur, you know perfectly well what I'm talking about.'

I continued staring at the ceiling. 'I swear I don't know. Mum got sick a lot. She was a cream puff.'

'Do you not remember the summer she got cirrhosis? You were a big girl by then, a high-school student. We were on the island and Dr Kemal came. Do you really not remember what he said? "If you have so much as a single drop of alcohol, Suheyla…" You must remember, surely? Nur, I'm asking you, please. Look at me. Look into my eyes. Dr Kemal was very serious. "If you have so much as a single drop of alcohol, it will kill you," he said.'

The anxiety inside me grew so intense that it passed out of my body and filled the room. I was going to suffocate. My heart felt like it was in a vice. I drank what was left in the cognac glass. Fikret had to leave, right away, but he wouldn't be going anywhere until he'd finished telling his stupid story. If he wouldn't go, then I would. It would do me good to get out of the house anyway, before that volcano of anxiety exploded, before I hurt somebody. I had to get out, go for a walk.

I looked at my watch, jumped to my feet and slammed the empty glass onto the table. My head was spinning.

'Oh, look at the time! Brother, I'm so sorry, I hadn't realized how late it was. I... um... I'm meeting Burak, to, um, talk about a new project. I took on a job, ghostwriting a historical novel, and I'm going to ask him to help with it. I'll ask him about your newspaper archives. He'll be able to help. Make yourself at home, just stay where you are. Ufuk will be back soon. We'll continue our talk another time, okay? So sorry.'

And without giving Fikret a chance to open his mouth, I stuffed my tobacco and Zippo into my handbag and left the house.

21

Burak

It was the first time Nur had come to our house in years. I say 'our' house even though it was just me living there and my mother had been dead for seven years already. I'd cleared out the back room where Mum used to sleep a long time ago. I'd got up on a ladder and painted the walls and ceiling, then I moved my desk from its corner in the living room, and my bookcase, into that room. I ordered a new armchair from Ikea and put that in front of the window overlooking the back courtyard, and I spread a green and orange kilim that I'd bought on the road to Assos on the floor. If you didn't count the novels on the top shelf of the bookcase, there was not a dust mote of Mum's left in that room. But still I referred to the apartment as 'our house'. Ours. Mum's and mine. Nebahat and Burak's house.

Nur plunged into the apartment as soon as I opened the door. There was something strange about her. She'd had a few drinks, I thought. I looked at my watch. A little after 9 p.m. It was a sweet spring evening, and with the lengthening days I hadn't noticed day becoming night. I'd been absorbed in my work. I'd done an interview with Madam Anastasia in her magnificent apartment on Balo Street the previous week, and I was writing it up for my column. My hips and waist were aching from having sat in the same position in front of the computer for so long. When I stood up, my left knee cracked. You're getting old, Burak, my boy. Though you might lose yourself in your work and forget all about time, your body is aware of every passing minute.

'Welcome, Nur. Are you all right?'

She didn't answer, just slipped into the wingback chair in the entrance hall and began undoing her sandals. She was wearing capri pants, which showed off her slender ankles, and a very becoming dark blue silk blouse.

'There's no need to take off your shoes. You can wear them inside now.'

She lifted her head and looked at the furniture in the little hallway. Mum's furniture. Then she bent down over her shoes again, as if out of respect for Mum's things she still needed to take them off. In spite of her stylish clothes, I thought she looked tired and a bit messy, and I wondered again if she'd been drinking.

Our ('our'!) apartment had two doors. One was meant for guests, because it directed you straight to the living room, without passing the kitchen, bathroom and bedrooms, and the other was what used to be called a service door because it was near the kitchen. It was a narrow door to the left of the stairway. When Mum and I first moved to Istanbul, years ago, I was very excited about having two doors. I remember that while the porter my uncle had hired was carrying our stuff upstairs, I was busy racing in through one door and out through the other. It's a happy memory, which means I must have forgotten what we'd lost: our village, our garden, the cherry tree, Dad...

Nur stood up. Barefoot, having taken off her high-heeled sandals, she was like a little girl, no matter her fancy blouse and well-cut trousers. As soon as we moved in, Mum closed off the service door and converted the little entrance into a space where she could sew, read a book or write a letter. A room of her own, but one without a door. She spent more time there than she did in her bedroom. Although I'd rearranged the back room long ago, somehow I couldn't bring myself to touch that space. I kept putting it off, even though it was a small area and didn't have much furniture. Her shawl was still hanging in the corner behind the wingback chair and on the bottom shelf of the small table was a basket with her wool in it. Seven years had passed in the blink of an eye.

'Forgive me, I've come empty-handed. I was going to drop into Divan, but...'

Nur reached out and touched Mum's sewing-machine case on the shelf. Pensively, as if she were playing the piano, she ran her fingers over the wooden box. She turned and, standing across from the chair she'd just sat in, looked long and hard at the shawl with its yellow narcissus flowers. The last time Nur had been there was the day of Mum's funeral. Seven years ago. Not with Ufuk, on her own. That was the year she got married. Ufuk had come to the mosque, but he must have left after that. My attention was elsewhere.

My stubborn mum had told me at one point during those last three months, when the cancer was consuming her, that she wanted to be buried in Istanbul, in the Ferikoy Cemetery, and definitely not in the graveyard near Erdek, just outside our village, where my father was buried, nor in the tomb in Edirne where her parents were. If she was buried in Ferikoy, I could visit her, and so could her students. That was her last request. I arranged it.

Nur didn't come to the Ferikoy Cemetery after the mosque. She went to the apartment with my aunt and the other women and helped prepare the tea. They made irmik halva, the traditional semolina dessert, which they then shared out into bowls and distributed to the neighbours.

I remember that detail, even though most things about that day are lost in a cloud of fog. It was a rainy spring day and darkness fell early. When I returned to the house with my male relatives, my uncles on both sides, the apartment was packed with other relatives I didn't even know, who'd come all the way from Erdek or Edirne for the funeral, and Mum's former students. Steam from the tea, human breath and the hum of voices filled the apartment. Shoes were stacked up in front of the door. In the past I'd have been embarrassed to have Nur see my provincial relatives' shoes with their backs pushed down piled up on the doormat, but that evening, when I came back from the cemetery, it didn't bother me. Maybe it was because she was married by then, so it didn't matter what she thought of me any more. In marrying Nur, Ufuk had given me my freedom. Or maybe it was because Mum had died. Whatever the reason, that's what went through my mind as I stood in front of the door, looking at the shoes.

My relatives, most of whom I didn't know, found it strange that Nur was walking around in her own slippers like the bride of the house and knew better than I did what was where in the kitchen and where the table napkins were kept. In the hidden corners of the living room the women were gossiping about her and probably about me too. Nobody spoke up and said, 'Nebahat loved her like her own daughter, ladies, so don't go on about it.' Who was there to tell them that? No relative had witnessed Nur and Mum sitting on the back balcony on summer evenings, eating cherries from a bowl and laughing. Only I had seen that, and I didn't say anything. I just stood there, near the chair where Nur was sitting right now, holding Mum's shawl in my hand.

Nur's fingers were now passing over the same knots in the shawl. Whether she was thinking about Mum or something else it was impossible to know. Her hands and eyes were roving from one piece of furniture to the next, like a frightened cat. I left her there and went to the kitchen. I turned on the light and stood in front of the fridge, not knowing what to do. The fridge door was covered in magnets advertising local restaurants and fast-food places.

'Do you want something to eat? Should we order something? We can get noodles, or fish. It comes from nearby, so it's fresh. Grilled sardines? You like them.'

When she didn't answer, I poked my head out of the kitchen. Nur was pale. She'd lost weight. She hadn't been like that when we'd had lunch together at Hunkar three days earlier, or had I just not noticed? Could a person lose that much weight in three days? Her face looked so small, it made her speckled hazel eyes look larger. Was she ill?

'Are you okay?'

'I'm fine. A bit, um, tired. I'm not hungry. You carry on and order something for yourself. I'll have a glass of cognac if you've got any.'

If you've got any... When did I ever not have any cognac, Nur? I always had some on the off-chance that you might come. I went into the living room, which I almost never used, not since I'd made the back room my study, opened the cabinet under the television, which I almost never turned on, got the bottles out and some glasses and took them out to the back balcony.

Nur had already sat down at her old place at the table.

She'd tucked one of her bare feet underneath her and was rolling a cigarette. I put the bottles on the table and filled our glasses. We clinked them in the dim evening light. She looked away. There was an awkwardness between us. We were like adolescents trying to be adults. Three days ago, when we were having lunch together, we'd been two forty-somethings having an intelligent conversation, two friends whose on–off relationship had spanned a quarter of a century. But not now. Actually, the reason for our awkwardness was obvious. It was the first time we'd been together in that apartment since Mum had gone, the first time we'd ever been there by ourselves. We were like shy teenagers who couldn't wait for their parents to go on holiday but then didn't know what to do once they were home alone. My childhood bed, in which I had dreamt of making love to her countless times, was just the other side of the net-curtained window. The ghost of our youthful desires, which we had suppressed because of my mother, was haunting that balcony. The tension was palpable.

I suddenly felt pleased about that. What we were experiencing now was more genuine, more raw than our adult behaviour during lunch at Hunkar. I was happy. From a distant station, passion blew its whistle. What if...? Nur and I hadn't made love since she'd married Ufuk, not since he'd come into her life, in fact. I was sure she'd been faithful to Ufuk. Why was I so sure? I don't know. Instinct, or maybe self-defence. If she'd been unfaithful to Ufuk, I'd have felt doubly betrayed, firstly because she hadn't told me and secondly because I should have been the man with whom she was unfaithful. Still... how many years had it been since I'd felt the excitement of that 'what if' and that pounding of my heart? A long, long time. Taking a sip of my whisky, I leant back and looked at the stars that were beginning to appear in the dark blue sky above the roofs of the apartment buildings.

Nur licked her cigarette paper and secured it. I heard the familiar sound of her Zippo and smelt petrol. She blew smoke at the windows opposite, where lights were coming on one after the other.

'This balcony is my favourite part of this apartment.'

'I know.'

She and Mum used to sit across from each other drinking tea, eating crackers and cherries and watching the goings-on in the apartments across the courtyard – food being cooked, tables being set on balconies, lights being turned on when evening fell, couples kissing on the terraces on summer evenings. I'd be lying on my bed in the back room, supposedly reading but actually listening to them.

'I wonder which school that girl goes to. She studies so much, it's given her spots from all the stress. What a shame. Poor girl, she only has one little life, and they don't even leave a slice of dry cake on the table for her.'

'Oh, look, Auntie Nebahat, the lady over there's had her hair done again. She's had it curled with tongs and lightened. She'd only just had it cut short and fluffed up.'

From my room I muttered, 'Do you two not have anything better to do than gossip about that poor woman's hair?'

Nur's laughter would bounce off the buildings opposite and come back to me. 'We can't see anything except her head so that's all we can talk about.'

Through the gauze curtain I could see Mum laughing silently as she slapped Nur's knee, visible in her cut-off jeans.

Nur used to drop by a lot. She'd show up suddenly, without warning, just like she had today. She'd park her Fiat Uno expertly in the narrowest of spaces between two cars and ring our bell, bringing with her a box of crêpes dentelles from Divan Pastry Shop. Those were the days before mobile phones, when it was acceptable for people to say, 'I was just passing and thought I'd come by.' Mum had got used to her unscheduled visits. When the bell rang, she'd run to the window and look out. Seeing Nur down there, with her hair cut hedgehog short and dyed flame red, she'd get another plate out of the cupboard and put it on the table. We'd eat together, then turn off the lights and watch TV. We'd take the slices of apple Mum peeled and cut, not like two lovers but like brother and sister. Nur was the daughter Mum never had. I'm sure in her heart she wanted us to get married, but she never once said as much. Maybe she knew that a rich girl from Macka, in spite of her left-leaning views, was out of my league.

'I can't bear this balcony without Auntie Nebahat. Don't get me wrong, but, you know...'

I nodded. She was right. With Nur there, I too felt Mum's absence more acutely. Those summer evenings with her and Nur sitting on the balcony, the three of us together, were gone forever. As life marched on, so we accumulated more and more losses to mourn.

'The artist who lived over there must have moved. Or did he get curtains?'

'That building's going to be demolished. It's part of the gentrification process. Everybody has to move out.'

'What a shame! Gentrification! Even in Kurtulus?'

We both stared at the back of the buildings. Some of the spaces that opened out from janitors' apartments had become rubbish dumps, but in others there were still lemon trees. One concrete area squeezed between several buildings had become a garden. There were lights in the windows and you could hear the clatter of knives and forks being set on the tables. In the alley, children were shouting as they played ball, and mothers were calling them in to dinner. The blare of televisions mixed with the clink of spoons against plates. Like Nur, the balcony was the place I loved most in the apartment. Behind those windows across the courtyard, life went on, unfiltered.

'Could I have a refill, please? It helped. If we're not going to commit suicide, let's at least have a drink.'

'Where did that come from?'

'Don't you remember?'

'Of course I remember. From that novel, *A Wedding Night*. I just don't understand why you're quoting it now.'

When Nur was young, she adored Adalet Agaoglu's books. She was so impressed by *A Wedding Night* in particular that she recorded herself reading the entire novel out loud. She filled numerous ninety-minute tapes and she'd listen to them while she was driving. When her car stereo was stolen, it was the fact one of the tapes was inside it that upset her the most. She never recorded books she loved again.

I filled her cognac glass. She took a sip and closed her eyes.

'My mother was an alcoholic. That's why.'

'What?'

She waved her empty hand.

'A textbook alcoholic. She'd drink, get merry, hug us, kiss us, then get angry, fight with my dad. Sometimes she'd pass out on the living-room rug. Then she'd swear to God she was going to quit drinking, and she would, for a little while, but soon she'd start again. It was like that all through my childhood. Dad took her to see a lot of doctors, and also psychiatrists – you know, back then, it used to be that only really crazy people went to psychiatrists – but none of them made any difference. We were forbidden from telling anyone at school, in our neighbourhood, or on the island that Mum had gone to a psychiatrist. Her being a drunk was very shameful. We'd wake up in the morning to find her passed out on the sofa, mouth open, saliva dripping onto the cushions, dressing gown gaping open at the neck. Dad would have gone out, having left her like that. We'd go and leave her like that too. Dad's driver, Sukru, would drive us to school, and neither Fikret nor I would say a word. I'd have stomach ache all the way to school.'

She stopped talking and relit the cigarette she was holding. Amid the gathering shadows I found her luminous eyes. Exhaling, her glance slid to the kitchen in the opposite building where a woman was washing dishes. I wanted to reach out and take her hand, but I couldn't. I was confused. For all these years I'd had this image of Suheyla Bulut in my head as a refined, kind, honey-eyed person radiating peace, even though Nur had never actually described her mother to me. On the rare occasions when she'd shared some childhood memory, her mother was no more than a cypher, and her father and Fikret made only the briefest of appearances. In the stories she chose to relate, she was always either alone or with Shirin Hanim, never with her mother or father.

I finished my drink and poured myself another. The whisky burnt my throat and then numbed it as it slid its way down.

'Why did you hide this from me?'

'I didn't hide it.'

'What do you mean? You told me and I forgot?'

'No, no.'

She laughed nervously, then pulled her chair forward so that she was close to me at the table and whispered, as if she were telling me a secret.

'I erased it.'

'What?'

'This... Mum... That she was an alcoholic. That she'd get drunk and yell at my dad. That my childhood sleeps were broken by wine glasses shattering against walls. That my ears burnt whenever the girls at school would look at me and whisper. Before she died, she'd not had a drink for seven years. Maybe that's why I never told you. But just when she was about to make it seven whole years, she...'

I reached out and took her hand. It was like ice.

'You're cold. Shall we go in?'

'No, it's good here. The cognac is warming me from the inside.'

For a while she gazed at her glass shining in the darkness, one hand still resting in my palm. The neighbourhood had quieted down and the sky was full of stars. An old tango was playing in one of the apartments opposite. I could sense the heaviness weighing on Nur's heart. She was exhausted. We sipped our drinks without talking and she began to roll another cigarette in the darkness.

'The human brain is a strange mechanism, isn't it? It covers your pain with a scab so you can forget. It protects you. Then, out of the blue, somebody makes a casual remark and the truth resurfaces.'

She went silent again. I thought she would say more, but she didn't. She lit her cigarette, then again looked at the windows of the apartments opposite, which were reflecting the blue of television light. The air had become quite cool. It would be good to go in, but what would we do inside? Sit in front of the TV and peel an apple? I downed my whisky and a sweet warmth spread through me. I loosened up, as if I'd come in from the snowy outdoors to a cosy stove.

'Oh well, what can we do? I've brought your mood down too. I guess we're getting old, Burak.'

'Darling, compared to the people I spend my days talking to, you're as fresh as a rosebud.'

She smiled. Leaving her cigarette in the ashtray, she leant across the table towards me and I was able to see her eyes for the first time since we'd gone out onto the balcony. They were large in her small, oval face, and they had a strange brightness about them. Or had she been crying without my noticing?

'Do you realize that's the first time you've called me darling in a long while?'

A bolt of electricity shot through me from the hand she was holding. It raced through my arteries, lighting up every cell it touched. Her face was very close to mine. Her perfect thin lips, her tiny teeth. What if...? I wanted us to stay in that moment where anything was possible, in that gap before an action was taken, a path chosen, a decision made. Could we not linger there a while? Maybe we'd kiss, maybe we'd pull back. We were suspended in time, in an eternity of possibilities. Nur always kept me there. That was why I was never able to let her go. She kept on offering me an eternity of 'what if...?' moments. Time was pulsating impatiently, ready to explode. Make up your minds about where you're going, it was saying. For a moment I felt that I was the master of time and fate. What could time do if I didn't make a decision? If I just stayed there in those swirling waters, motionless, where could it flow to?

But there was desire. Desire was not interested in intellectual pleasantries. I felt Nur's breath on my face. A thin haze was trembling around her body, engulfing me in waves. In the dark, my lips found hers, warm and tasting of cognac, tart and sweet, the most delicious thing they had ever savoured. I tried not to swallow her little mouth whole, but my heart was about to burst. I reached across the table, cupped the nape of her neck, exposed beneath her short hair, and pulled her head, her face, her lips, her mouth towards me. I was swelling inside. My stomach, my groin, my heart were frothing like a pot of Turkish coffee about to boil over. I took Nur's mouth inside my lips, sucking, biting, kissing. I was insatiable. I had missed her so much.

Without stopping kissing her, I pulled her to her feet. Her hand was still in mine and it was warm now, like a little bird in my palm. We managed to get into the bedroom without getting tangled up in the gauze curtain. I leant Nur against the wall behind the balcony door. She was in my arms and I held her tight, so she couldn't run away. I wanted to bask in the moment, the first time in seven years, but I was struggling to curb my desire. We'd passed the 'what if?' stage and our bodies had taken control.

I grasped her waist. The fabric of her blouse was thin and slippery, stretched taut against her skin. My head was spinning. I pulled her to me and buried my head in her neck. My hands were inside her blouse, caressing her skin, that beautiful skin which always sent me wild, seeking out the secret hollows of her waist, her rising and falling stomach, her ribs. I forced myself not to stroke her nipples yet, those sweet little plums; soon I would lay her on the bed and make love to her with all the youthful energy coursing through me. I was ecstatic, drunk with victory. It had been so long since we'd been on this side of 'what if?', we'd not even come close in years, but here we were, here she was, in my arms, up against the wall. We were gasping for breath, united in the pleasure that only we could give each other. She'd come to me again.

Rubbing my two-day beard on the sensitive spot behind her ear, I whispered breathlessly, 'This is why you came, isn't it?'

She moaned. I slid my hand into her pants, held the round cheeks of her buttocks. Cool. Two perfect globes. Maybe not as firm as before, but still smooth. Suddenly my desire intensified to the point of no return. I couldn't play around any longer. I threw her onto the bed, like a lion vanquishing his rival. I would take the pleasure she had withheld from me for years, always showing but never giving. She was twisting and turning beneath me, saying my name. She was hot and wet between her legs, pulsating. It was she who had taught me how to find those hidden places. I would delve into that nest without losing my way. Now. Right now. I never imagined that when I backed off for the briefest of moments, to get undressed, she would slip out from under me like a cat.

'Burak, no!'

She stood up and straightened her hair, her clothes. Her chest was heaving. I couldn't see her face clearly in the dim light reflected from the corridor. I didn't know what to do. My body was throbbing with the promise of pleasure. My heart was ready to burst. I was ready to burst. You can't say no, Nur! Not now. I could throw you on the bed right now and take what I want. I know you want the same thing. That's why you came here! You came here for me!

I sat on the edge of the bed. Nur was buttoning her blouse. She ran her hands through her hair. I was again in that moment when anything was possible, that gap, but this time I was the master of neither time nor fate. I was fading. Passion retreated, leaving in its place a broken and very familiar anger. It had always been like this. If we'd made love, it would have been the same. She would still have left me sitting on the edge of the bed, feeling incomplete and confused, while she went back to Ufuk. It was because she'd known that this was what would happen that she hadn't gone any further. Hopelessness was tearing me up.

I got up and walked to the entrance hall full of Mum's stuff. The raw light of the corridor dazzled my eyes. Nur followed me. She sat in Mum's chair and began to do up her sandals. Her white neck was red from my kisses. With her head bent, she murmured, 'I don't know what came over me there, Burak. I'm very sorry. I think I had too much to drink. I need to go now. I'll call you tomorrow.'

She stood up. She wouldn't look me in the eye.

Without saying anything, I opened the door, making sure that our bodies didn't touch. As she passed me, she wanted to stroke my cheek, but I drew back. I reached for the automatic light switch. Nothing happened. It appeared to have broken.

Nur ran down the stairs in the dark and disappeared.

I closed the door behind her.

22

Celine

'Hello? Celine? Are you there? Can you hear me? Celine?'

I held the phone away from my ear and Uncle Ufuk's voice turned into a mosquito's buzz. I was standing on a rock on St George's Hill, looking down over Viranbag, as still as a statue. The wind was blowing, messing up my hair, drying my skin, but I couldn't move. I stood there frozen, my phone in my hand.

'Celine? Celine? Hello?'

My uncle was obviously not going to give up. I was at the point of no return. Could I launch into some appropriate song lyrics? Nothing came to mind. I took a deep breath.

'I'm here, Uncle Ufuk. I can hear you.'

Okay, I'd said something now, so I couldn't play the 'pocket dial' card, couldn't say, 'Oh, my phone was in my back pocket and must have dialled you by mistake, I'm so sorry. Happy holidays,' and hang up.

'Celine, I can't hear you very well. There's a howling noise. Where are you?'

Where was I? Good question. I turned and looked at the

231

entrance to St George's. Was it the hum of the church service Uncle Ufuk was hearing? No, it was the wind.

I'm standing on a rock, Uncle, like a lost stork, and below me are nothing but bushes, rocks and brambles covering a steep hillside that drops down and down, all the way to the sea. The sea is as beautiful as a legend, like a silver skirt that's swirling and twirling around the island. At the horizon the water is purple, in the middle it's navy blue, and right below me, at Viranbag, in the shadow of the pine trees leaning over the sea, it's turquoise.

Would you believe me if I said I'd called you just so I could share this beautiful scene with you? No, you wouldn't. You once said to me that my generation had become limited as a result of being glued to our phones. Whenever we're at a loss for something to do, we gaze stupidly at the screen, looking for a distraction, and then we let the screen take us where it wants. We snap a photo of the scenery and WhatsApp it. It doesn't cross our minds to dial a number and describe the scene in words. We don't know how to laugh out loud any more – it's all LOL emojis, never a heartfelt 'ha, ha, ha'.

'Uncle Ufuk...'

Oh, my tongue had slipped again. I was going to say 'Ufuk', but I said 'Uncle Ufuk'. When I started university, they said, 'You're a young woman now, Celine. Forget this "Uncle" and "Aunt" business, from now on we are friends. Call us "Nur" and "Ufuk".'

I couldn't get used to it somehow.

'Celine, what's happened? Are you crying? Are you okay?'

I wasn't crying, but when he said that, my eyes filled with tears. My darling uncle was upset because of me. The only person in the world who cared about me was my uncle.

232

Maybe I should tell him about the argument I'd got into that morning. Those awful men were going to beat me up, Ufuk. Burak was my hero this morning.

But then... Burak? Umm, yes, Burak is here, Ufuk. And, right now, on the dining-room table...

'Celine, sweetie, please say something. What's going on there? Is everyone okay? Did something happen to Shirin Hanim?'

I sniffed. 'Uncle, Dad's disappeared. He left. We've lost him!'

Silence. And coughing. 'I don't understand. What do you mean, "lost"? How long has he been gone?'

'Since this morning.'

He chuckled softly, kindly. 'Since this morning? Well, it's not even evening yet. He'll come back soon.'

I jumped down from the rock and shook off bits of brush that had stuck to my shorts. The backs of my legs were dimpled from sitting on the stony ground. I walked towards the church. The smell of incense was wafting out of the open door. The hum had got louder. The priests were praying. There was something really sad about the candles stuck on the table at the entrance, flickering in unison. I didn't know what it was. My voice shook.

'No, Uncle, it's not like that.'

I passed through a crowd of people pushing and shoving as they tried to place their orders at a small outdoor restaurant, sat down at one of the furthest empty tables and told my uncle everything that had happened that morning. How Dad had come into my bedroom in the middle of the night and kissed my cheek, how he'd taken his backpack and gone. I left out the part about Burak and me planning to follow him. Anyway, our detective story had died before it was born. While I was telling him all that, it was hard to believe all those things had happened that morning. It seemed like months ago.

'Celine? Are you there?'

'Yeah.'

'Your voice comes and goes. Your dad's probably gone to visit some friend on the island. Have you phoned him?'

'I've been calling him since the morning. His phone is always off and he doesn't use WhatsApp. His phone is so old, I can't tell if he's read my messages or not.'

Uncle Ufuk took a deep breath. I could heard the rasping sound. His peaceful face came before my eyes. Blonde beard, green eyes. My Jesus-faced uncle. His voice was deep, like sprinkled water.

'Celine, sweetie, don't take offence, but I think you're making yourself anxious over nothing. I mean, maybe your dad just wanted to be by himself today, or maybe he's out doing yoga in the pine forest or something. You know he's got very interested in that kind of thing recently.'

'I know, Uncle Ufuk, but...'

I didn't know what to say. All around me at the outdoor restaurant people were having fun. Tables were being pushed together, and there was a hubbub of hustling, jostling men, women and children sitting on chairs that wobbled on the uneven ground. Trays loaded with sausages, French fries, thick slices of white bread, beer bottles, sour cherry juice, Coca-Cola, homemade wine and Greek salad were being carried in a line from the kitchen to the tables. The waiter, the son of the owner, was drenched in sweat, cursing behind pursed lips the brats that got in his way as he set a tray down on one table and then raced to another table to write down their orders with the pencil that was stuck behind his ear. Everyone was very cheerful. Holiday greetings were being exchanged between tables – the table drinking Coca-Cola and cherry juice were clinking glasses with the homemade-wine table and smiling at each other. Look, look – we can all live together, as brothers. Happy holiday! The same to you! And what did they call this holiday? Conservatives called it the Ramadan Feast and secularists called it the Candy Festival – fighting words that stayed under the table. What a charade! They'd strangle each other at the first opportunity, and would happily report their neighbours to the police.

'Celine, sweetie, is there something else bothering you? Is your great-grandmother all right? Her birthday's tomorrow, right? Is everything okay?'

Yes, right, tomorrow was Great-Granny's hundredth birthday. One hundred! Wow! That was the reason Burak was with us, to write an article in celebration of Shirin Saka. I don't think so! I knew perfectly well why he was there. Burak Gokce, you clever journalist, you trickster!

'Why aren't you here, Uncle Ufuk?'

I hadn't meant to sound so shrill. The headscarfed girl at the next table and the young man holding her hand turned and looked at me. I must have shouted pretty loud.

Uncle Ufuk was quiet for a while. He was probably stroking his moustache with his long, white fingers, his clean fingernails. He plays the guitar beautifully. He plays flamenco songs on a classical guitar. What were Burak's hands like? His fingers were stubby, as far as I remembered. Short fingernails. Ugly.

'Are you coming tomorrow, Uncle?'

It was a perfectly normal question. But why then was my heart beating so fast, as if I'd said something taboo? Neither Great-Granny nor Dad had once asked, 'Where is Ufuk, Nur? What's he up to?' Sadik Usta would have wondered, but he kept his thoughts to himself. I didn't include Burak. It was obvious why he wouldn't ask. And naturally I'd been left out of a secret everybody else was party to. Shit!

Finally the silence at the other end was broken.

'No, Celine, sweetie, I'm not coming tomorrow.'

Tears came into my eyes, my mouth and nose prickled, and my face was as hot as if I'd been in the sea. I hugged myself. 'But why not?'

The headscarfed girl at the next table was still staring at me. Why was she looking so anxious? Because I was like a bomb about to explode. If Uncle Ufuk had come to the island this holiday, everything would have been different. Totally different. He wouldn't have not cared about Dad's disappearance, for one thing. He'd have come looking for him with me, or at the very least he'd have thought it through logically. If Uncle Ufuk were on the island now, Burak and Aunt Nur wouldn't have shut themselves up in the dining room. They couldn't have. They couldn't have locked the door and made love on the dining-room table to the accompaniment of Albinoni.

My tears were gathering. At the other end of the line, Uncle Ufuk was explaining in a mumbling way why he wasn't there with us. He was spending the holiday with his parents and his sister who had come from America with his nephews. His nephews had missed him. They hadn't seen each other for years. He suggested we meet in Kadikoy as soon as possible and go to some record shops. I didn't say anything, just inhaled noisily. I don't know how Uncle Ufuk interpreted that noisy breathing, but all of a sudden his voice changed.

'Celine, is your aunt okay?'

I didn't know what to say. Was Uncle aware that Burak had come to the island? Or not? I needed this key information to give him an answer, but how could I get it? My silence made him anxious.

'Celine, what's happening? Tell me the truth right now. Is Nur okay? What's happening there?' His voice had got stern.

I stuttered. 'Sh-sh-she's fine. Yes.'

'Is she with you now? Could you call her to the phone?'

He was actually worried. If he only knew!

'No. I mean, I can't call her. I'm out. My aunt is at home. I mean she was at home the last time I saw her. She's fine. There's nothing wrong.'

She was fine. Perfectly fine. Snow white. Walking around the house in that kimono you brought her from Japan at all hours of the day. Hand in hand with Burak, she locked the dining-room door behind them. No, I couldn't be so cruel as to say that. I stood up and grabbed a sweating bottle of beer from the tray as the waiter delivered sausages and bread to the table next to me. I took twenty lira from the pocket of my shorts and slid it under the glass ashtray. With the beer in my hand and the phone to my ear, I headed down the hill towards the sea until I came to a big rock away from the tables, the sausages and the wary eyes staring at me.

'Uncle, I think Dad committed suicide.'

'What? What are you saying, Celine? What makes you think that?'

All at once I began to weep – saliva, snot and all. Little bubbles came out of my mouth and tears mingled with the bitter taste of beer on my tongue. Teardrops were pouring down my cheeks. I sat on the ground with my back against the rock and my legs stretched out. Stones and pine needles pricked my skin.

'Uncle... I'm in a bad way.'

As soon as I said that, I realized that I really did feel

terrible. It wasn't just then; I'd been feeling bad for days – for weeks and months, in fact. I felt like there was something missing, like I was incomplete, as if I was forever waiting for something, on the threshold of a life that somehow would never begin. Burak had brought it all to the surface. Shit! I missed Burak. How was it possible to miss a man I barely knew? It was ridiculous, but there was an emptiness inside me that only his attention and his love could fill. People could say whatever they wanted, but that emptiness could only be filled by one person in the world and that was Burak Gokce. I realized suddenly that this ridiculous feeling was what they called love. I'd fallen in love. I'd turned into the lyrics of a stupid, melodramatic song. I cried even harder.

'Celine, sweetie, please tell me calmly why you think your father would commit suicide. What makes you think that? Did Fikret ever say anything to you about taking his own life? Or did you find a letter, a note?'

My uncle's voice was calm. He's always calm anyway; he's like aloe vera lotion smoothed onto the skin on a hot day. No, I thought, Dad had never said he wanted to kill himself. There'd been no letter or anything, at least not that we'd found so far. I knew I was being ridiculous, but I wanted Uncle to give me some attention, to do something for me, something he wouldn't normally do. From deep inside me, a roar was rising.

'No, but...'

'But what? What was it exactly that made you jump to such a conclusion?'

He was definitely smiling. If we were together, he'd be stroking my hair. Suddenly I really missed my uncle. I could confide in him; I'd always been able to do that. When I was in high school, he used to listen patiently to all my troubles, without making fun of me.

'Be... because Great-Granny's father... Great-Granny's father... committed suicide. When Great-Granny was a child. It happened right in front of her. At the breakfast table.'

At the other end of the line, my uncle was silent. I sensed the smile on his face fading. I saw him in my mind as clearly as if we were on FaceTime. As I explained things, his long, thin, blonde-bearded face grew longer, and his green eyes darkened. As for me, with every sentence of my story, I believed it more and more. The more I believed in it, the more upset I became. Dad? Was suicide genetic? I tried to remember my Psychology 101 class. I thought it probably was. I put the beer bottle down by my feet. It rolled down the hill, hitting rocks as it went. I didn't care.

'It... it's in our blood, don't you see, Uncle Ufuk? I feel really bad. For months Dad has been obsessed with this great-grandfather. He goes to libraries and everything, searches through newspaper archives. Now I understand. He saw himself in this grandfather. The same tendencies. That's why he got so interested in the family connections and everything. There's a dark void inside him – not only in him but in all of us. That's the family curse. Dad has fallen into that void. He's committed suicide, Uncle Ufuk – I'm sure of it.'

I was crying violently now. The words in my mouth were like gravel. They tumbled out noisily and even I couldn't understand what I was saying. My poor uncle on the other end was swearing desperately.

'Celine, sweetie... Celine, listen to me now, okay? Are you listening?'

I nodded as if he could see me. The sun was going down.

The sea at the bottom of the hill was like a silly, carefree woman whirling and twirling, making fun of my troubles.

'Celine, are you there? Can you hear me?'

'I'm here, Uncle.'

'Celine, I want you to go home now. Where are you anyway? Are you far from home?'

'No, not really. I mean, um, I went out on my bike. To clear my head.'

I couldn't tell him that I'd come all the way up to St George's by myself because that would sound weird and I didn't want him to think I was weird.

'Okay, so I want you to ride back home very slowly and carefully, and when you get there, I want you to lie down and have a rest, drink some water. Okay?'

'Okay.'

'I'm leaving the house right now. I'll take the first motorboat from Bostanci to the island. Try to calm down a little. I'll be there in an hour. I'll call you when the boat gets close to Buyukada and we'll meet at the pier. Okay, sweetie? You understand, don't you? See you at the pier in an hour. In front of Hrisafi's Bookshop. Understood?'

I sniffed. It was a good thing we weren't on FaceTime. I wouldn't have wanted him to see my red nose and swollen eyes.

'Okay, Uncle.'

I got up slowly, took off my shoes and carried them in my hand. As I passed between the tables, people stared at me like I was a madwoman. I walked all the way down St George's Hill barefoot, like pilgrims used to. I'd stopped crying. A feeling of satisfaction that I hadn't experienced in a long time came over me. My mind had been detoxified, and like the stomach it was looking for fresh subjects, new plans to chew on. I was already dreaming about a bed and breakfast on Heybeliada or backpacking in Vietnam. Human psychology was so funny. Just a little bit of attention had been enough and now the knot inside me had been smoothed out. Not for nothing did they say that 'Love Is Everything'.

Uncle Ufuk was coming.

My uncle was coming to the island for me!

23

Sadik

Something compelled me to open the drawer of my bedside table. I felt the urge to glance over the interview which Mr Burak had conducted with me so many years back. I had folded the newspaper page into four and placed it neatly in the far corner of the drawer. From time to time I get the urge to see it, and so I open it up and read it. The sentences along the folds in the page have now been erased, but having read the paragraphs so often, I am able to fill in the gaps from memory.

Today, however, I was unable to find the newspaper. It was not in its place. This was impossible, of course. It was just that my eyes did not see it. It was old age. Having a tendency to become short of breath, I carefully inhaled and pulled the wooden drawer right out. I still did not see the newspaper. I removed the contents of the drawer one by one and lined them up on the bedcover. Unfortunately, among the old brown glass medicine bottles, the colourful old ribbons I had saved for some reason, the old identity cards of the kind issued by governmental organizations, the grocery lists, the telephone directories with their corners turned down, the two pairs of spectacles with no glass in their frames, and the pages taken from old calendars, I did not find that newspaper clipping. I was certainly doing something wrong. The newspaper article that I had cared for as for my own eyes had to be there somewhere. Perhaps it had fallen out of the drawer.

I straightened up, paying no attention to my dizziness, and removed the drawer entirely. I was not accustomed to seeing the bedside table, which had stood there for years, without its drawer. For a moment – how may I describe it? – it seemed to me that I was looking into the darkness of a mouth with missing teeth. I was a little frightened as my hand searched the darkness, but when it touched upon a piece of paper, my heart began to beat rapidly. Alas, it was a postcard. A postcard sent to me by Madam Nur from Canada, depicting several indigenous statues. In very small handwriting on the other side she had described at length the countries she had visited. She had written in such detail that there remained only the tiniest space for the address. At any other time it would have given me pleasure to read Madam Nur's postcard. But now I was in a hurry. I put the postcard on the bed; later, I would insert it into the mirror on the chest of drawers. Once more I passed my hand into the darkness of the bedside table, along its back, its top, the dusty sides. My flesh was pricked by a few splinters, but I paid no heed. However, it was all in vain. The page I was searching for was not there. I turned and this time emptied the drawers of the mirrored chest. I chanced upon many items – a tie that I had for some time been looking for, the missing half of a pair of socks – but I, your humble servant, was in no state to rejoice. The newspaper page that I valued so greatly was still missing.

For a time, I stood irresolute on the old kilim that covered the floor. If Mr Burak's interview was not in this room, then where was it? While cleaning the room, could I have placed it elsewhere? No, definitely not. When I cleaned, I did not touch it. In which case, where was it? The walls, the mirror, the wardrobe were spinning like a whirligig. I walked over to the bed with difficulty. The floor was sliding under my feet. I sat on the end of the bed. My head was roaring. An error, a great error, had occurred. I rubbed my temples with my hands. It was possible that I was having a nightmare. If I lay down and slept a little, when I woke up, hopefully Mr Burak's interview would be there alongside Madam Nur's postcard in the drawer where I had preserved it for seventeen years.

Under the spell of this idea, I lay down, and, although it was not my custom in the daytime, I closed my eyes. Upon closing them, I was drawn into the past. The bed was all but pulling me into the centre of the earth. In the middle of the bed a soft fissure had opened up and I myself had become like liquid and was flowing down into that fissure. I understood this to mean that death was paying me a visit. I became relaxed under the influence of certain sweet, long-forgotten feelings. Behind my closed eyes, a bright green colour made its appearance; the green of the needles of a spruce tree. And a woman's voice spoke thus: 'In nature, green is the colour which has the most tones.' Whose voice was that? A voice I had not heard in a very long time. It belonged to a tall lady, with water-green eyes. Her hair was uncovered, a hat was perched on top.

I remembered! I was very young. Mr Nuri was still alive. This lady would come to Madam Shirin's mother's mansion. She would give our little lady music and art instruction. She would take her on walks to improve the development of her lungs. Madam Shirin was rather delicate and was often ill.

They would include me in their forest walks. The lady teacher would raise her hatted head and look up at the tall trees. 'Look at the *bozger*,' she would say. Madam Shirin would giggle, and so would I, but I knew that *bozger* meant forest in the dialect that was spoken on our mountainsides. The lady teacher would show us the needles of the fir trees and the leaves of the oak, saying, 'Just look at the leaves of the *platanan* and the needles of the *akri*. Do they look alike?' We would lean over and look. The lady teacher always had paint smears on her fingers. When I touched the black resin seeping out from the trunks of the pine trees, she would slap my hands. 'Stop doing that, child! That's *pisar* glue – tar! You'll never get it off your skin.'

On my bed, I joined my hands over my stomach. A wind blew, bringing the smell of the wavy sea and the pines of our mountains, grazing my dry skin. I heard wild birds. Mama used to imitate bird calls very beautifully. It was as if I were falling deeper into the middle of the bed. This time the voice of my dear mama reached my ears. The word 'reached' is not appropriate, however. It was as if there was a rope stretched between my two ears and dear Mama's soul was seated there. She sounded so near. It was at that moment that I wondered if my spirit was being taken. Such an idea often comes to persons my age, and although I myself rarely contemplated death, at that time I was certain that death was paying me a visit.

For some reason, the scene of Madam Nur crying at the table appeared in front of my eyes. She was saying, 'I had an abortion, Sadik. I would have had a baby, but I killed it.'

Her voice merged with my mama's voice. 'There may not be babies in our story, Sadik, but it still needs telling. Tell our story, Sadikos. Tell it now. It is time Mr Burak wrote about it.'

'But I've lost it, Mama.'

The bed was swallowing me. Mama's voice was shaping the past.

'Sleep, my son. Sleep. Hush. The men of the gang were playing football, or *podosfero*, as we used to call it. I saw them through a crack in the door. I recognized them – they were Topal's men, acting out the orders of Topal Osman, militia commander. Our priest's head was being kicked from one end of the yard to the other, and the men were laughing. Our priest's head was bouncing off the rocks in the courtyard. Knock, knock. His eyes were open. Blue. I had hidden myself in the crypt and I was praying nonstop that they would not see me. But why should God, who did not protect the head of our priest, protect me?'

My feet were icy cold; I warmed them against Mama's legs. I was shaking with fear but could not stop myself from asking questions.

'And then what happened, Mama?'

'Nothing. Then I came here.'

'Did Mr Nuri save you from the armed gang, Mama?'

'Go to sleep now, son. Sleep.'

Mama stopped talking.

I myself never hid in a church crypt. I saw a priest, but no one was playing football with his head. Did I walk behind the women and the old people on that narrow path? I did, but Madam Shirin and the lady teacher were with me. They were walking in front of me. The past is confused in my head. The lady teacher was showing us leaves and orange blossom. She was talking, explaining. Then an eagle landed on a distant peak and she became absorbed in it. She stopped and looked, kept on looking. My little lady Shirin? Where was my little lady?

'My little lady Shirin, stop, wait, don't go! The teacher will be very angry. Little lady, don't climb that hill by yourself!'

'Come, Sadik, come.'

'No, little lady, you come down. I beg you. It is forbidden for us to go to the monastery. Strictly forbidden. Little lady! The monastery has been torn down, burnt, looted. Going there would be dangerous.'

'Come on, Sadik. Don't be frightened – come!'

I go. I climb up. 'Wait, little lady.' I am soaked in sweat. I am just a child. Small. I am gasping for breath. 'Where are you, little lady?'

'Shhh! Over here, Sadik. Over here. Don't make a sound. Come and hide behind me.'

'Little lady, what is that man doing?'

'Shhh! Be quiet, Sadik. That's not a man, that's a priest. See his black robe.'

'Little lady, what is the priest looking for? Why is he squatting on the ground? Is he digging the earth?'

'You stay here, Sadik. Don't come out from behind this column, do you understand?'

'Don't go, little lady! Don't leave me alone!'

'Shut up, Sadik. Shhh. You naughty boy, you'll reveal our hiding place. Why did you follow me anyway? Okay, hold my hand. We'll hide in this little niche. As soon as the priest bends over to dig again, we'll run. Do you understand? Don't make a sound. Nod if you understand. All right. Are you ready? If you freeze halfway, I'll beat you so severely when we get home, understand? Okay, one, two, three – run!'

We are running. The eagle is flying above us. I don't stop. We are running between the decapitated columns, from one grassy niche to the next. Gentle eyes follow us from beneath the soot on the scorched walls. We are surrounded by mountains and below us is a ravine. We are hiding. My hand is in my little lady Shirin's hand. I am still a child. She is my senior.

Are we in a crypt? No, we are in the ruins of the monastery. We are crouching down behind a column. There is no armed gang playing football with a priest's severed head; I never saw that. There is a priest, covered in dust and dirt. He is digging in the courtyard. Digging and digging, and finally... My little lady holds her breath. Without realizing it, she is squeezing my hand. Her cheeks are bright red and her blue eyes have grown so large, they take up her whole face. The end of her blonde plait is tickling my cheek. The priest has taken a painting with a silver frame from the hole he has dug. The little lady has forgotten we are hiding. She makes a small cry and takes a step out of the niche. This time it is I who pull her back by her skirt. She covers my mouth with her hand. The priest is crying at the place where he is kneeling. He is kissing the silver-framed picture and touching it to his forehead over and over again. And crying.

At that moment we notice that there are other men at the monastery. Above us, below us, everywhere. Gendarmes. I begin to cry. They are going to kill the priest. They will cut off his head and play football with it. They will laugh. I cannot stop crying. My little lady has her hand over my mouth. She presses harder. I cannot be silent. The priest is crying. I am crying.

'Shhh! Sadik, be quiet. Shut up, child!'

I cannot be silent. Sobs are gushing out, bursting from my throat. The priest must run. Right now. They will kill him.

My little lady does not know what to do. She kneels down and takes me in her arms. She has grown that year, but I am not that small and it is difficult for her. Still, she manages to run down the monastery path. I wrap my legs tightly around her waist to make myself less cumbersome. My nose is running and tears streak my cheeks. I am dirty. As my little lady runs down the hill, her chest rises and falls, her cheeks are flame red, locks of blonde hair fall over her forehead. My arms are black. I am ashamed to have them wrapped around her neck. I am sniffing continuously. The priest is pressing the silver icon to his bosom. He raises his head and looks at our high mountains. Run away, dear priest. They are going to kill you. My little lady is carrying me away from the monastery.

I was flowing into the centre of the earth through the fissure that had opened up in the middle of my bed. All my limbs were immersed in a holy basin. Only my head was free. I was a child. It seemed the soul was a child. When my head also flowed down the fissure, I would have surrendered to death. Madam Shirin took me in her arms at the centre of the earth. The autumn sun had turned her blonde locks ablaze.

Suddenly there was a great commotion. Doors were slammed. The bell on the garden gate rang. I heard my lady's voice. She was calling for me and banging her walking stick on the floor.

'My lady! Madam Shirin!'

Flinging death from my chest, I tried to stand up, but I could not control my body. I had fallen into a heavy, sticky substance. The teacher had warned me about this. 'It's tar, it's glue, it's *pisar*. You'll never get it off your hands.' I had been drawn into *pisar*.

I heard footsteps in the hallway. My lady's walking stick. I couldn't move my arm. If I screamed, would someone rescue me from this pit? Hear my screams! 'Madam Nur! Mr Burak! Miss Celine! Madam Shirin! I am here – me!' A sound like a moan filled my mouth. My lips did not move.

From far away there came an echo; from beyond our green mountains, whose peaks were eternally smoky, from the depths of our mad sea.

'Sadik! Sadik! Grab my hand.'

A hand touched my hand, a soft, slender hand.

'Dear Madam Suheyla, is it you? Is it you come to greet me on the other side?'

'Sadik, open your eyes! Do you hear me, Sadik? You're having a nightmare. Open your eyes!'

When my mind distinguished the owner of the voice, my body, together with all sensation, returned to me. Or I returned to my body. My bed disgorged me back into the world. My soul entered my body, found its bed and began again to flow. My eyes opened slightly. My arm was numb. My hand was still within Madam Shirin's.

Times were greatly confused in my head, the past ever cloudy.

24

Nur

When I left Burak's house, I decided I'd walk rather than take a taxi. From Kurtulus to Macka would take me about half an hour. I drew in a breath of cool air. It felt good. My ears and forehead were hot from the cognac. My brain must have short-circuited. Otherwise, what had I been doing in Burak's bed, with his hand between my legs? Burak knew how to arouse me and desire had scorched through my veins. In the arms of the man who loved me above all others, it was easy to focus on my own pleasure. There'd always been a strong sexual chemistry between us, since way back, but that didn't mean I was going to cheat on my husband of seven years. Burak knew that. He knew it, but he always tried to push his luck.

'This is why you came, isn't it?'

His bristly skin, his hot breath on my neck. He needed so much to hear that he was right, that I'd come with the intention of having sex with him. No, Burak, that was not why I came. It didn't even enter my mind that we would end up kissing and making love, that all of a sudden I would find myself underneath you. I should have told you that, but I just couldn't. I love you so much that I repeatedly lie in order to protect your feelings. I tell myself that you know the truth anyway, so I never disillusion you. I have never been able to love you the way you wanted me to, with passion, with desire. I've tried many times, but I've never managed it. I couldn't fall in love with a person who loves me more than I love myself.

No, I didn't go to your house to make love. I was going to tell you about a summer holiday long ago, something I'd never shared with anyone, something I'd struggled for years to forget. I was going to tell you how one sentence of Fikret's jumped up and hit me in the face. I was going to tell you how my mum committed suicide. I hadn't even told Ufuk. That's why I wanted cognac, to loosen my tongue. I didn't count on getting drunk.

Schools had just closed for the summer and we were still in our winter house in Macka. When I woke up, Sadik Usta and Fikret were in the kitchen. Fikret was eating breakfast at the table. The first summer winds were blowing in through the open window, Istanbul's intoxicating summer winds. I wanted to race outside immediately and go down to the water's edge, to the Bosphorus, to Bebek, to Hisar, or even to hop on a ferry and head up to Anadolu Kavagi. I couldn't get enough of early summer in the city. I needed to gorge myself on the blue of the sea, the smell of the fish in the nets, the gentle touch of the sun's rays in my eyes, on my skin, my nose. Istanbul was calling me.

Sadik Usta was putting steaks in the freezer and bagging up vegetables, fruit and salami. I didn't think anything of it at first. I was groggy. I'd been drinking wine late into the night with a friend from high school on the balcony of her house in Bebek, celebrating our having reached the last year of high school. University exams loomed like a giant mountain in front of us. Even though we were just starting the summer holidays, all our talk revolved around university preferences, points, preparatory lessons and private teachers. Let's have fun this summer, we said as we drank our way to the bottom of the wine bottle. When I got home, Fikret was asleep. I didn't go into the living room, just went to bed and stuffed cotton wool in my ears.

I slept with cotton wool in my ears all through those years, so that the rows that erupted at all hours between my mum and dad wouldn't wake me up. They fought that night after I got home, but I slept like a baby. Wine glasses were thrown against the wall, again. Shards of glass were scattered under the dining-room table and red wine had turned the champagne walls of the living room rose-coloured. The ashtrays on the coffee table were full to the brim. Sofa cushions littered the floor. I didn't care any more. I just glanced through the living-room door and headed for the kitchen. I was half asleep. Maybe that was why I didn't immediately register Sadik Usta's being in our kitchen as abnormal. Whereas actually he never usually come to our house. He was Grandmother's trusted servant, not ours, and he lived with her – in Moda during the winter and on the island in summer. They had migrated to the island the previous month, so his being at our house in Macka was a sign that this was an extraordinary situation.

'Good morning, Sadik Usta. How are you? Nothing wrong, I hope? When did you come?'

Sadik Usta closed the fridge door and with hurried movements opened the cupboard over the counter, took down a plate and placed it on the kitchen table across from Fikret. With a narrow-waisted tea glass in his hand, he walked to the stove to pour my tea.

'Sit down, Miss Nur. Have your breakfast.'

I sat down obediently in the place he had indicated. That was actually Mum's place at the kitchen table.

'Fikret, what's up? Where's Mum? Is she asleep?'

Fikret removed an olive stone from his mouth and placed it on the edge of his plate. I watched the small bite pass with difficulty down his thin, dry throat. He took a sip of tea. He'd eaten the crisp crusts of his bread but had left the soft white innards on his plate. I reached out and took them, then dipped them into the olive oil and oregano dressing that the sliced tomatoes were swimming in. My tea came. Some molasses and sesame paste had been mixed for me. As if having Sadik Usta at our house was the most natural thing in the world, I thanked him for preparing all my favourite things. Maybe Grandmother had sent him, I thought to myself. Maybe she'd said, 'You've looked after me long enough, Sadik. Go and help my daughter a little. Prepare my grandchildren's breakfast, make their beds in the morning, go to the market for them and buy some fish, some red mullet – Nur loves that. Fry it for lunch with a salad of fresh lettuce on the side.'

Might that have been how it went?

Unlikely.

I knew it.

'Fikret, where's Mum?'

He didn't answer. He couldn't. We were two children who'd sworn never to talk about Mum's drunkenness. Age-wise, we might have got beyond childhood, but on this subject our silence would go with us to our graves. Fikret threw a piece of cheese into his mouth. That too passed down his throat with difficulty. He screwed up his face. Gulp. Gulp. His Adam's apple moved up and down as if a green plum were stuck in his gullet. As darkness and deep silence descended on our spacious, airy kitchen with its window overlooking the palm trees and decorative pond of our well-tended courtyard, I realized I didn't really want to hear the answer to my question.

Sadik Usta brought my egg. He had peeled it and sprinkled it with salt and pepper, just the way I liked it. As he set the plate on the table with shaking hands, he blinked his bleary blue eyes.

'Your mother was taken ill last night, Miss Nur, and your father has driven her to hospital. It is not serious. God willing, she will return home today or tomorrow.'

Without saying anything, I began to spoon up my egg. I knew what was meant by Mum being taken ill. An alcoholic coma. Dad had driven her to hospital before. They put her on a drip and a few hours later sent her home. But Sadik Usta had never had to come to our house before. And we weren't children any longer; we often stayed at home by ourselves. I was sixteen and Fikret was at university.

When Sadik Usta went to clean up the living room, I looked at Fikret with questioning eyes. He cleared his throat.

'After you've finished your breakfast, pack a few things. We're going to the island. On the 2 p.m. ferry from Sirkeci.'

For a brief moment I was filled with happiness. We were going to Buyukada! Oh, how ready I was, even then, to forget my mother lying in the hospital. We were going to the island, which meant we wouldn't be going to the Aktur holiday resort in Bodrum. Hooray! The previous year we'd gone there for two weeks. We'd stayed in a white house with bougainvillea twined around the balcony. Mum loved it. The house was on a hill overlooking Bitez Bay and every day we watched surfers in their colourful outfits on the dark blue waters; they looked like exotic water birds. I was bored. I strummed my guitar on the balcony. The young people in the holiday complex all knew each other. They were summer friends who'd grown up together and not a single one of them wanted to get to know me. Maybe with my flat chest and skinny legs I seemed younger than I was and they thought I was just a child. I had brought Grandmother's four volumes of *Anna Karenina* with me, so I read that, and when Anna and Levin couldn't fill the emptiness inside me, I'd go and jump in the sea. I would swim from one beach to the next, rest a while on the rocks and swim back. When I was in the water, I was conscious of Mum's sad eyes gazing down at my burnt shoulders and puny hips. Once, a coquettish girl of about my age walked by our rented house and I heard Mum say to Dad, 'When will my daughter walk like that, I wonder.' She was disappointed that I wasn't flirtatious. Maybe she felt guilty that she hadn't taught me how.

When Mum wasn't being upset about my solitariness and childish awkwardness, she was having a good time. Since she didn't go in the sea, she spent her days at the bar, drinking gin and tonic and playing poker. Poker had been Mum's youthful passion. She'd learnt how to play at gatherings on Buyukada, where tables covered with green baize were set up in the gardens of friends' mansions and iced mint tea was served in pitchers. Fikret, meanwhile, was having the time of his life. He spent his nights in clubs like Halikarnas and Hadigari, and his days asleep. As for Dad, he sat by the fan in the living room, watching football on the little television set.

That year, we'd been planning to spend not just two weeks but the whole summer at Bodrum Aktur, far from Buyukada and my grandmother, something Mum had dreamt of doing for years. She believed that if we were outside Shirin Saka's realm of influence, Dad would spend the entire summer with us. At the beginning of every summer, she used to beg Dad to rent a house for the whole season, though he never did. But that year he had finally given in.

But now those plans had changed. If Sadik Usta was cleaning out the fridge, that meant we'd be closing up the Macka house. My happiness evaporated. Mum's condition had to be more serious than something a few hours on an intravenous drip in the emergency room could cure. I tried not to focus on the worst-case scenario. Everything would be all right on the island. I was a teenager, too wrapped up in myself to think about how distressing it would be for my mother to spend the whole summer under the same roof as her mother. I had friends at the Seferoglu Club. We'd play tennis in the midday heat, mess around in the pool, and I might even get asked to slow dance at the disco in the evenings. I'd grown a lot over the winter and I wasn't an ugly duckling any more. I hadn't turned into a swan exactly, but I wasn't awkward any more and my arms and legs had filled out. Maybe I'd get a boyfriend. I kept telling myself not to dwell on the negatives. Mum would get better. She always did. She'd stop drinking, again. Two months, three months. She'd be Suheyla Bulut again – courteous, friendly, as sweet as apricot nectar.

I'd walked as far as Kurtulus Street while I'd been thinking about all that, and the memories crashed into my heart like a violent wave. The shops had shut hours ago and the roads were empty. From the cheap nightclubs of Dolapdere dim lights fell onto the dark, narrow streets. The bouncers at the doors had ears so sharp they could hear the tapping of my sandals. As I passed the end of their streets, they turned and looked me over suspiciously, head to toe. I should have hailed a taxi at the Pangalti traffic lights. Istanbul at night was not safe for a woman on her own. It never had been, at any stage of my life, but there was now a new order of bully who knew how to bring a woman to her knees and they were present there, on those backstreets and on the main streets. My being out and about at night threatened their masculine power, their concept of what the social pecking order should be. I was trouble and they truly believed that teaching women like me a lesson would make society a happier place.

Just to defy them I turned towards Harbiye, hands in my pockets. A little beyond the Kenter Theatre, cars slowed down as they came alongside the pavements and rolled their windows halfway down. It was then that the transvestites came out of the shadowy doorways of the apartment blocks, exposing their lovely legs in tiny miniskirts. After sinister, hurried, anxious bargaining, they got into the cars. Their fees took into account, as they should have, the fact that almost all of them would end up getting killed. So many transvestites were murdered. For those self-appointed guardians of the social order, transvestites represented an even greater threat than I did. Even if they didn't do anything, their existence alone undermined the ruling power.

Dad's driver, Sukru, brought Mum to the island. Dad didn't come. He'd arranged an ambulance, which made its way to our house amid the horse-drawn carriages and bicycles. The garden gate was opened, the little bell rang, and Sukru and the ambulance driver picked Mum up and sat her in a wheelchair. I turned my head away immediately, but I had already caught sight of Mum. She looked like a bird. Her eye sockets were so sunken that I could have mistaken her for someone else. The whites of her eyes had turned yellow, her skin was greenish. Years later, when I was writing those articles about the hunger strikes in Istanbul, that scene in front of the garden gate came sharply to mind again. They didn't use the word 'died' for women who died in the resistance houses; they said 'extinguished'. Mum had been extinguished. Her soul was just about to fly away. Her eyes and skin were lifeless. In front of me was an empty bundle of bones, bereft of light or warmth.

But I could have endured that. I'd been eagerly looking forward to Mum leaving hospital and coming to the island. I was going to hug her. I was going to support her giving up drinking. We'd stop our horse-drawn carriage on the Grand Tour road and get out and pick the fruit of the strawberry tree like we used to when I was a child. We'd sit in Dilburnu Nature Park and breathe in the fresh air. I was grown up now. I could be her friend. I wouldn't let her feel lonely without Dad. I was ready to fill all her emptiness with my presence.

If the woman Sukru was pushing in the wheelchair had been my mother, I would have done all of those things. But the person I came eye to eye with in that brief moment was not my mother. Another soul had possessed the bag of bones my dear mum's body had become. This wasn't the peach-skinned mum who'd taken me to the children's theatre at the Ataturk Cultural Centre on Saturday mornings, who'd hugged and kissed me as we rode to Yoruk Ali Beach in a horse-drawn carriage. This sick woman was someone else and she didn't recognize me. With those thoughts in my head, I went out of the gate she'd just been wheeled through and made my way to St George's. I climbed the steep hill to the monastery and sat there all day, under the dome of the church, until evening prayers were over. Sadik Usta eventually found me there at nightfall.

Mum had cirrhosis. She was dying. Sadik Usta and Fikret had put her to bed in the room she had used as a young girl, on the top floor. She didn't want to see us, but on nights when I couldn't sleep, I'd slip into her room anyway. Mum slept in the brass-framed single bed with her face to the wall. In the moonlight filtering in around the edge of her curtain, I'd gaze at her long hair spread over her bare shoulders, at her backbone, visible beneath the light cover. What was it that made a person the being we knew and loved? Was it what they looked like, their voice, shared memories, a connection that both of you recognized and held dear? When one party severed that connection and discarded it, what happened to the love?

Hoping for a miracle, I would lift the covers and lie down beside her. Even her smell was different. I'd touch the mole on her back. When I was little and we used to lie side by side like that, she'd get me to scratch her back, everywhere except the mole right in the middle. Now the touch of that mole on my fingertip was my only evidence that this was my mother. I would fall asleep with my finger on the mole.

Towards morning she'd wake up and scream, and I'd jump up. She wanted a drink. She was swearing, crying, begging. As I backed out of the room, she'd start cursing – cursing my father for bringing her there and then leaving, cursing Sadik Usta, cursing life in general, but most of all cursing her mother. 'You whore, Shirin!' she would shout. 'You sold all of us! Soulless woman! Bitch! Impostor! Sadik, bring me gin! Nur, Fikret, children, bring me something to drink or I'll die.'

The summer passed like that. Grandmother never left her studio. She was painting like crazy. She'd have guests over in the evening and no matter how hot and humid the weather, she'd receive them in the alcove closest to the sea so that they couldn't hear Mum's shouting. Sadik took care of Mum. Fikret would escape to Istanbul, staying with Dad at our house in Macka. Knowing full well that it was forbidden, I'd go up to the pine forest. Bad things happened to young girls in the pine forest, but it couldn't be worse than what was happening at home. I didn't want to bump into my friends at the Seferoglu Club. They were the grandchildren of my grandmother's friends and their mothers had grown up with mine. At the green baize poker tables, Mum was gossiped about over the iced tea. A woman like Suheyla Bulut, famous across the island for her elegance and beauty, was now shut up in a room on the top floor, having fits and yelling, 'Bring me gin, you evil agents of God.' My friends would certainly have heard about it.

I was totally alone.

In the middle of August Mum got worse. There was a strong southerly wind and the island smelt of sewage and horse pee. The sea in front of our house was full of seaweed, jellyfish and rubbish. We were having breakfast in the dining room, Fikret, Grandmother and I. Because Grandmother had a headache, we weren't playing Albinoni. Fikret must have had a premonition. The night before he'd taken the late ferry from Bostanci and come to the island. Sadik Usta entered the dining room very agitated. He was stammering.

'Madam Shirin, Madam Suheyla is having convulsions. We should call Dr Kemal immediately.'

Fikret jumped to his feet and ran to the phone in the hall. Grandmother and I stayed seated at the breakfast table with the uneaten bread, the cheeses and the pistachio salami. Grandmother was grumbling to herself about Fikret, as if Mum's illness were his fault. More than my brother, she actually blamed Dad, and I have since come to understand why. My father seduced her daughter from her home, from her bright future. I don't know what bright future Shirin Saka had in mind for her daughter, but she couldn't accept that Suheyla had said yes to the first man she fell in love with in order to escape from her mother. As a child, I didn't understand that, but I could sense something. Hate. For Dad, and for Fikret as his son. It did not apply to me because I had come into the world as a girl, but I still had to breathe it in at the breakfast table. Maybe she felt like that about all men. Maybe, because of whatever her father did, she carried that anger inside and it extended to us.

I suddenly understood why Fikret had become obsessed with this great-grandfather. He wanted to find the reason for Shirin Hanim's anger. She had made him feel unwelcome ever since he was a child, a creature not wanted in her family, on the earth, in the universe. Even if what had happened to Mum wasn't Fikret's fault, it was the fault of men. Now Fikret was trying to lift this burden off his shoulders by uncovering the secret about our great-grandfather. Fikret's innocence would be proven and he would be forgiven. That was why he was so keen to unearth it.

I'm sick of feeling guilty all the time, Nur. Do you understand?

Oh, brother, I understood, but what a childish undertaking.

The day that the south wind hit the island was a turning point in our lives. Dr Kemal came down from Mum's bedside to the dining room. He sat the three of us across from him. His voice was cold, his face tense.

'Call her husband. She might not last until evening.'

Sadik Usta came in quietly and sat on a chair beside the door. He moved his lips as he sat there. We hadn't been able to reach Dad. Fikret, Sadik and I took turns at Mum's bedside. Sadik Usta used a cloth dipped in vinegar to bathe Mum's forehead and her ankles that had become as thick as wood. Dr Kemal spent that day with us. Grandmother shut herself in the library and did not come out the whole day. Mum's stomach had swollen like a drum, and the skin under her eyes was a dark purple. Her palms were red, her hands shook, and we couldn't understand what she said.

Then suddenly the weather changed. A violent wind beat the branches of the mimosa tree against the windows. Dust rose from the garden, the sea foamed and the sky went dark. I woke up from where I was napping on the kilim on the floor. Mum had opened her eyes and was looking at me. One of her hands was hanging off the bed. Our eyes met. Her gaze was like glass and my heart jumped. Was she dead? I turned to Sadik Usta, who was sitting at the foot of the bed with his eyes closed. The sound of that old lullaby came to me. I looked at Mum again, to be sure she was dead. She blinked. Then again. And again. The hand hanging down twitched. With my own eyes I saw a soul which was getting ready to leave its body make a sudden manoeuvre and return to its veins...

Then, in a whisper, 'Is it morning yet, Nur? Has the sun risen?'

Sadik Usta opened his eyes. Without moving he stared at Mum's hand reaching to touch my head. He stared and stared and stared. Then he covered his face with his dry, purple-veined hands and began to shake. Tears streamed down his wrinkled cheeks. It was the first time I'd seen him cry. I jumped to my feet, ran to the window and opened it. Wind filled the room. The mimosa rustled in my ears.

I yelled as loud as I could, 'Fikret! Come quick! Run! Run! Mum woke up. Run!'

Doors were slammed. There was the clatter of feet on the stairs. For the first time, Grandmother came into Mum's room, along with Dr Kemal. Behind them came Fikret, panting. Dr Kemal took Mum's temperature, looked into her eyes, at her tongue. From where we stood around the bed, we prepared ourselves for his judgement. He took some blood from Mum and filled a test tube. He felt her pulse, inspected her palms, pressed on her drum-like belly, listened to her chest. Then he straightened up and sat on the edge of the bed. We didn't move an inch. Grandmother was leaning on Sadik. We held our breath when finally Dr Kemal pushed back the hair falling onto his forehead.

Looking straight at Mum, he said, 'Suheyla, I was present when you were born and you are like my own child. I will not mince my words. You were on the brink of death and it is a miracle that your fever has abated and you have come through this.'

It was as if the room itself had been holding its breath. The brass-framed bed, the puffy pillows under Mum's head, the pink and blue rococo light fixture, the writing desk, and all of us family members lined up around the bed exhaled together. Dr Kemal must have seen the relief in our faces, our joy, for he raised his voice.

'Now, Suheyla, listen to me with the ears of your soul. If you ever drink again, there will be no saving you. Do you hear me, daughter? Your children are witnesses to my warning. Know that if you take so much as one drop of alcohol, your liver will fail completely and there will be no escaping death. Do you understand?'

Dr Kemal's serious, worried face.

Mum's eyes meeting the light.

Mum's body becoming my mum again.

'I am hungry, Dr Kemal. So hungry. Sadik Usta, is breakfast ready?'

Sadik Usta's agitated, veined hands wiping away his tears.

'Right away, Madam Suheyla. Right away.'

Just as I was about to turn into Valikonagi Street and go home, I turned around. I crossed the street again. I retraced the steps I had just taken, past the dark apartment entrances where the transvestites hid, past the dimly-lit signs on the cheap nightclubs guarded by burly bouncers, past the sleazy hotels. I got to Kurtulus Street. Fikret's words from earlier that evening, when I'd left home in a panic, echoed in my ears.

'Nur, don't you understand? Mum knew that if she drank even a single drop of alcohol, she would die. But she drank it anyway. She drank like crazy. That night she drank herself to death. Mum committed suicide, Nur.'

When I rang the bell to Burak's apartment, I realized that my cheeks were soaked with tears.

The door opened. I pressed the light button. No light. I walked up into the darkness.

25

Burak

We were in bed. We had long since passed the line of regret. I was holding Nur in my arms and we were naked. She was curled against my chest like a delicate-boned fish and as the wind blew through the open window of the back balcony it left goosebumps on her sweaty skin. She snuggled even closer into me. The place under my arm belonged to her. That bone and those muscles had been created solely to hold her body right there. It had always been like that.

When the doorbell rang for the second time, late at night, there stood before me a woman who knew what she wanted. Not a trace remained of the distracted hesitation of earlier. Slowly we undressed and stood naked in front of each other. We were not in a hurry. We had made the decision. We had crossed the line. I pulled back the bedspread and we got under the quilt. We were not like two shameless and hungry adolescents but like a husband and wife who slept together every night. I had my victory after all. I took her in my arms and beneath the dark of the quilt I passed my lips over her whole body, discovering once again the hidden places I had forgotten. She didn't try to direct me as she had in my youth.

I sensed that she was there for something more than sexual pleasure. She wanted a deep connection. In uniting with me she was hoping finally to fill the void. She gave herself to me.

As for me, I was as proud as a lion who'd laid his prey on the ground. While we made love, and later as I held her in my arms, my lungs were swollen with joy, like the gauze curtains puffed out by the wind. My muscles were pumped. Nur's tiny head was resting on the left side of my chest, right on my heart. As I stroked her short hair, her bare neck, desire rose within me again. I had climaxed just a short while before, but already I wanted her again. I wanted her, and I was going to take what I wanted. I was after pleasure. Simple, pure pleasure. I had longed for this body for years and now I was exuberant with the promise of its forbidden story. I was going to take it in my own time, as I wanted it, as much as I wanted. We were going to keep on making love, I knew it. We were going to make love until we dropped from exhaustion. Since we had crossed the line, we were going to stay on the other side until reality hit us in the face with the light of day.

I didn't care what story would be concocted for Ufuk. Anyway, it was clear something had already been made up, otherwise Ufuk would surely have called by now. Wouldn't a man worry if his wife wasn't home by then, or was he used to that? Did they have an open marriage? Did Nur phone him and say, 'Ufuk, dear, don't wait up for me this evening'? Inside me, jealousy stirred. No, impossible. In this country not even the most modern, most liberated woman could turn to her husband and tell him she would be spending the night in another man's bed. She couldn't say that and stay married. In lots of places in this country, she couldn't say that and stay alive. Ufuk wouldn't lift a finger against Nur, but still she would never say something like that. She wouldn't want the confrontation. She must have made up some excuse. Maybe she said she was going to the island. Even I knew she sometimes went to the island, shut herself up in Shirin Saka's house to finish ghostwriting a novel. Ufuk would believe her. He would choose to believe her.

So I relaxed. I passed my hand along her backbone. How thin it was. My beautiful, elegant lover. Years had only added to her beauty. I kissed her temple. It was sweaty. My heart ballooned with pride that I had made her sweat, had overcome her indifference. Her arms were entwined around my neck. The balcony door was open as we made love and she had tried to stifle her cries of pleasure by pressing her mouth against my shoulders, but moans and groans had leaked out. Sweat had gathered at her neck, her temples, her sacrum and now those places were softened by its sweet, cool moisture. I remembered the first time we'd made love, in a little tent in that remote valley. I hadn't been able to see her body in the dark. It was a moonless night and, outside the tent, waves were crashing on the sand. I got confused about where I should touch her. She had directed me with her hands, but after a while she gave up. I was ashamed of my incompetence. I was too hasty, too inexperienced. Still, she didn't run away. The next night she came back to me. And the night after that. She slept in my little tent every night until the day a storm burst over us and we gathered up the tents in a great hurry and took refuge in the village on top of the hill.

'What are you thinking about?'

'Nothing.'

'Your breathing changed. Something came to your mind for sure.'

She put her leg on top of my leg. Her hand grazed my cheek.

'That storm.'

'Mmm.'

'You know the one?'

'Of course I do.'

'Which one?'

Nur slipped out of my arms and stood up. Her skin gleamed like a pearl in the darkness. Wrapping herself in the red plaid blanket at the foot of the bed, she went out onto the balcony. I watched her through the gauze curtains as she collected up the bottles and glasses from the table. After she'd gone, I'd just left the balcony as it was. I was going to go to bed without even brushing my teeth. But then she came back. She came back to me! From the bed where I lay, I smiled.

'I enjoyed that storm. The rush, the running around, the way things changed from minute to minute. You and I were asleep in my tent. It had got light, but the sun hadn't risen. The air was ash-coloured, weird. Even the sea had lost that turquoise colour we'd got so used to. There was no safe, dry refuge for us; it was not a dream idyll any longer. What was humankind, I remember thinking, in the face of nature's power?'

She didn't answer. I reached out with one hand and tried to pull her towards me, but she didn't come, just continued to sit on the side of the bed. I wanted to believe that she too was thinking of that morning. More than that – I desperately needed to believe that she was. My euphoria of earlier had been erased. I was clinging on to memories.

Right before the storm, at daybreak, Onur had yanked open the zipper of my tent, making a great racket, and stuck his big head right inside, with zero concern for my privacy. I quickly tried to cover Nur's bare back with the edge of the sleeping bag. It was true that Onur had seen Nur coming out of my tent every morning, and he'd also seen her running into the sea in her skimpy, crocheted bikini, but there was a big difference between the bare back of a woman going swimming and the bare back of a woman who'd just been making love. The back might be the same, but the significance was not.

'Burak, mate, get up quick! A storm's about to break right over us. It's gone weirdly dark. Get up, Nur. Wake up the other girls. We've got to take down the tents right now. We'll go up to that village. Hurry! Wake up, man! The wind will pick up your tent and carry it out to sea with both of you in it!'

Nur jumped up as if she'd been thrown and ran to the big tent where the other three girls were staying. The waves had gone wild and the gentle valley which had held us to its breast for days had also gone crazy. The wind was bending the olive trees to right and left, leaves were flying, dust and sand were flying, everything was flying. It was impossible for me to take down my tent by myself. With Onur's help I pulled out the stakes and lowered the nylon, swollen like a balloon, then rolled it up with difficulty. We couldn't hear each other for the howling of the wind. Nur and her friends had taken down the big tent and the four of them were kneeling down, trying to roll it up. We'd made ourselves so at home on the empty beach, spreading our things all over the place, that in our haste to escape we had to leave behind the wine and tomatoes we'd suspended in the stream, as well as the coffee, salt and tinned food that the Bosphorus University girls had arranged so carefully in the rocky hollows. Nur hurriedly gathered up the camp stove and metal bowls. The clouds had descended and even the water at the mouth of the valley had turned into a foaming grey monster. The first wave crashed where I'd dismantled the tent that Nur and I had been sleeping in only a half-hour earlier and then raindrops the size of large grapes began falling from the sky, hitting our faces, our eyes.

'Leave everything where it is. We'll come back tomorrow and get our stuff. Grab your packs and let's go!'

We began to climb the steep hill in single file, Onur at the front, myself last, the girls in between. Nur was directly in front of me, and my eyes were on her huge backpack, to which she'd somehow managed to attach her tent. She was wearing a navy blue rainproof poncho that came down to her knees. All the BU girls were wearing raincoats actually. Onur and I, on the other hand, had set out on our adventure without remembering to bring things like salt, coffee, knives and forks, or raincoats. As we ascended the path to the village, jagged rocks on one side and a precipice on the other, we were shivering under the assault of hailstones hitting our heads like machine-gun fire. The city boys who had set off for an adventure in the wilds were being tested by the storm.

'Why are you smiling?'

Nur finally set her glass on the bedside table and lay down beside me, stretched out on her back with her arms crossed under her head. It was hard for me to let her be. I wanted to take her currant-like nipples into my mouth, but it wasn't the right time and she would have pushed me away. She was very sensitive about her nipples and wouldn't let them be touched until she was really aroused. I turned onto my back as well. Reflected lights were flickering across the ceiling, but I wasn't sure where from.

'I was thinking about the storm and us climbing up to the village on the hill and how Onur and I were so unprepared. You girls were like scouts, you'd come fully prepared. Raincoats, hats, waterproof boots.'

She didn't smile. She couldn't have forgotten. I continued.
'We were so inexperienced. Good thing they gave us
something suitable to wear in the village or we would have
got sick for sure. Our backpacks leaked too, if you remember.'

The scene at the village house we took shelter in came alive
in my memory. The elderly husband and wife set out food
for us and insisted that we spend the night there with them.
They brewed tea on the woodstove and cooked pancakes
with herbs and potatoes. The old man's name was Tevfik.
He brought Onur and me dry clothes, T-shirts and socks
belonging to their sons who'd left the village, and the old
woman brought out colourful handmade woollen slippers for
the girls. They'd taken off their raincoats and hung them on a
line tied between the stove and the couch, and our shoes were
lined up in the courtyard under an awning.

'Do you remember old Tevfik's house? That raki feast they
laid on for us? God, we drank so much!'

I pictured Nur smiling beside me. Old Tevfik turned out to
be a real night owl and his wife prepared the world's best raki
table. Our tongues and our tastebuds had shrivelled up after
a week of tinned beans and tuna. Tevfik's wife revived us with
stuffed zucchini flowers, broad-bean paste, various greens,
sardines, sausages, goat's cheese, water buffalo yogurt, and
pita bread baked in their outside oven. We all sat around the
low table on the floor and ate as if we'd come from a famine
area. We were young and always hungry and we'd got very
cold. Nur kept spreading butter on the hot bread and stuffing
it in her mouth. Rain was beating on the windows but the
woodstove was burning hot.

Tevfik kept filling our tea glasses with raki, and what great
raki it was! I don't know whether they made it themselves. My
head was spinning when I stood up to go to the bathroom.

I don't remember what time it was. I went outside, to the courtyard, and fresh air filled my lungs. The storm had calmed down. It was still cool, though, and the air smelt of wet earth and pine trees. A dark night had descended. Since the village had no electricity, we'd been using kerosene lamps, but down below on the beach it was dark, totally dark, and isolated. I had hidden my tent in a secluded place, along with my sleeping bag and mat. We'd go back down tomorrow. Onur and I were going to continue our holiday. Onur didn't use the word holiday – ours was an adventure. Man to man. The girls' classes were starting up again on Monday so they were taking the overnight bus back to Istanbul the following day. Thinking about that made my heart tighten. No, I couldn't leave Nur. I couldn't go back to that beach without Nur. The next day I would walk to the main road with Nur and her friends and then get on the bus with them. My tent and everything in it would stay with Onur. Onur would be angry with me for months afterwards, if not years.

The door behind me opened and Nur came out to the courtyard. We stood side by side looking up at the sky. The wind had scattered the clouds, completely cleansed the atmosphere of its hazy filth. Against the black background millions of stars twinkled in a sky that was more crowded than city people ever got to see. With her head tipped back, Nur blew cigarette smoke into the air. The sight of her silhouette in the darkness, her height, her elegant neck, drove me crazy again.

'Wow, look at that! There's not a single empty spot in the sky. The universe is completely full. And we think we're so damned important! Ha!'

I wanted to put my arm around her waist, draw her to me, kiss her, but I couldn't. We had made love every night of the past week, yes, but in the daytime, when Nur was with her friends, she kept her distance and didn't even let me hold her hand. I thought maybe she had another boyfriend. She would come to my tent at night, after everyone had gone to bed.

From the edge of the courtyard, Nur stared down at our beach and the valley squeezed between two steep hills. It was so far below us and looked tiny in the darkness. I was surprised that we could hear the waves crashing against the rocks. The storm was still raging out at sea.

'Man, how could we have stayed down there? It's so isolated. If a rowboat or a motorboat had come during the night, killers with knives could have sliced every one of us to death.'

I searched for an answer to that, something funny and flirty like, 'I'd protect you, baby.' Nur was a fan of humour magazines and I tried to remember a line from one of them, but nothing came to mind. I could have played up my background as a young roughneck raised in a fishing village – 'I didn't grow up in Macka like you did, missy' – but that probably wouldn't have gone down too well. I left the village when I was ten, grew up in Kurtulus, went to Istanbul Boys' High School. I didn't have any provincial roughneckness in me at all. I was a polite city boy, the son of a civil servant, a teacher, brought up without a father. In the ongoing silence Nur came closer to me. She was staggering slightly. With one eye on the window lit up by the yellow gas lamp, she tiptoed over and put her arms around my neck. She was still holding her cigarette and normally the smell of the smoke would have disgusted me, but at that moment I liked it. I hugged her waist.

'Burak.'

'Yes, darling.'

'Darling' just jumped out of my mouth. I waited for Nur's reaction.

'Burak, I… I'm really drunk. I think I'm going to throw up. Could you take me to the toilet, please.'

Did she not remember vomiting noisily in the wooden-doored toilet at the end of the courtyard? With great difficulty, I carried her to the bed Tevfik's wife had prepared on the floor and laid her down. She held on to my hand until she passed out. Mattresses had been spread out for the girls in the front room where the stove was, and Onur and I were given mattresses in the back room where Tevfik and his wife usually slept. I wondered where the elderly husband and wife slept that night. I didn't remember at all. In our youthful arrogance, we didn't even think about that.

As we were about to fall asleep under the cotton quilts in that small, dark room, Onur warned me about Nur and her gang, as if he knew I was going to go with them to Istanbul the next day. 'Bro, about these girls. Stay away from them, mate. Girls like that use blokes like you and me as if we were small change. I'm serious, man. Watch out!'

I opened my mouth to remind Nur of Onur's warning all those years ago. He'd been right, I was going to say, you've been using me for twenty-three years now, and you're not finished with me yet. But I decided not to say anything. What was the point of reproaching her? If she'd taken advantage of me, of my continuing love for her, hadn't I also gained by keeping her in my life? Had I ever asked her to get out of my life – had I ever even wanted to ask her to do that? Nothing could match the excitement of a night like tonight: the anticipation after so many years, the thrill of the possibility and then the wild joy and passion of the realization of that possibility. How many men could have that? If I'd married and had children, could my wife have given me the exhilaration and ecstasy I'd felt tonight? Definitely not. Even if the woman I'd married were Nur, she couldn't have given me that.

'Burak, do you realize this is the first time we've made love in this house?'

Nur had rolled onto her side and was looking at me. She was right. After Mum retired, she didn't leave the house much, and I wasn't the type to snatch any brief opportunity to sneak Nur in. And anyway there'd been many phases in our on–off relationship during which Nur had refused to sleep with me, when she was in love with someone else. In her youth Nur was totally monogamous. She wouldn't cheat on her boyfriends. When she had a serious boyfriend, she would still stop by our house and sit with Mum on the back balcony, eating cherries and crackers and drinking tea, and we'd still watch television together in the living room in the evening, taking the slices of apple Mum passed to her on the tip of a knife, but she wouldn't make love with me. So there had to be a very serious reason why she was now cheating on her husband. But I didn't want to think about that. It wasn't my problem and I wasn't going to make it mine. My sole concern was to make the most of this night of love and passion.

'Was this always your room? I mean, when you were a little boy, did you sleep in this room or did you move in here after you grew up?'

'No, it's always been mine, since we moved in. Why do you ask?'

She put a hand on my stomach and with her cool, slender fingers stroked the hairs around my belly button.

'Well, you know, this is the master bedroom. It's large, with a balcony, a wardrobe, a queen-sized bed, an ideal parents' bedroom. I'd have thought your mother would have taken this room for herself and given you the small one next to it.'

'Dad had already died by the time we moved here.'

'I know, but, well, your mum was a young woman back then. How old was she?'

'I don't know – thirty-two, thirty-three at most.'

She propped herself up on her elbow, turned her back and filled her glass with cognac. 'Thirty-two, thirty-three – what a shame to be a widow at that age. Do you know why she didn't marry again?'

I shrugged. 'Probably so that I wouldn't grow up with a stepfather.'

She turned to me, a teasing expression on her face. 'Do you think your mum ever slept with someone after your dad?'

'Of course not. What a question!'

She laughed and eyed me over the rim of her cognac glass. 'Oh, what a tetchy answer, Mr Burak! Are you jealous or something?'

I saw the twinkle in her eyes and felt angry. While I was trying to get her to relive the most meaningful memories of our youth together, her mind was clearly elsewhere.

'What are you saying, Nur? You're talking as if you didn't know my mother at all. She became like a grandmother before she was fifty. Her only entertainment was watching people from the back balcony.'

'Yes, but what about the years between thirty and fifty? You know that thirty-five is when we women peak, sexually, huh? Or forty, even.'

'You're being ridiculous. Mum was—'

'Okay, okay, don't get angry. You know best.'

She cuddled closer, settling her little head under my arm and clamping my legs under hers. She stroked my chest with her fingertips. I didn't respond. My libido had died. Was I upset – about my mother? Was I really one of those sons who was jealous of his mother? Could Mum have had lovers in that house while I was at school? She'd been very much in love with Dad. There was quite a big age difference, but she married him anyway, and the girl from Edirne with a degree in education left the city and moved to a little fishing village, just for him. She wouldn't have betrayed him. Why did I keep repeating that? Who was I trying to convince? Couldn't Mum have had a body full of life and desire like Nur? Why not? Because she wasn't like that. Crazy nonsense.

Nur changed the subject. 'One of your first ever interviews was with Sadik Usta, wasn't it?'

'Yeah.'

'What did he tell you?'

Her hand was moving now, making circles between my chest and my belly. I didn't feel like talking.

'I don't remember. It was a long time ago. At least fifteen years.'

'You don't remember anything at all?'

I took a deep breath. I'd been upset, but under Nur's hand my skin was waking up and my blood was pumping. I tried to speak in a calm voice.

'He kept talking about your grandmother – "Madam Shirin" this, "Madam Shirin" that. He didn't have a life apart from her. I tried really hard to get him to talk about himself.'

'And did you get anything out of him?'

'Not a word. He only talked about the house in Uskudar, its garden, Shirin Hanim's talent, her uncle, the house here, and so on.'

'What do you mean, "the house here"?'

'Apparently they used to live in your apartment in Macka.'

'How could that be?'

'That's what Sadik said. I was surprised too. I even made a note of it: "Macka since all the way back then."'

'Our Macka house was my father's. It has no connection to my mother's side of the family. Dad bought it when he married Mum, or maybe even before that.'

'I don't know. Maybe they lived in a different house in Macka. There used to be mansions there. He said they lived there.'

'Maybe. Anyway, that man is a closed jar of secrets. Think about it, he's spent his whole life loving Grandmother.'

'Where do you get that idea?'

'God, Burak! It's as clear as day, isn't it? I think Grandmother loves him too. What I wonder' – her hand had moved down between my legs and was stroking my penis, which had long since awakened – 'is whether they ever made love.'

With a sudden quick move, I flipped her over. She giggled. I lay on top of her.

'I see where your mind is.'

'I really do wonder about it.'

'Sure... Sure you do.'

I stroked the smooth skin of her inner thigh. Her tongue, her lips, held the tart sweetness of cognac. She was ready for me. A surge of joy rose within me again, wiping away my annoyance. She was mine. Until morning she was mine. The world could end tomorrow morning. The past, the future meant nothing to me. Nur was mine tonight.

26

Celine

Uncle Ufuk had come to Buyukada without a bag, but that was all right. Dad, Oguz and I kept some clothes at the island house, so maybe he did too. And I'd made such a scene, the poor man would have flown out of his house in a rush, with no time to pack anything. But when he said let's look at the motorboat timetable to see about a return ferry, I was very upset – panicky, even. What was happening to me, why was I acting like that? So what if my uncle left? Of course I knew what it was. It was as clear as day, but I just couldn't seem to admit it. Why had I called Uncle Ufuk all that way? Did I really and truly believe Dad had committed suicide? When I was on the phone to Uncle from St George's Hill, I did believe it. But now? Now I believed it a little bit. Or was I just an attention-seeking hysteric? Shit, that was a horrible thought. Even more horrible was the possibility that I'd called Uncle Ufuk so that he could rein in Aunt Nur. If he was busy with Aunt Nur, then Burak would be left to me. Yes, that was exactly what I was thinking. I was like one of those evil females in one of the soap operas.

Uncle Ufuk took a photo of the timetable hanging on the

door of the motorboat ticket office and turned to me. 'Boats leave for Bostanci until midnight, so that's fine. What do you want us to do now? Shall we start looking for your dad or should we sit somewhere and have a chat first?'

The normal thing to have done at that point would have been to have asked him why he wasn't staying the night. I mean, his wife was there, on the island, and tomorrow the family (plus Burak) would be celebrating Great-Granny's hundredth birthday. Why was he making plans to go back to Bostanci? But I couldn't ask him. Maybe something had happened that I didn't know about. For some reason I'm always embarrassed about showing that I don't know something, so I just nodded.

We started walking, not towards our house but in the opposite direction, towards the steep steps up to the club. Uncle Ufuk has long legs and he climbed the steps like a grasshopper. There wasn't a drop of sweat on the back of his off-white linen shirt. He was wearing lightweight tan trousers and soft suede shoes. Wise and honourable Ufuk Guney. I ran after him and was out of breath by the time we got to the top.

'Shall we have some tea here, Celine, and you can tell me everything, from the beginning. I'm curious.'

We were outside the Splendid Palace, the island's oldest, most fashionable hotel, with its white facade, red shutters and elegantly domed roof. I'd walked past it thousands of times, but it had never entered my mind to go in. It was like a forbidden garden for me, its staircase spread with a red carpet. There wasn't really a red carpet, of course, but that was the feeling it gave me. As soon as we went inside, we were in a different dimension. Outside was humid heat and the stink of horse pee; inside was cool, with an aroma of coffee. High ceilings, crystal chandeliers, smiling faces. Vivaldi.

One of the *Four Seasons* – 'Spring', I think – was playing. Welcome, come this way. Here, take the settee by the window if you like. Hushed voices, and a strong sense that though we might be on an island, standards should not be allowed to slip. I was ashamed of my cut-off cotton shorts, thin vest top and waterproof sandals. When I'd gone into Burak's room in the morning, I'd thought I looked really sexy, but now I wished I could wave a magic wand and find myself in a cream linen dress instead.

We went into a large and fabulous salon decorated with antique sofas, sideboards topped with ornate mirrors, stylish coffee tables and gilded armchairs. I edged around the perimeter like a crab until we reached the sofa Uncle Ufuk had indicated. The people sitting across from us, on the gilded sofa with matching table, and the ones perched on stools in front of the mirrored bar greeted us with nods. They didn't look at us for very long, but I could see question marks flashing in their eyes. Were we father and daughter, a man with a midlife crisis and his young lover, islanders or tourists? Definitely not day-trippers. Who were we? They analyzed us with their X-ray vision.

All of them were wearing ironed linen and pastel-coloured silk, as was to be expected. What was the word? Classy. I couldn't think of a better adjective to describe those people. If Uncle Ufuk hadn't been with me, they wouldn't for a minute have considered letting me in, I was sure of that. I'd seen myself in the gilt-framed mirror in the entrance. My cheeks were red from keeping up with Uncle and two lines of sweat ran from my temples to my neck. I was too suntanned as well. Being tanned isn't fashionable any more, it speaks of you not taking care of yourself, being coarse. We are in the era of porcelain skin, like Aunt Nur's. I felt like a different animal, like they were Siamese cats and I was a fisherman's huge mixed-breed.

Uncle Ufuk sat on the sofa, his leg crossed over his knee, and looked at me with a gently questioning expression on his long, thin face, in his calm green eyes. He never insists, just waits patiently. I was sitting on the edge of the chair. If they threw me out, I could get away fast. Our tea came. English Breakfast in a porcelain teapot, pink Chinese porcelain cups with gilt edges. Thin-waisted tea glasses were banished to beyond the hotel's red-carpeted entrance. We were in Europe now, Switzerland or somewhere. We were classy. I slid to one side of my fancy armchair and leant towards my uncle.

'Uncle... I mean Ufuk, don't get the wrong idea about how calm I seem. I am really super worried about Dad. You have no idea.'

He put his tea on the table and bent towards me.

'I'm listening. What happened? How did it happen? What's the story about that great-grandfather's suicide?'

I returned my cup to its saucer and acted as if I was thinking. Uncle Ufuk wouldn't be fooled. I was sure he was laughing at me under his beard and moustache. I raised my head and looked. No, he wasn't laughing. He wasn't laughing, but he was distracted. He wasn't interested in what I was going to say, in Dad, in that great-grandfather. Totally different things were going through his head. He was looking at me, but he wasn't seeing me. So I needed to start with the most dramatic story. I made my voice low and mysterious.

'So, Great-Granny's father shot himself, with a gun or a hunting rifle, I didn't quite understand which. Great-Granny was just a child, twelve years old, I think. They were having breakfast, sitting at the table. Tea was boiling in the samovar, and the man suddenly picked up his rifle and shot himself. Blood splattered all over the wall and never came off.'

Uncle Ufuk raised his eyebrows. 'Interesting. I've never heard that. Where did you learn about it?'

'Great-Granny told me herself. Today – this morning. We were in the library and then she dropped the bombshell. "My father shot himself." Those were her exact words.'

'Could she have been making it up, or hallucinating? Or maybe she'd been influenced by a book she read years ago or a story she heard. Wouldn't we have known about this suicide before now? When did you say it happened – did she mention the year?'

'No, she just kept repeating the same thing, like a parrot. Somebody called Servant Meryem was there. Then the man took his rifle off the wall, put it in his mouth and blew his brains out.'

Uncle Ufuk was jiggling his crossed leg. Then he scratched his head. I had got his attention! I felt it. Horses reared inside me. Bravo, Celine! You did it!

'We can actually figure out the year. If we know what was going on then, we can put it into context. How old was Shirin Hanim when she witnessed her father's suicide? Did you say twelve?'

When he asked that, I sat dumbfounded with my gilt-edged cup in my hand. Great-Granny was a child when she witnessed her father's suicide. Once, a long time ago, Great-Granny was a little girl who saw bits of her father's brain sprayed across the ceiling. Every time she sat down at that table, her eyes would get stuck on the bloodstains on the wall. They must have. The stain wouldn't come out. Shirin Saka grew into a woman who as a child had seen her father's brains splattered around the room. I was starting to understand Dad. Could a person who'd experienced a trauma like that as a child become a healthy adult? No way! Then that adult woman with a damaged soul had a child and raised her. A child named Suheyla. My namesake, the grandmother I never knew. Could that child's soul, psyche, be healthy? No, it couldn't. Suheyla was beautiful but depressed. How did I know that? Did I hear it from Sadik Usta, Aunt Nur? When I was little, people visiting Great-Granny – artists, intellectuals and all – would stroke my hair and say, 'But may the child not share her destiny.' Apparently, I looked a lot like the more grown-up Suheyla. I never let the adults know I'd heard their whispering, because I didn't want them to worry. I kept the upset to myself so that they wouldn't be upset at having upset the child. You see the burden on me! But, wait a minute, that was just the sort of burden Dad was talking about, wasn't it? It was passed all the way down to me from that great-grandfather. My God, Dad, I totally understand you now! You want to find out what happened with this great-grandfather so that you can get rid of the burden. Burden! Burden! Our burden is heavy and it's inside us. If we could find out why he shot himself...

'Where is your brain wandering to, Celine? Are you still trying to work out the year?'

'No, I was thinking...'

'Look, Shirin Hanim was born in 1917, so this event must have taken place in 1929. It was the beginning of the Great Depression in America. There were a lot of suicides on Wall Street then, but I doubt that your great-grandfather's suicide had anything to do with that. If we think about Turkey's economic situation in 1929... Where were they living then? In Uskudar? There was a mansion in Uskudar that Shirin Hanim mentions from time to time, am I right?'

I shrugged. What was the relevance of the time and the place? There was a twelve-year-old girl who saw the blood from her father's brains emptied out all over the wall. And then she raised a daughter, who had a son, my father, and a daughter, my aunt. And, last of all, Oguz and me. None of us were happy. Dad was right. There was a curse hanging over us like a cloud. I got my phone out and called him. I was going to tell him that I understood him, that he should come back and we'd find out about the curse together. That he wasn't on his own, that I felt the same way he did, that it was in all of us. I was going to say all that, but all I got instead was, 'The person you are calling cannot be reached.'

'I still can't reach Dad, Uncle.'

'Okay, don't you worry, we'll find him. I'm going to stay with you until we hear from Fikret. Are we agreed?'

I nodded. I had a lump in my throat. I took a sip of my tea. It was cold. Uncle Ufuk straightened up, slid to the end of the sofa nearest to me, reached out and held my hand. The lump was killing my throat. His hand was cool. I looked at his long, slender fingers covering my suntanned, thick-boned hand.

'Look, Celine, sweetie, I'll say this much. The story of your father's suicide is inconsistent from top to bottom, don't you agree? There's no letter anywhere, no suicide plan. Neither you, nor I, nor Nur has ever heard a word from your father about him wanting to kill himself. Are we agreed so far?'

Uncle Ufuk was speaking quietly, enunciating every word. His voice, like his hand, was cool. I felt like a soothing balm was being spread on an aching wound inside me.

'It's clear that you were affected by Shirin Hanim's sudden outburst. We don't know how much truth there is in her suicide story, but we'll look into it and find out. That's no problem. But it's only in your head that this is connected to your father having gone missing for a few hours. This shows that you are anxious. That your thoughts choose to focus on the worst possible scenario makes me think that you're under a lot of stress. Come, tell me, is there something else that's bothering you?'

I squirmed uncomfortably in the elegant armchair. What could I say now? Uncle Ufuk, I've fallen in love, deeply in love, head over heels, more than ever in my life. The ones I told you about before, they were just child's play. Now for the first time I want a real man, but he doesn't care a fig about me. If I can't be his, I will fall into a pit of despair and be lost forever. I want him like crazy. Whereas up until yesterday, it hadn't even crossed my mind, now it's like he's the only one in the whole world who understands me. It's ridiculous.

'Yes? Celine? Lift your head and look at me.'

'Umm...'

'Honey, is there something you want to tell me?'

My eyes filled. I can't tell you, Uncle. Because of whatever's going on between you and my aunt, I can't pour out what's inside me. Why aren't you coming home tonight? Why aren't you talking to Aunt Nur? If you tell me that, I'll open my heart to you. Otherwise, I'll just stay clammed up like a prisoner.

I shook my head. My voice came out hoarse.

'There's nothing else, Uncle Ufuk. Everything was fine until this morning. Then Dad went missing. Maybe you're right, I don't know, maybe I am making a mountain out of a molehill, but I have this bad feeling inside...'

Tears poured down my cheeks and dripped into the gilt-edged teacup, mixing with the English Breakfast. Oh shit, this was bad. My nose was running too. They hadn't brought a napkin. They had brought one, but it was beige linen. I wasn't about to blow my nose on that. I didn't raise my head.

Uncle Ufuk stood up.

'Come on, let's go and have a look at the places your father might have gone to. Have a think a minute – if Fikret wanted some quiet time on this island, where would he go?'

While he was paying the bill, I ran to the ladies. I turned on the gold-plated taps, splashed water on my face and blew my nose. My eyelashes were wet, my nose and eyes were red. I couldn't hide that I'd been crying, but I could still act like I hadn't been. And Ufuk would pretend he hadn't seen anything. My emotional turbulence would be like a third person walking with us. We'd pretend it wasn't there. We'd drag it along behind us. Our burden. My burden.

We came out of the Splendid Palace Hotel, turned left towards the Nizam neighbourhood, in the opposite direction of our house, and walked along the quiet, shady street behind the Anatolian Club. From the other side of the high wall we could hear the sound of happy children in the club's playground.

'Where shall we go, Celine? If we walk straight up from here, there's the pine forest. If we keep walking down Cankaya Street, we could look at the picnic area in Dilburnu. Lovers' Café is possible, but somehow I imagine your father in a quiet, calm, forested place. Somewhere on the Grand Tour road or in the tea garden at Viranbag? Or has he made his way down to the bottom of a steep hill and is right now swimming off a beach unsullied by other humans?'

'Let's go up to the pine forest. We can look around Hristos Hill. Dad loves the monastery up there. If he isn't there, we can come back on the Dil side.'

'Sure. You lead – you're the island native.'

Pink clouds passed over us. It was getting towards evening. Finally. What a long day it had been. At the top of the hill we turned left, where the forest started. In the bay below, where the gold-sparkling sea met the green of the forest, there were grand mansions with yachts and motorboats moored out front and gardens with pools in which red fish swam.

'Ufuk, do you think Dad might have gone to stay by himself in a bed and breakfast on a nearby island – on Heybeliada or Burgazada, say?'

'It's possible, of course, but he'd find it hard to get a room during this holiday period if he hadn't reserved one earlier, and if he'd booked ahead, why would he choose Shirin Hanim's hundredth birthday celebration? What made you think of that?'

'No reason. I just thought... Seeing Heybeliada across from us...'

The houses stopped. Now it was just pine trees to the left and right. There were young people all around us: the guys were focused on finding somewhere private so they could kiss the girls, and the girls were focused on how to keep the guys interested without going all the way. We just needed to get past them. We got past. They were walking slowly, getting on and off the outdoor exercise machines scattered alongside the path, shoving into each other, yelling to each other, saying we're tired, let's sit down here, then pinching and punching each other. Ufuk and I were quick, like a European couple, and passed them with athletic strides.

Uncle Ufuk kept his eyes on the ground while he walked. Pine needles made a crackling sound under his soft suede shoes and the air smelt of hot pinecones. The reddish-gold light filtering through the trees was really beautiful. If he'd

289

looked up, he would have got some glimpses of the sea, but he didn't lift his head.

'Celine, I want to ask you something. Does Nur ever mention me?'

I stopped. The sun was streaming through a gap between the trees, dazzling me. I used my hand to shield my eyes and tried to see Uncle Ufuk's face.

'What do you mean? I don't understand.'

'I mean, has she ever said anything to you about marriage, our marriage?'

I couldn't believe my ears. The great Ufuk was asking me, Celine, like teenage boys did about girls they liked! Stop the world! Make a note of this important moment: Ufuk Guney needed Celine!

He took off suddenly and I had to run to catch up with him. He spoke again without slowing down.

'Anyway, forget about that for now. Let's look for your dad for a bit. It seems to me we might find him up on that hill, meditating in front of the view.'

Come on, Ufuk, you can't fool me that easily. Really quickly, I tried to think of something my aunt had said about Uncle Ufuk, but I couldn't think of a single thing. My joy faded. I'd lost my advantage. The forest road came to an end and we turned left, up the paved road. A horse-drawn carriage passed us, and another one behind it. The old, abandoned Greek orphanage appeared in front of us, in all its grandeur, with all its ghosts. Whenever I passed it, I always felt like I was being followed by the ghosts of little orphan children with shaved heads and crazy looks in their eyes. They would be in my dreams that night, for sure. I looked the other way. Uncle Ufuk seemed sad. I had to think of something to make him happy. Aunt Nur had definitely said some nice things about her husband, I just couldn't remember them. If a person had such a sweet, cool husband, she'd talk about him, wouldn't she? My stupid brain just hadn't registered it.

'You know, Celine, Nur is a very lonely woman.'

Did I know that? Well, yes, when I thought about it...

'These last few years, she's distanced herself from her old friends, cut herself off. She really likes it that you've grown up and can be a friend now. That's why I thought she might have confided in you.'

I felt my cheeks getting red. A smile I couldn't stop spread over my face.

'Think about it. The only people she's close to are you and me. And Burak.'

When I heard that, I stopped dead in my tracks. Ufuk didn't notice. The monastery came into view at the top of the hill. Its tiled arches were caught in the light of the setting sun and the purple morning glories poking through the slats of the green shutters on the upstairs windows were in full bloom. Aunt Nur was a lonely woman, with nobody else but me in her life – and Burak. That was all! Aunt Nur was lonely and Burak was her friend. Since Uncle Ufuk could say that so casually, it meant Burak was a genuine friend of my aunt's. Like a brother. Best friends forever. He was her BFF. Of course! What a crazy imagination I had!

Suddenly I felt as light as a bird. I ran to catch up with Ufuk in front of the monastery. The sun was sinking down behind Heybeliada like a ball of fire. My excitement caught at my throat. I climbed the monastery steps and sat down. The bricks were warm. The warmth spread to the backs of my legs and little stones pricked my skin. I laughed like a crazy person.

'Ufuk, I've fallen in love.'

Uncle Ufuk took his eyes off the scenery and turned towards me. On his face was a surprised smile. He was so cute. I waggled my feet in a spoilt sort of way.

'Well, I never. Look at you! So all of this was just love's caprices, eh?'

'I don't know. Maybe.' Again, the same laugh from me. I was sort of mad at myself, but what the hell.

'Who's the lucky man?'

Ufuk came and sat beside me. Half of the sun had disappeared behind Heybeliada's green hilltops, but it was still very large and very red. As it dropped colourfully into the sea, it was painting the sky and the clouds pink. The crazy combination of colours and light was like a carnival. Yes, this evening was exactly like a carnival, a rave, a crazy parade of sensations, colours and emotions both inside me and all around me. My spirits, which had been on a rollercoaster since the morning, had now found peace. I was feeling peace and joy at the same time. I was in love. Totally. And when a woman is in love...

And when a woman is in love... Aunt Nur's voice in my ear. A day, years ago, when I was still in high school. We were driving to one of Istanbul's northern beaches, to Kilyos, in Aunt Nur's little maroon car. It was spring, the weather was crazy beautiful and the trees were full of pink and white blossom. Cigarette smoke was blowing back at me through the car window. I liked it. Alanis Morissette was on the car stereo and Aunt Nur was singing along. She'd just bought the stereo and was boasting that it could play CDs. Whenever we parked up, she would take the whole thing out and carry it with her so it wouldn't get stolen. I thought that was hilarious. We came round a bend and there in front of us was the endless blue of the Black Sea. We were in a globe of water and in the distance the dunes shone like gold. Aunt Nur was talking without taking her eyes off the road. She was describing what it was like to be a woman in love, how love was an altered state of mind, how you didn't feel like you any more because you saw yourself through the eyes of the person who loved you, which made you beautiful. You were a being that was loved. Aunt Nur had just fallen in love with Uncle Ufuk back then.

I looked at Uncle Ufuk out of the corner of my eye. Should I tell him that story? He was gazing at the view, expressionless, just like Jesus. His silence made me sort of uncomfortable. Had I said something wrong? Had I made him angry? I should have made up some love story to please him. We sat side by side on the old monastery wall without saying a word while the green hills of Heybeliada swallowed the blood-red sun and the pink sky began to fade. Eventually, Uncle Ufuk got down from the wall, brushed the pine needles off his trousers and reached out his hand.

'Come on, let's go home, Celine. Maybe your dad's waiting for us there. Shall we go home and surprise everyone?'

I should have been overjoyed to hear that. Uncle Ufuk was coming home, he was going to be with us. But for some reason I wasn't. Wasn't overjoyed, I mean.

Still, I took the hand he was proffering and jumped down from the wall.

27

Nur

We were in the dining room. Burak was sitting at the table, his face turned towards the door. I was on my feet, restless. The window was open but only heat and humidity were coming in, along with the hooting of the ferry and the beehive buzz of holidaymakers filling up the island. Inside, the house was cool and quiet. Time had slowed, reminding me of afternoon naptime when I was a child. The hardwood floors were hot, even the mosquitoes were lazy.

I walked over to the sideboard, bent down and pulled open its sliding door. Leaning into the familiar sound and smell of the furniture, I took out a jar of pistachio nuts, filled a bowl with a couple of handfuls and placed it between Burak and myself. He didn't eat any. He was gazing at me. Tiny little shadows were falling onto the wooden floor through the branches of the mimosa tree; black dots on the move. Burak was staring at me like a lovelorn idiot – I'd always hated it when he looked at me like that. Could he not find another expression?

I cracked opened a shell with my teeth. He immediately went on the attack.

'Don't use your teeth! You'll break one.'

I licked the salt from my lips and said, 'I got an abortion last week, Burak.'

My eyes were on his face, watching the stupid lovestruck expression explode into pieces. The shadows on his face changed place. I could read the thoughts going through his mind from the lines on his forehead. 'Abortion' was such a ridiculous word and 'I got an abortion' was even more ridiculous. It sounded like 'I got a promotion'. Or 'lotion'.

Ask the question, Burak! That question. What are you waiting for? Okay, I'll say it then. It was yours. I aborted your baby. I got pregnant that night. We didn't think about protection, did we? Whereas when we were young, we were so careful. No, I couldn't say it. Ask, Burak! Was it mine? Are you sure? Don't let the questions we presume we know the answers to hang like storm clouds between us. Let's have it out.

Damn it! My eyes were filling up again. Fast-flowing tears were overflowing from my nose, my eyes. I looked for a napkin. None. Sadik Usta had cleared the table, hadn't left so much as a crumb. Or a napkin. I fumbled in my pocket. Where was Sadik Usta's white handkerchief with blue stripes?

Burak was sitting like a statue across from me, his face as white as chalk. He understood. Otherwise he would have got up and held me in his arms. He wouldn't have left me crying there by myself. Tears were streaming down my cheeks and dripping off my chin onto my chest through the open neck of my kimono. Pistachio shells pricked my palm from where I was squeezing them in my hand.

'Burak...'

He got up and walked to the window, his hands in his pockets. Did I really have to tell him? So many things sank to the bottom of the ocean and stayed there. People lived right alongside such things – couldn't I have done that? Was it really necessary to have revealed all?

'Do you always have to behave like this, Nur?'

His back was turned. He was looking out the window. If we were in a movie, I'd have got up, walked to his side with my kimono billowing behind me, put my arms around his waist and leant my wet cheek against his shoulder. Without speaking, we'd have gazed out at the trees in the garden, the seaweed-encrusted well cover, the rotten mulberries on the ground, the bees whirling up and down. Whereas I didn't move, just continued to sit at the antique table left to us by the former Italian owner, cracking open pistachio nuts with my teeth.

Burak had grabbed hold of the dusty grey gauze curtain with one hand. I had a hard time hearing him because he was mumbling.

'Do you always have to make all the decisions by yourself? This... something like this... a huge decision like this... Couldn't you have consulted me? Couldn't we have thought it through together?'

I pictured that scenario for a moment. What if, instead of going to the clinic as soon as I realized I was pregnant, I had called him – Burak, I'm pregnant... Yes, it's yours... Yes, that night – then what would we have done? Would we have discussed having the child and raising it? What about Ufuk? Would we have put the child in Ufuk's name? Or Burak's? Would I have divorced Ufuk? Or would Ufuk have assumed the fatherhood of a child sired by Burak? Would Ufuk, who wanted a child with all his heart, who had for the past two years become more and more insistent that we do something about it, have jumped up and down with joy if I had gone to him and said I'd slept with Burak and fallen pregnant? Was that what we'd have talked about, Burak? No, of course not. Everything would have been clear-cut for Burak. Ufuk and I would get divorced, then I would marry him and we would raise our child together. A happy ending.

Taking a pack of tobacco out of my pocket, I began to roll a cigarette. I rolled it carefully, tightly, as I always did, and closed it with a lick of my tongue. I couldn't light it. Burak turned towards me. His face was a mess. I was sorry. I thought of Ufuk. When the snake-eyed doctor got her big-mouthed assistant to call our home phone and open with the words, 'Your wife's abortion', his face must have crumpled in the same way. She wouldn't have said 'abortion', she would have said 'procedure'. 'Your wife's procedure.' God, Ufuk, it makes my heart bleed to think of hurting you. All because of that snake-eyed woman's tricks. She realized I'd signed the 'permission from husband' form at a fast-food place nearby and she wanted to abjure herself of any legal responsibility. What a bitch! She took the form I'd signed but then quietly, politely, once I'd told her I'd be paying cash, in euros, took her revenge. Why did she call Ufuk once it was done? Did she not pocket the money herself?

'You, Nur... You! You... Damn it! Did you have to? Huh?'

Burak was gripping the back of the chair so tightly, his knuckles were white. For a moment I wondered if he was going to pick it up and smash it on the floor. The Thonet chair that Shirin Saka had brought from Vienna would be splintered into pieces. There was so much rage in his voice, rage that could only be satisfied by smashing something to bits. Anger radiated out not only from his face, but from his whole body, his skin. A strange smell that I didn't recognize was coming from his pores. It was as if his anger at my not being able to fall in love with him had been building in him all these years, and now... and now he was going to tear apart not the chair, but me. I was frightened. Would he? Was he blind with fury? He was looking at me like a mad person. Yes, Nur, you finally drove the man crazy. You toyed with him like a cat with a mouse. You made sure his relationships never went smoothly. When it looked like he was going to fall in love with someone, you came between them, flirting, being coy. You changed his mind; you scared off his girlfriends. If he were take his revenge on you now, would that be so much of a surprise?

But Burak didn't go crazy. He wouldn't allow himself to. He didn't have that macho anger. Burak was a boy who from a very young age lived alone with his mother in the big city they moved to. He would always be that boy. He didn't assault women, he protected them. He very quickly let go of the chair he'd been holding so tightly and put his head in his hands. Speaking from that position, his voice was hoarse.

'Does Ufuk know?'

I didn't answer. I looked at the fingers he was raking through his curly hair. Looked and thought. Thought about what I hadn't allowed myself to think about until then. Who would our child have looked like? Him or me? Was it a boy or a girl? At the time, I didn't want to find out, but now I wondered. Would it have had Burak's curls, or my stiff, straight hair, or was it a beautiful honey-coloured little girl like my mother? Was it murder? If Mum had aborted me, wouldn't that have counted as murder? I wouldn't have existed. I had made a person become nothing. No, I had made the possibility of a person become nothing. Burak was right. It was a serious decision that I shouldn't have made alone.

Somebody should have been with me. I wasn't strong enough to carry that burden all by myself. Nobody was.

Burak lifted his head. His eyes were red.

'Nur, how much does Ufuk know?'

In the mirror, as I walked to the sideboard to fill my glass with cognac, I noticed my face had become smaller. Shadows had filled the spaces where my cheeks had sunk. I pushed the 'play' button of the CD player. Albinoni began. First came the pipe organ, and then the double bass, like the beating of a heart. It was too early to hear a heartbeat, the ultrasound technician had said. I don't know why she was in that room. Maybe it never would have beat. The organ, the violin, the cello. I closed my eyes. Mum. Mum loved that piece. I never managed to be a mother, Mum. Rise up in me, Mum. You should have been with me when I went through that. You were the only one I wanted. You could have held my hand. You shouldn't have left so early, Mummy. Nobody has taken your place.

'Nur!'

'Um?'

'How much does Ufuk know?'

Men! Their biggest concern was always themselves. Life was one big pissing contest. I drank down my cognac. I wasn't going to refill it just yet. I set my glass down on the sideboard, walked back to the table and, standing there, lit my cigarette. Out of habit, I snapped my Zippo shut and held it tight in my palm. As I took my first puff, I wondered whether I was addicted to the smell of the Zippo's gas or to the tobacco. Cigarette smoke squeezed my lungs.

'He doesn't know I slept with you, if that's what you're asking.'

He would for sure have been mad at my having put it like

that. I should have said 'made love with you'. The unsaid sentence hovered like a ghost between us. It was there on the table, we were circling it. No, Burak, Ufuk does not know the baby was yours. Ask, Burak! You got me pregnant. Ufuk has been trying for a year and somehow it never happened. You, on the other hand, hit the target with one shot. Bravo, Burak. Now, instinctively, I should find you more attractive, right? But it isn't like that, Burak. Ufuk left me, he's gone. They called from the clinic and told him that his wife had had an abortion. She underwent a procedure. How could you not know? You signed the permission form. I'll fax it to you, of course. Ufuk's been gone ever since. And I miss him, Burak. Him. Not you.

'And you didn't tell him, did you? He found out afterwards. That's why he isn't here now.'

Now that's what I'd call a good investigative journalist. The music stopped. So soon! I pushed the 'play' button again. While I was at the sideboard, I poured myself a second glass of cognac and walked to the window. The garden was full of shadows. A light breeze had picked up and I bared my neck to it. Maybe the weather would cool down now. I breathed in the smell of rotten leaves, seaweed, sewage, the south wind and the shrieking of seagulls. You couldn't see the sea from that side of the house, but its sounds came, its coolness came. I wanted to swim. My throat and stomach were burning. What were Burak and I doing in that room? We were playing the roles of two adults. We said the necessary words on cue, were silent when silence was required, felt the pain we were supposed to feel. Even our wounds were where they were supposed to be. Come, let's go down to the jetty and swim. Let's swim way out, let's lie on our backs and look at the sky and let our arms and legs touch in the salty sea. Let them mingle softly, unhurriedly, like seaweed. Like in the past. Like those mornings when we first met and we ran into the sea from that beach at the mouth of that remote valley.

Burak was beside me. We stood side by side in front of the open window. I was holding a glass of cognac, a foolish choice in that heat, of course, but Mum... Albinoni and Mum. Mum, me and my daughter. It would definitely have been a girl. Maybe if it had been a boy, I wouldn't have been so scared. But I wouldn't have been able to form a bond with my daughter. I would have been defeated, because none of us have formed bonds with each other. Fikret was looking in the wrong place for the curse hanging over us. It wasn't with this great-grandfather. He should have been looking at the mother who abandoned Shirin Saka. Grandmother was just a little girl then. Her father had died and her mother sent the little girl off to someone called Uncle Nevzat, who had who knows what in the back of his mind. Yesterday at the breakfast table Grandmother had described a childhood deprived of love. The story Fikret was looking for was right there under our noses. This was a family tragedy of disconnection that reproduced itself through the generations. Maybe without realizing it, I had terminated the tragedy.

I drew close to Burak. Our arms were touching now. Put your arm around my waist, pull me to you, Burak. Protect me, watch out for me. Reassure me that when I'm with you, nothing bad can happen, that I am not alone, and I will rest my head on your chest. If I gave myself to Burak, would that mean an end to all the struggling, an end to having to repeatedly explain or risk being misunderstood, an end to finding solutions all by myself? Would it be like when I lay on my back in the sea? Would it?

Burak moved his arm away. Turning to the table, he picked

up his phone, earphones and notebook and stuffed them into his trouser pockets. I watched him fearfully.

'I'm going out to get some air, Nur.'

'I'll come too. We can get something to eat at Viranbag.'

'No, I want to go by myself, gather my thoughts.'

He reached for the door. I moved swiftly to his side. I missed Ufuk very much, yes, but I couldn't bear for Burak to go. I don't know, maybe I'd had too much to drink. I had turned into one of those women who knew what they didn't want but not what they did want. I didn't want him to leave me. I held the hand that was turning the key. He didn't stop. He opened the door, went out into the hallway and from there into the garden. I ran after him barefoot. Stones bruised the soles of my feet. As he was opening the garden gate, I grabbed his arm and twisted it, forcing him to look me in the face. He turned his eyes away. Talking to his shoulder, I murmured, 'Burak, please... Burak, I am so sorry. I beg you. Please don't leave me now. Please. I'm so sorry for everything.'

He didn't answer. He pulled his shoulder free and left. Sadik's bell jangled as the gate shut behind him.

28

Sadik

I opened my eyes a little. What time was it? Had dusk fallen? No, light was still coming through my small window. But it was as if it were evening already, for familiar objects had changed position, grown larger. There was no one holding my hand any more, although I thought there had been earlier. Yes, I was alone in my room now.

I sat up in bed. For how long had I slept? I looked at the clock tick-tocking beside my head. My eyes could not distinguish anything. Could it be that I had died? Death had come. Was it a dream – the dear priest and that little hand holding my hand? Outside my door I heard tapping. Madam Shirin's cane. I made an effort to get to my feet, but my head was spinning. I was swaying. I needed to sit a short while longer. When my eyes began adjusting to the light, I discerned my lady's silhouette in the hall. My door must have been left ajar. In the light seeping in, an angel with white hair and twinkling blue eyes was looking at me. Or was I still in my dream? When I lifted my head again, Madam Shirin was not there. The bell on the garden gate was ringing. I recalled that I had heard it earlier. It was possible that it was not a hand but the noise of the bell that had pulled me from the dark pit of that subterranean world. My clothes were in a miserable state. I brushed down my shirt, trying to smooth its wrinkles with my hand, and ran my fingers through the two strands of hair that remained on my head. In vain.

The bell rang again. Still swaying, I left my room and, holding onto the furniture as I went, passed into the hall. The kitchen was filled with the evening light which was pouring through its window and striking the entrance, the hall, the dining-room door. Where was my lady? Even if I couldn't see her, I could always sense where she was, but not right then. I was disoriented. Why was the house so silent? Where had everyone gone?

I went down into the garden. A light breeze was filtering through the grapevine and I could hear the sound of laughter and music from the neighbouring garden. Evening was descending; the earth was continuing its journey around the sun. At that moment I knew I hadn't died. Death had spared my soul. I felt happy, which meant that I still wanted to live. No, that was not the reason. The reason was my lady. If I were to pass to the next world, what would happen to Madam Shirin? It was my duty to wait on Madam Shirin on this earth. If I should go before her – may God prevent that from happening – my soul would not find peace in the next world. That was why my heart was relieved that death had not taken my soul. The grey kitten appeared from under the gate opening onto the street, ran to me, and standing on its two back feet, rubbed its head against the cuffs of my trousers. It was hungry. I suddenly came to my senses – I had not prepared the evening meal! Oh, dear God, what a disgrace!

'Stop! Stop, I say! Don't break the bell. I am coming!'

I made my way slowly to the garden gate, impeded by the grey kitten jumping up at me and weaving around my legs, and saw that it was the boy from the hardware shop who had been ringing the bell so furiously. His forehead was wet with sweat, and the basket on the back of his moped was full of tins of paint, an empty oil drum, brushes…

'What is all this?' I asked, nonplussed.

'The mistress of the house ordered them by phone.'

'Are you sure there hasn't been a misunderstanding?'

'No, Shirin Hanim called the shop and spoke with my father. She ordered all these tins of paint. It comes to 350 lira.'

'What hardware shop is open on a holiday? Where did Madam Shirin find your telephone number?'

'I don't know, old man. The lady talked to my dad.'

I led the way up to the house and the boy followed with the tins of paint, the bags and the oil drum. Madam Shirin was waiting at the door of the dining room with a smile on her face. If I was not mistaken, she winked at me, just as she used to during her parties in the past. A tiny moment, but enough to make my heart jump.

When she spoke, her voice was loud and clear.

'Put it here, my boy. Bring everything. Yes, under the table, beside the table, like this. Did you bring the oilcloth? Then spread that out first. Cover the whole floor. Move the table over here, but don't scratch the floor! Well done. Here, take this money and keep the change for yourself. That's your holiday treat.'

When Madam Shirin opened the double-door of the dining room as far as it would go, the bright light from the kitchen window directly across from the door hit the floors, the table and the mirror above the sideboard. It was then that I saw the bowls on the table. They were filled to the brim with nutshells. There was an empty cognac glass, and Madam Nur had extinguished her cigarette in the dark blue ashtray beside it. I immediately gathered up the ashtray and the bowls and swept away the nutshells that had fallen onto the table with my hand. I took them to the kitchen and tipped them into the rubbish bin. Seeing the empty pans lined up on the stove, I remembered again that I had not yet prepared the evening meal. I had served my lady's lunch on a tray. Chicken and noodles, with a salad of grated carrot on the side. But hours had passed since then. Although Madam Shirin ate nothing but fruit on summer evenings, it was my duty to always have a light repast prepared. I could cook artichokes. Or October beans. Where was Madam Nur? More importantly, where was Mr Fikret? He'd said that all the food for tomorrow's tea party had been ordered from a friend's shop, but one needed to look over the list. There might have been omissions, and one could not be certain everything would be delivered on time. Both Madam Nur and Mr Fikret were required.

'Sadik, Sadik! Where are you, for God's sake? Come here. We have a lot of work to do.'

Hearing Madam Shirin's bell, I shook off my thoughts, placed cherries and apricots that I took from the refrigerator into a bowl, and left the kitchen hurriedly. The hardware shop boy was getting onto his moped and I called to him to close the garden gate behind him in case a passing cow might stray inside. The bell on the gate rang as he shut it, leaving me with a bad feeling inside. Where was everyone? I closed the front door and the light changed. The entrance became dim and sadness enveloped me. I went into the dining room, which was directly opposite the kitchen, and set the bowl of fruit on the sideboard. Madam Shirin had had the hardware shop boy move the table in front of the window and she was now looking at the opened-up space and at the wall behind the table. The evening shadows were shifting across the wall. The floor was covered with oilcloth. Madam Shirin was wearing navy blue high-heeled velvet slippers with tiny pearls embroidered on them.

The late Mr Halit came to my mind. May he rest in peace. He was sitting there at the head of the table, where he always sat, and bang! His head fell. The mountainous man capsized onto the floor. Then little Suheyla. How she cried. In moving the table from its place, it was as if we had disturbed both their spirits. It made me uneasy. There was also Madam Shirin's strange behaviour, but I was familiar with that, for she was always like that when she started on a large painting. I knew that. However, it had been years since she'd painted anything other than her own face on the mirror. The old paints had all dried up and we'd thrown them away. Was she preparing to work on a canvas with the paints the hardware shop boy had brought? Where then was the canvas? The canvases I had stored between the desk and the wall in the library remained in their place.

'Sadik!'

'Yes, Madam Shirin.'

Her head was still turned towards the blank wall and her thin white hands were moving among the shadows projected there, like a blind person feeling her way. Or perhaps she was seeing things I did not see.

'Close the door.'

She looked at me. I was alarmed. A shiver ran down my spine for it was as if we had gone back in time. My lady was a young girl again; her cheeks bloomed like roses and her eyes sparkled as if with electricity.

'Bring the jars, towels, rags and my old brushes. Fill the drum with water. Then come. Oh, and I want my stool.'

'Should I bring a canvas, Madam Shirin? And your palette?'

'Not necessary. Did you close the door? Good. Prepare the table. Bring the plastic tablecloth.'

No matter how old I become, I shall never forget what is required when Madam Shirin begins a painting. I covered the dining table with the plastic tablecloth with the fruit design. I lined up the paints and the brushes. How many glass jars would she want, I wondered? I brought ten. I brought the hand towels with which she dried the brushes after they'd been dipped in water. I looked for the turpentine. That would not be required. She would work with watercolours. I again enquired as to the canvas. She reached out her translucent, purple-veined hand and gestured at the ether.

'Prepare the green.'

Normally she would at this point have been asking for her palette, but today she did not desire a palette. I now understood. The hardware shop boy had brought plastic mixing trays, the sort used by house painters. Lots of them. I opened the metal lid of the green paint and poured a little onto a tray. Speedily I stirred the paint. My hand shook somewhat. My lady's hand was poised in the air, waiting, like an impatient bird. Did Madam Shirin not require a canvas or a sheet of paper? Could my lady have overlooked this? I prayed that this would not turn out to be an accident similar to the one suffered yesterday morning. An accident of the mind. May God preserve us.

'Emerald, tea leaf, rain-drenched grass, seaweed on a rock, spring bud. Give me the thick brush. The thickest.'

I opened the lids of the yellow, white, black and red paints, mixed them slowly, poured the mixture into a jar, dipped the thick brush into the paint and handed both jar and brush to her.

'Here is the emerald green, Madam Shirin.'

Hurriedly, hungrily, she dipped the brush into the jar and withdrew it. Then she closed her eyes and took a deep breath. In the darkness beneath her eyelashes she was envisaging the picture she would draw, in all its detail. Another deep breath. A rasping sound came from her throat and it was then that I understood what it was my lady was about to do. And I was astounded at myself. How had I not thought of this before? In my mind I had dared to accuse Madam Shirin of absent-mindedness, of an accident of the mind! However... Are you sure about this, Madam Shirin? My lady? My lady's eyes remained closed. She was holding the jar full of green paint with the brush in it up to the empty wall, as if it were a wine glass and she was raising a toast to someone I could not see. All at once, she began. She gave me no opportunity to intervene. She struck the wall with the brush. Again she struck. She dipped, she struck. Again and again. Upon the wall, at the place she had struck, a mountain appeared. At the foot of the mountain a forest. Where the forest ended, fields. I trembled. I took a backwards step.

'Tea leaf!'

Hastily I mixed a little black, a little red into the green and poured that mix into another jar. The brush was proceeding swiftly across the wall. Behind the mountain, other mountains were appearing. My lady's arm was rising, descending; she was moving to the left, to the right, without the aid of her walking stick.

'Mix the green of the grass drenched by rain. Come on, Sadik, make haste. Finish the green. Then I want the yellow of corn. After that, the brown. Quick. Don't delay with the blue.'

Gradually my hands regained their former speed. Time had turned inside out. We were young. Our eyes could see, our legs could carry us without aching. My hands were no longer trembling, my fingers were as strong as ever. I prepared the shade Madam Shirin needed the minute she asked for it. I got the proportions right without fail. I could determine my lady's reaction by the nod of her head when her brush touched the wall. One by one the mountains materialized, the yellow flowers, the fields, the blue of sunny skies, and, far below, the foaming sea. Even the wind manifested itself on the dining-room wall.

I noticed that Madam Shirin held her back perfectly straight as she sat on her high stool. She was wearing a navy blue scarf, the same colour as her slippers. Thin wisps of her white hair had become detached from her bun and were floating softly around her head. Some had fallen onto her neck. How white, how delicate her neck was. Our childhood came to my mind. A memory from long ago. The hair around Madam Shirin's neck was blowing in the wind. We were leaning over a ship's rail, looking down at the pier below, where two women were waving handkerchiefs at us. The ship's whistle blew. Rivers tumbled down into the sea from faraway mountains and stone bridges spanned the frothing waters. Yes, I remembered. As Madam Shirin drew, the past took shape in my imagination. I remembered it all.

After having worked with vigour and speed for some time, Madam Shirin stopped. I was familiar with this state also. In order to capture the scene in her imagination, she always began by drawing and painting furiously, and then she'd stop and take a good look at what she'd done. If she was pleased with it, she'd work on the empty areas, slowly, slowly. A period of time would pass in this manner, and then she would again rush joyously, speedily filling in the gaps. We stuck to our old, familiar tempo. Give me stormy blue. Here you are. Rain cloud. Ready, madam. Crow? Lead grey? Copper pail? Tobacco and weeds? Yellow gold? Here you are, my lady.

The atmosphere in the dining room had become heavy. Time had slowed. We were like the wagons of a long-distance train, and the silence of the house no longer made me uneasy. I had ceased to wonder where the other members of the family were. I felt that Madam Shirin and I had passed into a world that contained just the two of us, and I hoped that no one would come into the house, that we two could remain alone in that world forever.

Just then, my lady spoke.

'Sadik, listen to what I have to say to you.'

She was in one of her slow phases. On her high stool, with her face so close to the wall it seemed to be glued to it, she was painting the windows of a two-storeyed stone house.

'A passage has opened into the past. You realize that, do you not?'

I did not answer. What could I say? Sometimes, especially when she is in the middle of a creative endeavour, Madam Shirin makes abstract comments that are beyond the comprehension of your humble servant. Generally, I am not personally offended by such esoteric remarks. After the windows of the two-storeyed house she began to paint the ivy that twisted across its walls. For this part she requested spring-bud green. All of her attention was given to the strokes of her brush. Without turning her face from the wall, she continued to talk. Certainly, she was speaking not to me but

311

to the scene arising from her imagination. But she spoke in a way that confounded me.

'Sadik, I know that the priest came to you also. Just like he came to me. He came because the passage to the past has opened. Perhaps you remember that there were passages between some of the mountains. The old folks used to call them mountain passes. Don't you remember? It's not important. The important thing is the opening of the passages. The dear priest passed from there to this side. And listen to what I say to you: Fikret has passed through and fallen into the past.'

My tongue and my brain were frozen. Should I be concerned about my lady's mental health? Yes, she sometimes forgot everyday things, she got confused over what she ate in the morning, but I had never before witnessed her becoming carried away by otherworldly ideas. It frightened me.

'Sadik! You understood what I said, did you not?'

Then this thought came to me: from whom had Madam Shirin heard that Mr Fikret had left the house in the pre-dawn darkness? Did Miss Celine tell her? Or Madam Nur? I myself had not let a word on the subject of Mr Fikret pass my lips for I did not want to disturb my lady's peace of mind.

'Sadik, give me foamy blue. Mix purple for verbena. Do you not hear me?'

I prepared the colours she desired in an agitated manner. The balance was not correct. It was the purple of violets. My lady understood but said nothing.

'Listen now, Sadik. Since the passage has opened, there's a story that will pass from there to this side. Stories are never forgotten, Sadik, they merely stay silent inside us, that's all. The time comes, some pressure is exerted, the passages open, and the past flows into the present.'

A breeze stirred within the room. My lady was painting.

She was speaking as if she was humming a song. Once upon a time when pigs had wings and horses could talk... Her face was so close to the wall that I thought her sounds would be echoed by the green mountains, the forests, the gusting winds she was drawing.

'There were two young men who lived in a very fertile land squeezed between the sea and the mountains. Give me the black, and a clean, fine brush. Where is Celine?'

I handed her the tin of black that the hardware shop boy had brought. There was no need to mix anything. Without looking at me, she took the brush and the tin. She drew two young men wearing baggy black trousers, vests, and red belts. They were drawn quite large in comparison to the mountains and the houses. Madam Shirin's art is like that. She does not adhere to proportions as they are in their natural state but rather magnifies what she finds important. The two young men were the same size as the mountain range behind them. They were important. They had moustaches, broad shoulders, smiling eyes. Their arms were held high in the air as if in a joyous dance. I do not know how it happened, but I heard it. A musical instrument was playing. This was not like the instruments Mr Halit and Miss Suheyla used to play, it was rougher and louder; it made you want to dance. It unnerved me. Madam Shirin drew some other people behind those two.

'One of the young men was from this village by the seaside. He was clever. The other was the son of a rich gentleman from a village carved out of the mountainside; he grew up in a stone mansion, from where, if you went up high enough, you could see the sea. As soon as summer came, all the villagers moved up to the high meadows. Those from the seaside and those from the mountains met and got to know one another. Can you see them?'

I nodded. It truly was as if I was watching the column of people winding their way joyfully up the mountainside. They had loaded cloth bundles, trunks, kilims and babies onto the backs of their animals and had stopped on the banks of a fast-flowing river to rest. Women were stringing up cradles between two trees to rock their little ones. Who were these people? Why was Madam Shirin drawing them? How was it that my memory held the sound of their songs?

'If you went down from the mountains to the sea, you came to a large city. There, the buildings were as finely worked as pearls, and ladies did not leave their houses without putting on their most beautiful silk dresses. The streets, like those in Europe, were pretty with pastry shops, stylish restaurants, elegant hotels. And in that city there was a large school to which every family wished to send its sons. The school was housed in a magnificent building on the seafront. It was called the Phrontisterion. Mix dusty pink. Light redbrick.'

Madam Shirin had now moved to the side of the wall nearest the library and was drawing the city she described. From her brush emerged slim-waisted women in hats, strolling beside the sea. They were carrying parasols to protect their faces from the sun. Others were getting in and out of stylish carriages. Then she painted a majestic four-storeyed building in dusty pink. She put glass in the windows and gave them white frames.

The two young men met at this boarding school. As students, they dedicated themselves to the ideals of freedom and swore an oath that they would liberate the villagers of their homeland from cruelty and oppression. They were so young, so innocent. But before they could complete their education, a great war erupted, a war that would make the whole world miserable.

Madam Shirin had scarcely finished her words when, from behind the mountains on the wall, flames burst from an exploding bomb. I heard the screams of soldiers whose legs had been blown off. My lady was both drawing and talking. Or perhaps she was not speaking, only drawing, and I was hearing the story. The large city by the sea fell into enemy hands. This was not a defeat but a positive stride forward for the young men and their struggle for freedom. We are finally liberated from the rule of the Sultan, they said. They celebrated. However, in a short while, bad news began to arrive. The Sultan's army was emptying all the villages in the areas that were still under their rule. The order had come that those villagers who had served the enemy would be evicted from their homes.

Right above the beautiful city on the sea, on the right side of the mountain she had painted first, she drew half-naked children fallen in the snow. A line of people with bowed heads was marching, and at each end of the line there were armed guards. Gendarmes. My mind went to the dream I had had. I saw my dear mama. She had hidden in the crypt of a church. A gang of bad men were playing football with the dead priest's head. The bells of the church were silent, its tower had been blown up. Someone had decreed that these people be entirely erased, that a hundred years hence there should be not a trace that they had ever lived on that land. No one would remember them. Who had spoken thus? How could Madam Shirin know all this? The times being spoken of were far back in the past. Those terrible events happened to other people. Then why did this recollection live in my memory?

Madam Shirin slowly got down from her stool. She swayed briefly as she found her balance. I raced over to hold her arm, but she crossed to the far corner of the wall, where the dining room met the library. The joyful phase had passed. She was covering the entire wall, from one side to the other. She asked for red, for gold, for orange, for pomegranate blossom. She was talking nonstop. Her voice had become shrill, thin, reinvigorated. Thousands of villagers died of exhaustion – the white plague, she said. The villages of the people who had been singing happily just a short while before were now being burnt. Smoke was devouring houses full of women and children. The sea was going crazy, wild and foaming. Dark ships passed.

My hands were shaking and I was unable to measure out the paints correctly. My lady paid no heed. She was consumed with drawing, painting, talking. Maybe she was not talking. Maybe I was reading. Reading the wall. Reading of blood flowing over the snow-covered mountains, of the purple legs of children, of bodies left behind unburied, of crimson rivers, houses in flames. Stop, Madam Shirin! It is enough, my lady, enough! You too will collapse from exhaustion. That was what I wanted to say, but my lips were sealed and not a word came out of my mouth. This was a story that should not be told. Madam Shirin was not doing a good deed by making this wall painting.

However, I knew from experience that when my lady was thus engaged in a painting, one should not approach her. She might respond unpredictably. I sank onto the chair at the head of the table. Shadows were flitting about in the garden. I heard the screeching of seagulls, the rustling of the mimosa leaves in the evening breeze. My lady was now painting without looking at the colours, from memory. As for me, the scenes I had grasped had put me in a troubled mood. In spite of this, I was able to make out the young girl following the sad young student down the mountain. I recognized her from the two black plaits beneath her white headscarf. My heart beat rapidly.

'One of the young men rescued a girl from his village,' said Madam Shirin. '"I saved one life," he said. "One life is worth the world for the one who lives it. We will keep our people alive. We will begin anew; we will rebuild our village, our lineage."'

My mind completed the story. The area around the big city was safe and it was there, in a village in the mountains behind the big city, that the young man's friend lived, in a large house. They would begin a new life there, he and the girl he had rescued. He did not know then that he would climb the mountain and fight a war, that he would be trapped in a cave and killed like a wild animal. My dear mama's voice. A story whispered in my ear. My papa. Papa saved Mama from the church in her burnt-down village. Mama had not gone up into the mountains, where everyone froze to death; she had hidden in the village, and Papa took her to a place where she would be safe. As the colours and shapes of Madam Shirin's mural appeared, doors opened in my memory. Was it possible that this was the passage that Madam Shirin had mentioned?

Madam Shirin fell silent and turned to me. I recoiled at the angry expression on her face. What had I done?

'Sadik, your father hid your mother in our house, when she was pregnant with you. A safe place, he thought. But later? Later what happened? You know what I am speaking of. A man living like a body of dark water...'

In the dim light I kept my eyes on my feet and murmured, 'How can I know, Madam Shirin? These are painful events from before I was born. It is not the past which is important, but the happy life we have lived. However, if they have

inspired you, there is undoubtedly a wisdom in them. You
have created a great masterpiece. Such a powerful painting.'

I did not know how to continue. My lady's sudden flame of
anger had made me so uneasy that my stomach was cramping.
In desperation I looked at the last of the daylight fading in
the mirror above the sideboard. It was no longer possible to
distinguish colours and shapes and yet my eyes caught the
blue of my lady's eyes as she stared directly into my face.
Certainly, I had unknowingly committed some grave error. I
had made her angry. I had upset her. It had been the same in
the past. When Madam Shirin was making her art, she would
get cross very swiftly.

With unexpectedly agile strides Madam Shirin approached
the table and sat down next to me. I immediately stood up,
picked up the bowl of fruit and offered it to her. The apricots
had turned red and speckled in the heat. Madam Shirin took
a sour cherry, chewed it for a long while, and spat the stone
on the floor – onto the oilcloth, in fact. I sat down and ate
an apricot. For a while we sat without speaking amidst the
opened tins of paint, the random drips of paint, the brushes
and the jars, and ate fruit from the bowl. From time to time
I glanced at her from the corner of my eye to check whether
she was still angry. Her face was turned to the wall. As she
chewed on her cherries, she examined her painting. When she
spoke, she sounded worn out.

'Now do you believe me, Sadik? I told you a passage had
opened between the past and the present. All these people
came here through that passage. Fikret has gone and fallen
into that passage. Let us hope he finds his way back.'

I did not hear what my lady said next, for just at that
moment the door creaked and revealed Miss Celine's tall, thin
silhouette. She looked in and for a brief time could not see

anything, but then her young hand found the switch. Electric light spilt from the crystal chandelier across the ceiling, the sideboard, the table and chairs. Like glass marbles, it scattered whenever it hit something. My eyes hurt. Miss Celine gazed around in astonishment. I closed my eyes. I heard the rumble of Madam Shirin's breathing beside me and smelt her lavender perfume. Miss Celine's footsteps pattered across the oilcloth.

'God, it's so messy in here! Are you guys setting up a street market or what? What's going on? I heard the two of you when I was passing the door just now – not that I... but... what language were you speaking? I couldn't understand a thing. Was it bird language or something?'

Upon hearing this question of Miss Celine's, I too believed that a passage had opened between the past and the present, and I prayed that Mr Fikret would find his way and return to us.

May God keep him safe.

29

Burak

Mingling with the crowd at the pier, I felt good.

Very good. Too good.

My stress dissipated as I walked down the market street, dodging the grocers' boys on their mopeds, the mothers pushing prams. I rubbed shoulders with the day-trippers – yes, Nur, those same day-trippers that you are always so disparaging about – and wondered whether to do what they were doing and sit down at one of the tables made out of old beer kegs and eat stuffed mussels. And you know what, Nur, I was happier being in that unsophisticated crowd than I was being in your house with its rare antique furniture and the same weird music playing over and over. That's where real life is, on the street, in the outside world. You should know that.

I approached one of the beer-keg tables and immediately a chubby young man materialized with a menu in his hand.

'Sit here, sir. You will be comfortable. What can I get you? French fries? Stuffed mussels?'

I realized that I was hungry. I hadn't eaten anything since the cheese toast at the Horoz Reis Tea Garden. And before that I'd had another cheese toast with Celine at the crack of dawn, at another tea garden at the pier. The morning seemed like weeks ago now.

'I'll have the lot. And a beer.'

'At your service, sir. Shall I make you a Greek salad? With lots of lemon and olive oil?'

'No, thanks. Bring the beer right away and make sure it's cold.'

I sat down on one of the uncomfortable stools at the keg table and watched the waiter swinging though the dark door. People were surging past in throngs. Happy, carefree people with nothing on their minds beyond what to do next, where to eat, whether they might have a beer, or, since it was a religious holiday, whether perhaps they shouldn't. Was that true? No, of course they'd all have their own problems, but they didn't dwell on them when they were on holiday. These were hard-working people who didn't ruin their days off by worrying about things. Keep the problems for the week and let the weekends be for living.

The chubby waiter brought my beer and mussels. The beer was flat, but I enjoyed its ice-cold passage down my throat. I squeezed lemon onto the stuffed mussels, used a shell to spoon up the pilaf and meat and threw it in my mouth. Delicious. The pilaf had absorbed the smell and taste of the salt, the sea, the lemon and the seaweed. I suppressed the thought that eating a mussel from the Sea of Marmara was like eating a leaking battery.

As I piled up the empty mussel shells on the side of my plate, the bowl of discarded pistachio shells on the table in Shirin Hanim's dining room came into my head. The shells Nur had stubbornly opened with her little teeth. I examined my feelings. Nothing remained of the burning emotion I had felt as I left the house and walked rapidly down to the pier. I replayed Nur's following me to the garden gate, her pleading for forgiveness, her crying, her begging to come with me. 'Don't leave me!' The bell that rang in your ears when you opened the gate. The iron gate closing behind me. Nur's little white feet through the bars.

I was furious. As I took quick, angry strides between the horse-drawn carriages and bicycles, the same record was playing crazily over and over in my head. Nur had killed my child. She hadn't even given me the chance to have a say in the matter; I was of no more importance to her than an insect. She had stolen my chance to be a father, obliterated a human being that carried parts of both of us. How selfish was that; how arrogant. How could she have made such a decision without consulting me? Did a father not have a voice when it came to his child's life? Half of that child was mine, a product of my genes. It would have carried parts of my mother, my father, the grandparents I never knew. That child was ours. How could she have done this to me?

So why didn't I feel anything now? Did my thoughts just pour out of my head and drain away as I went over and over it, like muddy water from a tap? Nur's feet... Her pleading voice, her wretched, half-conscious glances after two glasses of cognac, her dark red toenail polish through the bars of the gate.

'Shall I bring you another one, sir?'

The waiter placed the French fries in front of me. How quickly I'd finished the beer.

'Sure. It was nice and cold, did me good.'

'Right away. I'm leaving the ketchup and mayonnaise here.'

The sauce bottles bothered me. I didn't like having the red, white and yellow plastic bottles on the table, even though it was a beer keg and not a real table and I was sitting on a stool fit for a child. Still, the bottles didn't look right beside my plate, my glass, my fork and my food. I'd put a little ketchup on the edge of my plate and send the rest back.

Suddenly, I don't know where it came from, maybe from the smell of fried potatoes, a scene from my childhood dropped into my head. We were in our house in the village. My father was still alive. I was in primary school, year five or six, and it was a Sunday afternoon in early spring, or maybe it was still winter. The television was on. Back then, Sunday was the only day when TV programmes were broadcast in the daytime as well as the evening. I was trying to finish my homework in the room that doubled as the TV room, the dining room and the living room, but the homework seemed to keep on expanding every time I turned a page, like when you chewed a mouthful of okra.

Mum had set up the ironing board in front of the woodstove. We didn't have central heating in that house and Mum would sometimes complain to Dad that she wished we'd moved to the better-appointed company housing in Erdek. Dad was looking at a football game on the TV – not watching it, just looking at it. He wasn't interested in football, but he liked to be able to join in the conversations about it with his co-workers at the factory. The television was black and white and there was only one channel. I didn't know that football was played on grass because the field on the TV was grey and I thought they played on dusty soil just like me and my friends did. I liked playing football, but I didn't like watching it. It was hard to concentrate on my homework with the annoying buzz of the commentator's voice filling the room. Dad was still in his pyjamas. There was a plate full of orange peel in front of him and he'd stubbed his cigarette out on it.

The weekend was over and I felt like crying. The two days I'd spent a whole week dreaming about were coming to an end on a Sunday afternoon of cigarette smoke, steam from the iron and noisy football commentary.

The dream of a life with Nur was like the way I used to feel on those Friday lunchtimes full of promise, whereas if I were to actually have that life with her, would I not end up feeling like I used to on Sunday afternoons? I heard her begging for forgiveness again. 'Don't leave me, Burak.' If I hadn't left her, if I'd gone to the pier with her beside me (actually, Nur wouldn't have gone down to the pier, she'd have taken me to some wooden shack of a bar known only to islanders and she'd have been proud of herself for that), if I'd said, 'All is forgiven, Nur. Come into my arms,' then wouldn't I have laid myself open to that Sunday feeling for the rest of my life?

I was mulling this over as I sipped my beer. Suddenly, in among the crowd surging past me, I saw Fikret. I jumped up, put my beer on the keg. My child-sized stool fell over backwards. Yes, it was definitely him! His distracted, passive face, the rucksack on his back and his slightly hunched way of walking set him apart from the tourists. Weaving hurriedly between the beer kegs, without considering whether he'd be able to hear me above the din, I called, 'Fikret!'

He didn't hear me. Knocking over the stools that blocked my way, I slalomed round people so as not to lose him. At least he was tall, and his gait was distinctive. But just as I was catching up with him, I saw a vision, or rather a ghost. It was as if I had to stop this ghost or Fikret would be erased from the face of the earth. When, gasping for breath, I finally tapped him on the shoulder, I feared he might have someone else's face when he turned around. But it was Fikret. Yes, it was Fikret Bulut in front of me, with his wide forehead, his moustache, his beautiful, sad hazel eyes, so like Nur's. The mysterious absentee we'd been searching for since morning. I was so happy to see him, I almost put my arms around him and kissed him.

'Fikret! Fikret, where have you been? We've all been so worried about you.'

'Hello, Burak. What are you doing here?'

For a moment I didn't quite understand what he was asking. His voice was so strange, his gaze so distracted, that I thought he'd forgotten we'd had breakfast together yesterday morning and that I was there to celebrate Shirin Hanim's hundredth birthday, even though it was he who'd invited me. But he was probably asking why I was there in the marketplace, at the busiest time of the evening, instead of at Shirin Hanim's quiet house, away from the crowds. Or maybe he wasn't thinking about anything, or not about me, anyway. It was obvious that he was preoccupied with something.

'Are you okay, Fikret? Everything all right? Shall we walk home together? Wait a minute while I settle my bill.'

Taking my wallet out of my back pocket, I looked over at the beer keg where I'd been sitting. The chubby waiter spotted me in the crowd and somehow, even from that distance, he managed to communicate with his hands and eyes that it was okay, he knew I hadn't run off, not to worry.

Fikret grabbed my arm. 'Burak, could we sit down somewhere and get a bite to eat? Talk a bit. What do you say?'

What could I say? The sadness in his eyes again reminded me of Nur. That doleful look. Definitely inherited from their mother, Suheyla.

Ten minutes later we were at one of the touristy fish restaurants at the pier, sitting inside. 'It'll be quieter inside, we can talk more comfortably,' Fikret said. I was grateful. Ever since they banned smoking indoors, it's been horrible being stuck behind plastic sheets in supposedly open-air places, enveloped in smoke. We sat at a window table and the air conditioner immediately neutralized the heat and humidity.

'What shall we drink – beer, raki?'

Since I had just drunk two beers one after the other, I didn't really want either, but to be polite, I said raki. I'd just have a little. It was clear that Fikret needed it more than I did. As a matter of fact, I thought he'd quit drinking after he took up yoga and all, but Nur could have been exaggerating. Or maybe it was just coffee he'd given up, because he went on to order every one of the cold appetisers the white-haired head waiter was recommending from the tray his assistant was holding. After which, Fikret added, 'And bring us a large bottle of the green Efe Raki, some feta cheese, some melon and a rocket salad with the tomatoes peeled. You don't have seaweed salad? Oh, you do? A portion of that too. We'll start with those and order the hot appetisers later.'

We didn't speak until after the raki was served. In silence we watched the families passing by the window with ice cream cones in their hands. Fikret's eyes were red with tiredness, his face ashen. I was impatient to hear his story but didn't want to appear overly excited. Disingenuity is a professional habit; the more indifferent I appear to be, the more information I'm able to obtain. But really, what information could Fikret have? I had some for him, though. His sister had aborted my child. Did he know that his sister had come to my door last month, drunk, and shared my bed until morning? I stopped myself from sharing that.

I took a sip of raki. It was good. No water. I ate a cube of feta cheese. Fikret was prodding the appetisers on his plate with his fork but not eating. My eyes focused on his Adam's apple. In our youth, when Nur and I were by ourselves, we used to make such fun of Fikret's Adam's apple. Young people can be so cruel.

Fikret leant back and rubbed his cheek. He hadn't shaved that morning, which was in part why his face looked so grey.

'Burak, I've found out something quite incredible. Unbelievable.'

He drank down his raki in one gulp and motioned with his head to the young waiter. His glass was immediately refilled.

'Actually, you know, it's all thanks to you. I mean, yesterday, during breakfast, we were sitting at the table, and you were talking to Grandmother...'

I nodded.

'No, wait a minute, I should start at the beginning. As you know, I've been curious about my great-grandfather's story for a while. I had this feeling inside, a heaviness. I've been doing these self-development programmes, with Freya, and they're like psychoanalysis, only it's not just your own subconscious that's analyzed. You also look into the subconscious and genetic records of the generations that came before. They analyze your inherited memory. Nur thinks it's all hocus-pocus, but what do you think? I believe it has a healing effect. You know, when Freud first came up with his psychoanalytic theories, many people thought that was hocus-pocus too. A hundred years from now, transpersonal psychology will be a popular approach for the healing of the human soul, I'm sure of it.'

The waiter brought our seaweed salad and Fikret added a squeeze of lemon and a drizzle of olive oil. I ate a piece of melon, then took a spoonful of pinto-bean pilaki and some spicy mashed tomato paste. My stomach would start burning soon – bar-burn. Hard-to-digest foods along with raki always spelt digestive disaster. I tried to focus on what Fikret was saying. I'd never heard of the psychology discipline he'd mentioned, but I was relieved to hear it wasn't some New Age fashion like quantum healing but a known school of thought with a specific identity and some respectability. Still, I was hoping he'd get on with his story. I took a mouthful of seaweed salad. It was delicious: greens with the smell of sea salt and iodine.

Fikret had picked up on my impatience. 'Let me get to the point. I've asked Grandmother countless times about her father, but to no avail. I never get an answer – it's always a blind alley, an empty well. But then yesterday, for the first time... Yesterday at the breakfast table, did you notice that Grandmother revealed a very important detail about the past?'

'You mean her father's suicide?'

Although I hadn't learnt about the suicide from Shirin Hanim's own mouth, it hadn't been difficult to work out from what I'd witnessed between Celine and her great-grandmother in the library that this was the big secret.

Fikret's fork was suspended in mid-air, seaweed hanging untidily from it.

'Where did you hear about that? Grandmother didn't say anything about that yesterday morning, I'm sure of it. How, where, did you get that information?'

His voice had got louder, but not from anger. He was shocked, disappointed. This was no doubt the big story he'd brought back from wherever he'd gone at dawn, whereas if he'd stayed with us, he'd have heard it from Shirin Hanim, if he was lucky, or if not, Celine would certainly have dropped the bombshell. Celine! I should tell her that her father had been found. The proper thing would have been for Fikret to call her, but it didn't look like that was on the cards. But if I were to text Celine right then, she'd be there within minutes. She'd waited for news of Fikret all day, she could wait a bit longer. In any case, Fikret's story probably wouldn't take too long, then we'd finish up and go back to the house.

'Shirin Hanim told Celine. We haven't been able to confirm the story, but if you've been given the same information... Really, where have you been all day, Fikret? We were worried, especially Celine. She's been looking for you since morning.'

Fikret shook his head sadly. 'I know. She's sent me a ton of messages. I've got a sensitive daughter.'

'Where did you go? Where did you learn about this suicide?'

'Hang on, I'm getting to that.'

Our raki was replenished. Fried calamari and tiny pastry parcels stuffed with cheese and spinach arrived. Reddish clouds were drifting across the sky. It was going to be a pretty sunset. Suddenly I was sorry we hadn't sat outside, in a corner with a view of Heybeliada across the sea. I guess in the second half of our lives we start to regret every missed sunset.

'As I was saying, I heard something at the breakfast table yesterday and... I was following up on that, actually.' He laughed. When he laughed, his sad, serious face lit up. He looked like Nur. I glanced at him. There was some colour in his cheeks now and the distracted dejection of earlier was lifting. When someone has a story to tell, they come to life. Stories bring a person to life, give a person life. Without stories, we fade away.

'You know, Burak, when a person reaches a certain age, it can be the little things that point to the really important issues.

We find the true meaning of life through small coincidences. You asked Grandmother a question – I've forgotten what – and she answered you. Then Sadik Usta interjected. "It wasn't like that, it was like this," he said. They both claimed different things, but it might have escaped your attention – just two old people arguing about an insignificant detail. Do you remember?'

I thought about it. Then I tried to remember the tape I'd been listening to in the Horoz Reis Tea Garden. Yes, they'd disagreed about something. I'd been just about to listen to that bit again when Celine had raced up on her bicycle and distracted me.

'I'll tell you,' said Fikret. He was excited. 'They were talking about a priest. Grandmother said it was an autumn day when they saw the priest, and Sadik tried to get her to stop talking.'

Yes, of course, now I remembered. She said something about a church and a priest, but the flow of her story was interrupted when she was asked for details. Nur had got angry with Fikret about that.

Fikret continued. 'While they were arguing about the priest and the icon, the interview you did with Sadik years ago suddenly came to my mind.'

'Interesting. How did you make that connection?'

He dropped his voice, leant forward and whispered mysteriously, 'If I said I made the connection, I'd be lying. It was as if it was already recorded somewhere deep in my subconscious and all of sudden I located the place. I knew that Sadik kept that newspaper clipping in the drawer of the bedside table in his room.'

'You don't say!'

I couldn't keep from smiling. That interview I did with Sadik Usta was one of my first ones. Back then, 'Portraits' was just a column, whereas now it takes up the whole of page two in the *Saturday Extra*. But it seems to me that when I had less space I wrote deeper, more meaningful articles. I was strangely moved by Sadik Usta's keeping that clipping in his drawer for seventeen years. Maybe I was drinking my raki too quickly. Fikret was drinking swiftly too and wasn't aware of the comings and goings in my head. He was busy finishing his story.

'After breakfast, while Sadik was in the kitchen, I quietly went into his room, found the clipping and took it up to my room. I was sure it contained some information that would be helpful to me. I read it carefully from beginning to end. At that point, nothing struck me, but that night, while I was pacing up and down in my room... suddenly... voila! The information I was looking for was right in front of my eyes. The strange thing is that it had been there my whole life, but I'd chosen not to see it.'

He stopped talking, sat back and threw the calamari ring on the end of his fork into his mouth. A self-satisfied smile spread across his face.

As was expected of me, I leant forward with curiosity and asked, 'What was that information?'

'Macka!'

He laughed again. I didn't understand anything. Was he laughing at the expression on my face? No, it was as if he was saying, come on, you're the clever journalist, you find the connection. I finished my glass of raki. How quickly one's mouth gets used to the aniseed taste. I always take little sips at first, but by the second glass it flows down my throat as smoothly as water.

'Macka, Burak! Macka! You don't understand, do you? Then hold tight and listen! It was you who found the connection. And what's more, damn it, it was seventeen years ago that Sadik told you himself. Look, take this!'

He took the folded newspaper clipping from the pocket of his short-sleeved checked shirt. The paper gave off the medicine and cologne smell of old wooden drawers. It had turned yellow and the writing along the folds had been erased. The colours of the photograph taken in Shirin Hanim's living room in Moda, in front of one of her oil paintings, had faded and blended into each other.

Fikret pressed his finger on a sentence at the end of the article.

'Look, right here. You ask, "Where did you live before you moved to the mansion in Uskudar?" And he says, "Macka." Just like that. "At Madam Shirin's parents' house in Macka."'

I shook my head. There was a mistake. 'But I talked to Nur about that and it seems there's no connection between Shirin Hanim and your apartment in Macka – I mean, the apartment where Nur and Ufuk live. Apparently, it was your father who bought that apartment.'

Fikret's hazel eyes were shining. 'Exactly! The Macka where our apartment is has nothing to do with the Macka Grandmother and Sadik spent their childhood in.'

'Yes, of course. That area has changed dramatically. When they were children, it would have been full of mansions and villas.'

Fikret guffawed. He refilled our glasses with raki. I smiled too. I wasn't used to seeing him so jolly. He'd always been the epitome of seriousness. Nur was flighty and wild and Fikret was the big brother with both feet on the ground. As he clinked his glass against mine, his voice grew louder with happiness.

'Burak, what are you saying, man? I'm telling you, that

Macka wasn't this Macka. That Macka isn't even in Istanbul, Burak. It's in Trabzon. The Macka that Sadik was talking about is a district in Trabzon. On the Black Sea, in the Pontic Mountains of the northeast, near the Georgian border. The church, the priest, the icon and everything were all in Macka, at the Panagia Sumela Monastery. You understand? Yes! I stood with my mouth open just like that when I discovered that. But that's not all! Listen now: Sadik Usta and Shirin Hanim aren't Turks. Don't say anything, Burak. Wait. The two of them – the man we know as Sadik Usta and the woman we know as Shirin Hanim – are one hundred percent Black Sea Greeks!'

30

Celine

I was so stoned when I turned on the light in the dining room and found Sadik and Great-Granny. I'd just smoked a whole joint all by myself. But don't get the wrong idea – I'm not one of those potheads who rolls joints morning, noon and night. The reason I brought weed to the island was because I was going to write some songs while I was here and I thought the weed might inspire me. But to be honest, I smoked that joint just to forget everything, to escape from myself. I was really depressed.

Uncle Ufuk and I came home laughing and chatting. Maybe my laughing at his jokes was kind of forced, but he was obviously in a good mood. Was it me telling him I was in love that made him get carried away, or what? He asked a lot of questions about the 'guy' I'd fallen for, and when I said there wasn't anything worth talking about between us yet, he laughed suggestively. According to him, there was nothing better than being in love in your early twenties. This was my golden age. Love was the greatest thing. And so on. I just couldn't tell him that the guy I was in love with wasn't a 'guy' at all but the great Burak Gokce. And the more I kept on not saying that, the more miserably ridiculous the whole situation became – in my head, of course.

As his mood lightened, so mine darkened, but I didn't let on. Walking down from Hristos Hill, I made up all sorts of stories. I said the guy I was in love with was studying journalism. Kind of a white lie – not so far from the truth. I said I'd met him at a bar in Kadikoy where our band was the opening act. A total lie. Curly black hair, glasses. True. Was he attracted to me? I wasn't sure yet. When I said that, Uncle Ufuk laughed sweetly.

'You're certain you're in love with him and yet he's not attracted to you? That's against the laws of nature, Celine.'

That should have made me happy, but I felt really low. We'd just got to the garden gate and although it was twilight I could still see people moving behind the dining-room window. Maybe that was why I felt so desperate. The lovemaking scene on the dining table resurfaced in my imagination. I was supposed to have got past all that. They were best friends, remember? Aunt Nur was a lonely woman and Burak was her BFF. No. Aunt Nur opened her cherry-patterned kimono for Burak like a... a... I was filled with hatred and jealousy. But an even more overpowering emotion was rising inside me. Panic. I hadn't told Uncle Ufuk that Burak was there with us, that he had arrived yesterday, had done an interview with Great-Granny at the breakfast table and then in the evening had sat on the jetty with Aunt Nur and me, drinking wine, smoking a joint, getting high and going for a dip. I hadn't been able to tell him.

Uncle Ufuk followed me into the garden and was about to go into the house when I ran and grabbed him. I did everything I could think of to stop him from looking at the billowing gauze curtain in the dining-room window. How could I tell him now? I had no choice but to dive in, head first.

'Uncle Ufuk, um, Ufuk, I forgot to tell you earlier – you know anyway, I'm sure – that Burak's here. He came to do an interview with Great-Granny. He stayed here last night. For his newspaper c... c... column.'

I had trouble finishing the sentence because Uncle Ufuk's arm under my hand turned icy cold. Tilting his head a little to the right, he looked into my face. His eyebrows were raised.

'Why didn't you tell me this earlier, Celine?'

His voice was like ice too. He jerked his arm away from my hand, and instead of going into the house, he turned towards the sea.

'You go on in, Celine. I'll come in later. Please don't tell Nur I'm here.'

He was going to leave. As soon as I went into the house, he'd go out through the gate. I would hear the bell ringing. My insides were in shreds. What about his promise not to leave me until we found Dad? Yeah, right, what did I expect? I built the man up, only to drop him like a burst balloon. It was all my fault. Was that the right time to be talking about love, just when his wife was cheating on him?

With my head down, I went into the house. I didn't even slow down when I passed the dining-room door, but I still heard their murmuring. My eyes filled with tears. Uncle Ufuk shouldn't be having to go through that. It was so unfair. Here we were again, back where we started.

When I got to my room, I took out the weed I'd hidden in my pencil case, broke open one of the cigarettes I'd bought while I was waiting for Burak yesterday morning, put in my earphones and played Massive Attack's 'Teardrop'. It fitted. I crumbled the weed, trying to save every crumb, put the filter in, fumbled around for a match in the bottom of my bag, found one, lit it and inhaled. And again. It felt good. It was sort of like mint, or thyme. What harm could it do?

Later on, I left my room and went downstairs. I was observing myself. I was in the hallway. It was dark. I was at the dining-room door. I put my ear to the door. Would I hear moaning? Could you make love for that many hours? How should I know? My only experiences had been rushed, unsatisfying encounters; that was as far as my repertoire went. Oh, Burak, if I could make love with you even just the one time, I'd know what it was like to be a woman. Who was I kidding? Burak would leave me as soon as he'd slept with me. He'd run off, get out, wouldn't answer my messages. If I persisted, he'd respond in a silly, friendly, even fatherly manner, as if nothing had happened. He'd deny every move, every word, every intimacy. I was looking for a serious connection, not just good sex, but the only reason he'd get close to me would be out of lust. He was a middle-aged Turkish man, after all. Lust and a serious connection would push against each other and I'd fall into the hole in between. Shit.

As I was envisaging these scenarios, I noticed something strange about the sounds I was hearing through the door. What language were they speaking? Mumble, mumble, mumble. I leant down and looked through the keyhole. Still blocked. Enough! I grabbed the door handle. It opened right away. It must not have been locked. How could that be? So what was going on now? There were two chairs in front of me and two people were sitting on them, side by side. Had they been sitting there the whole time? What was that smell? But these two... these two... I'd been expecting to see Burak and Nur on the dining table acting out an illustration from a

Taoist sex book, but it was Sadik and Shirin who were sitting there in the dark! I got the giggles. It was terrible. The more I tried to stop myself, the more I laughed. I was doubled over with laughter. How to explain to those two what the giggles were and why I had them?

I turned on the light and the crystal chandelier sparkled. I rubbed my eyes. The two of them were looking at me like a pair of deer caught in the headlights. What was going on? The dining room was a disaster area. They'd somehow managed to drag the massive table over to the window and there they were, perched on high-backed wooden chairs like two exhausted sparrows. I stopped laughing. I felt like crying at the sight of those two little oldies sitting side by side. Oh God, they were so old! Two bodies whose life force was almost spent. It was so hard to imagine that they'd ever been young. It was like they were born old, like they'd always looked at the world in that same old-fashioned, ignorant, incompetent, incomprehensible way. But of course they must have been young once, must have felt the same things I felt. Really? Had life battered them the way it battered me? Hard to imagine.

They were staring at the wall opposite. I didn't see the picture at first because I was staring at them. It took me ages to see it, or so it seemed. I'd lost all sense of time. Suddenly, I was filled with happiness. Of course! If the people in the dining room were Shirin and Sadik, then... If p was q, then... It was like I'd woken up from a nightmare. None of the things I'd thought had happened in that room had actually happened. Life could start afresh. I had to go and find Uncle Ufuk. I'd drag him there if I had to. Right away. I had to go. Immediately.

'Romeika,' said Great-Granny.

Sadik was startled. 'Madam Shirin!'

I took two steps towards them and the weed hit me like a ten-tonne truck. My feet left the floor; I floated, crashed into the ceiling. Then I was looking down at all of us from above – Celine, Sadik, Shirin, the dining room. It was like watching a film. I listened to the dialogue with interest.

'What is Romeika? Is it something like eureka?' The giggling Celine had forgotten all her troubles, her plans, her uncle Ufuk.

'It is not a thing, little lady. Your great-grandmother is totally exhausted.'

'The language we were speaking is called Romeika. Also known as Pontiaka or Pontic Greek.'

That meant I hadn't made it up. It meant the murmurings I'd heard were not my imagination and that I'd asked them what language they were speaking. Yes, of course I'd asked them – just now, when I came into the room. I thought I'd just thought about asking, but I'd actually done it, like, with words. Would they notice that I was stoned? Hopefully not. I assumed an air of complete seriousness.

'What is it, this language? How do you know it?'

I was suddenly reminded of the made-up languages that twins use with each other. We'd studied that in my Psychology 101 class. It's a real thing: nobody knows what they're saying, not even their mothers. I looked again at Shirin and Sadik sitting there, next to each other. Their wrinkled cheeks, their dry, deep-set blue eyes. Sadik had a dark complexion, Shirin's was pink and white, but the way they sat, the way their necks tilted to the right, even the way they sighed was the same. What if those two turned out to be twins! I giggled. Oh God, I was so high.

'Celine, come over here and sit down.'

Great-Granny pointed to a chair behind her, next to where

she'd hung her stick. Yes, Your Majesty. I passed to my proper place. Now all three of us were sitting in a row, like birds on a telegraph wire. Part of me was still on the ceiling watching the scene. They were sparrows, I was a seagull. Our faces were turned towards the wall. Our faces. Our faces to the wall. The wall! Oh, my God! Celine got to her feet. What! Aha! There was an un-be-lievable painting in front of her. She took two, three, four steps towards the wall. Mountains, clouds, frothing sea, ships blowing out black smoke. She had an irresistible urge to touch them.

'Don't touch! It's not dry yet.'

'Yay, Great-Granny! Wow! This is amazing! This... this... What is this? Did you do this? How? When?'

'Little lady, your grandmother is very tired. You may talk to her tomorrow. With your permission, I will now clean up.'

'Sit down, Sadik! There are things we need to tell Celine. She is Fikret's daughter, after all.' Great-Granny's voice was stern.

'What? What do you need to tell me?'

I was intrigued. But I couldn't take my eyes off the wall. It was as if, were I to go through that wall, I wouldn't find myself in a hall off which the ground-floor rooms opened but in a real place, in the mountains, beside the sea. Not in the kitchen or the pantry.

'Tell me, Great-Granny!'

'First of all, tell me what *you* see.'

Oh God, Shirin, what don't I see! You've poured it all out. Okay, you painted as far up as you could reach. The top half of the wall is empty, an irritating champagne colour, but the lower part is magnificent. There's everything you might want – bombs, mountains, forests, stone bridges, rushing rivers. Giant-sized men in the Shirin Saka style – moustached, with black vests and red belts. One of them is holding up a black handkerchief, ready to launch into a dance. Then he takes the hand of the other man to get him to join in. Hey! Hey! That's what it looks like. Classic Shirin Saka, defying all dimensions and conventions. And behind them is a house. Do I know that house? I go closer. A big house. Pink and purple flowers growing up the stone walls. Have I seen a photo of it or did I see it in a dream? Then, look, a sad young girl is walking down the mountain. Her two plaits hang down from beneath her white headscarf. It's not just her; there are other people walking. As I look, they become visible. It's like a computer simulation. The more I pay attention, the more I see. All the people are tired. I don't know how Great-Granny manages to make you feel the tiredness of these people or, you know, the joy of the young men dancing. The woman's not famous for nothing.

'Don't close your eyes. You'll only hear if you're looking. Go closer. What does this scene say to you?'

Hear? Those two had to be as high as I was. Okay. I got really close. What did the artist want to say here? I looked and looked. I didn't hear anything. Bombs were exploding on the mountains. Some people were crying. Maybe it was the howling of the wind. The sea was so rough. But I didn't hear any if that. My mind returned to the language they'd been speaking together.

'I can hear that language you were just speaking. These people are speaking that language.'

Sadik Usta gasped. Great-Granny stood up, leaning on her stick. Sadik Usta remained sitting where he was. This was strange. Normally, he springs up, takes Great-Granny's arm, hands her the stick, straightens her skirt, and, you know, waits on her. Whereas now he was leaning his elbow on the table and just staying there like that. Like he was frightened or defeated, something like that. But by what? He'd surrendered. But to whom?

'Do you see these two men, Celine?'

Great-Granny walked slowly over to her magnificent painting. I went nearer and looked at the place she was pointing to with her stick.

'I'm going to tell you the story of these two friends. A story of betrayal. Because if I do not open this box now, the passage to the past...'

From where he was sitting, Sadik Usta moaned. I turned to him, frightened. Things were getting very weird. For a start, could those two old people really have painted that whole wall so quickly, even if Shirin Saka's speediness was as legendary as her style? Dad did tell me once that she had on occasion produced five masterpieces in a single night. Then there was that thing they spoke, whatever it was. That language. That was also weird; it did something to the mood in the room. And now she was saying something about a passage and it was all getting very deep. We had some work to do here.

'Sadik Usta, are you okay?'

The poor old dried-up shell waved his hand hopelessly. Great-Granny nudged my leg with her stick.

'Celine! Are you listening to me? I need to tell this story to you. Not to anyone else. To you. Give me your arm so I can lean on you.'

After that, things got even weirder. Great-Granny takes my arm and we start walking away from the door. But it isn't the door any more, it isn't our dining room. Shirin and Celine, arm in arm, enter the painting. I begin hearing things: crying; bombs exploding; live music. Music that's like an excited heart beating to an insane rhythm. Piercing violin strings going crazy. Is that a fiddler, Shirin? Great-Granny's voice sounds like the fiddler. Fighters are making their way up the mountainsides. Look, she's saying, this one is heading up into the mountains. She points to one of the giant men she's drawn. We pass right by him. If we reached out, we could grab his arm. He's going to join the rebels and fight the men who massacred his parents and razed his village to the ground. The other giant man will remain in the mansion with the women and children. He'll send aid to the one on the mountain. Provisions, clothing, weapons. Do I understand?

I don't understand, but what does it matter? I've gone into the painting with you, Shirin. We're like two young girls wandering around in the mountains. Is this what you meant by the passage? We're walking. Crows are flying from the branches. There's a battle somewhere. I hear other voices. Militants, guerrilla fighters, gangs. From one mountain ridge to another. Great-Granny pulls at my arm and we stop in front of the house adorned with pink and purple flowers. Beside the house there's an arbour and beneath the arbour are men in boots. Soldiers. They're holding a little girl in their arms. They've taken all her clothes off and they're stroking her blonde hair. Is that me? She looks like me. Why did you draw me, Shirin? I shiver. I'm afraid. They're going to hurt me. Tears fall from the little girl's eyes. Tears are falling from my eyes. The man sitting at the table under the arbour has his head in his hands. He is desperate. He is the little girl's father. He is one of the joyful young men we just passed. The men are threatening to take his daughter unless he tells them where his traitor friend is. I can hear them. Or Great-Granny is relating it to me. They're pinching the child. I shudder as if it's my own skin being pinched.

Let's go, Great-Granny!

Let's get out of this passage!

Impossible! You need to hear this story.

I'm not hearing the story; I'm in it. I'm living the story. I'm shouldering the burden of the wretched father sitting under the arbour. I feel the pinching of the child, the bruising of her skin. I know. I know everything. I know, although no one has told me. It is a story registered in the spirals of my DNA. Everything is recorded in the archives at the bottom of the well. Registered and forgotten. Yes, the desperate father, in order to save his daughter from those soldiers, is going to reveal the location of the mountain cave in which his friend who joined the rebel forces is hiding. He will be an informer. For the rest of his life, he will be the man who betrayed his friend, his people. The story of his betrayal is being worked into the spirals of his DNA. Ha, you're one of us now, the soldiers will say. I am there. I hear them. They laugh cruelly. We'll leave a guard at your door. We look after those who work with us. The day will come when your people will be crammed into a boat and dragged from this land, carrying nothing but a bundle each, but we will protect you. That's what they're saying. One of them kisses the little girl. His disgusting saliva drips down my cheek. Then they let her go. She falls down. Her bare knees are covered in dirt; dirt mixed with blood. I am falling too. Great-Granny holds on to my arm.

'Madam Shirin!'

It wasn't me who fell; it was Great-Granny. She fell down against the wall, one hand on her chest. Her voice cracked.

'I'm fine, there's nothing wrong. I had a palpitation.'

There is a howling in my ears. The sound of the fiddler is growing faint. Its frenzied rhythm is calming down. Sadik Usta has run and knelt beside her. He has found lemon cologne from somewhere and is rubbing it on the insides of Great-Granny's wrists. Great-Granny has leant her back against the wall. Her eyes are closed and her lips are moving as if she is praying. Just where her head is leaning, a great building rises up from a ledge on a cliffside high up in the green mountains. I hadn't noticed it until now. It is beautiful. It is not tall but rather spreads out along the rocky ledge, embracing the mountains. It is so much a part of its surrounds that at first glance you don't see it, but once you have seen it, you can't take your eyes off it. It is a monastery, but quite unlike the ones on Buyukada. This is a magical monastery. It could be in a fairy tale. In the courtyard of the monastery are two little children, hand in hand. They are looking intently at something. The girl is blonde-haired, the boy has blue eyes. I take a step back. Another step. Their eyes are focused on Shirin, fallen on the floor, and on old Sadik rubbing her wrists. The thing they're looking at as if they're under a spell is... Holy shit! That thing... that thing... is the future! Their own future. The children are looking from inside the painting at our dining room, at Sadik and Shirin collapsed at the foot of the wall. They are looking at their future selves. Because those children in the monastery courtyard are Sadik and Shirin themselves.

Oh my God, I was so stoned!

31

Nur

I was sitting on the edge of the pier, staring at the sea and eating potato balls wrapped in wax paper that I'd bought at the overpriced delicatessen. People were still getting on and off the ferries in droves, pushing, shoving, laughing as they passed behind me. I had my earphones in. With the noise of the outside world suppressed by music, I could observe my thoughts as if they were somebody else's.

Where my mama left me, hold me tight,
Where I've given up on love, set me right.

Even though I've been listening to that album for years, I've never tired of it. Metin Altiok was such a talented poet, and yet what happened to him? They burnt him alive in the Hotel Madimak with the rest of the poets in 1993.

I leant over the concrete side and watched the jellyfish caught up in the seaweed swaying back and forth as the waves washed in and out. The sea was dirty and I couldn't see the bottom.

My memories gather with the snow,
Slowly...

It was at exactly that spot that, years and years ago, Mum had me throw my dummy to the fish. It had become an issue in the family that I still walked around with a dummy in my mouth, even though I was already at kindergarten. My father used to get especially angry about it. He somehow managed to connect my addiction to the dummy with Mum's family, seeing it as another example of the perversity he associated with Shirin Saka's family, and so he considered it Mum's responsibility to get me to give it up. Since it's because of your genes that the child is like that, you should sort this out, Suheyla!

I leant over a bit further, closer to the water. Were there any fish down there, amongst the seaweed? Mum had persuaded me that fish much littler than me needed my blue plastic dummy – the Little Black Fish from the children's storybook that she read me before bed, for example – and after I'd thrown it to them she would buy me cherry-rosehip ice cream from the ice-cream seller in front of the club. I lay on my stomach, my chest pressed against the warm concrete, and gripped the dummy tightly in my fist. The greeny-blue sea was clear and sparkling, but the Little Black Fish was nowhere to be seen. When I finally screwed up the courage to throw the dummy into the water, I was expecting little baby fish to immediately come swimming into view, wagging their tails at the present I'd given them. When none appeared, I was confused. I cried. Mum had tricked me. Did fish suck on dummies? And what would Little Black Fish be doing at our island, beside our pier? For one thing, a fish's mouth was too small. They weren't coming. I'd seen how they rushed in as soon as you chucked a single crust of bread into the sea. So Mum had lied to me. She lifted me up into the air by my armpits, but I didn't want any ice cream. I was all alone in the big, wide world. I cried.

And now I was crying again. What had changed since then?

Always, a part of us is missing,
For some reason

I was still all alone in the big, wide world. Even more so, because my gentle mum, whose presence had once been as sweet and refreshing as the juice of an apricot slipping down my throat, was no longer with me.

And when you say
Let me fill that void,
What you have
Slowly loses its value
In time

When I turned my head, I saw them. They were coming out of one of the seafront restaurants. Burak and Fikret! What was going on? Fikret was gripping Burak's arm, talking to him and at the same time pulling him away from the pier, towards the fish restaurants lined up alongside the boardwalk. Burak went along with Fikret for a few steps, then changed his mind and stopped. Fikret stopped too, but carried on talking. Two minutes later they repeated the same performance. Fikret pulled Burak, Burak resisted. I turned off my music, took out the earphones and put them in my pocket, and watched the strange scene for a while. Both of them seemed unsteady on their feet. They must have been drinking together. When and how had Fikret appeared and how had Burak found him? Or had he known all along where Fikret was?

Eventually, Burak freed himself from Fikret's grasp and with a serious expression on his face said something to him. They both turned and looked at the ferries waiting at the pier, and it was then that Burak and I caught each other's eye. I smiled, but he looked away, angry, hurt and resentful. He glanced at Fikret, said something else, and Fikret nodded. Then they embraced each other, not with a bear hug but rather they patted each other on the back, in the way guys do when leaving a bar. Take care of yourself, brother. And so on. So they'd become best friends. Fikret had a rucksack on his back, Burak was empty-handed. Presumably his wallet, phone and notebook were stashed away in some of the many pockets in his trousers. In the old days, he would carry rolls and rolls of film in those pockets, back when he was a fearless young reporter. Now he was the slick, wary writer of 'Portraits'.

After Fikret had disappeared into the crowds in front of the fish restaurants, Burak came over to me. I smiled again. Come on, Burak. We've loved each other for such a long time. Forgive me. I needed so much to be forgiven. My smile was about to turn into a foolish, pleading grin, but Burak stayed serious. I love that about men, how they don't feel the need to respond to a smile.

'You found Fikret!'

'Yes, he just appeared in front of me in the crowd.'

'Where's he been all day? Did he explain?'

'I'm leaving, Nur.'

I tried to suppress the wave of panic rising inside me. 'What do you mean, you're "leaving"? Where are you going?'

'To Istanbul. Home.'

Inside me, something shattered. My eyes filled. It always felt like a part of me was missing. Altiok's lines were still playing in my head:

> *Though I have reached this age*
> *There is still a child inside me,*
> *Yearning for love*

Burak paid no attention. He glanced anxiously at the ferry, then back at me. Something in his expression had changed. He wasn't angry, hurt and resentful any more, but nor was he like he used to be either. There was such a thing as too late, and I had crossed that line.

Still, I made one last attempt. 'But tomorrow?' I said. 'Tomorrow is Grandmother's hundredth birthday. Won't you be here for that? What about your interview?'

As if I cared about Burak's interview, his writing, the 'Portraits' page in the weekend supplement. What I really wanted to say was, won't you stay for me – we can talk it through, and then you'll forgive me.

'I have my story already. I don't need anything else.'

What could he mean? Okay, so be it. I wouldn't ask. What was that new look in his eyes? Burak never looked at me like that. Something was missing. Passion? Desire? I couldn't tell. There was a purity there, unclouded by other emotions. I was upset. The ferry whistle sounded and the familiar announcement came over the scratchy loudspeakers: 'The ship now approaching will depart immediately for Eminonu, via the islands and Kadikoy.'

Burak started moving. 'That's my ferry. I don't want to miss it. You should run and catch up with Fikret. Don't leave him on his own.'

Without giving me a chance to answer, he leant and touched his lips to my cheeks. Swiftly, softly, and not at all like he'd intended to kiss me on the mouth but had misfired. Then he left, his hands in his pockets, his eyes forward, his steps rapid. I watched him from behind. With one hand I felt for the trace of his lips on my cheek, but there was none. Damn! He'd kissed me the way I used to kiss him when things were good between Ufuk and me. As a friend, plain and simple. Not on the mouth.

I didn't move until the ferry had left the pier. I would have stayed longer still if I hadn't seen Fikret buying roasted chickpeas from the street seller near the motorboat landing. I dragged myself over to him. I was utterly exhausted. I wanted to lean on someone or fall into someone's arms; I wanted to feel physically supported the way I do when I lie on my back in the sea with my arms wide. In truth, though, I'm the sort who can only really be myself when I'm by myself; I've never known how to give my weight to someone else. Still, I wanted to find out if Burak had made things even more complicated by talking to Fikret about me, and if so how much had he told him?

'Fikret!'

'Hello, Nur.'

He wasn't at all surprised. He must have seen me. He'd have to have walked past me to get to the landing from the restaurant anyway.

'Burak's gone.'

'I know. Would you like some?'

I looked at the paper cone of chickpeas he was offering but didn't take any.

'Shall we walk a bit? It's cooled down at last. It's going to be a lovely night.'

I didn't say anything. Venus was now winking behind Heybeliada, where the sun had set an hour earlier. Because Venus follows the sun around in the sky, we don't see her in the day, but after sundown she has the chance to show herself briefly in the twilight, before she too disappears. The sun doesn't wait for her. Burak waited for me for so long and now he was on the ferry, approaching Heybeliada.

Fikret and I walked to the clocktower square, past the ice-cream parlours and trendy waffle shops, past the enticing aromas and 'Welcome! Welcome!' greetings. The place I longed for was quite different from all that and I doubted it could be found anywhere in the world now. Fikret would say that I needed to look inside myself to find what I was looking for. Fair enough, but could the outside world also not be more like the world I dreamt of? Ufuk would say, what are you waiting for, go find it, secure in the knowledge that I wouldn't actually be going anywhere, or if I did, that I'd come back to him. Only Burak would ask me to describe the place I wanted to wake up in.

We walked past the Old Acacia Hotel and went into Anadolu Club. The people sitting at the tables on the elegant terrace cast sidelong glances at us, looking us over. Fikret smiled at a few of them, nodded in greeting. The club was busy, but we'd left the noisy holiday crowd outside. The floor lamps gave off a soft yellow glow like old Parisian streetlamps, and from loudspeakers hidden behind palm trees Richard Clayderman's gentle piano could be heard. Elderly ladies were playing cards at round tables, and healthy, handsome parents, having let their children loose in a safe area, were drinking Blush with friends who looked just like them. Despite the refined ambiance, Fikret decided to stick with raki; without a second's hesitation, he ordered a double. Bravo, brother! His personal development journey had obviously got him to a point where he no longer cared what others thought. I asked for cognac. In that heat? Of course, the waitress said nothing; she had obviously been taught not to question anybody or anything.

'Throw in a couple of ice cubes. And could you bring us some bitter chocolate, if you have any.'

Fikret laughed again. There was a lightness about him, perhaps because he'd been drinking with Burak, or maybe for some other reason, I didn't know.

'You're incorrigible, Nur!'

I grinned and leant back in the wicker chair. It was like we were in Havana. We were sitting in the courtyard of the hotel Hemingway used to stay in. Outside were ordinary people, exhausted from the heat, the crowds, life's troubles, trying to make the most of a short holiday. Inside, here we were, the elite, leaning back in our wicker armchairs, listening to the rustle of palm leaves accompanying Richard Clayderman playing 'Let It Be'. I clinked my fat cognac glass against Fikret's raki glass. It made me happy to see him drinking, but I didn't say anything. I didn't want to remind him of his yogi self. We were good like that. We were good.

'Well, tell me, brother, where were you all day?'

Ensconced in our wicker chairs, we both sat staring out to sea. I couldn't have coped with sitting across from him and talking face to face. I felt crushed. Perhaps it was the thought of Burak getting on that ferry and leaving, or perhaps it was Ufuk not returning my calls; I didn't know. A thin, sharp knife was carving away at my heart. Did you call that a carpenter's knife? A chisel? One used for fine work, anyway. Slicing tiny slivers from my heart.

'I went to Macka.'

Macka? To our house? Ufuk? Had Fikret gone to see Ufuk? But Ufuk wasn't in the Macka house. He hadn't been back to the house since he left that night. The chisel gouged out another slice and drew back.

'The Macka in Trabzon. On the Black Sea – in the northeast.'

My eyes must have opened wide in surprise.

Fikret explained. 'Did you know that our people – I mean Grandmother and Sadik Usta – were born and grew up in Trabzon's Macka?'

I thought about it. Did I know? Yes, I probably did. At some point somebody had mentioned something about the Black Sea, but was that Trabzon, or Samsun or Rize? I hadn't paid attention. They sold something up there so that they could buy the Buyukada house. Was it land? No. There'd been a big house somewhere. But all of that happened long before I was born, even before Mum was born. Grandmother was newly married then. Okay, but what was Fikret doing there? No, I wasn't going to be so foolish as to ask that. Fikret had become obsessed with our genealogy, with this great-grandfather called Nuri, so he upped and went to Trabzon, to this Macka, on the second day of the holiday. He was the incorrigible one! Deep down, I envied him. He did what he wanted and didn't care if people thought him crazy. When he set his mind on something, he did it. He didn't give up.

'You went there this morning and just got back, right?'

He nodded, took a big gulp of raki, and then another. Drink, Fikret, drink! Drink and let's see your true self.

'I couldn't sleep last night, Nur. You were all sitting on the jetty in front of the house, laughing together, but the voices in my head just wouldn't let up. I knew that I'd be at peace only once I'd completed the puzzle. The solution was right there in front of me, I could sense it, but though I could fit the second piece with the third, I couldn't finalize the whole picture. There was always a missing piece.'

'What piece?'

Fikret stirred and turned towards me in his wicker chair. His eyes were bloodshot.

'Do you seriously want to know?'

What he meant was that he would tell me if I didn't make fun of it, make fun of him. He was burning to tell someone, and that was why he'd been so reluctant to let Burak go. But Burak had gone. Another cut from the chisel. A deep breath. A swallow of cognac, that cure-all, slipping down my throat, sweet and warm.

'Of course I want to know.'

Tell me, Fikret. Distract me. If my thoughts are diverted, this knife inside me will stop whittling. Come on, entertain me with your Black Sea stories, with what happened behind closed curtains, with family secrets we've sworn not to reveal even though we have no idea what they are.

Fikret took the cone of roasted chickpeas from his pocket, threw a handful into his mouth, and sat back.

'So... yesterday morning at the breakfast table, while Burak was asking Grandmother about her childhood, they had a heated argument. Did you notice?'

'Who do you mean by "they"?'

'Grandmother and Sadik. It was some story about a priest who came to the place where they were living. They mentioned a church icon. To be precise, Grandmother tried to bring up the subject, and Sadik glossed over it. Do you remember? Well, right then, I suddenly remembered the interview Burak did with Sadik Usta years ago.'

'Sadik Usta cut out that interview and hung it beside his bed, as I recall.'

'Yes, I remembered that too. That's why I went to his room after breakfast.'

'Fikret! That newspaper clipping is very precious to the poor chap. I hope you didn't tear it off the wall and pocket it.'

'It wasn't on the wall. He'd taken it down, but it wasn't hard to find.'

'Brother!'

'So what? It's right here.' Fikret unzipped the front pocket of the backpack that was on the floor beside him. He took out the old newspaper clipping with its faded edges. 'Tomorrow morning when Sadik Usta goes shopping, I'll put it back where I found it. The man doesn't open his drawer every day and reread what he said to Burak! It's been there for seventeen years – he won't miss it for one day.'

That made sense. I threw some chickpeas into my mouth, then downed another mouthful of cognac. Evening had crept into night, so we could get drunk without feeling guilty. I felt the courage that comes with the darkness. A person can do all sorts of things after nightfall, then be shocked at themselves when daylight arrives. Could you please refresh our drinks? Merci.

'I was right. I had remembered correctly. Sadik had told Burak years ago. Look, here. Take it, read it yourself. He talks about "Shirin Saka's parents' house in Macka". That's the second piece of the puzzle. A priest, an icon, her parents' house in Macka. I was looking out the window and thinking about all that. I realized I wasn't going to fall asleep, so I opened my laptop, typed those words into Google, and what do you think came up?'

Our drinks were replenished. They didn't have any bitter

chocolate, of course. Not even any regular chocolate. It didn't matter. Stars had filled the sky. The sea across from us was dark, the ever-present ferry lights shining bright in the blackness.

'What came up?'

'Sumela!'

For a second I thought he'd said, 'Suheyla!' Suheyla. Our mother. The perception of the familiar. All doors lead to you, Mum. Fikret must have seen the surprise on my face because he felt the need to explain.

'Panagia Sumela Monastery.'

'Oh, okay, I get it. The Greek Orthodox monastery, you mean? The one up on the cliffs, in that really dramatic spot, near the Georgian border?'

Fikret studied my face to see whether I was prepared to listen to what he had to say. I opened my eyes really wide to show that I was interested. I must have convinced him. He raised his voice.

'Listen to this, Nur. It's the time of the Turkish War of Independence and the ultra-nationalist Topal Osman and his gang of thugs are massacring the Eastern Black Sea Greeks. The priests at Panagia Sumela Monastery bury a very valuable icon of the Virgin Mary somewhere so that it won't be looted or burnt. One of the priests manages to escape and when he gets to Greece, he tells the priests there where the icon is. Meanwhile, Turkish nationalist gangs are looting the Greek villages and razing the churches to the ground. The beautiful Panagia Sumela Monastery bears its share of this savagery, but nothing happens to the icon of the Virgin Mary, which is safe in the earth. Years later, when the Black Sea region has been completely cleansed of its Greek population and all traces of them erased, a priest comes from Greece, finds the buried icon, embraces it and takes it to Salonica. Our Shirin and Sadik, who were children then in Macka, witness this event.'

A star fell, dropping out of sight behind Heybeliada. It was huge. It looked like a plane, disappearing from the dark sky. 'Amazing!' I muttered.

'Yes, it is, Nur. An amazing story. What were Sadik and Shirin doing at the Panagia Sumela Monastery then? One possibility is that they were playing. Their house wasn't that far away. Another possibility is that this was a game orchestrated by fate so that you and I would eventually get to hear the story. At any rate, when all the pieces came together, I couldn't ignore it. I bought a 6 a.m. ticket from Sabiha Airport to Trabzon.'

'How did you get to the airport at that hour?'

'I called a water taxi to take me to Pendik, and from there it's no distance to Sabiha, so I took a cab.'

My brother has never balked at spending money on his passions. I had to admit, it was an interesting story. I envied Fikret his enthusiasm and courage.

'What did you find when you got to Macka? I assume you didn't just ask whoever you met about Shirin Saka's father? What was your plan?'

'To be honest, I didn't have a plan. I just went with the flow. It was as if someone was whispering the next steps in my ear, so I just tuned in and did as I was prompted.'

Oh, dear God, the New Age talk had begun.

'It was the whispering voice that got me on that plane to Trabzon, and I didn't even think about what I'd do once I got there. I've come to realize, Nur, that we're not in control of our lives, that everything is predetermined. And even if it isn't, the place where the storyline is managed can't be accessed; human will has no effect on it. When your intuition gets sharper, your sensitivity to the story increases and you simply take the next step without trying to change the game or waste effort by pulling it in the direction you want to go or wondering where it's taking you. You don't have a specific goal.'

'It seems to me that a person should have a specific goal if he leaves Buyukada to catch the 6 a.m. flight to Trabzon.'

'Yes, of course. But I didn't have any expectations as to what that goal would or should be. I just knew I had to go there, even if nothing came of it. Maybe I'd never know why I went, but that was immaterial. I didn't need a reason.'

'That's sort of an opportunistic approach, isn't it?'

I was teasing him, but Fikret didn't take the bait. He didn't notice. He polished off his second glass of raki and set it down on the glass table with a bang that almost shattered it. I was starting to have fun. It had been so long since my brother and I had gone out drinking together. I rolled a cigarette and lit it.

'How did you get to Macka?'

'I took a taxi from the airport. The driver was a young man, very young. When I told him I was going to Macka, he presumed I wanted to visit the Panagia Sumela Monastery. "The monastery is closed for restoration work," he said. "Professional climbers from Istanbul are scaling the cliffside, clearing away the rockfalls, making it safe for visitors and cleaning its facade. But if you want, I can take you to the villages where they still speak Black Sea Greek." It turned out that last year an English woman travelled there, a university professor like me, and wanted to go to those villages. And that was how the taxi driver discovered that the strange-sounding dialect he heard his grandma and grandpa speaking was actually an ancient language about to be extinguished from the face of the earth and therefore a potentially valuable tourist attraction. So now he takes people coming from the city, teachers like me, to those villages. Since Sumela was under restoration, he was sure I'd want to visit them instead.'

'Are there still people speaking Greek in the Black Sea region?'

'It's not Greek as such, it's Pontic Greek – what's known as Pontiaka or Romeika. On the way back, I looked it up online. There's even a documentary about it – I'll send you the link. Some people say it's the closest language to Ancient Greek. And, yes, it's still spoken in some villages.'

'That's interesting. I thought there was no Christian population left up there.'

'There isn't. Everybody is strictly Muslim in the villages that speak Pontiaka.'

I sat up to stub out my cigarette. Fikret had sunk into a meaningful silence. I gazed out at the lights reflecting on the dark waters from the small windows of the approaching ferry.

'Did you actually hear this language being spoken?'

'Yes. At the coffeehouse in one of the villages in the Macka district where the taxi driver dropped me off, several old men were speaking Pontiaka to each other. They stopped talking when I walked in. We exchanged holiday greetings, and the taxi driver introduced me as a teacher doing research.'

'They didn't like that, I assume.'

'They didn't. A few young roughnecks were quite threatening. What did I think I was researching? Some of the old men were watching TV and paid no attention. Others were deep in card games or backgammon. Tea was coming and going. The doors and windows were open, and there was a nice breeze.'

'I can't keep quiet any longer, Fikret – I have to say

something. It's like you're describing a film. Did you really experience all this today?'

He laughed. 'I can hardly believe it either, but, yes, this all happened today. Really. Look, we're here now. You and I are having a drink together in familiar territory.'

I felt like getting up and giving him a big hug. It was something I'd never done, even in my dreams. Had we ever hugged each other? I mean, from deep down, heart to heart? Had we ever shared our sadness by leaning our heads on each other's shoulders? Fikret lost Mum too. Was the knife that was slicing my heart into shreds also doing its work inside him?

'The rest is very strange. Every one of the old men at the coffeehouse had something to say about our great-grandfather Nuri. I'd assumed that nobody would be able to talk about him, that nobody would remember him, but it was just the opposite. Somebody said that he got what he deserved. That he was a rat. He shot his fellow resistance fighter in the back, they said. Some of them argued about that. Should he have helped a terrorist? they said. When the younger people there heard the word "terrorist" they got all riled up. "Are you the great-grandson of a Pontic Greek terrorist?" they said. A few said he had to do what he did for the struggle for independence. Others said he was an outright traitor and that this was obvious from what happened. Because in the end he—'

'Fascinating! But how could they remember all that from so far back? Are you sure they weren't just making up stories to impress you?'

'It's a small place and stories get passed round by word of mouth. And there are lots of old people there, Nur. People so old the light in their eyes has gone out, the skin of their hands

has been lost to brown liver spots, all their teeth have gone
and they're leaning on canes even while they're sitting down.
The Black Sea soil is amazing. People live long, like trees. We
treat Grandmother like a piece of rare Indian fabric because
she's a hundred years old, but up there, believe me, some of
the granddads look like they could be Great-Grandfather's
age. You assume they can't hear anything, and then they're
the ones who lay the golden egg.'

I wasn't convinced. Fikret wanted a story and the men in
the coffeehouse – men of all ages with nothing better to do
– mixed a lot of old tales together and presented it to him.
'Here's your great-grandfather's story' – and Fikret fell for it.

'There were people there who personally knew not our
great-grandfather but our great-grandmother.'

'Who?'

'Shirin Saka's mother. When her husband died... Great-
Grandfather Nuri's death... well, that's a story in itself. I'll
come to that. But first you have to hear what I'm going to tell
you, for context. So, Nuri dies and his wife, Shirin's mother,
remarries. You know that. Grandmother has told us about it.
In order not to bring an adolescent girl into her new husband's
house, she sends Shirin to a distant relative in Istanbul.'

'To the mansion in Uskudar. They send Sadik with her. I
was thinking about that today actually – about what a painful
experience that would have been for a young girl. Her father
dies and her mother, for some obscure reason, immediately
packs her off to a so-called uncle's mansion. We never took
into account this trauma of Grandmother's – when we were
accusing her of being a bad mother, I mean. Poor child. At
least they sent Sadik with her. Maybe that's why—'

Fikret waved his hand impatiently. 'Yes, that's interesting.
Because they actually sent Sadik to Istanbul to be educated,

not as a servant. I mean, at the beginning. His mother always expected that he would complete his education and work as a clerk in the shoe factory.'

'Really? Where did that come from? How did you learn all this, Fikret? Are you sure you didn't shut yourself up in a hotel room and spend the day dreaming up this story?'

Fikret laughed. He was excited. He was like a little boy all impatient to tell his remarkable story. His insides were all churned up as he tried to decide which bits of the story to tell first and which to save until later for maximum dramatic effect. His words came tumbling out one after the other without him taking a breath. If my eyes started to drift somewhere else, he would suddenly raise his voice to secure my undivided attention.

'As I just said, when Shirin's mother's first husband, Nuri, dies, she, in your words, gets rid of her daughter and marries one of the prominent men of the village. She takes Sadik's mother, Housekeeper Meryem, and settles in her new husband's home. She has children with her new husband. Housekeeper Meryem brings up these children, and as she's doing so, she tells them about her own son. Over and over. How Sadik went to school in Istanbul, how he would return to the village one day, wearing a suit and polished leather shoes and carrying a briefcase. He would kiss his mother's hand. Thanks to Meryem, these children – Shirin Saka's half-siblings, that is – grew up hearing the story not only of the lucky Shirin and Sadik, who were sent to Istanbul, but also of Meryem's husband, his past, which had been erased from the collective memory, and the shame behind Mr Nuri's death.'

Startled, I sat up straight and brushed the table with my hand, almost knocking over my cognac glass. It was empty anyway.

'What are you saying? That Shirin Saka has half-siblings in a Black Sea village?'

'Yes, she does. Siblings that share the same mother but have a different father. We have three great-uncles.'

'Did you meet them?'

'How do you think I learnt this story? From my Black Sea cousins, of course. Now, hold tight, Nur – are you ready? This Great-Grandfather Nuri, his wife, his daughter Shirin, even Housekeeper Meryem, Sadik, and Sadik's father, do you know what they all actually were?'

I leant forward to hear Fikret, and as I did, I caught sight of my phone on the table. I had a message. Involuntarily, I reached out my hand. It was from Ufuk. Ufuk! I straightened up. I had a message from Ufuk! For the first time in days. I had missed him so much; I felt it deep inside me, on my skin, in my bones. My hand shook as I slid the screen to read the whole message. I was sort of drunk, I guess. Otherwise I wouldn't have started crying when I read it.

'I'm waiting for you in our usual room at the Splendid Palace Hotel.'

I stuffed my phone in my handbag and got to my feet. My ears were roaring and my head was spinning. Fikret was anxious too. He stood up.

'No, nothing's wrong, Fikret. Everything's fine. More than fine. But I have to go now. Don't forget what you were going to tell me. We'll talk tomorrow. I have to go now. No, no, everything's fine.'

He bowed his head. He had a story to tell and that story would come alive only if he told it to someone. My brother needed me, needed my ears, but I had to go. Ufuk wouldn't wait. I stood on my tiptoes and hugged him. He was surprised, but he didn't draw back. On the contrary, he put his arms around my waist and held me tight. I leant my head against his bony chest. Oh, Fikret, who do we have in this life except each other? Maybe he'd been right. Maybe this story had to be dug up from where it had been buried and brought into the light in order for us to overcome the lack of connection between us. Our believing in a story concerning our ancestors would bring us closer together, regardless of whether it was true or not. What he had called a curse was in reality the dearth of intimacy between us, our continuing silence and detachment, our estrangement from each other and also from others. Now we could embrace each other. And, most importantly, Ufuk had called me! I was in love – with Ufuk; with Burak. I loved my brother. No, not one person, not one thing. I was love. Period.

I skipped out of the club like a young gazelle, crossed the street and ran up the steps to the Splendid Palace Hotel.

Ufuk was upstairs, in our room, waiting for me.

32

Sadik

While Miss Celine accompanied Madam Shirin to her bedroom, I put the dining room in order. I closed the lids of the paints and washed the jars, the mixing trays and the brushes in the kitchen sink. I was unable to move the table back on my own, but I arranged the chairs around it. I gathered up the oilcloth from the floor, folded it and put it away in a cupboard in the garden shed where the hose is kept. I carried the tins of paint out to the shed one by one and placed them on the shelf.

As I went into the dark garden, I was overcome by sadness. Laughter was coming from the next-door neighbours' property. They were grilling meat and the wind always blew the soot and smoke onto our side. My mouth was dry. I could not recall when I had last eaten, and it was not only my mouth that felt dry but my limbs too, as if my stomach had shrunk from my flesh. Over there, our old ones used to say that death crept up from the legs. My legs were aching. I decided I would take a chair outside and sit in front of the door for a spell, as I used to in the old days. Back then, Madam Shirin's black dog would come and put its head on my knee. Its eyes were blacker than the night, unchanged even when its fur turned white with age. It was when a white film grew across those black eyes that I knew it was going to die, but I did not say anything to Madam Shirin. She was devoted to that animal, perhaps because she found it after there was no one else left in the house. We were carrying on with our lives as if we'd forgotten dear Suheyla's death. As if one could forget such pain. Of course, we hadn't forgotten. That sweet, elegant, thoughtful child melted away like a candle. She burnt herself out.

I went inside to get the chair. As I walked into the tiled entrance hall, I felt its coolness on my face. Old furniture smells differently in the cool of evening and its scent grazed my skin. The house was silent. I passed the rooms opening off the hall, rooms with their familiar daily sounds and shifting light patterns, their laughter, their arguments, the ghosts of their dead, and closed their doors one after the other. Madam Shirin was asleep now in her bedroom overlooking the garden. No matter how lightly she breathed, my old ears always heard her. The kitchen. Clean. The pantry, all in order. Then my small room. I checked the door leading to the back garden. Closed. I glanced up the stairs. Where was Madam Nur? Mr Burak was also not present.

I entered the library, turned on the light. A few photographs had fallen under the table across from the fireplace. I collected them up. Miss Nur and Mr Fikret on the swings we hung from the iron posts supporting the grapevine, with Madam Suheyla's shadow fallen across them. Miss Celine and my lady had been looking at those earlier. I put the photographs into their box on the shelf. Time was such a strange thing. It seemed to me only yesterday that Madam Nur and Mr Fikret were children, whereas in their opinion those years were a long way in the past. As for my own childhood... I needed to go bed. I needed to just lock the front door and go to bed. Madam Nur would have her key with her, and if she didn't, she would remember that a spare key was kept hidden under a stone in front of the pantry window.

I turned off the light in the library and closed the door. I would rinse my face in the bathroom and retire to my room. However, after that, I do not know how it happened, I found myself again in the dining room. By the light reflected from the neighbours' brightly illuminated garden, I perused Madam Shirin's wall painting. In the darkness the mountains were higher, the forests denser. The teeth of the young men dancing the horon, our Black Sea folkdance, and the froth on the wild sea shone whitely. Madam Shirin had drawn the men life-sized. They were tall, well-developed, handsome men and they were standing right in front of me. If I spoke, they would speak. The more one looked, the more one had to continue looking. There was truly something magical about the way my lady had achieved this.

With my finger I touched the two plaits swinging from my dear mama's head. The paint had not completely dried. Perhaps my finger had left a mark. I could not tell in the dark. Madam Shirin had painted the details of my dear mama's hands and feet, her unsteady gait, so beautifully that I had no doubt that this was indeed my mama. The young man dancing the horon in front of her, the one with blue eyes, was my papa. I did not know him, but I knew that story. I knew it, but I did not know that I knew it until tonight. It seemed one did not forget.

Suddenly I heard the front door of the house being opened. I recoiled as if I'd put my hand in the fire. I had not heard the garden gate. The light in the dining room was not on and I had closed the door. No one would come in there at that hour. Even so, I crouched in a corner and waited. There came a few unsteady steps outside the dining-room door. Was it Madam Nur? Her footsteps were light. Perhaps it was Mr Burak. Had they given him a key too? I strained to try and catch any words or laughter, but whoever it was had remained standing where they were, without making a sound. I crouched there for a while longer, listening to the screeching of the seagulls that had nested on the roof and to the loud laughter of the next-door neighbours and the clatter of their plates, bowls, knives and forks.

Finally, when I was convinced that whoever had been in the hall had silently gone up the stairs, I got to my feet and opened the dining-room door. The stained-glass window above the front door filled the hall with a dead light and so at first I did not comprehend what I was seeing. When I did, a scream rose involuntarily from my throat, for it was Professor Halit's ghost who was standing there in the middle of the hallway! I hung onto the handle of the door to stop myself from falling.

'Mr Halit!'

The tall, thin silhouette turned slowly in my direction. I thought my heart would fly out of my chest.

'Sadik Usta! What are you doing there?'

'Mr Fikret!'

Gasping for breath, I leant against the doorframe. It was Mr Fikret. In truth, I am not one to believe in ghosts and passages to the past, but it seemed I was still under the influence of Madam Shirin's work and words. Unsure what to say, I quickly closed the door to the dining room. I was greatly relieved but did not want Mr Fikret to know how anxious I had been.

I switched on the night light on the console table to the right. My hands were shaking, but fortunately Mr Fikret did not notice this. I perceived that he had been drinking alcohol. Miss Celine had left her shoes at the foot of the stairs and while I was picking them up to take them to the cabinet under the staircase, Mr Fikret held my arm. I thus saw him from close up. His eyes were red, and his nose too. In order not to reveal that I smelt the raki on his breath, I turned my head slightly to the side. Where had he been all day? Hopefully not drinking alcohol the entire time.

'Sadik Usta, come and sit here. Let's talk a little.'

He pulled me to the chair beside the console table where the telephone lived.

'Welcome home, Mr Fikret. I have something to do in the kitchen. Let me complete my tasks and I will bring a jug of water to your room.'

Meaningless talk. Mr Fikret looked blankly into my face.

'Would you make me a coffee, please, Sadik Usta?'

He followed me into the kitchen. While I was bringing coffee and sugar from the pantry, he sat at the table where Madam Nur had sat earlier in the day, where she had cried and then fallen asleep with her head in her arms. My back was turned, but I sensed him looking in my direction. Mr Fikret might look, but he does not see. Since childhood, his mind has always been somewhere else; rather than being involved in what is happening around him, he is always preoccupied with his own thoughts. I glanced at him from the corner of my eye as I took a cup from the shelf near the table. He was sitting with his head cocked and propped up on one elbow, as if listening to words that were being whispered into his ear alone. I put the coffee and sugar into the small pot and added water from the jug. From the kitchen, the laughter from next door sounded louder. Seeing the colourful lightbulbs they had strung up in their trees made me sad. I wished that I had left the light in the dining room burning. From outside it would then have appeared that Madam Shirin and her grandchildren were celebrating the holiday properly. Attending to such details had been important in the past.

'Sadik Usta, do you know who Ioannis of Espiye is?'

Upon hearing Mr Fikret's question, my heart skipped a beat. I lit the stove with the long taper kept in the drawer rather than with a match so that he would not see that my hand was trembling, set the pot on the flame and stirred it carefully to ensure the coffee and sugar were well blended with the water. I coughed slightly to clear the knot in my throat. Perhaps Mr Fikret took this as an answer. I had no answer to give. He raised his voice.

'I don't know what they told you, Sadik. You're so tight-lipped, it's impossible to know what you're thinking. By all means, keep your back turned and don't look me in the eye, if that makes you more comfortable, but please listen to what I have to say. The way we see a person depends on our perspective, does it not, Sadik Usta? For example, in this family we've always thought of you as a servant because you've always waited on us and stood two or three steps back from our table. It never occurred to us to look at things from a different angle. A person doesn't question the knowledge he has memorized like a poem, does he? Particularly if a community wants to forget its crimes. Or a family. If I were to look through a different lens, would the truth as I have always understood it still remain the truth? Or have I been believing in a false reality? People don't think about that. What do you say?'

Mr Fikret was talking to himself. He certainly did not

expect an answer from me, and so I stayed silent. I placed his coffee on the table in front of him, returned the coffee and sugar to the pantry, washed the small pot in the kitchen sink, carefully dried it and hung it on its hook on the wall. Then I leant my hands on the cool marble of the counter and thought.

Perhaps my old ears had misheard some of what he'd said. I knew of Ioannis of Espiye. My mama used to speak of him at night when we lay side by side in our bed inside our hut that was connected to Mr Nuri's mansion by a secret underground passage. Ioannis has gone up into the mountains, she would say. He sleeps under a dark sky full of stars. He carries firewood and weapons on his back and leaves no trace of where he's been. Over there, the mountains are many and steep, their peaks are capped with smoke, their caves are innumerable, and they swallow up those who do not know the way.

Mr Fikret drank his coffee in one noisy slurp.

'The thing I don't understand is why you chose to be Grandmother's manservant. Did you feel you weren't Grandmother's equal because your mother came from a village, from Espiye, whereas Grandmother's family were from Macka and lived in a mansion? But your fathers had overcome those differences and became friends. Then your mother sent you to Istanbul with Shirin so that you would be educated. She expected you to become a clerk in the shoe factory. Why did you quit school? Why did you undervalue yourself like this, Sadik Usta?'

I felt dizzy all of a sudden. I staggered, took a couple of steps back and held onto one of the chairs that was pushed under the table. My ears were roaring. I know no prayers... The boys at school... Recite the Shahada! Pull down his trousers so that we can see what you really are. They trapped me in a corner. If a teacher had not come out into the yard right then, if the bell had not rung...

My hands and legs went floppy. Mr Fikret jumped to his feet and sat me down. He filled a glass with water from the jug and held it as I drank. I hadn't realized how thirsty I was. Mr Fikret was agitated. He knelt on the floor in front of me, muttering.

'Oh my God, are you all right, Sadik Usta? Forget about all this. Just look at me. Lift your head and just look at me, Sadik Usta. I've worn you out. I shouldn't have done that, especially not so late at night. But I learnt so many extraordinary things today that I couldn't contain myself. We have worn you out. We have worn you out and we shouldn't have, Sadik Usta.'

From so close up, Mr Fikret looked very much like dear Miss Suheyla. The same slanted, half-closed hazel eyes casting the same wary, tremulous gaze. They did not see what they were looking at, but what did they see? I tried to say something so that he would not be anxious on my account, but all I could manage was an incomprehensible rattling sound. With difficulty I got to my feet. Mr Fikret held my arm and we went out into the hall. The house was quiet, so quiet. I opened the door into the dining room and turned on the light. Then I walked in, pulled out a chair from the table, which was still not yet back in its place, and sat down.

Mr Fikret remained frozen in front of the wall. He stood like that for a time. Then, slowly, slowly, as if he was under some sort of spell, he passed his hand over the misty mountain peaks, the clusters of purple flowers, the turbulent sea.

'The paint may not be completely dry yet, Mr Fikret. Your grandmother—'

'Ioannis of Espiye!' He pressed his finger on one of the young men that my lady had painted life-sized. 'This... this is him, isn't it, Sadik Usta? Tell me the truth! This is your father!'

I nodded. Mr Fikret was most excited. Light had returned to his eyes. He was joyous as he looked at the painting, and he kept saying, 'But this is incredible, this is a miracle,' as he raced from one part of the wall to the other. As for me, I had no strength left. My bones felt as if they had been crushed to powder under a heavy load. I would never be able to rise from that chair. Death had come to take my soul earlier that evening and had changed its mind, but now it would not depart until it had completed its task.

Mr Fikret's finger stopped on the other young man.

'And this is Haralambos, isn't that right? Haralambos of Macka. Ioannis's closest friend, his blood brother. They had studied together at the Phrontisterion in Trabzon. Later, in fear for his life, Haralambos had no choice but to go over to the Turkish side and assume a new identity as a Muslim named Nuri. Grandmother's father.'

Again I was only able to nod my head. I could do nothing else. I now perceived that my lady had painted those two young men in such a way that anyone studying them carefully would see myself and Madam Shirin in their faces. She was truly a great artist.

Mr Fikret walked the length of the wall, touching and interpreting the different scenes as he went – the mountains, the monastery, the children crying for their grandfathers who had died on the path to exile. He knew all about them and described them in such detail that there could be no explanation other than that which Madam Shirin had asserted: Mr Fikret must have passed through the passage to the past.

'Ioannis and Haralambos: two young men, both Pontic Greeks. The year they finished high school, Trabzon was captured from the Ottoman Empire by the Russians. There were joyous celebrations in the streets, for everyone thought that at long last an independent Pontic Greek state would be established – the Republic of Pontus. They did not know, however, that the Ottoman administration, as part of its ethnic cleansing campaign and in retaliation for the Russian victories in the region, would over the coming months empty the Greek villages of the empire's western Black Sea region, which the Russians had not reached and therefore remained under Ottoman administration. They forced the villagers to flee inland, to the mountains. Many people died along the way, of sickness, from the cold, and at the hands of armed Turkish nationalist gangs. Ioannis's family in Espiye were among those exiled to the mountains. Ioannis only found out later that his mother and father had died of typhus on the road. The truth about this death march of the Black Sea Greeks was not known about until much later and was never officially acknowledged by the Turkish Republic. Ioannis returned to Espiye, where he found his neighbour's daughter, Maria, hiding in the church among the looted, burnt-out houses. He took her to his friend Haralambos's mansion in Macka, and, leaving her there, joined the Pontic militia in the mountains. Up there, he fought the Turkish gangs, gendarmes and soldiers, anyone who had colluded in the persecution of his mother, his father, his people. He was a romantic figure, a guerrilla fighter... Does all this resonate with you, Sadik Usta?'

I closed my eyes. I thought of my dear mama lying beside me in bed. She was certain that Papa was still alive. He will come back, she would say, but she worried that he might not find us with our new names, and sometimes she would cry. Once he returned, we would have our own house, Mama said. We would no longer live in the hut in Mr Nuri's garden like servants, and she would not do the grand lady's housekeeping as repayment for her gratitude towards Mr Nuri. She waited for the war to end, for the forced migrations to stop. The war had finished long ago and those who had been exiled remained in exile. Even as a child, I knew that, but Mama would not believe it. She used to say that when the time was right, the resistance fighters would come down from the mountains and attack. It is of no significance, she would say, that they are silent for the moment. The prospect of being separated from my little lady made me very sad. I was happy in Mr Nuri's mansion and did not know the meaning of 'servant'. I used to light a candle in front of the mirror late at night, as I had seen Mama do, and pray that, with our new names, Papa would not find us. In the secret corridor connecting our hut to the mansion, many candles burnt. Papa never returned to us.

Mr Fikret touched the people gathered in front of the clusters of purple flowers covering the walls of the mansion.

'See here? They are threatening Haralambos. The armed gangs, instruments of the high-ranking officials of the new Turkish army, have come to his house. They have stripped his little daughter Sofia naked in front of him and are about to take her away. Greek girls were often sold to prominent families in those days, or they might decide to kill her, throw her body in the river, or do something even worse. How convincingly Haralambos's despair has been depicted.

When I look at him, I feel the impossibility of his situation, how he had no choice, faced with the inevitability of fate in all its clarity. He had no option but to lead the soldiers to the cave where his dearest friend was hiding. In doing so, he would save not only his daughter but also his wife and Ioannis's pregnant wife, Maria, whom he was hiding in his own home, thus also saving you. That's right, isn't it, Sadik Usta? Haralambos changed everybody's name. Your mother became Meryem. For himself he chose Nuri, which means "Light", as does the name Haralambos. His daughter Sofia became Shirin. The Turkish soldiers kept their word. If he became a Muslim, he, his family and his retainers would be exempt from the compulsory population exchange programme between Greece and Turkey. And so Nuri and his household stayed in the mansion while tens of thousands of Christians died miserably on the road to exile. By the time you were born, there was not a single church left in the area in which to have you baptized. Drunk with victory, Turkish nationalists even pillaged and burnt the beautiful Panagia Sumela Monastery. A few of the priests managed to bury some of the precious icons in the earth before fleeing for their lives. Years later, they returned to dig them up. The former Haralambos of Macka, subsequently known as Nuri, lived for ten years with the terrible burden of what he had done, but after that he could endure it no more. Am I right? When you were ten years old, he took his rifle and blew his brains out in front of all of you.'

The roaring in my ears ceased. I opened my eyes. In my head there was a brief and sudden silence, similar to the silence that descended on the table in the moment after Mr Nuri's rifle exploded and before his shattered skull dropped onto the plate in front of him and smashed it in two. A thin, grey rain was falling. The windows were steamed up from the heat of the stove. The pine forest outside was obscured. We had just finished our breakfast. My little lady had mentioned our chance encounter with the priest and the icon at the monastery. There were olive stones on our plates, bread crusts on the table, some leftover dried meat, a slab of feta cheese. Mama was leaning over the samovar, refilling the tea glasses. She was excited to hear that the priest had come. For years no priests had visited our area. This was definitely a good sign. As the tea glasses clinked in her hands, she recited a prayer of thanksgiving. She believed that the time had come for my papa to come down from the mountains. But then Mr Nuri spoke.

'They tortured Ioannis and tore him limb from limb, Maria. They fed his flesh and bones to the wild animals of the mountains. Do not wait in vain. It was I who delivered him, my dear friend Ioannis, into the hands of our oppressors. May God forgive me my sins.'

The rifle exploded. The grand lady closed her eyes, covered her ears. The glass of hot tea fell from Mama's hand, hit the floor and shattered. Steam spiralled up from the floor. I saw everything from the corner where I was throwing logs into the stove. The only thing I didn't see was my little lady getting to her feet and coming over to me. I missed that. It was only when Mr Nuri's head fell forward, breaking the plate in half, and Mama screamed, 'It's a lie!' that I felt my little lady's hand in mine. Her fingers were like ice, but two drops of sweat dripped down her flame-red cheeks as we stood in front of the stove. She was trembling. With one hand I squeezed her palm. With the other I wanted to cover her eyes. I wanted to say to her, 'Do not be afraid, little lady. Do not tremble. As long as I live, I will protect you from evil. I will remain with you forever; I will always be near you, always behind you, always in attendance. I will never allow anything horrible to happen to you ever again.'

How could I explain that to Mr Fikret?

I could not.

I lowered my gaze and remained silent.

33

Burak

Just as I was getting on the ferry, I came face to face with Ufuk. He was in the crowd that surged down the wooden jetty as soon as the boarding gates opened. It was obvious from his expression that he was surprised to see me. As for me, I was annoyed – not because it was Ufuk, but because I wanted to be by myself just then. I wanted to sit by the window and watch night descend on the sea as I thought about Fikret's story and tried to work out what my feelings were regarding Nur. I would have felt the same had it been any one of my acquaintances who'd bumped into me there on the ferry.

Our eyes met. We couldn't pretend we hadn't seen each other now. We would travel together; we were both too civilized to do otherwise. We spoke casually as we exited the stairs side by side. Going to Istanbul? Yes. You? Of course. I'm going back to the city as well. Obviously, I'd not got on this ferry only to get off again at Heybeliada, the next island. This last was said silently, to myself.

We sat outside at the back, on the open deck, on what they used to call the luxury seats. The questions we couldn't ask were all lined up, hanging in the tense silence between us. The engine started. The hawsers were unwound. We drew away from the pier. Ufuk murmured something. I leant over to hear him. He's one of those men who speaks softly, in a low voice.

'I thought you were staying on the island tonight.'

There it was – the first bit of information. He knew I'd been invited to Shirin Hanim's birthday celebration and that I'd spent last night at their house.

'I was going to stay, but then something urgent came up, which is why I'm going back.'

Not exactly a lie. Out of the blue I'd been given a great story: Shirin Saka's true identity, discovered on the eve of her hundredth birthday. I would get up early tomorrow and start writing it up, or maybe even when I got home that night.

Ufuk nodded. He looked unhappy. His lean face, hidden behind his blonde beard, seemed to have got even longer, and his eyes were lost in thought. Tension sat between us like a glacier. We watched as the view through the window became more and more lovely. As the island receded, the sky turned navy blue and lights came on in the windows of the villas. Tea arrived. We both reached out and took a glass, leaving the sugar cubes on the tray.

Why had Ufuk been on the island? When did he come and why was he going back to Istanbul? Had he seen Nur? He must have. He wouldn't have gone to Buyukada just for a bit of peace and quiet; he'd gone there to see his wife. And then? Then something happened and he decided to go back. But I'd spoken to Nur just before I got on the ferry and she didn't say anything about having seen Ufuk. She wouldn't have told me in so many words, but I'd have understood. Nur couldn't have seen Ufuk. Ufuk came, changed his mind, and was going back.

'Nothing wrong, I hope? Why are you going back? It's Shirin Hanim's birthday celebration tomorrow morning.'

He looked at me in such a way that I felt embarrassed and turned away. The pine trees of Dilburnu Nature Park were visible in the distance. A beacon was alight on St George's Hill. Ufuk knew everything. Knew and was heartsick. I suddenly felt sorry for both of them. On one side there was Nur, who was miserable and in need of love, understanding and a shoulder to lean on. On the other side was a sad man with his head bowed. Their separation pained me, which was a new situation for me; always before, I'd been desperate for them to break up. Since the day they'd met, I'd hoped that Ufuk would turn out to be just another one of those men Nur thought she was in love with but then got tired of. I hadn't just hoped that, I'd believed it. I'd assumed that, yet again, Nur wouldn't find the love she was searching for. She'd get close, but she wouldn't succeed. Even when she told me she was going to marry Ufuk, I thought she was still playing her old games, even then, in her thirties. I thought they'd split up, get divorced, because Nur didn't know how to be in love. I'd never known a person who was so thirsty for love but who couldn't let herself succumb to it. In the end, she'd come back to me. She would realize that the love she was looking for was the love she'd had since the beginning, with me. Even as she searched for love in other bodies, she knew that she and I had a special bond, but she somehow didn't understand that our love endured, would always endure, no matter what. One day she would understand. I had continued to wait for that day.

Until now.

'Ufuk, I know it's not my place, but, with your permission, I'd like to say something to you.'

The ferry was approaching Heybeliada. Ufuk put his empty tea glass on the seat and turned to me. How clear the look in his eyes was.

'Nur...'

I didn't know how to say it. Time was running short. We were now parallel to Heybeliada's jetty. The lighthouse lamp was on, and a few yachts were meandering around the inner harbour. I stared at the spiral steps of the Naval Academy.

'Ufuk,' I murmured, 'I don't know what's going on between the two of you, but what I do know is that Nur is very unhappy.'

He turned his head away. The water between the ferry and the pier was as smooth as glass; a calm, dark blue. The restaurants lining the seafront came into view. Compared with Buyukada, everything looked clean and quiet. What if Ufuk and I were to jump off the ferry and go into one of the simple tavernas wreathed in colourful lights, have a drink together, say all the things that never get said... What if we just poured it all out?

The ferry came to a standstill and the chunky hawsers were thrown over as the engine roared noisily. Down below, the crowd that had gathered behind the railings on the quayside was restless, ready to attack the ferry as soon as the gates opened. I spoke very quickly.

'Ufuk, you should get off here. We're only ten minutes from Buyukada. There'll be a motorboat from Bostanci soon and you can take that back to Buyukada. Nur needs you. Even if she can't bring herself to say it, believe me, she needs you more than ever right now. Go back to her.'

Ufuk was looking at Heybeliada's seminary atop the dense, pine-covered hill. He was looking but saying nothing. The gates opened. Day-trippers raced onto the ferry, hurrying to grab a seat. The door to the back deck kept slamming open and shut. I had to speak rapidly. If Ufuk was going to get off, he had to act immediately.

'Nur is unbearably lonely, Ufuk. She's waiting for you. She has her eye on her phone the whole time – every minute, every second – hoping to hear from you.'

Finally, he turned around. There was a familiar expression on his face, a hurt and sorrow that I immediately understood. He too thought the baby Nur had aborted was his. Who knew, maybe it was. At this point, who could prove otherwise.

'If Nur has hurt you,' I continued hurriedly, 'you should know that she didn't intend to. She acted the way she did out of loneliness and despair, because she was in distress and didn't know what else to do. For the sake of my old friend of so many years, Ufuk, I beg you to forgive her. She needs you so much right now, more than you can ever imagine. Please, go back to her.'

The engine roared again. As Ufuk got to his feet, he squeezed my shoulder. For a brief moment we looked into each other's eyes. I think we both gave a slight smile. Then, taking his hand off my shoulder, he turned towards the steps. From where I sat on the back deck, I saw him jump onto the pier with a single stride of his long legs just as the ropes were being gathered up. I waited to see if he would look back at me. No. He kept his eyes forward, entered the pier building and disappeared from sight.

And then?

And then I moved.

To a very small penthouse apartment in bohemian Cihangir with a distant view of the Topkapi Palace peninsula from the balcony. It was the home of a journalist I knew who'd had to leave the country. He wanted someone to look after his cat and his belongings. 'I'll come back and stay here whenever I'm passing through,' he'd said, a little hopeless, a little desperate. But one doesn't 'pass through' this country any more. Most can't come back. Their passports get cancelled, or they don't even try for fear that the moment they enter the country, they'll have handcuffs slapped on their wrists and be thrown in prison. I hadn't thought about moving at all, but as soon as I said to my desperate friend, 'I'll take it, I want to get away from Kurtulus anyway,' I realized that I had actually wanted this change for a very long time. To leave the house I'd lived in since I was ten years old meant a new life for me. It forced me to get rid of all the stuff I somehow hadn't found time to go through since Mum died. I distributed everything in the entrance hall to neighbours and friends. The only thing I took from Kurtulus to Cihangir was Mum's shawl from the back of the armchair.

Fikret was a great help when I moved. While we were making separate piles of what was to be thrown away, what was to be sold and what was to come with me, he taught me a new approach to material possessions that he'd recently come across. If something didn't spark joy when I saw it or touched it or heard its sound, he told me, I should drop it from my life. Thanks to that principle, I got rid of hundreds of plastic bags, rubber bands and ribbons that Mum had saved, thinking she might need them someday; and I also sent to the wastepaper collectors my notes from university and my old notebooks full of newspaper clippings that I'd thought might come in handy one day. In applying the joy principle, I threw out most of my CDs but kept all of my cassettes, including the famous *Memories 9* compilation tape. At first I was embarrassed to discover that I had not one but two copies of this album that girls used to swoon over and boys made fun of. But Fikret picked up the cassette and smiled. Both of us knew that though the songs had originated with famous American bands, they were recorded in a studio here in Turkey by some Turkish singers in order to avoid copyright payments. This shared memory of the lost years of our youth brought us closer together. Sometimes you can have a closer bond with your peers than with your family. I gave Fikret one of the cassettes as a gift.

It was while I was moving that Fikret began insisting that we go to Macka together. It was the middle of summer. The special edition of 'Portraits', published in honour of Shirin Saka's hundredth birthday, had been received with great interest. Along with the interview with Shirin Hanim, I'd written up the story that Fikret had unearthed in Macka. I wrote it exactly as he'd related it, at length and encompassing the whole family saga: the suicide of Shirin Saka's father, who was actually a Pontic Greek; and all about Sadik Usta's father, who'd fought against Turkish armed gangs in the Black Sea mountains, and Housekeeper Meryem and Sadik Usta himself, and how they'd relinquished their identities and continued to practise their faith in secret, underground, so as not to be exiled from their land. It was truly a remarkable story, no question about it, and considering my emotional attachment to the family, I managed to put out a good article. However, the reason it got such a lot of attention was not down to my stylish prose, nor even to the excitement about Shirin Saka's mural, which came to be described as her 'eleventh-hour masterpiece'.

I entitled the article 'Face to Face At a Hundred Years Old'. It came out on a Saturday in the middle of July, a day so hot even the children stayed at home. Celine had sent me photos of the birthday taken with her new phone, which had a lens so good that it would consign all cameras to history. I'd already sent the portrait photo of Shirin Saka and the photo of her new mural to the paper, together with my article. The third photo Celine sent was just for me and she requested that it remain private. I laughed when I read that. In a world where every conceivable image can be found at the touch of a finger, who would you be hiding your face from? I downloaded the high-resolution photo onto my computer and enlarged it.

The family was lined up, posing, behind a table set for Shirin Saka's birthday tea. The centrepiece was a sour cherry and whipped cream cake that rose like a palace from the middle of the table and was surrounded by cupcakes and steaming glasses of tea. I couldn't count them in the picture, but Celine had written in her email that there were exactly 101 candles encircling the three-layered cake. On one side of the cake sat Shirin Saka, in front of her latest work of art, the mural, with an imperious expression on her face. Her thin white hair was held in place with ivory combs, she had applied pearly pink lipstick to her lips, and she was wearing a pale blue blouse whose quality was apparent even in the photo. She was staring into the phone's camera with great seriousness, as if she didn't know that this celebration was in her honour.

At the other side of the cake, on the far end, was Celine. She'd set the self-timer for ten seconds and had then run to the table and was hugging Fikret with both arms. Fikret had laid his cheek on his daughter's head. Nur was next to Fikret and on her other side was Ufuk. She had taken Ufuk's arm. I enlarged the picture to get a close-up of Nur's eyes. They were slightly swollen, a bit red, the green very clear. Tired, but peaceful. Her pupils held a subtle expression of submission, which only I would understand. There was a promise of happiness, if not happiness itself, in those eyes. I touched the screen with the tip of my finger. It was as if Nur winked.

I zoomed out.

The most surprising thing about the photo was the smile on Sadik Usta's face. It was thin and vague but definitely there. Maybe even more surprising than the smile – or maybe not – was that Sadik Usta was not standing in the background, somewhere near the door, but sitting beside Shirin Hanim at the centre of the table. Their hands lay side by side on the white tablecloth, wrinkled, veined, covered with brown spots. In between them was the cake knife.

I'd anticipated that the article would elicit interest, but I had no idea that I'd exposed a deep and significant wound. By midday that Saturday I'd received close to a hundred emails. By evening it was more like two hundred. The interview was being shared unbelievably quickly on social media, with hundreds of comments. This continued for days. What had transpired between the fathers of Shirin Hanim and Sadik Usta, once close friends, was not such an extraordinary occurrence, it seemed; my having scratched the surface was enough to bring into the light numerous similar accounts. The grandchildren of men who, just like Shirin Saka's father Nuri, were Pontic Greeks but had been forced to change their names, and the grandchildren of elderly women who spoke no other language but Pontiaka their whole lives, shared their stories with me and thanked me for bringing the subject into the public arena. I was shocked.

The great majority of the emails came from the Black Sea region of Turkey. Hundreds of people wrote to say that they actually had a different identity, that they had never even told their children the truth. Some were crypto-Christians who continued their worship in secret; others were people who lived in strict Muslim villages but spoke only Pontiaka. In their effort to integrate, they had raised the next generations to be more nationalistic, more religious than anyone. Some of those children and grandchildren, when they discovered the truth, went to court and officially changed their names on their identity certificates.

A few people wrote from Greece, having somehow found my name, and asked for my help in tracing relatives – children hidden in a neighbour's house at the time of the forced migration, grandfathers who died on the march, lost babies whose names mothers had murmured until their dying day. In every story there was appalling cruelty and heartbreaking desperation. Without realizing it, I had lifted the lid on a cauldron of fierce emotion.

On a day as hot as hell, while we were clearing up the house in Kurtulus, Fikret suggested we go together to Macka, travel to the neighbouring villages and talk to the people who had got in touch with me, promising to keep their names hidden. I could write a series of articles. This was an open sore and it was obvious that every one of them had a story to tell. Plus I liked talking to old people, Fikret added when he saw how wary I was. He would come with me. He had anyway already promised his cousins, the descendants of Shirin Saka's half-brothers and sisters, that he would come back.

My editor at the newspaper was not as keen on this idea as Fikret was. Not only had my 'Portrait' piece on Shirin Saka deviated from its original brief, but it might conceivably be co-opted for political ends, and this new project unquestionably had a propagandist element to it. Even if I had the best of intentions, it was possible that the people I planned to interview would take the opportunity to promote their own political agendas. In our current times we needed national unity and togetherness more than ever, and so on and so forth.

When he heard that I'd given up on the idea of writing a series of articles, Fikret was upset, but he didn't push it. He merely mentioned that if I wanted to produce a book out of this project, he was sure Ufuk would be happy to publish it. In which case, I could just resign from the newspaper. I told him that we should forget it for now. The emails continued for a while, then tapered off.

One evening at the end of the summer I ran into Nur in the city. I had last seen her at the Buyukada pier, right before I got on the ferry. Both of us had stayed quiet since then. She was trying to work things out with Ufuk and I had buried myself in my writing. Both of us needed time before we could rekindle our friendship and start afresh. Our relationship had been wounded, and not only because of what Nur had done. My insistent desire, my stubborn belief that Nur could only find love with me had exhausted our friendship. But the foundations were strong, the DNA was solid. If we gave it time, it would recover and live on.

Nur was walking towards Tophane. She smiled when she saw me on the street corner. She looked tanned and rested. I leant against the building on the corner and watched her coming. The sun was setting behind her, bathing the rooftops, the towers and the water in a golden glow. We didn't hug, just stood facing each other. The fragile peace I'd seen in her eyes when I'd enlarged Celine's photo had now suffused the whole of her face. Her eyes shone like two emeralds.

'Congratulations. I hear you've moved.'

With her head she indicated Batarya Street, on whose

corner we were standing. She obviously knew which street I'd moved to. She and Fikret must have talked about me. She must have also heard about the repercussions of the article I'd done on Shirin Saka. Even if she wasn't on social media much at all, she'd have found it hard to ignore, and there was no way she'd have bypassed news that concerned her family. Yet she hadn't written me a single word about it. In all that time, she hadn't phoned, hadn't even left a message. Maybe she didn't like the public interest. She'd not been pleased at Fikret's persistent attempts to uncover their family secrets anyway.

She had a large folder under her arm.

'Is that the Fat Cat's novel? You finished that quickly.'

She'd been going to write a historical novel the last I knew. For a rich businessman. She'd told me a little bit about it when she came to my house in Kurtulus.

'No, it isn't.' She dropped her head, looked at the ground and smiled. 'This isn't a commission.'

'Oh, really? What is it then?'

'My own novel.'

'What are you saying, Nur? Finally! That's great. Tell me about it. What's it about?'

She was still staring at the ground, still smiling. Her shyness worried me. The wind coming up from Tophane ruffled her short hair, causing the wisps around the nape of her neck to fly here and there. She raised her head. Her cheeks were flushed. Hesitantly, she looked into my eyes.

'I don't want to talk about it until it's published, Burak. Nobody's read it yet except my editor at the publishing house. I'm going to meet her now, at Café 6.'

I was surprised. 'Really? Ufuk's not publishing it? Did you sign up with a different publisher?'

'Yes.'

Now that was big news. I was really happy when Nur told me the name of the publisher. She'd done well.

'So that's double congratulations, Nur. This time you won't be ignored by the critics, right?'

As soon as I said that, I regretted it. Nur's first novel, *The Stationery Shop*, was like a child who'd died young. She never mentioned it. Any hint of its existence reminded us of its death, so we acted like it had never been written.

But Nur laughed.

'You know, Burak, I really don't care whether the critics notice this book, whether they scrutinize it in their serious magazines. I don't even know why I wrote it. It sounds sort of Fikret-ish, but let me put it like this: I had to write it. I had to take this step. And I took it without having a specific goal in mind.'

'Good for you. I can't wait to read it. Have you decided on a title?'

'Yes, but you'll have to wait until it comes out.'

When we went our separate ways, we hugged each other. I inhaled the smell of the sun on her skin. Nur was fine. Happy. Peace and contentment rose like delicate smoke from the body I held in my arms. I let her go. I bought food for the cat, a tuna sandwich for myself from the grocery shop on the corner, and went home.

My apartment in Cihangir is small. Where the ceiling slopes down, it's impossible to stand up straight, and so, because of that, the shower isn't in the bathroom but in a corner of the bedroom instead. At first this seemed weird to me, but I've got used to it now. The architect put a little window in the shower wall so that while you're showering you can gaze out over the rooftops and to the sea beyond. When I'm behind the counter in the open-plan kitchen, washing lettuce and tomatoes for a salad, for example, I also get a tiny glimpse of the sea through the balcony door. I watch the ships as they pass. It takes from four to six seconds for a ship to come into view and pass out of view. The Topkapi Palace peninsula is the fixed point. While I watch my slice of the sea from my kitchen as I prepare my salad, the cat – left in my charge by my journalist friend and owner of the apartment – winds around my feet. He is a grey-and-white stray cat, a sad creature. A car hit him when he was a baby, leaving him with a crippled leg. We've got used to each other and he sits with me at the table I have set on the balcony.

That night, however, I was to have a guest. I was expecting Celine. I hadn't seen her since Buyukada. After Shirin Hanim's birthday, she took her backpack and went travelling by herself. She camped on beaches so remote they didn't even have mobile phone reception. She went to Castellorizo Island with some young Australians she met in Kas, and from there she went on to explore some other Greek islands. She was on the road for two months, on her own, and had just recently come back. She wanted to come by for a housewarming visit. How polite you are, Celine, I said on the phone. Well, I am a descendant of Pontic Greeks, am I not, she replied. Perhaps that was why she went to those Greek islands and stayed there so long, to find out more about her newly discovered identity. Or for some other reason. Maybe love. I would learn more when she came over. She also wrote two songs while she was away, which she would let me hear. One of them was called 'Guesthouse Rooms' and the other was 'At the Breakfast Table'.

While I was waiting for her, I called the house on Buyukada. I'd been wanting to check on Sadik Usta for some time. Did he read the article, and what did he think of it? I wasn't sure what to make of his silence. As I waited for the phone to be answered, I could hear in my head the ringing of the old green telephone on the console table in the hall echoing into the emptiness. After quite a while, Sadik Usta's rasping, anxious, 'Hello, how may I help you?' came down the line. The eccentric old chap was very happy to hear me.

'We are sitting here with nothing to do, Mr Burak. Everyone has gone away, and the house is silent. Madam Shirin is in good health. All those people who stopped by through the summer to view her mural tired her somewhat, but she is fine now, thank the good Lord. We cut your article out of the newspaper and glued it right here, Mr Burak, on the mirror above the console table on which the telephone sits. Miss Celine read it to us. From time to time Madam Shirin puts on her glasses and we read it again, from start to finish.'

'Thank you, Sadik Usta. That makes me happy.'

Silence. Sadik Usta is the sort who doesn't say anything unless he is asked a question.

'Will you be spending the winter on the island?' I asked. 'Won't you return to the apartment in Moda?'

'No, Mr Burak, we are fine here. The gardener's wife and children will do our shopping and our cleaning. They will lay the fire for us, although, in fact, this will not be necessary as Mr Fikret has had radiators installed in the house. They work with natural gas. The house is warm. We only light a fire in the fireplace to gaze at it. We give thanks that our stomachs are full. We lack for nothing.'

My insides twisted as I imagined those two old folks,

centenarians, sitting across from the fireplace in the library of the island house. Sadik Usta must have read my thoughts from the other end of the line, for he said, 'Mr Burak, please do not worry about us. After clearing the breakfast table, we become absorbed in Madam Shirin's painting. It is wonderful to think about the past. Even more wonderful is to be able to relive the past over and over again thanks to that picture. We have passed the age for reading books, our eyes can no longer distinguish the letters, but you must continue to write, Mr Burak, so that others may read about the past and experience it like that, from the very beginning. Do not be anxious for us. We are fine, Mr Burak. Fine.'

After we ended the call, I stayed out on the balcony a while longer. Sadik Usta was right. We can't live our lives again, but we can write about them. And that's not all. For me, writing is not just about shedding light on the past, it's also about connecting with the present, a way to immerse oneself in the here and now, a way of living life to the fullest. Writing helps reverse the losses. If you don't jump right in and embrace life, you'll never escape the emptiness inside.

The phone was still in my hand.

A seagull landed on the balcony railing and eyed the meal I'd prepared. The cat at my feet prepared to pounce. Right then I made my decision.

I would go to Macka.

And from there to different villages, mountains, cities. I would lend my ear to the hundreds of people who'd emailed me. I would bring the secrets of their pasts into the open of the present day. I'd have to resign from the newspaper, but they were sure to have fired me one day anyway. I could get by on the rent from the Kurtulus flat for a while. I wouldn't write a series of articles, I'd write a book. Those who wished to could reconstruct the past; those who wished to could turn back to the beginning and read it over again.

I took a deep breath and dialled Fikret's number. As I waited for him to answer, I watched the ships coming and going in the little slice of sea I could glimpse from my balcony.

Glossary of Turkish words

Abi	Brother
-ada	island
Bey	Mr
Hanim	Mrs
raki	sweetened alcoholic drink, often anise flavoured
Usta	Master

THE SILENCE OF SCHEHERAZADE

DEFNE SUMAN

'Unique and enveloping... Utterly delightful' BUKI PAPILLON

Also by Defne Suman

The Silence of Scheherazade

September 1905. At the heart of the Ottoman Empire, in the ancient city of Smyrna, Scheherazade is born to an opium-dazed mother. At the very same moment, an Indian spy sails into the golden-hued, sycamore-scented city with a secret mission from the British Empire. When he leaves, 17 years later, it will be to the smell of kerosene and smoke as the city, and its people, are engulfed in flames.

Told through the intertwining fates of a Levantine, a Greek, a Turkish and an Armenian family, this unforgettable novel reveals a city, and a culture, now lost to time.

'This rich tale of love and loss gives voice to the silenced, and adds music to their histories.'
Maureen Freely

'Utterly delightful.' **Buki Papillon**

About the Author and Translator

DEFNE SUMAN was born in Istanbul and grew up on
Buyukada. She gained a Masters in Sociology from the
Bosphorus University, then worked as a teacher in Thailand
and Laos where she studied Far Eastern philosophy and
mystic disciplines. She later continued her studies in Oregon,
USA and now lives in Athens with her husband.
Her English language debut *The Silence of Scheherazade*
was published by Head of Zeus in 2021.

BETSY GÖKSEL is an American teacher and translator
who has lived in Turkey since the 1960s. Her translations
include *The Hate Trap* by Haluk Sahin and *The Silence of
Scheherazade* by Defne Suman, as well as several books on
art and architecture for the Istanbul Municipality.